Jonathan Gash is a docto[...] medicine, and lectures wo[...] developed his love for antiques during his years as a medical student when he supplemented his income by working in the London street markets. He lists his hobbies as antiques and his family. He is married with three daughters and three grandchildren.

PAID AND LOVING EYES

A Lovejoy Novel

Jonathan Gash

ARROW

First published 1993

1 3 5 7 9 10 8 6 4 2

© Jonathan Gash 1993

First published by Century in 1993

This edition published in 1993 by Arrow,
Random House, 20 Vauxhall Bridge Road, London SW1V 2SA

Random House Australia (Pty) Limited
20 Alfred Street, Milsons Point, Sydney,
New South Wales 2061, Australia

Random House New Zealand Limited
18 Poland Road, Glenfield
Auckland 10, New Zealand

Random House South Africa (Pty) Limited
PO Box 337, Bergvlei, South Africa

Random House UK Limited Reg. No. 954009

A CIP catalogue record for this book
is available from the British Library

ISBN 0 09 922771 1

Printed and bound in Great Britain by
Cox & Wyman Ltd, Reading, Berkshire

'What none can prove a forgery may be true;
What none but bad men wish exploded, must.'

William Cowper (1731–1800)

'What none can prove a forgery may be true;
What none but bad men wish exploded, must.'

William Cowper (1731–1800)

1

The lovers were making the van sway. I had to get out, from seasickness. The night was perishing cold. Donk found me sheltering under trees in the drizzling dark. He's the antiques trade's only profit-making messenger, has a rotten old motorbike.

'Lovejoy? Your pot's tonight. Nine o'clock in the harbour barn.'

My heart fell and rose. Armageddon time, and me minding a pair of illicit fornicators in a furniture van.

'Sure, Donk?' I looked at the van as it reached orgasm. Just my luck. First paying job for a fortnight, and paradise – antiques – spoils the money. No, that's not right. It's gelt that does for antiques, not the other way round.

'Josh said hurry. That'll be a tenner, Lovejoy.'

Donk's messages are all ten quid, payable on delivery. I climbed up into my passionate van's cabin and fired the ignition.

'I'll owe you,' I called as he yelled after me. People don't understand. Antiques are urgent. Anyway, the lovers inside wouldn't notice that their trysting-place was barrelling through the rainy night at sixty. Passion is mostly oblivion. I'm an antique dealer, the only real one left. I know passion, and passion knows me.

There's a wharf in town. Not much of a harbour, but its access to the sea is well used these two thousand years. Four furlongs of paving overlooking an estuary, two cranes, a few warehouses. Ships come from the Continent – two thousand tons, max. They bring fertilizer, we send grain. The system, and the cargoes, are unchanged since before Caesar landed. I drove slowly into the barnyard, and parked by the railings. Five posh motors, I saw. The gang was all here.

The orange cabin light had buzzed on miles ago, querying the journey. My lovers must now be replete, ready for off to their separate homes. I sighed, reluctantly pressed the release. Just when you wanted ardour prolonged, lust lets you down. I'd wanted them to orgy on so I could referee the battle of the pots in the barn.

'Where are we?' the woman was asking as they stepped down, looking about.

The man said, 'I felt us moving.' I should hope so. They came at me together, under the shelter of the loading bay. I'd not seen either of them before. Secrecy's the hallmark of Gaunt's Tryste Service.

'Driver!' the bloke snapped, tapping my chest. I hate that. 'What's the meaning of this? We . . . boarded at a countryside lay-by. And you put us down . . . *in a harbour*? Where are our limousines?'

Door-to-door limo service is included in the price with Gazza Gaunt's luxury fornication pantechnicon. You get a well-stocked bar, an opulently furnished interior, and cosy privacy wherein to wreak your savage sexual desires on your lover's willing body. (Lover, like batteries, not included.) Then you primly return home to your husband/wife/children worn out saying you've had a hard day at work/college/committee. It costs a mint, though folk keep coming back for more. Well, a woman wants first a lover, then a husband, then a lover. It's love's roundabout. Guess who confessed that her nature was 'too passionate', her desires 'violent'? Queen Victoria, that's who. Gazza, the shrewd operator who runs the waggons, says four-fifths of his customers are regulars.

'Lovejoy?' somebody called from the barn doorway. 'Fight's on. Josh says come now.'

'Get me your head office?' The bloke was outraged. He was a stout glary sort, with the familiar non-face of a TV politico. 'I'm supposed to be at a sales conference in Nottingham.' Well, lies stay cheap.

'Look. I'll bell you taxis,' I offered desperately. Two bulky goons loomed in the light. Silhouettes threaten, don't they?

'Lovejoy,' one goon intoned, quiet with menace. 'Life or death, lad.'

'Coming,' I cried, shuffling anxiously on the spot. Threats make me do that. 'Look, mister. I promise – '

'Fight?' the woman asked. 'What fight?'

2

There was relish in her mellifluous, husky words. I recognized the response. Women love conflict more than men. In the oblique light of the loading yard she looked stark somehow, black and white yet languid with the serenity of the well used. Lovely. Money's easier to spot on a woman. They like it to show more. Smallish, slender, intense, voluptuous. I loved her.

'Diana.' Her bloke was furious because of my prolonged stare at the bird. 'You can't surely – '

'*What* is life or death?' She actually licked her lips.

'Counting, Lovejoy.' The goons were moving down the loading bay. Diana glanced at me, at them, her excitement growing and showing. God, but women interrupt your thoughts.

I swallowed, looking from him to her. You can't help wondering how they made love. I mean, her on her side, her back, hands and knees, with him. . . ? 'You can wait in the van. I have to go.'

'Can we watch, Lovejoy?' She was thrilled.

'They'll wait inside,' I told the heavies, passing them the van keys to prove I was obeying. The goons shrugged as brains failed to raise the game. I went up the wooden steps, the man behind me expostulating every pace.

'What's the contest?' Diana asked, eyes alight.

'Between two pots, love.' I added sardonically as she exclaimed in disappointment: 'The prize is everything.'

'You said life or death, Lovejoy. Whose?'

'Always mine, love,' I said, and went into the light where the contest was to be fought.

'Wait – ' the woman was saying behind me. I heeled the door shut in her face.

2

God knows how gamblers do it, but they fill any place with smoke. It's beyond belief. I can't see the point of smoking, which only proves I too was once an addict of the stuff. Fear beats craving in the craven, hey?

The barn is ancient, oak beams and wattle and daub. Hereabouts such buildings can't be altered – unless bribes bend law. Josh Sparrow, the barn's owner, is a fierce upholder of preservation laws. They've given him a rich living. He competed with avaricious builders to buy this bit of the waterfront years ago –then announced it was to be East Anglia's Folk Epicentre. Conservationists rejoiced. They even gave him some award for Caring Commitment. Since then, the barn's been used solely for illegal activities, gambling, meetings between factions of villains, general mayhem. Josh gets really narked when Pennine pipers and Lithuanian dancers want to hire it. I keep telling him to change its name, but he likes the classy sound.

'About frigging time, Lovejoy!' said our paragon of epicentric culture.

He's always got a half-smoked fag dangling from one side of his mouth and goes about half blinded by his own smoke. Josh is forty, twitchy, always smells of fruit gums, plasters his hair down with some oily stuff. It must come free because he's a stingy sod.

'Been driving for Gazza. They're outside.'

He tutted through his smokescreen, this devout Episcopalian who deplores sin. He owns twenty-five per cent of Gaunt's Tryste Service. The holy quarter, I suppose.

Of the half-dozen people here, I saw I could ignore seventeen straight off. They were the brawn, the retinues, recruited duck-eggs with less than one neurone apiece. I hate them. Why do these ham-and-blam brigades line walls everywhere from the UN to the White Hart tavern nowadays? The world's getting like mediaeval frigging Florence, I've-more-assassins-than-you. Two birds, fifteen blokes, the usual ratio since equal rights dripped into the well water with the fluoride. They've all seen Ronald Colman films and dress early United Artists. I was cold, chilled, wet, hungry.

Three cheap chairs were arranged in a row in the middle of the barn floor under a cone of yellow light. The gelt sat there, idly contemplating the infinite, certainly not speaking.

Josh didn't count. The two protagonists standing to one side twitching nervously didn't count. I went forward into the light and stood before the prile. Grovelling's served me pretty well on the whole. I quelled my sense of degradation. Shame's no big spender, so doesn't count either.

'Evening, John. Sorry I'm late.'

Big John Sheehan's an Ulsterman. He actually should have counted several, but morphologically notches only *uno*. That is to say, he sits in a casual attitude of unsmiling threat. He clears his throat, you shut up until you're sure it's not the prelude to a sentence. His sentences, however you define the word, compel attention.

'?' his expression asked.

I explained about the Tryste job. He examined my face for perfidy, nodded okay after a heart-stopping moment.

'Josh gets docked half-crown in the pound,' he pronounced in that soft Belfast accent I like. Half-croyn in the poynd. 'Sloppy, Josh.'

Sweating slightly – well, muchly – from relief, I said hello to the other two gelties sitting alongside him. Strangers. During politenesses I worked out what forgetting to remind me about tonight's battle would cost Josh. Big John lives in pre-decimal money because he hates confidence tricks, unless they're his. Two shillings and sixpence out of every quid was an eighth. Of all Josh Sparrow's income for the month! Christ. For me, that would have been zilch. But for me it would have been a different punishment.

'Evening. I'm Lovejoy,' I said humbly.

'Good evening,' one said. 'Jan. To assess the antiques.'

Elegant, suave, twenty press-ups at dawn, cholesterol-watcher. Tanned and immaculate. Had a gold-headed walking stick. Fake Edwardian, so not all that good an antiques assessor. Cosmetics stained his fizzog. Well, takes all sorts.

'Get on with it,' the other growled.

Rotund, heavy breather, thick features veined with thin purple lines. His teeth would be mostly gold, if ever he laughed. His cigarette slummed beside John's cigar and Jan the Assessor's slim panatella. But I bet No-Name could do as many press-ups as anybody else. And weighed heavier. He wore an overcoat that could buy three weeks in Gazza Gaunt's sexy conveyances, bird included.

'Right, right,' I fawned swiftly. The two contestants came nervously forward. Their big moment.

'Who's first?' Big John asked. And when nobody spoke decided, 'Home team.'

'No,' the bulky geltster gravelled out. 'The Yank first.'

I didn't start to shake, but came close. Six suits leaned away from the wall. Big John's line did likewise. The two gangs looked at each other with that serenity hoods wear before war starts. We all froze, except for trembles.

Big John nodded. 'Right, Corse.'

The world relaxed, thankful it could orbit safely until next time.

Josh Sparrow dragged on a couple of floodlights, falling over wires and needing three goes to get the plugs right while his serfs carried a small japanned table in. I couldn't help staring at Corse. I was thunderstruck. I'd never seen Big John countermanded before. And he'd backed down. It was like learning that God picks his nose. Feet of clay, or something.

'Lovejoy.' Josh was telling me things, and I wasn't paying attention.

'Eh? Oh, aye. Ready.' I stepped out of the limelight.

The American advanced. She was dressed casually but clever, if you follow. Frocks can look almost exactly the same, cheap or rich. But some slight difference instantly tells you that one is a shop-bought end-of-sale good-riddancer, and the other classy and extortionate. This was the latter.

'Phoebe Colonna,' she announced, cool as you please.

She faced the three, standing for all the world like a girl about to recite. Small, hands folded. The pool of light made an arena of the flagged floor. No other lights, just the single shaded bulb above. The japanned table gleamed. I could make out the pale shirts and collars of the nerks around the arena. A mini-circus.

'Before I begin,' she preached, 'I particularly want to thank you gentlemen for the opportunity of presenting my work here in East

6

Anglia. You will observe that I have paid particular attention to the composition of the glass incorporated – '

'Get on with it,' Corse growled. His catch-phrase.

Phoebe gamely kept up her prattle as she hurriedly beckoned a serf forward. He carried a covered object.

' – questions of design integral to the complexities of rationale, creativity-wise . . .' Et mind-bending cetera. I bet she'd slogged, postdoctoralwise, to be that slick in balderdash.

I watched her reach out, still lecturing away, and gently lift the cover as floodlights splashed on . . .

Only on the Portland Vase.

'Lovejoy?' Josh timidly interrupted her to warn me, stay where I was, but by then I was already across and staring down at the object. Lovely, truly bliss. I started smiling. Time hung about for a minute or several.

'Can I?' I asked.

Phoebe checked with the three by a quick glance. Josh tutted, coughed away a smoke spume. I lifted it from its stand. Flat disc base, not the knobbed amphora type. Beautiful work. She made to point, guessing I was some sort of referee.

'See where I effected the cameo relief carving – my own patented blowing process – of the white outer layer?' She was so proud of her work. I could have eaten her.

'Thank you, Phoebe,' I said. My eyes had filled for some reason. Eyes are stupid.

She was moved. 'You appreciate beauty, Lovejoy.'

Her vase was covered, I retreated, Phoebe smiled out of the way, and on came Steve Yelbard. He was a real artisan, decisive, no cackle, just put his piece down, lifted the cover and stood aside.

Thin, in overalls, scuffed boots, pencil behind his ear, he looked ready to make another ten soon as somebody got a furnace started. Another Portland Vase. Fake, of course. Which is the truth word for a copy, look-alike, reproduction, simulant.

I didn't need to go over to it. Excellent work. Interestingly, his was the full amphora type, base dropping to a rounded point in its stand.

Now the Portland Vase is famous. Everybody knows it, and its story. Any Roman cased glass – layers made separately then heat-fused – is beautiful. The most gorgeous of all is the Portland.

Cobalt-blue translucency, it looks solid black unless you try to shine a light through. Opaque white glass figures adorn it – Peleus and Thetis, a tree, a cupid, some sort of sea dragon, you know the sort of thing; all those deities whose names you can never get the hang of. That's about it, really, *except that there's only one*. The British Museum has it. And here we were with two. Isn't life grand?

Corse the charm-school graduate grunted, 'Shift. Let's look.'

I stood aside. Steve Yelbard waited, talking technology with Phoebe. His eyes never left her Portland. She talked attractively and laughed merry laughs. The three rollers stalked round, looking at the two glass pieces. They hadn't a clue. A roller is a big investor in antiques. Any old, or even new, antique will do as long as it's worth a lot. They're nerks on the whole, but usually dangerous. I cleared my throat. Nobody stopped talking. Steve was the only one who looked at me.

'I saw your exhibition in St Edmundsbury, Steve. Not bad.'

He brightened. 'My prototype?' He grimaced. Real glass-makers always apologize, knowing nowt is perfect.

'Two prototypes,' I reminded him. 'One's base was disced, like Phoebe's. You decided against it?'

'I believe the original was in a true Greek amphora shape. The point removed and later replaced with a disc. Lovely, but twelve centimetres – '

'Twelve point one.' I nodded. 'And a different blue.'

He took instant offence. 'I wasn't shunning the challenge, Lovejoy. It's a question of what's artistically right.'

'No talking!' Corse snarled.

I leapt away and shut up. Jan was chattering, displaying his awesome vocabulary, making an impression on everyone listening, chiefly himself.

'There's a positive vibrancy of intellectualization, risk for risk's sake, atavistically speaking . . .'

And all that jazz. Phoebe was smiling, pointing out features of her superb vase. Lights were being trained while the gelt men peered and squinted at the two Portland Vases. Talk about a bloody pantomime. They got fed up after a few moments and strolled back to their chairs. Josh fetched me, plucking at my elbow as if trying to unravel my shabby jacket.

'Well? Which, Lovejoy?' Time for me to point the finger, and get either Steve or Phoebe a fortune or penury.

The floodlamps were extinguished. The shade cast its golden cone over me. I stood there like on trial. For an ugly second I thought how frigging unfair this all was. I mean, just because I'm me, they shovel this responsibility –

'Yelbard.' I ahemed to clear the squeak, tried again.

Jan swivelled, looked at Sheehan, Corse, then me.

'That's preposterous!' he exclaimed. 'The American piece is fabulous! It's perfection! Why, the Yelbard replica is . . .'

Silence is refuge when tyrants differ. I stayed silent.

'Lovejoy?' Big John interrupted.

Corse was darting suspicious glances. His goons came off the wall. So did Big John's. Jan pranced to the table desperate to prove me wrong.

'What's the point of asking Lovejoy?' He indicated Phoebe's piece. 'I've made a lifetime study of ancient glass. I tell you this divine piece could be the original Philip Pargeter replica! It's totality is perfection – '

'What's this pansy mean?' Corse grated. 'I came here for a 'ckin' definite. No maybes! You can't put money on a frigging maybe!'

'I think you'll find, gentlemen,' Phoebe interposed smoothly, 'that Mr Fotheringay is correct. I based my work on the famous reproductions of the original Portland Vase made by Pargeter and John Northwood, dated 1876. You will find – '

'Lovejoy,' Big John said quietly. 'The arts man says you're wrong. Why?'

I'd rather have stayed in the rain to catch my death of cold among the trees. I swallowed to get my voice going.

'Because he's right, John. Because the American girl's right, too.' I nodded at her Portland. 'It's beautiful. But she didn't make it, did you, Phoebe?'

'What's this beautiful shit?' Corse spat a stream of saliva in disgust. I moved my foot in time. 'We're here to back the best *fake*.'

'There's only one fake here.' I glanced at Steve, who was starting a slow smile. 'Steve's.'

'I don't know what you're trying to pull, Lovejoy – '

Phoebe's face suddenly went ugly with fear. Her voice pitched higher. Odd that terror uglifies a bird, when passion beautifies them so. But it was either her or me, with Corse signalling his suits into their ominous lean. I cut in.

'There are several copies of the Portland in glass, Mr Corse. Not counting Josiah Wedgwood's famous pottery jasperware efforts. It started with Edward Thomason at Birmingham Heath, 1818 – unfinished. Then Pargeter and Northwood had a few goes. Some bloke called Locke in mid-Victorian times . . .'

I petered to silence, not because I'd run out of things to say, but because Big John had frowned slightly. Slightly's enough, to cowards.

'How come the lassie knew his name?' he asked.

'Whose name?' Jan said, face draining. Big John meant him.

Nobody answered, far worse than uproar.

'Look,' Jan said, trying a laugh that convinced nobody. 'I'm well known. I write for a dozen periodicals. I – '

'As Tiffy Tiffany,' Sheehan said. 'Your newspaper name. His voice goes softer, the more threat within. 'You're anonymous.' Hurt showed in his brogue. 'I *paid* for that information.'

All the suits were edging closer now, glaring. I looked about but there was nowhere to go.

'Please,' Jan was saying, tone ascending like a prayer. 'Please. I *had* to make sure. Don't you see, Mr Sheehan? I *couldn't* leave an investment this big to mere chance!'

He was squeaking in fright. The girl was trying to get out but the circle of hoods closed. She struggled genteely a second, then tried indignation.

'Well! If you can't listen to reason . . .' All that. Useless.

'We been done, John?' Corse scraped a cough, cast his fag end in rage. 'The Yank bitch and this poofter?'

'It isn't like what it seems!' Jan was shrilling, frantic, appealing desperately to Big John. 'This is serious money! A fortune – '

'Ronnie,' Big John said.

Three cube-shaped hoods came and hauled Jan away. When I looked, Phoebe was already being bundled out of the rear door. It slammed with echoing finality. I tried drying my clammy hands on my trousers. Steve seemed frightened. It's the safest way to be. I know.

'Lovejoy?' My cue from Big John.

'Phoebe was showing you a genuine old Pargeter copy. She'd not made it herself. That way, she'd win this contest and get the job.'

'And our money . . .' Corse choked, his face a vast sweaty plum.

'Josh,' Big John intoned.

Josh Sparrow came at a low creep, quivering and bleating. 'John, I swear to God. On my mother's life. My baby's head. I never had any notion there was a scam. I honestly don't know what's happened – '

'What did?' Corse grunted.

Happen? My turn. In a wobbly yodel I managed to start. 'Your competition was to fake the Portland Vase. Phoebe submitted a repro made in the 1870s, by famous old glass-makers. Steve here submitted his own work.'

'You sure?' Corse loomed over me like solid cumulus.

'Positive. Hers felt antique. Steve's doesn't.'

Corse's great puce visage cleared. He rotated, looked at Big John. 'Here, Sheehan. Is Lovejoy a divvy?' And got a nod, thank God.

'I am, yes, I am!' I said, desperate to show I was agreeing with everybody, especially BJS. I'm pathetic. I was still cold.

'That's okay, then,' Corse said, to my vast relief.

'Josh,' Big John said, as everybody relaxed and started shaking hands on unknowable deals. 'Six and eightpence in the pound. For four months.'

'Right, John!' Josh croaked brightly, grinning as if he'd just been awarded a knighthood instead of having to cough up thirty-three per cent of his income for the next twelve weeks for letting mistakes happen on his territory. Still cheaper than death, though.

They paid me a groat and let me go, into that slippery old rain. That was the start of it.

Sometimes a vehicle can seem a real pal. A goon gave me the keys as rain chilled my face and motor-car doors slammed and serfs lurked about the loading bay. I stood watching them go, weakly raising a hand – ignored – in salutation to Corse, then Big John. The vehicles splashed past. Other saloons started up, roared after. No sign of Phoebe Colonna, or Jan Fotheringay of great renown. Gulp.

Alone and safely out of it.

I got in the cabin and sat there in the darkness to let my sweat dry. Escape comes in many guises. Across the estuary, lights winked. The harbour's opalescent sheen toned the night sky. Peace. I started the engine, drove out, heading along the wharf towards our town's orange sky glow.

Then the customer's buzzer sounded loudly in my ear, frightening me to death.

'Lovejoy?' a woman's voice said on the intercom.

Diana? Still here? I thought the goons had run her and her tame shag back to the limousine-riddled lay-by whence they'd come.

'What the hell are you doing still in there, silly cow?' I swerved nastily, yelled into the squawk-box. 'You made me jump out of my frigging skin.'

'Thank goodness,' the intercom said with relief. 'For one moment I thought you were one of those hulks, Lovejoy. Find a quiet place where we can talk.'

'Get knotted, missus,' I said. I was blazing, really narked. 'You're going back to Gazza Gaunt's garage – '

'Or I'll complain that your incompetence exposed the Tryste Service to the police, my influential husband, the Vice Squad . . .' Women's voices go sweet when they threaten.

'The Drum and Fife's got quite a nice secluded lounge,' I said politely, swallowing a bolus of pride.

'Good, Lovejoy. You learn quickly.' It was a purr. She'd never swallowed pride in her life. I could tell. She'd defend her pride with blood. I wish now I'd remembered that, but once pathetic, always.

3

The Drum and Fife is a posh roadhouse, a cut above spit-and-sawdust. To my dismay the place was heaving when I parked in its ancient flagged courtyard. I was too fed up to try anywhere else, and went to undo the passion waggon's rear door.

The lady stepped out, tutting because I'd no umbrella for her. I'd have used it for me, if I'd had one.

'Does it never stop raining?' She drew her collar round her.

'God left the taps running when he built East Anglia.'

'Well?' She gazed at the tavern. 'What are we waiting for?'

'Your, er, gentleman.' He hadn't emerged. 'Worn out, is he?'

She smiled in the exotic coloured lights that taverns string about themselves these days. 'Jervis left,' she said, and walked among the gleaming wet carapaces of the motors.

I scrambled to lock up and ran after her, hunched, through the worsening downpour. Why is it that hotels and suchlike spend a king's ransom on their fronts, yet their rear view is all drainpipes, steaming windows looking into horrible kitchens, rusty tubes?

Naturally, my 'nice secluded lounge' was thronged. Upstairs rollicked to the thump of some band. People dressed to the nines stood about chatting. You'd never seen so many carnations. A couple snogged in the coffee alcove with the abandoned passion reserved for strangers at a chance meeting. This wore hallmarks of a wedding.

'Sorry, missus,' I said, catching my streamliner up in the foyer as she stood looking about where to go. 'We picked a bad night.'

'No night's bad, Lovejoy,' she said, smiling. 'Days are hell.'

Her eyebrows demanded action, so I found us a place in an inglenook, a phoney iron grate with a cold fire. I looked my disgust. Spinning tin reflectors and a threepenny red bulb in plastic, pubs think they're Designer of the Year.

'Get me a martini, Lovejoy. No lemon.'

Bloody nerve. I nodded obediently, signalled with exotic mouthings to a puzzled wedding guest in the crowd. I'd complain

13

about waiter service when it was time to go. She should get her own frigging drink. I was hired to drive the blinking love truck, not flunkey drinks for her.

I gauged her as a crowd of youngsters tore whooping through the foyer. Balloons ballooned, streamers streamed, dresses flounced. Upstairs, cymbals crashed and an announcer bellowed something inane to prolonged applause. God, but weddings have a lot to answer for.

She looked different in the tavern's subdued lighting. Lovely, yes, but harder than her voice had suggested. I'd only seen her in rainy darkness before. Now, she was thirty, give or take a yard. Small but gorgeous. And so confident you could only admire her. Legs you could eat, figure you couldn't leave alone no matter how you tried. Skin alabaster perfection. Hair a delight –

'You approve, Lovejoy?' she asked.

Sarcasm makes me go red. I must have been staring.

'What d'you want, missus?' The description I'd been looking for: lush, but hard.

'Get me a cushion,' she said, extracting a cigarette from a handbag worth the whole Drum and Fife and expecting somebody to leap forward and light it. A bloke did, smiling eagerly.

She jerked a plume of smoke slowly, pursing her mouth in a way that almost stopped the show, and ignored him. He went his way, dazedly delighted to have been spurned by so gorgeous a creature. Aren't we daft?

'Get your own frigging cushion,' I heard myself say, and thought, oh, God. Now a bad report to Gazza.

She looked at me – actually at, as opposed to including me in the scenery. She did the woman's no-smile hilarity, the appraising gaze that makes you feel a prat.

'I meant, er, what do you want, lady?'

Driving Gazza's Tryste vehicles can be a real pain. He has three of the damned things. They're known among us by a crude double nickname – the first word rhymes with truck. You can land right in the mire. Reason: the course of true love does not run smooth. Whoever said that knew a thing or two. The last time I'd driven for Gazza was to a beach near Brancaster. The lovers inside had had a terrible fight – the woman a black eye, bleeding nose, the bloke scratched to blazes. Both had appealed to me in yells and screams

14

to judge the rightness of their separate causes. The police wahwahs had come. A right shambles, me declining any knowledge of the battling lovers. Luckily, Gazza has an understanding with the chief constable, so all was smooth bribery and corruption. Gazza blamed me and didn't pay me, the swine. Tonight's success was my attempt to show new-found efficiency, and I needed the money.

'What happened in the barn, Lovejoy. I'm intrigued.' A direct order. Tell, or else.

'It's like this,' I began.

'Excuse me, sir. Madam.' A real professionoil suaved up, three trainee slickers in tow. 'Mr Prendergast, manager. Do I have the honour of addressing one Lovejoy?'

'One has.'

Jodie Danglass smilingly raised her glass to me from a stool in the long bar. I pulled an ugly thank-you-for-nothing grimace at her, for bubbling me to this yak. She's pretty, new to the antique trade, with thrilling legs. She talks crudities in her sleep. I mean, she looks as if she might sometimes possibly do that.

Prendergast smiled, tache, dark pinstripes, teeth a-dazzle. I smiled back, scenting fraud. It's the one thing I'm good at, being one myself.

'The Drum and Fife welcomes you! Could I offer your lady and your good self a complementary drink, sir?'

'No, ta. We're just going.'

Fraudsters have to do the driving. I was interested to see how he'd put screws on me.

He twisted with a smirk. 'Could you value the antique painting on display in the foyer? Naturally, the D and F would recompense you. Perhaps a complementary sojourn . . . '

'There is no antique painting in the foyer.'

He gyrated, darting his assistants a quirky tight-mouthed smile. I'd said something he hated. 'Did one pause to look?'

'One didn't need to.' If there'd been an antique painting in the foyer, it would have pulled me like a magnet. It's the way we divvies are. Folk only believe you if you put on an act. That's why police look menacing, bank managers dress sterile, judges pretend deep thoughts. Everybody goes by appearances. I should have remembered that, too.

15

I sighed, made my excuses to Diana. The foyer was only a step. The painting was beautiful, a Turner watercolour of Venice. Scratched, rubbed, the paper's surface scarified just right. The colours were exactly his, the dark-tinted paper brilliant.

'Lovely.' You can't help admiring class. I felt smiling.

Prendergast blossomed, beaming. 'There, sir! Thank you! I knew that you would authenticate – '

'No, Mr Prendergast. It's nice but naughty. Fake. But done clever. She used the right watercolours, see? She had the paper made specially – '

'Fake?' He reeled. Minions rushed to support him, but I was fed up and moved away. What do folk want, for Christ's sake? He'd thought the painting miraculous – all in a second it's ugly? Like everybody else these days, blinded by money. Disgusting. I felt sick.

'Come on, love.' I grabbed Diana's arm and hustled her through the departing bride and groom's mob. Confetti snowed from balconies. People screeched and hollered. Delight was everywhere. It can really get you down.

Somebody had glee-painted my van and tied balloons all over it. *Didn't Tarried – Just Got Married!!!* in pink clung to grammar and my van's sides. Joy abounding's pretty depressing stuff. Sometimes I wish it would bound off somewhere else. I rammed Diana into the cabin, climbed after.

'Budge up, love.' I fired the engine and we moved off to a clatter of tins tipsy nerks had tied to the rear bumper.

'Who's this she, Lovejoy?' And when I looked at her blankly in the dashboard glow, 'You said she.'

'The faker? Oh, aye. Looks like Fanny's work. Runs a children's society. Husband's a parson. She's a friend.'

Her lips went thin. 'Friend? And you betrayed her, for a night's free stay in a tavern?'

Women are born judges – of everyone else, never themselves. Ever noticed that?

'It was either her, or Turner.'

We drove in silence for a few miles, during which I got wetter still by pausing to remove the tins. I got us on to the trunk road. I was dying to get shut of Diana.

'You didn't look at the painting, Lovejoy.' Women never let

things drop, do they? 'When we arrived, you just pushed into the lounge.'

'I never said I did look. In fact, I said the opposite.'

She was getting me narked. I should have returned her and the van hours ago. The evening was becoming supportive psychotherapy.

'You betray friends, yet you won't betray Turner, who's *dead*?'

'Dead?' That did it. Deliberately I slowed the van. I always start going faster in a temper and police radars skulk everywhere after nine o'clock. 'Ever seen a Turner painting, love?'

'Several. A friend of mine has at least two – '

'You've seen the greatest paintings in the history of the universe, and have the frigging nerve to say Turner's dead?' I should have chucked her out there and then, fifty miles an hour. If I'd any sense, I would have. 'You silly ignorant bitch.'

'*What* did you – ?'

I closed my mind to her. I was too tired. 'Tell Gazza, love. And your influential friends. And your famous Jervis bloke. But let me be.'

Fame is shame. I suddenly realized I'd recognized her paramour, the mighty Jervis. He'd triggered off that sense of something shameful, so he must be famous. Fame really *is* shame. Aren't the most famous football teams simply the ones who've kicked everything over the grass, season after season? Aren't Olympic champions merely the ones on the biggest dose of corticosteroids? The most famous politicians the crookedest? Except in antiques, where fame measures beauty and true human love, fame is shame.

Now, here's the really odd thing about that night. She didn't mention the argument to Gazza Gaunt at all. Not a word. I reached the bypass, pulled in, transferred her to the waiting limo, and saw her off without a single cross look.

More amazing still, I reached Gazza's depot and signed off about ten-thirty with no trouble. He was pleased, because cleaning ladies come to repair love's ravages in his Tryste vehicles, eleven to midnight. And I got a bonus.

'Bonus?' They're usually what other folk extort from me. An incoming bonus was a novelty. '*For* me? You sure?'

Gazza laughed, slapped my back. He's a great back-slapper, is

Gazza. He has a brother who clubs non-payers and uncooperative workers, so I didn't mind this sign of approval.

'Double bunce, Lovejoy. You really created an impression on that lady.'

Here was the odd thing. Gentleman Jervis had been very definitely miffed at my harbour detour. And the bird Diana had taken the hump when I was rude. So a *bonus*? Really weird. Gazza's never given a bonus in his life. Extracted a few, yes.

Doubtfully I inspected the notes. Strangerer and strangerer. I must have done something right, but what? Like a nerk, I forgot this vital question, pocketed the wodge and went on my way tiredly rejoicing.

This particular night, rejoicing meant Almira. She has a grand manor house in Birch near the church, and this quiet little cottage by the sea inlet. Mansion for august familial propriety, nook for nooky so to speak. Says her husband runs a chartered bank's investment company or some such.

Dinner was planned for seven-thirty, then passion till dawn. Arrangements don't have the accuracy they used to, I sometimes find. I think it's mainly because women don't get their act together. I was starving, could have eaten a horse. I got the bus down the estuary to Burnhanger, and walked into a flak storm. Luckily, Almira accepted my explanation that the taxi I'd got from town had run over a badger, and that I'd insisted on taking the poor injured animal to the vet's at Lexton. Naturally, I'd had to stay with the creature until I knew it was going to live. I was so moved by my tale I welled up. Finally she forgave me, and said I was just a lovely, sweet thing. Back on the right lines, thank God, I had the grub. In my honour she'd come off her perennial staples – whittled carrot and a lettuce-wrapped nut – and cooked food instead.

The passion began about one in the morning, and lasted to six-forty-five a.m. That's when she gets up to feed her bloody horses and bully the serfs.

She barely had time to make my breakfast before she had to streak off in her Jaguar. And even then she forgot my fried bread. Women really nark me. All night to work out the right breakfast, and still she gets it wrong. Can you believe it? Typical, that. It's time women learned to get organized. Probably comes from having nothing to do all day. I slept on, the sleep of the just.

4

My cottage is a short distance from town, slumped beneath thatch in its overgrown garden wilderness. Our village isn't up to much. Historically a recorded failure over two millennia, it's shown no improvement since King Cymbeline, another local loser, lost all to Rome. I don't like countryside, but for once was glad to get back to my bare flagged floors even if I did have to pay the extortionate fare on the village bus. Almira would go berserk when she found me gone – I'd promised to wait until eleven, but once you're awake you can't just stare at the ceiling, can you? And I'd money in my pocket, my bonus from Gazza.

The phone was cut off, and electricity. Par for the penniless. This narks me. I mean, what if I'd been an old-age pensioner, shivering, wanting to call Doc Lancaster? Lucky for them I wasn't, or I'd have pegged out and made them feel really sorry. The post was on time, eleven o'clock delivery. I brewed up as the post lass shovelled bills into the porch. She came in.

I'd built a fire of beechwood, starting it with yesterday's unopened letters, and got a kettle on.

'Burning evidence, Lovejoy?'

'Some old logs, Mich.' They were beechwood. Two pounds of beech soot to a gallon of water, boiled briefly, then decanted and evaporated to dryness, is the ancients' recipe for bistre, the pigment Old Masters drew with. A lot of forged antique drawings were due to appear in the next antiques auctions, after which my electricity and water supply might miraculously get switched on – if Fanny delivered the fake antique paper on time. Some local swine was testing my Old Master forgeries for the right antique watermark, using beta-radiography, so I'd had to pay Fanny's exorbitant prices and she'd never even seduced me, the cow. I ask you. Beta-radiography's simple: you put a radioactive source under any paper, with a film on top. Leave it a while. Develop the film. And presto! A photo of the paper's watermark! It's a cheap and simple foolproof test of antique

19

paper (which is why, of course, antique dealers avoid it like the plague).

She was telling me off. 'Michelle, not Mich. It's our anniversary, Lovejoy. Don't I get a card? Flowers?'

I stared. She laughed, a tiny sprite of a girl with a smile that makes you forget how hopeless the mail is these days. I like her, a red-haired pest.

'Two years I've been teaching you my name.' She disapproves of my habitat's coarser features. 'Never a word of thanks.'

'Who needs letters?'

'I'm valuable, Lovejoy.' She perched prettily on the divan, wrinkled her nose at its unmade condition. 'You didn't sleep here last night. Nor the one before.'

'So what? I was, er, busy,' I said lamely. Women make you feel guilty even when you've done nothing.

'You still with that rich tart, Lovejoy? You didn't ask me why I'm valuable.'

'Why're you valuable, Mich?'

'Because I'm a winged messenger. Tinker's at the Treble Tile, very urgent. And a posh lady in a monstermobile is asking Dulcie where is Lovejoy Antiques, Inc.'

That would have been almost worth another stare, but the kettle boiled just then and I had to dash to find my two mugs. Michelle lay in an *Olympia* by Manet posture. Dulcie's our village postmistress. Michelle has a phone thing on her pedal bicycle. I groaned inwardly, except Michelle heard me. It'd probably be Diana repenting of her bonus.

'Tell Dulcie to get rid.' I held up the mug as a bribe.

'No sugar.' She smiled and waggled provocatively out, doing the trailing-fox-fur mime. I felt worn out. Not even noon, and already hunted. Is it me? Everybody else has such control.

Tinker's my barker, a filthy shuffler who lives partly on ale and pickings, but mostly on me. He's my rumour-ferret for antiques. The best in the business, he assimilates news by osmosis. I mean, he can stand in a remote village pub all day long, gradually getting more and more kaylied, then tell you just before he falls down paralytic at midnight what's gone on at auctions in Ipswich, Norwich, even the Midlands. My part of the contract is to see his boozing slates are paid, every tavern in the Eastern hundreds.

Magee's Brewery should send me a turkey at Christmas.

Michelle came back inside, closing the porch door, I noticed. She's almost a pal, as far as the Royal Mail services go. I gave her the cracked mug because it cuts my lip.

'Now, Lovejoy,' she said. 'Blackmail time.'

'Who're we doing over?'

'Me,' she corrected. 'I'm blackmailing someone.'

That sprawl out of Manet's famous painting was almost exact, except there was no Nubian slave, no black neck ribbon. And Michelle was clothed. I looked about for blackmailees. Me?

'Me?'

'You, Lovejoy. Pay up, pay up, and play my game. Two years' flirting is two years too many.'

'Or what?' Gawd, I'd not even had a swig. I tried to sound defiant.

'Or your parcel goes missing.' She smiled, laid her mug aside, beckoned with a crooked finger. 'It's registered, stamped, sealed, insured – '

'Parcel?' I licked my lips. I wasn't due any parcel. No antiques come through the legit post these days. I wondered about my past scams. Had that bloke in Ribblesdale finally decided to sell me his assortment of children's rattles? I'd been after them for a twelvemonth. Mainly silver Regency, but with two North American Indian tribal baby rattles the most valuable of all. Sounds daft, but they'd buy a decent house, freehold, with furniture thrown in. Or had that Amsterdam dealer weakened, and sent me his Napoleonic prisoner-of-war bone sailing-ship model on approval? Worth a new car any day, especially with slivers of horn –

'Interfering with the Royal Mail's illegal.'

'I'm unscrupulous. Yes or no?'

I hesitated. It had to happen, of course. Women always have the final say. It's really only a question of when. It wasn't right. I knew that. I mean, Michelle had just got wed. Her new husband is a tough road-mender, all brawn and beef, this week labouring on the village bypass. And women always blab. I sometimes think that's why they do this. All these arguments totalled a resounding no. But antiques are antiques.

'Okay.' Being cheap costs, I find.

'The door.'

Obediently I went to wedge a stool behind it – the lock's wonky – and bumped into Jodie Danglass. She was entering briskly.

'Hello, Lovejoy. I knew you'd want to thank me for last night's . . .' She saw Michelle and beamed even brighter. 'Should I say sorry, or offer congratulations?'

Michelle swept out. Even a post lass can flounce if she's a mind to.

'Look, Mich,' I tried lamely after her, but got nothing back. She seized her bike and pedalled off in disdain.

Jodie was done up to the nines. I eyed her. 'You're not winning my heart, Jode. You're down on points.'

'Come, Lovejoy. Wear your very best. You've a customer. Sports centre in Ladyham.'

'This gear is it.' The new recreation place she mentioned was for the megamoneyed, not scruffs the likes of me. But a rich antiques customer must be obeyed.

She looked me up and down. 'Well, they said come whatever.' She smiled, brilliant with intimacy. 'At least *I* know you're spotless underneath.'

See what I mean? They can't help bragging they've nicked the lolly. It narks me. She had her motor at the gate. I got in, asking who the customer was.

'Not the foggiest, darling. Thought you'd tell me. She phoned me ten minutes since. Offered more than I make in a week to get you to Ladyham.' Jodie squeezed my leg, a cruelty with her shapely pins scissoring seductively as she drove. 'Didn't your persuasive tactics work last night, then?'

Last night? She'd seen me in the inglenook at the Drum and Fife with good old Diana, of bonus fame. Was Diana the customer? I settled back for the journey.

'Not my knee when I'm driving, Lovejoy.'

'Sorry.' She'd started it, then blames me. See what I mean?

The Nouvello Troude Sports and Recreation Centre dwarfs Ladyham, a village of insignificant size and zero fame. More of a hamlet, really. One pub, a stream, a church, a gaggle of houses old as the hills. And, new on the outskirts, a giant complex of tennis courts, buildings filled with desperates pumping iron, swimming

22

pools and diving boards. They've even flattened fields into running tracks and steeplechase courses. It's obscene.

Jodie parked by the slummer's entrance – the smallest motor in the proper car park was a Bentley – and we entered the perfumed interior. Talk about plush. A log fire – no rotating tinsel glow lights at the Nouvello Troude, thank you. Wilton carpets, a glass display case of genuine Manton flintlock long arms on the wall, chandeliers. The reception hall was baronial, panelled and adorned. Very few of the loungers looked athletic. More of a club atmosphere, really, broken only by the sound of quiet chatter and somewhere the tap of a ball.

A couple of women gazed up, smiling, sipping interesting liquids, waiters hovering to bring more. Conversation resumed, with low laughter at my scruffiness.

'Mr Troude, please,' Jodie told some serf.

The kulak practically genuflected into the carpet's pile at the name and swayed ahead of us, giving backward glances like a keen collie.

'Who's Troude?' I asked in a whisper. We passed along corridors with original watercolours every few yards, Doulton decorative moon flasks, oviform vases and figures on small pedestals. This was class.

'Somebody who wouldn't bring your Diana into a place like this, Lovejoy.' Why *my* Diana? Why were we whispering like spies?

On to a glamorous balcony, plusher than any West End hotel. Beautiful people strolled, in or out of dressing-gowns. Some lounged, drank. Others basked under lovely complexion-gilding glims, and drank. Still others stayed in their designer dresses, and drank. All ogled, looked, drank. I felt uncomfortable. We sensitive plebs do, among the surreal and glorious.

'How d'you do. Lovejoy?' Troude was a slender, sun-crisped Latin, gold bracelets and chains against chestnut tan. His shirt alone could have bought my cottage, its two dud mortgages included. 'Welcome to Nouvello Troude.'

'Ta.' I felt I had to say that, though he'd only shaken my hand. Wiry was the word. A bullfighter's physique. He'd be a natural on a horse. Maybe, I thought hopefully, I should introduce him to Almira, get her off my back, so to speak.

23

'Miss Jodie. I thank you for conducting Lovejoy hither.'

A faint bow, no handshake. Get thee gone, Jodie, was his message. She made a smiling withdrawal. Conducting hither? Christ Almighty.

'Please sit, Lovejoy. Drink?'

'Tea, please.' I'd been done out of my home-brew, not to mention Michelle. The world owed me.

A sudden screech made my blood run cold. I thought, oh, no. Not here, the one time in my life I'd made posh. But it was. Sandy, as always larger than life.

We were on a balcony above a swimming pool. The plunge was not one of your echoing glass-domed halls filled with floundering Olympic hopefuls. Beautiful: palms, small courtyards with exotic plants, rimmed with natural walks, genuine grass (indoors? How the hell?). And a few dozen glitterati, the men shapely look-I'm-stupendous, the women mouth-wateringly luscious. No more exotic plant, however, than Sandy.

'Coooeee! It's me! Lovejoy!'

In a bikini, for God's sake, and a floral see-through dressing-gown, off the shoulder, with high-heel sampan shoes in magenta-studded gold. I went red. I honestly can't see the point of making yourself look a pillock, but it's how he is. Everybody was tittering.

'Hiyer, Sandy.'

He came over, doing a sexy slink. I moved back a bit. His eyelashes raked the air of his advance. God, he looked a mess. Mascara, rouge, lipstick. And . . . I stared.

'You *love* my earrings, Lovejoy!' he crooned. It was a threat. With Sandy, everything's a threat. 'Aquatic motif! I'm a prince – well, *princess* – between two frogs!'

A live frog sat dismally in the bowl that dangled from each ear loop.

'Er, great.' I hesitated. You daren't offend Sandy's dress sense. He and Mel – you always offend Mel anyway, no matter how hard you try – are antique household furniture and Georgian-Regency antiquers of mighty opulence. They inhabit a converted school-house and barn not far off, and despite appearances are shrewd, aggressive dealers. 'Do they hurt?'

'My earrings?' He tittered, gushed round to see everybody was paying close attention. 'I'd *love* it if they did!'

Folk chuckled. Sandy shrilled a laugh.

'The frogs, I meant.'

He rounded on me, spitting malice. 'More worried about reptiles than about *me* you hideous *ape*, Lovejoy! You spiteful, inane, inept *failure* you!'

To my dismay he burst into tears, teetered off at a lame sprint in his high heels. I called a sorry, Sandy, after him, but knew I was for it. He'd not forget that, or forgive. I sighed an apology to Troude.

'Sandy's an old friend, sir. Not', I added anxiously in case it got back to Sandy and landed me in still deeper trouble, 'old as in aged. Old as in good.' Good as in . . . ? I gave up. I'm hopeless explaining at the best of times. With all these sweet-lifers smiling at my discomfiture, I began to wish I'd stayed at home. At least there I'd have got ravished by Michelle, and earned my parcel.

'You really did mean the frogs, Lovejoy!' Troude was interested.

'Course. The poor buggers were . . .' I cleared my throat, rubbed the words from the air with a gesture. 'The poor things were trapped. It must be horrible.'

He paused to allow three uniformed varlets to serve tea. Sterling silver, I saw. Other balcony tables had silver plate. Troude must be a high-flyer. You can't count new silver, new gold, new anything. Only antiques matter. But society assays worth as wealth.

A peasant stayed to pour, grovelled in withdrawal. I eyed Troude. A man of multo wealth and much, much more. That explained Troude's aura. Confidence? Authority? In that instant, Troude became my rival. Don't misunderstand me: I don't mean pistols-for-two-coffee-for-one, all that. But this man was the focus of the whole Nouvello Centre. Kicking order having been established, we sipped tea and admired the decor. My one advantage was that I could wait longer than he. Like Prendergast of the Drum and Fife, an antiques perpetrator has to put the screws in. Your screwee's job is to wait, and hope to get out in one piece.

'This leisure complex cost a fortune, Lovejoy. You like it?'

'Sumptuous.'

'You hate it.' He sighed, not put out in the slightest. 'It's a curious feature of civilization that administrators escape blame.

Future archaeologists will clear the rubble, and reconstruct, what you see about you. They will be appalled at its sheer bad taste, find my name on the foundation stone, and blame me for crassness.'

'You own it, eh? I'd rather have had the fields.' Which is saying something because I hate countryside. It's superfluous. I can't honestly see what's wrong with concrete. The Nouvello was still a good argument for environmentalists, though, even to me.

He smiled, made that open-palmed gesture that isn't quite apology. Italian?

'To the *salotto buono*, appearances are everything.'

The business oligarchy, the ancient blood line of the gentry. No, not Italian. That hint of sarcasm revealed more than it hid. It sailed close to contempt, but what for?

'Look, er, Mr Troude. I'm sorry I spoiled that scene. I didn't mean to annoy Sandy. And I am sort of busy – '

He allowed a fawner to hurtle forward and light his cigarette. His glance swiftly backed the girl out of earshot. 'Lovejoy. The reason I invited you is that I hear you have a precious gift. I wish to use it. Would you be agreeable?'

'Use how?'

His expression was nearly amused. 'Your gift only works in one way. I know, you see. It is not a skill that can be passed or taught.' His cigarette hand paused, but only for an instant. Two waitresses clobbered furniture aside racing to supply the missing ashtray. I felt the waft of vitriol in the air. They left, to tremble somewhere else, guilty of omission. Jobs would roll.

'You know a divvy?' I was interested.

There's not many of us. You can always tell people who've see it before. Folk who don't believe are the majority, and simply don't want to believe.

'Yes, one. He suffered an unfortunate accident.' He shrugged without visible expenditure of energy. I wish I could do that. As soon as I got home I knew I'd be trying to do it in the mirror, quirky smile and meaningful eyebrows. I'd fail. Comes from living near the Mediterranean, I think. 'I miss him.'

'For what?'

'His divvying gift worked for most antiques, Lovejoy. Not all types, but enough.' He exhaled smoke. Studious, but it wasn't scholastic learning. Monetary reflections hung in that smoke, not classicism. He was a roller, not a caring antiquarian.

'Will he get better, your divvy?'

Troude hadn't called divvying a skill, or an aptitude. Gift. He'd said gift. A believer, all right. Suddenly I wanted him to be a cynic, and me far away from here.

'Alas and alack, regrettably no.' Hither, *and* alack? Maybe he liked Errol Flynn remakes. Play is life, for the rich. 'Our divvy was old, and his gift sadly fading. I immediately started looking for a, forgive me, Lovejoy, a substitute. A full year ago. Even before he . . . became unavailable.'

'I don't know if I'm up to doing a lot,' I told him frankly. My hands were sweating. I managed not to shake. That was pretty good, seeing I now wanted to know if he'd killed old Leon in Marseilles. 'And I've some deals on.'

'Cancel them, Lovejoy.' He was so pleasant, smiling with teeth off a dentist's advert. 'You will be splendidly recompensed. Unless, of course, your display with the Portland was a deception, and you yourself a fraud.'

How did he know about the Portland Vase fakery contest? I smiled. I quite like caution. 'I'd have to think about it.'

'I shall arrange to appraise your gift Lovejoy, if you don't mind. You will be given a generous retainer.'

'Doing what?'

'A small task. Judge a few antiques, maybe move a little antique silver.'

Sounded easy. I often did such jobs, vannies we call them. 'Get my old Ruby out of hock, I'll shift anything anywhere.'

He smiled at my quip and gave his non-shrug shrug. 'Ruby? An auto? Very well. There is one small question.'

There always is. I stilled. 'Yes?'

A crowd of elegants strolled on to the balcony. They chattered less noisily when they saw Troude, but just as happily.

'You are a northerner, yes?' He was French. Definitely. He'd nearly said *oui* like they do, the yes a reflex terminal. When I nodded, 'Your parents? Grandparents?' He was very intent about it. Still, whatever turns folk on.

'One granddad a wild Irishman from Kilfinnan. One grannie

Scotch, from Kinghorn in Fife. A granddad and grannie darkest Lancashire back to the year dot. Mixture, really.'

He relaxed with disproportionate relief. Funny, because grampa talk bores people for miles around.

'That accounts for your gift. A Celtic element. But no French?'

'Sorry.' I did the only sort of shrug I know, a feeble imitation of the real thing. I was thinking what gunge. He declined my offer to write down my address, inferring he already knew it by heart or that his minions would.

Sandy carolled a farewell from the upper balcony as I took my leave. His shriek of laughter made all heads turn. He'd replaced his frog earrings with on-off neon fishes.

'Naughtily nautical, Lovejoy!' he trilled. 'You admire?'

I just hoped the electric fishes were not alive. I left, muttering an apology to Troude. He came with me to the entrance to see me off. I swear even the squash balls muted as he passed.

'Sandy is not our most serious Nouvello member,' he said. 'Everybody is fond of him though.'

We parted amicably enough. His giant limo took me to town, dropped me off at the Antiques Arcade by the war memorial.

Safe now among crowds of shoppers, I watched the motor recede. I felt vaguely tainted, as if my skin was about to erupt. Troude had come unnervingly close to saying something else instead of Nouvello member. I desperately needed Tinker and a phone. I'd kill Jodie for landing me in all this, silly cow. I saw Almira's car approaching, and ducked into the Arcade. It's safer among antique dealers. At least you know they're sharks and out to get you. Friends and lovers are infinitely worse.

5

There's a main trouble with anything good. Like with women my question is, why can't they see how much we crave them, for heaven's sake? (The answer's that maybe they do . . .)

The trouble with antiques is fakes. The trouble with fakes is antiques. Just as in any war, greed is the instigator, and dithering uncertainty the determinant, of success. Thus antique dealers become a happy band of mourners at the funeral feast for casualties in an unending conflict.

Our local merry mob of antique dealers occupies a few crevices of dereliction. They've installed a small bar since the boozing law changed, to sell liver-corroding liquids at extortionate prices. The whole Arcade is nothing more than an alcove of many alcoves. You'd walk past it with hardly a glance. Wise folk do just that.

The usual chorus of jeers and imprecations rose to greet me. They were all in, bemoaning (a) the cheapskate public, (b) being broke, and (c) having this priceless Rembrandt/Wedgwood/Michaelangelo genuine antique that they're willing to let go for a few quid as a special personal favour to you/him/her/anybody . . . The siren song of the dealer.

Frederico grabbed me first, looking more like Valentino than Valentino. He's from Wigan, but cracks on he's never been to gaol. He wore a green suit by mistake, because he's only Irish on Fridays. Mondays he's from Tuscany.

'I've got a couple of things, Lovejoy!' He hisses this terse sentence, looking furtively round shoulders, trying for Fagin in the next amateur *Oliver*.

'Over here when you've a minute, Lovejoy,' Liz Sandwell called. I waved, brightening. Her tough boyfriend wasn't with her. 'Got what, Fred?'

Fool for asking. You need never ask, not with Frederico. His act's something to do with the ferries from the Hook of Holland. They dock at Harwich bringing loads of tourists. He gets caught out sometimes, finds he's claimed to speak a tourist's own lingo.

Also, he only talks gibberish, a handicap for so determined a communicator. It's not my fault if I get confused. He dragged me to his alcove – a plank, a chair, a battery light, two boxes.

'Lovejoy,' Donk interposed, breathing fury. 'You owe me. That message – '

'Sod off, Donk. I'm busy – '

But he wouldn't be put off with IOUs, promises, tales of misery. Only when Frederico shelled out the dosh did Donk leave. I think civilization's got a lot to answer for, now trust's gone. Which raised the interesting question why Frederico paid up for me. He's never done that in his life.

'It's genuine old glass, Lovejoy. Honest. Every sign!'

'Oh, aye.'

One of his two boxes yielded a lovely little sweetmeat glass, its stem faceted and its foot scalloped. The dealers all around went quiet and started drifting over. Frederico made insulting gestures to repel them. It worked. They retreated muttering, narked and envious. Old glass is valuable beyond common sense these days. If you find one, order your blonde and two-litre Morgan and spit in your general manager's eye.

'See? Genuine 1780.' He sounded as if he was offering me surface-to-air missiles, peering about.

'Sorry, Frederico.' His paddy green kept getting me on the wrong track. 'It's duff.'

'No!' A cry from the heart. The other dealers chuckled, resumed chatter, pleased their friend would lose a fortune.

This is always the hard part. The glass simply didn't reverberate in me. Therefore it was dud. How to find explanations other people would understand. . . ?

'Look, Frederico.' I held it up against the bulb, though daylight facing north's best. 'Glass isn't a solid. It's a supercooled liquid. Think that, and you're halfway there.' Pointing, I showed him. 'Old glass – anything before 1800 – *must* have tiny air bubbles. Modern glass has virtually none.'

'But the iridescence, Lovejoy!' He was almost in tears.

You feel like knocking their heads together sometimes. Can't the blighters read? Being basically fluid, glass interacts with air and whatever crud's around. So over the years, wetness – in air, ground – causes its surface to iridesce, due to laminations. Think

30

of microscopic scaling, and you've almost got it. Light gets bounced about wrongly in the glass, causing the effect. Sadly, dealers and the thieving old public jump to conclusions, the daftest but most constant folly.

'Somebody's dunked this in a cesspool.' It can take two cesspool years to get the right quality of iridescence. I've had three good fakes – Laurela at Dovercourt makes them for, er, friendship's sake – steeping in a marsh near here since last Kissing Friday. I sluch them out to check, every fortnight. It's grim, because one of those yellow-beaked black ducks has nested on the very spot, interfering little blighter.

'I've a certificate, Lovejoy! The industrial chemists – '

Now he was really agitated. I looked at him with real surprise. He's a con artist, so should know that every antique fake doing the rounds has more certificates than an Oxford don. The trick is to slice a piece of genuine ancient iridescent glass surface from some antique, and have it analysed – then sell the certificate to a dealer, who'll pass the testimonial off as belonging to some fake drinking goblet he happens to have.

The other box made me hesitate. He was so miserable. I waited. He waited. Liz Sandwell called. I looked expectantly at Frederico. He said nothing, forlorn with his dud glass.

'Look, mate,' I said, with sympathy. The poor bloke had pinned his faith – his greed, really – on scooping the pool. 'Get a few fakes from some old genuine piece, and cement them to your fake. The old trick. Then it'll sell at any provincial auction. And you can use your certificate to authenticate it.'

Hope filled his eyes. Avarice works wonders. 'Cement how?'

Narked, I walked off. Dealers are useless. I mean, Theophilus wrote how in his *De Diversis Artibus* in the eleventh century. The world hasn't read it yet.

Liz Sandwell was better value. I kept looking back at Frederico's other box. It pealed chimes in me, reverberating.

'Eh?'

'I said go halves, Lovejoy.' She smiled, a lovely offer. But you have to be sure what a woman's offer actually is. I keep making this mistake.

My throat cleared. 'Halves of what?'

'Not me, Lovejoy. This illuminated panel.'

'It's rubbish.' I turned on my heel.

She caught me. 'Why, Lovejoy?'

Because it didn't utter a single boing. Except Liz wanted a reason reason. So I looked at her neffie panel. A parchment egg tempera painting, St Sebastian dying heroically for something or other. Lovely, the right style and everything. If I'd been a buyer I'd have said Early English, worth a small house. Then I looked across at the dejected Frederico.

'I'll tell you why, Liz, if you persuade Vasco Da Gama there to show me the antique in his other box.'

She went and wheedled, returning in a trice with the box. The closer it came the more certain the chime. I swallowed to wet my throat for speech. Talk is problems.

'Can I look?'

Frederico, offhand, nodded. I reached inside the humble cardboard and felt a warm loving living thing slip smiling into my palm. I lifted it out, my soul singing.

It was beautiful. Besides glass, the one class of antiques that has stormed ahead of the world price spirals is that of scientific instruments. This was superb. For sheer price it could have bought the whole Arcade, and the street too I shouldn't wonder.

A travelling sundial. Octagonal base, incised with lines and numbers, with a recessed compass. Its gnomon – the little raised bit that casts the shadow – was shaped like a bird. Four hour scales, and latitude marks for 43 and 52 degrees North. You would adjust the bird gnomon for whatever latitude you were sailing in.

'Michael?' I heard my voice ask. 'Is it really you?' I rubbed the grime, licked a thumb, tried again. And it was.

Michael Butterfield – spelt right, thank God; contemporary fakers got his name wrong, like Smith the great porcelain faker did with Wedgwood – was an Englishman in Paris. For over fifty years he turned out superb works of genius. Naturally, from 1670 on his brilliant creations have been forged, stolen, faked, copied, like all things bright and beautiful. A true hero of talent. Can you imagine him, striving for perfection by candlelight when all around was filth and degradation, with –

'Sit down, Lovejoy.' Liz was holding me.

'No.' I pulled away from the silly cow. They treat you like a cripple, women. 'How much, Frederico?'

He looked amazed, me to the sundial. 'It's only brass, Lovejoy.'

'Butterfield made in silver and brass, nerk. How much?'

A distant cough sounded, coming nearer with a pronounced Doppler. The vibration shuddered through the Arcade. A flake of paint gave up clinging to the wall under the force. Tinker was approaching along the High Street.

'You sure, Lovejoy?'

He was asking *me*? Gawd above. 'How much?'

He licked his lips, tried to take his dial back. I kept it. Just because an instrument's made of brass doesn't mean lunatics can't damage it.

He glanced at his duff glass. 'I thought it was the other . . .'

The other way round? I might have known. A put-up job. Who'd given him the two boxes? No wonder he'd got the wrong suit on today. With tears in my eyes I replaced the Butterfield dial in its box and handed it over. Neither the fake glass nor genuine instrument was his to sell. Life is a pig.

'Sod off, Fred.' Where was I? 'Your parchment, Liz.'

' 'Ere, Lovejoy.' Tinker came in, shuffling behind his thundering cough like infantry following a creeping barrage. 'There's a tart wants you over at – '

'A sec, Tinker.' I gave the filthy old devil the bent eye, to restrict my trade secrets to a few square miles. His idea of tact is to pluck my sleeve in a theatrical mimicry of stealth, while booming out anything confidential as if yelling from a distant shore. I'd promised Liz a reason reason. I scanned her illuminated parchment.

'Blue, love. They should have used lapis lazuli instead of Prussian blue. Diesbach discovered Prussian blue in 1704, centuries too late for your mythical mediaeval monk.'

Actually, I'd have given modern French ultramarine a go, made up in egg yolk. Better still, I'd have re-re-remortgaged my cottage, and bought quarter of an ounce of genuine lapis lazuli. I hate fakers who're too flaming idle. So what that genuine lapis lazuli's the costliest pigment on earth? Ha'p'orth of tar and all that. Tip: get round the experts on this vital point by mixing a proportion of Guimet's synthetic ultramarine, available since 1824 for heaven's sake, with twenty per cent ground-up lapis. You finish up with an almost perfect faker's blue –

33

'That posh tart with the big knockers, Lovejoy,' Tinker interrupted. 'Her's a frigging pest. Wants you outside.'

'Thank you, Lovejoy,' Liz Sandwell said sweetly, retrieving her parchment. 'You may go, seeing duty calls.'

I leaned away from Tinker. His breath emerges very, very used. Must have been drinking solidly since dawn. His old army greatcoat was stained, his mittens filthy, rheumy eyes bloodshot, his stubble encrusted with food residues. I was pleased to see him in such good shape.

'Same one looking for me round the village early on?'

'Nar. That was just some whore, Lovejoy.'

'Can I listen?' Liz was enthralled. 'Or are you inaudible?'

Tinker got annoyed. ' 'Ere, miss. You keep yourself to yourself. We've work to do, if you haven't!' His attention returned to me. 'Young folk. They're all on tablets. I blames this free education.' He has theories like hedgehogs have fleas.

'Come on.' I got him out of the rear entrance, and we made the Three Tuns by diving among the alleys.

'That posh tart, with them frigging nags.' He inhaled half a pint at one go, settled back with a sigh. 'The one you've been shagging since Wittwoode's auctioned them funny frocks.'

Which being translated meant Almira. Tinker was reminding me that she and I met at a local auction of funny frocks – Tinker's phrase for the most beautiful collection of Continental eighteenth-century dresses ever seen in the Eastern Hundreds. Tip: embroidery's still the cheapest way to buy into the antiques game, but not for long, not for long. I thought deeply.

'Who was the woman asking at the post office?'

'Told you, Lovejoy. That whore.'

It wasn't right. Tinker's very strait-laced. He didn't call people whores, unless . . . What was it Jodie'd said? About Diana being not quite the sort of woman a gentleman like Troude would allow in the Nouvello? To me, Diana'd come over as a bonny bird simply having sly sex with some magnate who couldn't risk scandal. What more natural than to use Gazza's lovemobile, driven by that pillar of virtue Lovejoy? Surveys say seventy-two per cent of us are hard at illicit love affairs, surveys say. I wonder how they missed the remaining twenty-eight per cent. To work.

'Something's niggling, Tinker.' I fetched him another three

pints, lined them up on the table. 'Sandy showed up yesterday in Ladyham – '

'He would, bleeding queer,' Tinker snorted. 'Never out of that frigging Frog centre since it opened. Put up a tithe of the gelt, he did. Like your tart.'

My headaches usually come on pretty gradually, unless they get help. I pressed my temple to slow things down. Tinker was rabbiting on.

'Wait, Tinker.' Tart and bint are simply females in his vocabulary, but a whore was a whore was a . . . 'You mean Almira?'

'Aye. Know how they got the land? Did the old dole shuffle from that poxy club, Mentle Marina.' He growled. I raised a finger just in time. He spat phlegm noisily into a drained glass, gave a pub-shaking cough, and recovered, wiping his eyes on his shredding sleeve. 'It only worked because that poofter's pal's some rich Continental git.'

Too much. Both temples were pulsing now. I was a nerk between two throbs . . . My mind finally clicked into gear. Sandy's earrings. Princess, between two frogs. I tried to recall Troude's comment. He was observing that I hadn't got Sandy's joke. One, Troude. Number Two . . . Who was Number Two?

'Almira? She financed the place?'

'Her and that frigging pansy. They got a kitty up for some Frog. Has his bleedin' nails done at the barber's, just like a poxy tart. Don't know what the frigging world's coming to, Lovejoy.' He spat expertly on to the carpet before I could restrain him. 'Her lawjaw's got four houses. Did you know?'

'Who?' Now quite lost.

'Always at frigging Ladyham, him. Says he once rode for England.' He snorted in derision, which from Tinker is a pub-clearing operation that nearly blew me off my stool.

'Rowed, like boat?'

'No. *Rode*, Lovejoy. Frigging horse!' He cackled, wagging his head. A couple of brown pegs trying to pass as teeth littered his gummy grin. 'How can you ride a horse for England? That's not proper racing, like the Grand National. What a berk! Him in Parliament. He's never there. What we pay him for, eh?'

It would take more than a casual chat to disentangle Tinker's rumours. I gave up. Almira's husband an MP, and a banking company lawyer to boot?

'Antiques, Tinker.' I tried to get back on the rails.

'Oh, aye.' He grimaced. 'Sorry, Lovejoy. Baff's dead.'

Silence for the departed, mostly to absorb shock. It was like a blow on the temple. I honestly couldn't see for a second. My vision slowly cleared.

Baff's a talkative, friendly sort of bloke. No more than twenty-five. A refugee from the army – some regiment giving up its colours after half a millennium. Baff settled locally with a bird called Sherry down the estuaries. Nice bloke. I like, liked, him a lot. He hadn't a clue about the porcelain and jewellery he tried to sell, of course. An average antique dealer, mostly by theft. Tell you how he stole in a minute.

'What happened?'

'Got done over last evening. Some yobbos. He was working a seaside ice-cream stall. They did him for the takings.'

Dully, the facts clunked in. Baff died on the way to hospital. The spoilers vanished in the crowds. The Plod were questioning some youths, but nobody was charged yet. Fat chance, in a thirty-acre seashore all caravans and holiday-makers.

'Watch it. Your tart, Lovejoy.'

Almira was alighting from her motor. She's so splendid-looking that folk slow down to watch – blokes to lust, women to tot up the cost of her clothes.

Alacrity called. 'Tinker. Find Steve Yelbard. You know, the glassie. And Phoebe. Donk should know, if anybody.'

'Dunno, Lovejoy.' I slipped him a couple of notes, so he could keep supping ale, his only source of calories. 'The Portland Vase final? That Phoebe's a snotty cow. That bugger Yelbard's worse – he's honest.' He spoke with the gloom of the antiques barker, to whom honesty's the ultimate cheat.

'Get on with it.' I made for the door, preparing a smile of welcome for Almira.

' 'Ere, Lovejoy!' Tinker was rolling in the aisles. One of his jokes loomed. Wearily I waited in the doorway for the hilarity. 'I'll bet you give her a better ride than her nags!'

And he literally fell off his stool. I eyed him gravely as he recovered, cackling helplessly, blotting his eyes as he climbed back up. A couple of blokes down the bar looked at each other uncomprehendingly.

'Very droll, Tinker,' I said sombrely, and left to the tender mercy of Almira.

She was there, glowering on the pavement. I started with surprise and rushed to embrace her with thankful exclamations.

'Doowerlink!' I cried, giving her a buss. 'You're there! Where did you get to? I left the note saying definitely ten-fifteen at the war memorial! I was absolutely frantic – '

It's the one way to cast doubt into a woman's mind, hint that she's mislaid some vital message.

'Ten-fifteen?' she asked, mistrustful.

'Yes, love!' I was so impatient. 'We've missed our chance, doorlung! The holiday I was planning!' I sighed. 'The last places on the flight went at twenty-to. Oh, hell!' I took her hands, gazed sorrowfully at her. She looked about guiltily, tried to recover her fingers from my vice-like grip.

'Not here, Lovejoy.' She was trying to look casual for appearance's sake.

'They couldn't hold the seats. It was a charter flight.'

She was looking hard, seeing pure truth shining nobly from my eyes.

'You've been planning a holiday, Lovejoy? For us?'

I went all soulful. 'It's little enough, Almira. I mean, you take me out to lovely meals. And that weekend on the coast.' I looked away, biting my lip. 'This was all I could afford.'

'Oh, Lovejoy.' She started to look guilty. I was pleased, making headway. 'I'm so sorry. Was it very dear? Only – '

'No, love.' I went proud. '*I* wanted to treat *you*.'

'A lovely idea!' she said mistily. 'Where did you leave it?'

'Eh?' People were pushing past on the pavement. I kept having to move aside for prams and pushchairs.

'The note.'

'Oh, by the window. Propped up, where . . .' Where it could easily blow away, so ending the lies necessary on the subject.

She drove me to my cottage. Where my ancient Austin Ruby waited, glamorously restored and out of hock. I was overjoyed. Suddenly frightened, too, for who could afford to settle an expert

37

car restorer's six-month bill? Overjoyed, yes, but aware of how deeply I now was in Troude's scam. And its enormity.

'Is this old car yours, Lovejoy? I didn't know you had one.'

'Neither did I, love.' I said weakly. We went inside and made smiles. I couldn't help thinking of Baff Bavington.

6

Women talk in the pluperfect vindictive, as the old crack has it. All the same, there's not much wrong with malice – as long as the arrow falls short if it's aimed at me. Why it's such a constant for birds, heaven alone knows. They relish the stuff.

'Who gave you that car, Lovejoy?' Women never let go, but I've already told you that.

'Eh? Oh, had it years, love.'

She padded about the room shivering, moaning about draughts. Finally zoomed back, freezing, complained I'd pinched her warm bit and trying to manoeuvre me out of it.

'Whose bed is it?' I demanded. Frigging nerve.

'I've never seen your motor before.' All suspicion.

'The Ruby? It got cindered. Thought I'd seen the last of it.'

'Restored by loving hands, I see.' Rich women see a lot. 'Who paid? Another woman? Seeing your electricity's off, and the phone.' She lifted her head from the pillow. 'And seeing you were going to take me on holiday, Lovejoy.'

See what I mean, about women never trusting people? She'd be on about this for months. Luckily we'd not last that long.

'Some bloke forked out. Part of an antiques deal.'

Shrewd Lovejoy's quicksilver brain was equal to the task. I took her delectable body in my loving embrace, and raised her head so our eyes locked. I said, most sincerely, 'There is no other woman, dwoorlink.'

'You're sure?'

'How could there be? To prove it, we're going to a superb new place for supper tonight. The Nouvello Troude at Ladyham!'

Her relaxed body went a fraction unrelaxed. 'Ladyham?'

'You know it?' I smiled, still most sincerely. 'I expect you wealthy landowners dine there all the time.'

'Nouvello? No, darling. I've never been. But Ladyham's rather a way, isn't it? When there are so many places nearer.' She burrowed beneath the sheet, ready for a new smile. I felt myself weaken. 'Let's go to Barlfen. It's on the waterside.'

'I'd like to try the Nouvello. I've heard it's really posh.'

'Can I persuade you, Lovejoy?'

I was determined to get her to Ladyham, the lying cow. She co-owned the massive new leisure centre, whose boss, Troude, had just hired me. She and Sandy had partly financed it. Yet she's never been?

'Can I, darling?' Her mouth was everywhere, her hands crawling up my belly.

'Right,' I said weakly. Being ridiculous is my lifestyle. 'Barlfen. Sevenish okay?' Pathetic.

The Ruby was lively as a cricket. They'd done a good job at Sugden's garage. I called on Suggie. He came grinning to meet me. His two apprentices were overjoyed to see my Ruby, God knows why. They always say they're sick of it.

'Nice old crate, Lovejoy.' Suggie's always wiping his oily mitts on his overalls.

'Ta for doing it, Suggie.' I tapped its bonnet. 'What's the fastest I can do?'

The apprentices laughed out loud. They were itching to undo it again, start afresh on the damned thing. Barmy. Imagine mending engines all day long.

'Eject if you hit fifteen mph, Lovejoy. Downhill.'

'Ha, ha,' I said gravely. 'The bill get settled, Suggie?'

'All done.' He was over the moon. 'Thankful to get cash in hand these days, with that bloody tax.'

'Great, great.' No receipt, no trace of payment. 'Who collected it?' I asked casually. 'Only, the bloke left a letter on the driving seat.'

Suggie's grin faded into wariness. 'Best post it to him, Lovejoy.'

Kicking myself, I beamed, nodded. 'Why didn't I think of that? Cheers, lads.' I should have thought up a better story.

Just to show them, I notched a good twenty mph leaving their lane, but cut down to my usual sixteen when the Ruby started wheezing. The clatter still came from under the rear wheels, but elegance has to be paid for. I drove with pride into Sandy and Mel's gravelly forecourt. The Ruby trundled to a halt, silenced thankfully.

Mel was packing a big estate car. Cases on the roof, the interior stuffed with gear. Pot plants too, I saw with dismay. Oh dear.

'Wotcher, Mel. Going on a sweep?'

A sweep is a swift scouring of the countryside for antiques. Whether you use fifty technicians like the BBC in its *Antiques Roadshow*, or a series of village halls like Sotheby's, or even if it's just yourself, it's basically foraging and returning loaded with antiques, the joy of mankind. But this was no quick trip. My heart sank. Had Sandy and Mel fought again?

He paused, strapping the cover over the heaped roof rack.

'No, Lovejoy. Leaving.'

Sandy and Mel are constants in the antiques game. I mean, they're forever quarrelling, parting in tears and temper. Then it's the big reconciliation and they resume dealing – shrewd, money-mad, but knowledgeable. They have a knack. Their latest success was finding a collection of wrought-iron German snuffboxes. Don't laugh. These were only half an inch tall, but were gold-inlaid, damascened, and genuine eighteenth century – if they're genuine eighteenth century. You know what I mean. Sandy and Mel's nine boxes were brilliant, original, and authentic. Their like in one handful will probably never be seen again. I nearly cried when some undeserving Yank bought them for a fortune. I eyed Mel. The less exotic of the pair, unsmiling, always cross. I was unhappy, seriously.

'Leaving leaving, Mel? Or just leaving?'

'Leaving squared, Lovejoy.' He tested the strap, stepped back. 'That's everything.'

He looked at me. Sorrow began to creep about. This looked truly grim. I'd seen the scene a hundred times, but never quite like this. The long silence made it worse.

'Mel?' I said, nervous.

He gazed about. 'Just look at it, Lovejoy. Converted school-house, a barn. Not bad, decoratively first rate. Three hundred years old, sound as a bell. Stock at valuation.'

A notice board announced it was for sale. My spirits hit my boots. This was real. Mel and Sandy, splitting? Like Tom and Jerry going separate ways. Unthinkable.

'Why, Mel?'

He knew I wasn't asking the price, and smiled deep woe.

'Sandy's gone in over his head, Lovejoy. You know how he is. Anything different.'

'I saw him at the Nouvello.'

'Mmmh.' The non-word spoke volumes of mistrust, almost fear. He tossed me a bunch of keys. 'He doesn't know I've gone, Lovejoy. Give him those.'

His anguish was all the worse for being quietly veiled. I mean, I don't understand how two blokes and all that. But love's a pretty rare plant. In this life there's nowt else – except antiques and they're the same thing anyway. I don't know what I'm trying to say, except I was upset. You can't really believe the Sandys and Mels of this world, not really. Like, they've parted every four or five days, tantrums and sulks, as long as I've known them. But when any partners finally separate, there's a terrible dearth. Almost as if two such transparent phoneys were really among the few genuines in the whole Eastern Hundreds.

'Mel, look,' I hated this. 'How about you phone Sandy and maybe meet him in the Marquis of Granby?' It always worked before.

He was already firing the engine. I felt cold. 'No, Lovejoy. It's over.'

He had sunglasses on. We'd not had any sun all week. For a minute he said nothing, while I tried to think of some magic phrase to cure all this. I get desperate when things suffer.

He said, 'You were kind, Lovejoy. So many aren't, you know. True kindness leaves no place for gratitude.' He glanced around the barnyard. 'It's only a small token. You'll do their gambado anyway. It's your nature. But advice from a friend, if I may?'

'What?'

'For once, just this once, don't help, Lovejoy. Not anyone. Friend or foe. Or you too'll finish up baffled.' He meant don't do what Troude wanted, now Sandy was his backer. 'I'm at my auntie's in Carlisle.' He hesitated, then smiled that terrible smile. 'Can you take another word of advice?'

'Yes?'

He indicated the steps up to the small office he and Sandy shared. 'Steal the Kirkpatrick. It's the best piece left.'

'Steal?' I yelled indignantly after him as he drove out. 'Steal? I've never stolen a single thing in my life! I'd not stoop so low . . .'

Gone. I heard the motor slow by the dairy, turn near the Congregational chapel. Its sound dwindled. Nothing. I looked at the forecourt. The jardinières were gone. The lovely Roman terracotta in the window was gone. I was furious about what Mel'd said. For Christ's *sake*! Cracking a malicious joke like that. Surely it was a joke? A sad attempt at humour as he'd driven out for the last time, to conceal his heartache? As long as he didn't really mean it. I mean, what sort of a rat would rob his friends?

The forecourt was empty, except for me. Nobody about. I looked at the bunch of keys he'd given me. At the steps. At the For Sale notice. And thought. Kirkpatrick?

Cornwall Kirkpatrick was a stoneware potter. American, Illinois. He decorated his jugs and whatnot with cutting satire – snakes as politicians, with biting inscriptions saying how horrible they were. His fantasy urns and geographical pigs (I kid you not) make you sleepless, give you bad dreams. Skilful, but alarming. And very, very pricey. So rare, they'd buy a good month's holiday any day of the week. I always sell them – give some other poor blighter the nightmares instead.

But to *steal*? From friends? That's the action of a real gargoyle, a despicable cad.

Only to test the door handle, I went up the steps. That meant I had to try the keys, open the door. And have a quick look round, see the Kirkpatrick was still there. Only for security and all that, because you can't be too careful. I found it in my hand, Mel's Kirkpatrick jug. Criminal to leave it. I mean, clearly it needed looking after, right? I decided I'd better take it home. Not stealing. No, honest. Not genuinely *stealing*. Only, somebody had to care for it, right? So I wrapped it up and hid it in the Ruby's boot, just so it wouldn't get stolen. There are thieves everywhere these days.

Baff's house was on the way, so I drove there, more by instinct than anything else, wondering how much I'd get for the Kirkpatrick jug. Only 1870s, but packed with potential. I felt truly heartbroken over Sandy and Mel, but notched an exhilarating twenty-two on the bypass, in a lucky wind. Omen?

Baff Bavington's a breakdown man. He's a lazy devil, is Baff. My brother used to say that lazy people aren't lazy – they're merely clever. Breakdowning is a way of nicking antiques from unsuspecting ladies who live alone. You can do it to elderly couples, too, but Baff never did – after one incident when some old geezer turned out to be a dead-shot colonel with a twelve-bore.

Sherry's his missus. She used to help him out, for authenticity's sake. Baff's standard trick was this: break down, engine boiling over or something, in the very gateway of some old dear's house. Baff knocks – can he please have some water for his radiator? (Sherry smiling anxiously from the motor.) Baff takes the pan of water, while Sherry nips round the back and susses out the house. She slips a window catch, or inserts a sliver of comb into a lock to make it easier to pick. There's even a spray you can get that makes a window impossible to close properly – I'd better not tell you its name, or you'll all be at it.

That night, back comes Baff, cleans out your antiques and other valuables while you kip. Easy.

The boyos – real hard-liner antique robbers – despise break-down merchants because police always have their number. Within an hour of waking up, the robbed old lady's on the blower to the Plod. Who of course have a score of other reported breakdown-style thefts in the vicinity. Somebody always has the car's description. And Baff's. And Sherry's. Who suddenly need alibis . . . et relentless cetera. No, the boyos want scams you can do unscathed and often. Breakdowners are the lazy antique thief's theft. It's also risky. Which is why Baff's done time.

Sherry was grieving in her mother's cottage, which is where she and Baff live. Mum's their chief alibi, forever in court testifying to the innocence of her daughter and Baff. I knocked, went through the sordid courtesies folk use to ward off grief.

'You were a real friend to Baff, Lovejoy,' Sherry told me, sniffing. My friends were having a hell of a day. Was it just me?

'That's true, right enough,' her mum said, dabbing her eyes fetchingly at the mirror. 'You'll miss Baff's trade, Lovejoy.'

The ugly old bat showed all the grief of a road sign. A pro. And Sherry, a lovely plump woman with a penchant for old-fashioned hairstyles, scrolls on her forehead, was only going through a let's-pretend sorrow, half an eye on a telly quiz show. She knew I knew, only too well. She hostesses with excessive zeal on the town bypass, between helping Baff's breakdowner jobs. I discovered

Sherry's exciting pastime accidentally, when doing a night valuation for Big John Sheehan. The Ulsterman had taken a liking to some display silver at The Postern, a crude hotel of creaking antiquity. He'd told me to drainpipe in and suss the silver, see if it was (a) genuine, and (b) worth stealing. Everybody knew it was in three cabinets, second floor. That night, I'd started out to obey – only to step on two heaving fleshly protuberances in the darkness. Both turned out to be Sherry, plying her hostessly trade in a manner unorthodox and a mite unexpected. Next morning she'd sought me out, frantic lest I divulge all to Baff. I'd gone along, because women have hidden persuaders. Anyway, silence spared Baff heartache, right? But why was an idle sod like Baff – sorry, *requiescat in pace* – why was he doing an extra night job?

'I'll see the lads have a whip-round, Sherry,' I said gently.

Her face lit up, instantly shedding sorrow at the sound of monetary music. 'You will? Oh, Lovejoy! That would be marvellous! I don't know how I'm going to manage, what with . . .'

She petered out, pinkly remembering our first nocturnal encounter and its mutually beneficial consequences.

'Never mind.' Embarrassed, I made my farewells, paused at the door. Mum absently borrowed her daughter's eye-liner. 'Here, Sherry. Baff actually working, was he?'

'Baff?' Her mind reluctantly left thoughts of how much money the more sentimental antique dealers would chip in for her newfound widowhood. 'Yes. He was doing a sea-front stall. They'd phoned him. Good money, Lovejoy. Of course,' she added hastily, in case word got back and diminished Baff's friends' generosity, 'I haven't had it yet.'

'Look,' I said. 'Let me collect it for you. Where'd you say it was?'

She got the point instantly. 'Selveggio Sea Caravans. On the Mentle Marina waterfront near the funfair.'

'Er, did Baff leave any antiques around, Sherry? Only, he owed me a couple of items . . .' He didn't, but it was worth a try.

'No, Lovejoy. We'd had a run of bad luck lately. So many people have dogs and burglar alarms these days.'

'Never mind, love,' I said nobly. 'Forget Baff owed me a thing.' I felt really generous, pardoning Baff's non-existent debts to me.

Sherry came to see me off. She closed the door and stood on the step in the darkness.

'Lovejoy. I'm quite free now.' She straightened my jacket lapel – no mean feat – and smiled beguilingly. 'It's hard for me to accept. But you've no regular woman, have you? Maybe you and I could get together. I could pop round, see if you needed anything.'

'I'll bring your money round later.' I bussed her, cranked the Ruby out of its moribundity, and chugged out of the tiny garden heading for reality.

This is half my trouble. I can cope with more or less anything, except with events that change in mid-stream. Like, here I was expressing my genuine sorrow over Baff's mugging/killing, only to find myself propositioned by his bird who was more interested in hitching up with a replacement bloke and getting a few quid. It felt weird. Sandy and Mel actually separating, Baff getting done.

When I'm bewildered, I head for antiques and sanity. The auction called. My best-ever fake was back in town. But first, a fake historical interlude, at a genuine knight's gathering.

Because I'd promised, I went to Sir Edward's Event. I didn't want to go. It's near Long Melford. Every year they select some historical date by chucking dice, then re-enact the trades and village life of that particular year. The whole village is at it. They wear period garb, serve period-style food and drink on trestle-tables. They dance to reproduction musical instruments. It's a bit too hearty for me, especially if they get things wrong. It's still quite pleasant to see the children done up in a make-believe old schoolhouse, farriers shoeing horses with a travelling forge, all that.

The grounds at Sir Edward's are given over to the Event, two whole days. There must have been three hundred people there, counting us visitors. Admission costs the earth; this year it was to raise gelt for Doc Lancaster's unspeakable electronics that he tortures us with. A good cause, our luscious choirmistress Hepsibah told me, laughing, as she took my money. I wandered in among the mob, hoping nobody would see me slope off after a token grimace at the jolly scene. Enthusiasm has a lot to answer for.

At Pal's joiner's bench, though, I really stopped to really look. He had a table.

'Wotcher, Pal.' He's an old geezer, does the woodwork scene every Event. 'Rain held off, then, eh?'

'Thank God, Lovejoy. Want a genuine antique table, Anno Domini 1770?'

The table was lovely. I stared at it, worrisome bongs not happening in my chest. It was labelled *Sideboard Table, Chippendale Type, c. 1770*, with all manner of fanciful descriptive balderdash; *from the home of a Titled Norfolk Gentleman* . . . The surface got me, though.

'Genuine is it, Lovejoy?' Jodie Danglass, no less. Sir Edward's Event was a burden for me; it was extraordinary for Jodie.

'Course it's genuine,' Pal groused. He's pleasant, until you differ with him on some opinion. 'Think I'd kill myself doing a surface like that, do you?' He went on lathing a piece of wood, using a rigged-up sapling drill. That's only a rope stretched from a stooping sapling to your instep. Grudgingly I watched him. Better skilled than me. 'Borrowed it from Sir Edward's Hall.'

Well, the local bigwig might have had a fake made by the original methods. But nowadays? Except . . .

'Are you all right, Lovejoy?' Jodie asked.

'Stop nagging.'

We went to get served by a little girl. Dilute mead, quite good. 'That surface, love.' Perfect, with the sheen only the hand of man can create. 'I'd heard somebody say last week they'd seen a mint Sheraton side table in the Midlands, the surface unflawed, perfect, original. I didn't believe him. But for some craftsman still to be faking so good these days – '

'Looked genuine to me.'

She sounded quite indifferent. I nearly choked. Antique dealers think nothing of the things they're supposed to know, understand, admire. I saw red. 'Listen to me, you silly cow. See over there?' The little girls serving the mead had a kitchen table, virtually a plank of chipboard with four machine-made legs. 'That'd take any nerk less than an hour to make, household drill and buffing pad. But that. . . ?' I looked across to where Pal was pausing to light a fag. Somebody shouted a criticism, were cigarettes in period? He waved back apologetically, took no notice, grinned with an addict's afront. I was to remember that grin, in far, far different circumstances.

47

'That?' she prompted. She looked as disturbed as I was, probably thinking how near she'd come to making an offer for it.

'You buy a log of mahogany, love.' I described its huge shape with my hands. 'Not the forced spongy wood they import nowadays, but the slow-growing natural unforced trees you have to pay the earth for – if you can still find one in the raped wild forests. Then you – top dog, as they used to say – straddle the log over a saw-pit. Some poor sod – bottom dog – climbs down into the saw-pit. You get an enormous woodman's curved two-handled log saw – itself a valuable antique, because nobody makes them now. Hour after hour, you saw the log lengthways to make a plank . . .'

It takes me like this, the shame, the ecstasy of antiques. I'm the only man living to have done the whole thing, start to finish. I couldn't move for a week afterwards. I paid a fortune for seven stalwart farm lads to partner me on the saw-pit I'd dug in my garden wilderness. They'd given up, one after the other, and left calling me barmy. I'd slogged on, hands like balloons, bleeding and blistered.

'Then you take your sawn plank of mahogany. You plane it flat. Takes three days.' Jodie was looking at me, mesmerized. I could have swiped her one. Antique dealers and fakers think of automatic electric planers, gouging drills you work with a button while having coffee and a fag. I heard somebody shouting for me from over where the horses were. I yelled back a sod off, pressed on. 'Then comes the hard part.'

They'd worked barefoot, mostly, those ancient cabinet-makers. All heroes to me. When the table's surface was smooth as any hand-plane could make it, they'd got children – often their own – to beg or buy fragments of broken brick. The children ground the brick pieces to dust in a pestle and mortar. They'd then winnowed it, casting the dust up into the air.

'Coarser brick-dust particles fell first – resisting the air, see? The children, toddlers to seven-year-olds, caught it on bits of fustian, in a bowl, anything. The finer particles were caught separately.'

The bloke was still shouting. Torry from Beccles, pockets full of phoney silvers as usual. I rose to move away, sickened by my tale anyway. Jodie caught me. Her eyes were huge. 'Wait, Lovejoy. The children?'

'No sandpaper in those days, Jodie. The maker smoothed it

48

with brick-dust. I've done it. You rub the flat tabletop – coarse powder first. Your bare hands, to and fro along the wood's grain, hour after hour.'

'But don't your hands. . . ?'

'Aye, love. They swell, blister. The skin shreds. They weep on to the dusty wood. The dust becomes a paste, of skin fragments, brick-dust, blister water, sweat, blood. Think how it must have been. Virtually naked at the finish, dripping pure sweat. But you kept going. You had to, or you and your children starved, literally.' My voice went bitter. 'I had delusions at first. I would do it exactly as those ancients did. What a pillock! I lasted two hours. After a week's rest, another two hours.'

My skin had peeled first, then blistered from my raw palms. I'd used my elbows. Then I'd stripped naked, and stood on the tabletop with bare feet, shuffling the brick-dust up and down the wood.

'See why it's special, having a genuine Sheraton table? A modern Formica job's machined in a trice, virtually untouched by human hand. But the heartwood of an antique table's *still got the craftsman in it*. His blood, sweat, flesh, it's there in the living wood. Is it any wonder a genuine antique *feels* different? Modern furniture is chemical-covered chipboard. The real antique is a person. It's a friend living with you.'

'That's . . . lovely.' But she'd started out to say something very different. Well, truth takes you different ways.

'Know how long it took me, Jodie? Sixteen weeks, to repeat three days' work of a seventeenth-century man.' I tried to give her a grin, defuse the talk. Her face was all alarm. 'I had to keep resting to battle on. Pathetic. You women have it easy, love. The work of your sisters three centuries ago is still within your reach. Look around.' Across a patch of grass two milkmaids were hand-milking some Jersey cows, admired by a small crowd. Other girls were washing clothes in the fountain, beating garments on stones. People wandering among the stalls were laughing, joking. Oh, so very merry. 'You women can still give it a go any time, cook, wash, bake, skivvy for fifteen hours a day. You'd be tired, aye, but could still congratulate yourself on how marvellously you'd relived your grandma's routine.'

'And you?'

Answering took a long time. 'Ashamed, Jodie. I'd thought myself fit. I knew what to do, God knows. But the long-dead craftsmen defeated me.' I looked across at the village church. 'Yon graveyard's full of the old bastards. Any one sleeping there could wake today, step out, and produce brilliance like us modern clever clogs couldn't do in a month of Sundays. Admitting that is the shame of my life. It does something to a man. See, love. A woman can always claim she's prettier than the Queen of Sheba, that Lady Hamilton's hair was a mess and her own isn't. We blokes have more absolute comparisons. And we lose out every single time, to those that've gone before.'

'Can nobody do it nowadays?'

'That sideboard table Pal has on show there is a fake, Jodie. But it's been done using the old methods. Must have killed somebody.' I snorted a half-laugh. 'Until now I'd thought I was the only bloke alive who'd ever made a genuine fake. Get somebody able to repeat the old processes nowadays, you'd be a millionairess by teatime.'

'Then why don't they, Lovejoy?'

'Because the old methods use up people, not gadgets.' Well, I should complain. I'm the one who always argues people first, things second.

That is all I want to say, for now. We saw Sir Edward tottering towards us. He's a boring old devil, so I left Jodie and went to watch the morris dancers. That's something else I'm no good at, either.

7

Once upon a time, antiques were a rarefied pursuit for scholars. Oh, don't misunderstand. A few titled gentlemen really did pursue antiquities all over the ancient world. They spent fortunes, founded private museums in attics. Great, but kind of chintzy.

Until July, 1886.

In that month the great antiques hunt began, when an auctioneer intoned 'Lot One' – and the Duke of Marlborough's Blenheim Palace's magnificent art, furniture, statuary went under the hammer. That gavel was gunfire that reverberated round the world. The Great Antiques Rush was on. Think of a rocket soaring upward, that's never yet begun to fall. Okay, it's levelled off now and then, but always resumed rezooming prices into the stratosphere.

Now, we're all at it. Clever people draw graphs of antiques' values, starting back in that lovely summer of 1886. Don't be fooled. It's not a mathematical proposition. It's not philosophy. It's a scramble.

Umber Auctions took over from Wittwoode less than a month after he got nicked for 'discretion', that hoary old get-out by which auctioneers absolve themselves of blame for trickery. They behaved like a new Prime Minister. Wholesale sackings, Under New Management posters everywhere, advertising campaigns – then no change. The same whifflers drift aimlessly about hoping to make a few quid on the side, crooked auctioneers, crooked vannies, crooked antique dealers moaning that the antiques are pure unadulterated gunge. It still sank of armpits and stale smoke. I love it. An auction has paradise within. All you have to do is look.

'Lovejoy.' Practical was over like a shot, trying to pull me to see. 'What d'you reckon?'

Even before we pushed among the grumbling dealers I knew it would be the same old fake. You have to laugh at blokes like Practical because they're a waste of time, yet sensible in a weird kind of way. He fakes only the cheaper end of antiques. Not badly, but not well either. Fortyish, thin, stained with his famous watercolours. He uses his jacket for a rag, so half of him is always rainbow, the other half taupe tat.

'Good?'

I looked. The famous George Cruikshank, who died in 1878 or so, illustrated Charles Dickens's works. He also sketched as he wandered, producing little watercolours that have never really caught on. You can get genuine Cruikshank for less than a week's wage. This is the sort of thing Practical fakes – hence his nickname. Old Masters 'aren't practical'. Cheaper, less risky forgeries are.

'Not bad, Prac. Not, definitely not, good.'

My tone disappointed him. 'Give me a tip, Lovejoy?'

'Get a couple of decent old frames from Farmer. New fake frames are a dead give-away. And stop using tea to mimic foxing. Everybody nowadays knows to look for a sharp rim. Leave the watercolour surface undamaged. Say it's just been cleaned. And for heaven's sake stamp its reverse, Prac – you can buy a fake Agnew's stamp for ten quid down the market.'

I turned away, exasperated. Folk drive you mad. Then I paused. Seeing Diana enter from the street, swivelling every head, made me think.

'Here, Prac.' Voice low – antique dealers have three-league ears. 'You still a neb man?'

Door-to-door con tricks come in many guises. The commonest among antique dealers is the 'neb man'. The old game where you pretend to be a council/social worker/health inspector – some kind of semi-authoritative official. You talk your way into somebody's home, filch a small antique, and scarper lightly on your way. It always works. In fact, it's so easy I sometimes wonder if people actually want to be tricked. 'Neb' comes from the old word for the peak of a cap – as once worn by officialdom's intruders. You still see market barrowboys and bus crews surreptitiously touch their foreheads, symbolizing touching a neb, to signify an inspector's on the way.

'A bit. Why?'

Practical hates doing it since he lost his teeth. No smile. A con man needs a smile. Too much booze had rotted his fangs, and pot teeth were looming from the dentist on Chitts Hill. For Practical, it had been the Year of the Tooth. I watched Diana out of the corner of my eye. She was urgently questing, not strolling. Drowning, not waving. I ducked. I'd my own problems.

'Done anything round Mentle? Ladyham?'

'Me and Baff did turn and turn about. I sold him Mentle a month since.'

'Ta, Prac.'

I promised to see Farmer, persuade a frame out of the stingy old nerk to help Prac out, and eeled towards the door. It was then that Donk saw me and yelled my name. A right pest he was turning out to be. I had to stand upright and pretend I'd been casually inspecting an Eastern mirror mounted in a brilliantly cut mother-of-pearl surround. Diana came over as soon as she could, all the oafs deliberately not getting out of her way.

'Hello, Lovejoy. I thought I'd find you here. Can we speak?'

'What do you think of this?' I seethed with disgust. 'Leave mother-of-pearl in sunshine, you never get its glisten back. A waste of all that lovely carving.' Actually, there are ways, but they're not good.

I went with her, but only so she wouldn't give me that can-we-talk? routine. I hate it. It's all they ever say on telly soaps: *Can we talk?* As if you have to set up a Security Council before telling a bird her dress is a mess and you love her. God, but the world needs me.

'My own fake's here, Di,' I said shyly. 'Want to see it?'

'Which is it, Lovejoy?' our greatest failed lover butted in to ask.

Dicko Chave. He's hopeless, which is to say an average dealer. A pompous, bluff bloke, he's proposed to every woman in the Eastern Hundreds, rejected every single time. Nobody knows why. He's begged me to tell him where he goes wrong. I'm stumped. I mean, an ex-officer, doesn't drink much, his own house, keeps accurate tax accounts would you believe, church-goer, shoes polished, reliable as a Lancashire clock. You'd think women'd find him a good prospect, if only for economic reasons, but no.

'Sorry, Dicko.' I now regretted boasting, even quietly, to Diana. Already dealers were sidling up to listen. The auction prices would fall now, from general suspicion. My Sheraton would

53

have to wait for its deserved adulation until after it was auctioned.
I took Diana's arm.

'Lovejoy. Won't you introduce me?' Dicko asked, wistful with
his unmarried smile, drawing himself up for social niceties.

'I'm sorry,' Diana snapped. 'We're busy.'

'Oh. Perhaps some other . . .' We were out of the door, which
wafted after us: '. . . time'.

See what I mean? Diana hadn't given him a glance. Yet Dicko's
polite as well. Strange.

We went, brisk with purpose, to the Tudor Rest across the road.
Not far enough, but their coffee's the only drinkable coffee in East
Anglia. Hank the Yank runs it, needless to say. A triumph of
caffeine-soaked heredity over environment. She chose a corner
place after prolonged inspection.

'Expecting being stabbed, love?'

No levity. My heart sank. Deadly earnest time, and an auction
about to start a hundred yards away. I have rotten luck.

'No time for wit, Lovejoy. What did he tell you?'

A pause while Hank TY himself served us. He has three
waitresses, but they do sweet nothing – as far as observers can see,
that is. But Hank is a very happy proprietor. He admired Diana,
tried to extend his delivery with chat, and failed at least as badly as
Dicko Chave. He retired hurt to his kitchen, but not too hurt.
Giggles arose from there within seconds.

'Troude?' I wondered about the wisdom of this meeting. I
mean, why was she asking? 'Why're you asking?'

'I suggested you, Lovejoy.' She did that woman's head-shake
that loosens their hair but makes you feel they're girding for war.
'I have to know if he hired you.'

'Is he your pal, Di?'

She lit a cigarette with aggressive intent, spouted smoke. She
was mad all right. I began to regret that bonus. She was here to
cash in on the obligation. No need to ask whose obligation, either.
It's always on mine.

'If you call me Di once more, Lovejoy, I'll throw you under the
next bus. Understand?' I nodded, to get the rest of the ballocking.
'Monsieur Troude and I are good acquaintances. We have
difficulty keeping in touch, under the circumstances.'

'Mmmh.' She'd said about some husband. Maybe a club

member? Investor? Or was that Member of Parliament's wife a regular iron-pumper there? I had to go careful. 'Mr Troude just said he'd be in touch.'

'That means he has hired you, Lovejoy,' she translated for her own, not my benefit. 'Have you a pen?'

She lent me a gold pencil from her handbag. I wrote the address on a menu. She held out her palm, but I honestly wasn't trying to pinch her pencil. For God's sake, everybody forgets to return pencils, don't they? Anyhow, I'd swap her rotten gold propelling pencil any day for a genuine Borrowdale graphite, the best writing tool ever made since the world began. It was back in the 1560s that gales uprooted an ash tree in Borrowdale, Cumberland. A man happened to see pieces of a strange solid in its up-ended roots. Curious, he felt it, and saw how easily it blackened his fingers. He used it to mark his sheep, and graphite – stone that draws – was born. Sensibly, folk began enclosing slivers of graphite – 'English antimony' – in a lathed wooden tube and hey presto! I hadn't realized I'd been telling her out loud. She clipped her handbag closed. I think I was beginning to like her. She smiled at something achieved, and I was sure.

'I'll make it worth your while, Lovejoy. Keep me informed. In more ways than you can imagine.'

Her hand touched mine, a promise on account. Promises have the half-life of snowflakes, which makes me wonder why I fall for them. You'd think I'd learn.

'Won't Troude be narked, if I blab to you?'

'He'll be glad, Lovejoy. No need to let on, though. Let's keep it just between ourselves.' She rose to go, leaving that red crescentic reminder of lust on her cup rim. 'Oh, Lovejoy. *Parlez-vous-Français*?'

'No, love.'

'School slanguage, though?'

'*Plume de ma tant*ie's all very well, love, but teaching doesn't get you very far. Here, love. You forgot the bill.'

'Oh.' She paid up with a kind of surprised amusement. 'You know, Lovejoy, I rather think we're going to get along. It's some considerable time since I've had a partner I could rely on.'

We said goodbye, me promising – I do it too – to let her know the instant Troude showed up. I found Hank beside me watching her walk up the brough into town.

'You're a lucky swine, Lovejoy,' he said. 'She looks a really great lay. How much a trick?'

First Jodie Danglass thinks Diana's socially unacceptable. And now Hank jumps to the same conclusion. Most be some allergen in the pollen.

'She's my client, Hank,' I said airily. 'Antiques buyer from, er, Michigan. Paid quarter of a million for a collection of Philadelphian teapot lamps last week.'

'An American?' he cried delightedly. 'And I thought she was Paris France! Nice trace of accent.'

'Educated there, Hank. Cheers.'

He went back in to resume his onerous labours making waitresses giggle in the kitchen. I went across the road more thoughtful than before. Suddenly there seemed a lot of France about, where France wasn't.

The world restored normality when Tinker caught me up and dragged me into the Ship Inn. He had Steve Yelbard waiting, victor of the Portland Vase competition.

'Hello, Steve.' I let my delight show. 'Congrats. Your glasswork's beautiful. Here, let me get these . . .' I ordered ale for the three of us, which was numerically equal to six – four for Tinker, one each for Steve and me.

We spoke for quite some time. He was a nice bloke, not able to tell me much. Genuine, as far as I could tell. More interested in glass than breathing. An enthusiast after my own heart. I asked if he'd visited anywhere locally besides Long Melford where he was staying, was told no.

Steve told me about Jan Fotheringay. 'I got a note saying he had a commission for me, copying some varied-knop bell-mouthed wine glasses, but he didn't show.'

'Newcastle, eh?' I sighed. Even a fake 1734 vintage glass, with its knops shaping the stem with lovely variation, yet in exquisite proportion, would send me delirious. Newcastle's glass has never been bettered – and I do include Venice. They are nearly priceless. 'You do your own wheel engraving, Steve?'

'No. Got a Dutch bloke.'

I laughed. 'Traditionalist, eh?' Even that long ago, our glasses were sent to Holland for engraving. The real difficulty is making sure the air-beaded ball knop isn't a fraction too large. Some

glass-maker fakers run amok when they try for the most valuable –
'Eh? What, Steve?' He'd said something.

'Jan. Terrible luck.' Steve tutted. 'His motor home. Didn't know he was a drinker. You can't tell, can you?'

'Mmmh,' I went. I'd get it from Tinker later.

And that was that. Steve knew nothing about Phoebe Colonna, despite strong views on her morals, substituting a Victorian replica for one of her own. Unscrupulous, he called it.

'An American trait, Lovejoy. Spreading all over the world.'

So we parted, me and Tinker waving off this pure-minded forger who'd discovered America was to blame for all our wrongdoing. God knows what the Old World would do without the Yanks to blame for everything – blame our horrible old selves instead, I suppose.

'Tell, Tinker,' I ordered.

'Dry old day, Lovejoy.' He threatened a rumbling chestiness. I flung a couple of pints down his throttle in the nick of time. 'That poofter Jan lives in a motorized caravan. Its engine caught fire driving through Archway. He lost the lot.'

'What's this about drink?'

'Pissed as a newt, Lovejoy,' he said inelegantly. 'The Plod checked his blood. Insurance'll shell him like the bleedin' plague. Out of hospital, magistrate'll chuck the book at him.'

'That bad?'

The long hand of Fortune? Or the longer, more decisive hand of Big John Sheehan, Corse, both?

I remembered then I was going to Barlfen with the lovely Almira, and made a run for it. From my chat with Steve I was practically sure there was no connection between the Portland Vase competition and this Troude bloke. And sure too that Almira was only pretending she had no investments in the Nouvello venture in Ladyham. After all, she might have an old flame on the board, and simply be doing him a favour, right?

It came on to rain about then. I saw no new omens.

8

That evening was straight out of *Casbah*, me staring soulfully through candleglim at the beautiful Almira, who smiled mistily and whispered sweet everythings. The Barlfen Rest turned out to be the nook to end all nooks. No diner could see any other diner unless she was at his table. It was like a rabbit warren. You wended among ferns and carved ornate screens. Clever old Almira, to suggest – well, insist on – this place.

'Lovejoy, darling.' Almira was all for cottage work again. 'It's time to go.'

I'd had her pudding, disappointingly non-filling sorbet stuff. She'd seemed to expect me to eat it, the way women do. 'Wait, doowerlink. Please.' I pretended to temporize, slipped in an order for profiteroles. 'I have something to say.'

'Yes, darling?' Women love appetites in action. Almira was happy to see me nosh. I waited for the discreet serf to retire. It took longer than I wanted, because I'd had to wrestle the waitress to the best of three pinfalls for enough cream.

'Our holiday,' I said. I wanted to appear soulful, but you can't when scoffing your third pudding, so I let instinct guide me along. 'France. Next Friday. Can you get away?'

'France?'

She went faint. Her hand crept to her lovely throat. She was wearing genuine amber – orange-coloured, not Chinese red, no trace of that ugly sectoring that gives amberoid mock-ups away in oblique light. Lovely thick complete beads, matching near as amber ever can. Low-cut, her swan neck without a blemish. No wonder women rule.

'I checked. There's another flight next Thursday. I paid a deposit.' I looked proud.

'But Lovejoy . . .'

'I know exactly what you're thinking.'

'You *what*?' Now pale as well as faint, her voice going.

'Don't worry. I've made the arrangements through a

58

travel agent near St Edmundsbury. You husband will never trace it.'

'Oh, darling,' she said, frantic. 'I couldn't possibly come, not to . . .'

Not to France? I thought, but did not say. I watched her scrabble out of the pit I'd dug.

'It's the . . . the competitions, Lovejoy,' she said with bright invention. 'I'm training three showjumpers for the point-to-point. I'm so sorry, darling. You're so sweet to think of it. I must recompense you for all the cost you have put into the idea, darling.'

'That's kind, love.' I eyed her. I was really narked. What if I really *had* paid a holiday deposit? 'Promise me you'll come some other time. How about Greece?'

She reached across the table and squeezed my hand, eyes glowing with unbridled love or something. She almost collapsed from relief. 'I promise, darling. Greece sounds lovely.' If I'd said Greece first we'd already be on the Great White Bird. 'Anything you want, Lovejoy,' she offered, gay now the threat of France was all done.

'Doowerlink,' I said mistily.

Anything, but keep off Troude's properties at Ladyham and Mentle where Baff got killed by louts, and book for anywhere but France? I was suddenly out of my depth. I told her to settle the bill because I was in a hurry. She obeyed with suppressed excitement, and we scurried from Barlfen with unseemly alacrity to make savage passionate smiles at my cottage.

She was sound asleep when I eventually rose and stole away with all the stealth of a fairground. I cranked the Ruby into life, and had it clattering resentfully through the drizzle towards London in minutes. I'd hidden the matches, so even if Almira heard me she'd have had a hell of a time lighting a candle to get dressed and catch me up.

Four o'clock in the morning, I was chugging down Highgate Hill when the Ruby croaked to a standstill next to the stone marking where young Dick Whittington had paused with his cat on his dispirited retreat from London and heard the bells chiming out promises of Lord Mayorality and fortune. I paused to listen. Only the tap of the rain on the wheezing Ruby's bonnet. It looked fit for

Casualty. I went in to find the nearest unvandalized phone box. Enquiries gave me Jan's newspaper number. With a lot of shinannikins I got somebody on a night desk and explained I was Jan Fotheringay's doctor with urgent news for the next of kin. They had a conference of some sort, reluctantly gave me a number in Tooting Bec. I rang.

'Hello,' I said sternly to the sleepy but harassed bird who answered. 'This is the Whittington Hospital. I'm Dr, ah, Pasteur. Some confusion has arisen about Jan Fotheringay's, ah, designation status.'

'Yes, Doctor. This is Lysette, his next of kin,' she said breathlessly. 'I knew there would be trouble. It's this dual nationality, isn't it? He *was* born in Switzerland, but has lived here all his life. The tax returns are in such a mess from it.' A sudden switch as she realized the hour. 'He's still in a stable condition, isn't he?'

'Well, his condition is . . .' I crackled and hissed like a failing phone. We in East Anglia know the sounds only too well.

Armed now, I entered the Whittington Hospital and asked to see the night sister. I was Jan Fotheringay's long-lost estranged brother who'd just heard the bad news.

'Hello, Sister,' I said, going all desperation when they found her for me. 'I can't thank you enough for looking after my brother, Jan. Lysette in Tooting Bec says he's had a terrible accident. Can I see him, please? Our poor old mother does pine so . . .'

'It's just as well you came, Mr Fotheringay,' the night sister said sadly. 'A terrible accident. You can see him. But you must fill in this form. Name and address, please.'

I complied, narked. I mean, I'm basically honest, so why all this malarkey? Women ought to realize they have an obligation to trust me, but they never do.

The ward was long and thin with dismal green walls. Patients snored, rumbled, twitched, groaned. Gruesome machines did their blinks, wheezes, clanks. The hospital reverberated to clicks and clashes, the whole nocturnal symphony of dins combining to make healthy innocents shudder. If they don't use ether any more, why does its perfume linger?

Jan was unrecognizable. He lay on a bed that seemed a complex tangle of tubing in a plastic bubble. The bubble itself was tubed up like an astronaut. Jan was riddled. Even his tubes had tubes, fluid dripping in and fluids dripping out. Shiny metal cylinders squeezed and relaxed. Monitor screens bleeped and blooped. Dials showed numbers. Mad dots chased other mad dots across green glowing oscilloscopes. I felt ill.

The nurse caught my arm, helped me to a chair.

'I understand, Charles,' she said quietly. 'Seeing your brother like this is bound to be a shock. Put your head between your knees. I'll bring you a cup of tea.'

Silly bitch thought I was queasy. Ridiculous, because I'm not the sort to go giddy seeing somebody who's poorly. My vision returned slowly. My clammy hands eventually stopped shaking. Sweat dripped down my chin on to the floor. God, but hospitals have a lot to answer for. It took me half an hour to feel myself again, and even then the sight of Jan was enough to make me emigrate.

'Can I speak to him, Nurse?'

'Yes. But you won't go too near.'

She retired back to her illuminated desk, a pool of light in a sanctuary straight out of Goya, head bent beside the lamp, all else in darkness.

My head was bent too. 'Jan?' I said to the plastic sheeting. My breath condensed on it. 'It's me. Lovejoy.'

The figure didn't move. You could see bits of his features, mottled and scaly like a fish gone bad. Couldn't they cover his burnt bits up, for God's sake? He seemed to be lying uncomfortably, and not on proper bedclothes either. Didn't they give sick folk a proper mattress? Hell flaming fire.

'Anything you want me to do, Jan?'

'I haven't got a brother.'

Barely audible. I found myself looking about guiltily, but the night nurse wasn't in earshot. 'I lied. They wouldn't have let me in otherwise.'

An arm moved – well, some place the limb should have been shifted slowly. Tubes trailed with it.

I said, a bit apologetically, 'Stop frigging me about with this Jan the Critic gunge. You're from Tooting Bec.'

'How did you find out?' No laughter, but I felt he'd be amused if they lifted the hospital off him.

61

'I phoned the newspaper. Said I was your doctor. They told me your address. I phoned the girl there. Lysette, isn't it?'

Astonishingly, I saw an eye open to hold me in its gaze. Not such a nerk after all, lying here with that alert bright orb steady on me.

'Why're you digging, Lovejoy?'

This was the hard part. I hesitated. 'I have to know what happened after they took you out of the barn that night down in the harbour.'

Silence. No feeling of a would-be smile now. More like would-be fright.

'Listen, Jan. I'll guess. You just tell me if I go wrong.' I licked my lips, planning ahead. 'The hoods threatened you. You got scared, decided to make a run for it. You commissioned Steve Yelbard as a decoy, didn't show. You got your motorized caravan, and heading through Archway had an unexpected accident – '

'Accident.' The limb moved.

'Was it Corse's men?'

'Not even a crash.' He sounded so tired. 'They made me watch while they burned it. They threw me in the door. I heard them laughing. I hit my head and couldn't move. It was all afire. Some passing football supporters pulled me out, the nurse told me.'

'I'm scareder than you, Jan. I'll say nowt, and do less.' But I'd had to know. I mean, I've worked for Big John Sheehan quite a few times. 'Was it Corse, or Sheehan's lot?'

'Neither. They set me running, Lovejoy, but they wouldn't care where I went.'

Odd. 'Where were you going?'

'Back to Geneva. I thought I'd be . . .'

'That's enough, Charles,' the night nurse said, quietly interposing. She looked ready to deal with a million tubes in a million horrid ways. I'd learned enough. I thought.

'So long, Jan. Keep going, eh?'

'Lovejoy.' I bent my head to hear the whisper in spite of the nurse's tutting. 'My address, my – '

'Safe with me, Jan. Cheers.'

On the way out, I almost bumped into a bonny dark-haired girl. She was hurrying towards the ward from the lift's cacophony of clashing doors. She didn't spare me a glance, just hurried on past. Lysette? I'd bet a quid.

*

Sometimes, I wonder if everybody doesn't go through life desperately trying to avoid being seen. It's as if we've all committed a murder, and have a nagging terror we might get spotted. Oh, I know we go about pretending the opposite, wearing fashionable clothes, sprucing ourselves up to catch the eye. But that's only surface ripples. Deep down, we strive for anonymity. At least, some do. Like me. I'm a chameleon in search of a colour against which to stand and vanish.

Especially to Cissie.

Lovejoy, her note said, as if I hadn't enough to do. *Come immediately. It's urgent. I shall be in until eleven.* No signature. I knew who.

Yonks since, I mentioned a wife I once had. Cissie'd become a half-remembered dream. I couldn't even recall her face, not that I'd tried. Like a pillock I drove obediently through Lavenham, wondering why the hell I was bothering. Marriage isn't what folk say it is. Bonding's pretty loose stuff, and marriage knots aren't. In the first place, it's hard to find any spouse who behaves as if morality's there in strength. Second, married couples never agree on what marriage actually is. For me, I simply hadn't understood that getting married to Cissie did not constitute a proper introduction. Mind you, who can fathom birds? Why, for instance, was the Marquis de Sade's missus Renée unswervingly faithful to him all the years he was in the Bastille, only to leave him the minute he got sprung? You tell me.

Their house is enormous. I'd only ever been there once before, to deliver her share of the belongings. She'd banished me, her belongings and all, threatened me with the police if I ever showed again. I'd been delighted to comply.

'My usual Tuesday visit, Katta,' I said to the maid.

She emitted a brief tubular screech, her signal of humour. A vast emporium of a maid, is Katta. She never stops spreading across your field of view. She's been with Paul – more about him in a sec – since he went to school on the Continent. Probably rescued her from Castle Perilous, and kept her on ever since.

'Oh, you!' she gave back, wittily. It's all she's ever said to me. It comes out. O keeyoo.

'Announce Lovejoy, Katta, if you will.'

She rolled ahead like a billowing cloud fast-forwarded in a

nature film. You have to admire a bird who grapples anorexia to a frazzle.

'This way, Lovejoy,' said Cissie, walking sternly between us, not glancing at me. I was deflected into a drawing room where Paul stood, trying his distinguished best to seem in command. It was doomed to fail within five furlongs of Cissie.

She walked sternly to the fireplace and swivelled sternly. (If any spaces happen in the next few sentences, insert sternly; it'll save endless effort on my part. Cissie is stern personified.) Blondish, exactly the right height-to-weight Quartel Index from working at her figure in pools and leotards, exactly the right height, clothes, teeth, attitude. She's the most depressing example of perfection that ever crippled a bloke. Imagine a gorgeous death ray, you're close.

'Lovejoy,' she snapped, 'you have to help Paulie.'

'Why'd you not invite me to your wedding?'

Note the absence of greetings, won't-you-sit-down. What the hell was I doing here? I make me exasperated. I mean, I'd had two whole months of being wed to her Churchillian imperatives, enough to last several reincarnations, and here I was reflexly coming back for more. I'm beyond belief. I honestly get me wild.

Paul is a posh lawyer, investor. City gent. He looks the part. I say that with all the derogatory effect I can muster. It's all Paul ever does, look the part. I think he's just a suit. Occasionally, like now, he can seem really lifelike when despair shows through, but he's still only a Madame Tussaud replicate escaped from gene control.

'In trouble, Paulie?' I kept pretty meek at this stage, because I can fly off the handle.

'You must do as Philippe Troude says,' from Cissie.

'In trouble, Paulie?' Me, still meek.

'I said you must work for Philippe,' from between Cissie's perfect teeth.

'In trouble, Paulie?' Still meek, still on that old handle.

She swung on him in fury. 'I *told* you he'd be insufferable!' she honed out. There's no other word for her speech. It's a whine, a mosquito in your earhole at night that wakes you up flailing air, or a distant forester with a band-saw in the woods of an autumn. But the word doesn't work for Cissie. She never, never ever, whines. She shrills, screams, shrieks, thunders, but never whines. Honing, that scrape you get from metal on a honing stone, is the best words can manage.

'I. T. comma P.?' I said, so affable.

'Listen to me,' she honed. I stepped back. The band-saw had moved closer, and forests give absolutely no protection from the likes of her. 'Paulie has invested a great deal – a *very* great deal! – in Monsieur Troude's enterprise. He's not going to suffer on account of a worm like you, Lovejoy!'

Like at The Hague and the UN, her arguments always plead her own case in the guise of philanthropy. I listened with a sudden glim of interest. Why me?

'Why me, Paulie?' Still a meek handle-hanger.

'*Tell him!*'

Half the trouble was, I've only to see a couple and my treacherous mind starts asking absurd questions. Like, how *do* they make love? Does he ever ravish her over the breadboard? Or in the garage unloading shopping? What do they say during grunts of passion? Have they ever wept in prayer? What charities do they support? Does he squeeze his blackheads? Hers? If so, what does he do with the end-product? Is he a mattress-wiper, or a surreptitious flirter of the rolled-up. . . ?

'Lovejoy! Pay attention!' honed in my ear. I honestly swiped at an imaginary mosquito. Paulie had been droning for ages. What with Paulie droning and her honing, they were a concerto of sound Schönberg would have envied with his mere twelve tones. Tone, hone, drone. I stood there, an imbecile amid exhortations.

'. . . investment opportunities balanced against shortfall fiscal inputs retrograded leverage-wise . . .' he was saying. (I'm making this up; I haven't a clue what actual words he was using. Like I said, an investment lawyer. You get the idea.)

'. . . cullage from antiques reinvested across the board,' he said. And stopped.

'And?' I prompted. He'd got to the only word I could understand, antiques.

'And what?' he asked. He even managed to drone that.

'What do you want me to do?' This is so typical, rich people greedy to be richer. If you want to become rich, don't invest

65

everything, and don't spend virtually nothing. Simply buy a good, rareish antique. That'll do the job. You want to know how? Right, a tip: Knocking around this old kingdom of ours are some thirty white-enamel-face long-case (so-called 'grandfather') clocks, with the most unusual dusty pinkish floral decoration on the dial. Birds, vines, leaves, the odd tendril, all painted so very slenderly. Simply go and buy one, average market price. What a rotten tip! you exclaim angrily, because the average long-caser is a whole month's wages – expensive, no? Answer, no. Because that delicate manganese decoration signifies a value ten times that of the average grampa clock. See? Instead, prats like this Paul–Cissie molecule want to be moguls overnight. Hence the contumely.

He looked pleadingly at Cissie. She glared. 'Lovejoy knows all the time, Paulie. He's just being aggravating.' She made me sound like a tooth abscess.

'Words of one syllable, please.'

'Help Philippe to identify certain genuine antiques overseas, Lovejoy. So he can reimport them here, for auction on the international market. Otherwise the profit vanishes.'

She paused, to my relief. I felt like I'd got clogged ears from swimming underwater. You know how your hearing goes thick after being in the plunge for an hour?

'The percentage return is – '

'*Paulie!*' from honer to droner. He fell silent. Very, very wise of him. Disobedience was not tolerated in her ranks.

'Why aren't the antiques being auctioned off on the Continent?' I should have asked Troude that.

'*Lovejoy!*'

Exasperation's not much of a response, is it, but it's sometimes all you can get from marriage. Escapers know that.

'Can't be done for the price,' I said blithely, but still with a dollop of that good old meekness.

'What kind of financial package are you – ' droned Paulie.

'Shut *up!*' from not-tell-you-again Cissie. 'He means he doesn't want to, Paulie.' She rounded on me. 'You know Paulie's invested our life savings in the scheme, Lovejoy.'

Everything polarized. What some folk'd do without the first person singular, God alone knows. Cissie's policy is, third person = abuse; first = the cause of righteousness. I thought, blimey.

Then got intrigued, because I couldn't remember ever having thought that Cockney expletive before. Blimey, from the old English curse, blind me if I lie. Why blimey now? I'm no Cockney. Some trigger had set me off.

'Shake him, Paulie!' she was honing.

'Do if you dare, Paulie,' I said evenly. 'I didn't come up the Stour on a bicycle.'

He lowered his hands. I felt sorry for him. He should have got out while he was still alive.

'You have to, Lovejoy,' he said. 'Please.'

How desperate it had all suddenly become. I was intrigued. I mean, for Cissie even to summon me to her presence was a step of grimsome magnitude. What an interesting scheme Troude's was. Maybe the way to obtain more facts was to play hard to get?

'No, ta.' A little unmeekness had crept in after all, which only goes to show you can't depend on practically everything. 'See you. May you live for ever.'

It's the Chinese backhanded compliment. I chatted all the way to the front door with Katta. She did her soaring yell of a laugh and said, 'O keeyooo!' I liked her. She's the only one talks right in that house.

The Ruby for once sparked at the first crank, and was off the starting grid like a racer. It was glad to be out of it.

9

The lamp hours were ended when the Ruby shuddered to a stop.
Almira's Jaguar had gone. Even so, I entered the cottage like a
night-stealing Arab, in case. She'd vanished all right. Hadn't left
any grub, thoughtless cow. Sulking, I bet.

I went to bed. The divan was cold, but I didn't mind. No tubes,
no plastic bubble. Over and out.

This tube machine was coughing, regular as a metronome. I
came to in a sweat, realized it was only Donk's motorbike in –
repeat, actually inside – my porch. Motorbikers live on the
damned things. Makes you wonder how they go to the loo.

'Lovejoy?' Donk yelled at me, peering round the door. 'Get
your skates on, you idle sod. It's eleven o'clock. Sun burning your
eyes out.'

The old squaddies' shout made me feel queasy, remembering
what had nearly happened to Jan Fotheringay, chucked into his
burning caravan by anonymous arsonists.

'Urgent message, Lovejoy. Pay up. And you still owe me.'

I lay and thought while Donk's wretched machine spluttered
and fumes enveloped the world. Diana, Troude, or even Big John
Sheehan? Or a normal thing like an antique, *Deo volente*? What
choice does a bloke like me have?

'Right, Donk.' I roused and paid up.

'Ta. Message is, get to Mentle Marina. Noon. Jodie Danglass'll
be there.' He backed his bike, stuffed the notes down his jacket
front. 'You're a jammy sod with the birds, Lovejoy. I saw that
MP's missus leaving.'

Diana? Probably still paranoid about Troude hiring me. I was
halfway back to bed when I paused.

'Hang on, Donk. When?'

'Three hours since. I come up earlier.' He paused as an idea
struck. 'Ought to charge double, two journeys.'

'Donk,' I yelled to stop him. 'What d'you think of her motor?'
Donk's engine mad.

'Give anything for a maroon Jag, Lovejoy. Who wouldn't?'
And silence.

Five long minutes I stood there naked as a grape, staring unseeing at the garden where the robin flirted for its morning cheese and the bluetits mucked about and the hedgehog trundled.

My mind kept going: Donk saw Almira – she of the posh motor – leave my cottage. He'd called her, what, that MP's missus. I'd thought her husband an investment banker. She'd explained his absences by fluctuating share prices and such. What had Tinker said, in his confusing report that day? Now, I reckoned Diana's bloke was an MP. Hadn't Diana said as much, Jervis somebody? Was *he* that pompous Jervis, love in Diana's lap? It flickered in my memory. Donk is only a messenger, admitted. Motorbikes think only of haring down the bypass at ninety so they can go even faster coming back. But they see an awful lot of people in a day, and know more than most. Was Almira Jervis's tart on the side? If so, why did she haunt *my* restful hours? *Or was she Mrs Jervis?*

Having deducted only bafflement, I drove to Mentle Marina in time to meet Jodie Danglass at noon. I was worn out.

She came to meet me, handbag swinging and hair blowing in the onshore breeze. I warmed to her, though I still hadn't quite worked out why suddenly she was so prominent on my horizon, so to speak. Children were watching a Punch and Judy. Those weird nasal voices and everybody getting hanged or beaten put the fear of God up me, so I refused to advance towards her and waited where I could see the donkeys trotting across the sands.

'Have I got the wrong accessories, Lovejoy?'

'You look exquisite. This where Baff bought it, Jode?'

She looked about, didn't point. 'No. That caravan site on the north shore. They have a funfair, disco dancing, open-air pub, amusement centre for the yokels.'

We could see it, three furlongs on. First time I'd been at Mentle for a couple of years, when I'd bought a fruitwood lowboy – as the American dealers always call these 1720-ish small tables. I love applewood furniture, and paid a fortune in IOUs for it to a seaside landlady. (Don't be daunted by the rather lopsided appearance of the little drawers, incidentally. It's bound to happen to gentle woods like apple after about 150 years. In fact it's a good honest clue to authenticity, in a trade which badly needs such.)

'The south shore being where we're heading?'

'Yes. Two distinct halves, Mentle these days. BT.' We started walking. 'Before Troude.'

The sands gave out midway along the sea promenade. There a few geological pimples, which pass for cliffs in flat East Anglia, rose with obvious effort to form a headland. A walker's path climbed its contours through flower arrangements and decorative bushes so you could stroll with your ladylove while avoiding the ice-cream sellers and balloon touts.

'He own this Mentle Marina too?'

'The lot. North-shore funfair, caravan site, pubs. He's the big shilling, Lovejoy.'

With Almira Galloway and Sandy among his backers. But backers for what? The thing that worried me most, though, was the knowledge that Baff wouldn't have got his part-time job unless the boss said so. Not only that – around here you obeyed this Troude prude. For some, or any, reason. Even if it meant taking a duff job that ended in a planned blagging by yobbos. How had Baff, your average minnow, mortally offended a marina mogul to earn that doom?

We walked the prom, short-cutting the headland, coming on the marina itself with unexpected suddenness.

The place had been all fields, until excavators dug out a series of shallow bays and opened seacocks to let the tides in. Then it became a mesh of inlets, jetties on a mathematical grid design. Seagulls love it. Posh folk sail yachts down the coast to throw parties for other nauticals who throw parties back. There's a lock gate, but only to charge boats entering and leaving. These seaside places are catchpenny.

'See the building? Only finished three weeks ago.'

A feast of modern architecture, the squat ugliness was breathtaking. Wrap-around windows gave a monster view of artificial bays. Its artificial lighthouse blinked red and green port and starboard lanterns from artificial masts. Artificial sails stuck up from the deck-hatch roof, across which artificial spray whisked every few seconds. Artificial rigging displayed signal flags depicting some non-message. Only the seagulls weren't artificial, and I wasn't sure about some of those.

'I love it,' I told Jodie. She looked at me with a ? in her eyes. 'Only practising.'

We were expected. Jodie was given a polite thank you by Troude in a blazer-and-Henley rig. Neckerchief with gold anchors, and a flying pennant blazer badge. The lounge was extravagant with ships' wheels and marlinspikes and capstans and two of the most grotesque figureheads you could ever imagine. No place to get drunk. You'd wonder what you were looking at.

'See you, Jode,' I said, smiling to show I wasn't daunted by the lady sitting with Troude. He even had a captain's cap nonchalantly on the couch beside him.

'Thank you for coming so promptly, Lovejoy.' He smiled differently in daylight, but still the ruler of all he surveyed. Or, in present company, possibly not?

'How do you do, missus?' I said politely. 'Lovejoy.'

She gazed with utter indifference. Not at me, note, but vaguely in my direction. But there were a few boats gliding the briny behind me, so I couldn't be certain.

'This him?' she asked Troude. She didn't care one way or the other if I was me or not. I could tell.

'If it's me you want, missus.'

She looked at me, not quite hailstones but getting that way. 'I won't tolerate idiocy, Philippe,' she said.

'He's nervous, Monique.' He introduced her. 'M'selle Delebarre, Lovejoy.' I sat at Troude's gesture of invitation, thinking, she's the boss and he's only her nerk, captain's cap or no captain's cap.

Surprisingly, I didn't think I was. Nervous, I mean. In the lounge, staff were preparing for an influx, but keeping quiet and respectful. No customers, which was odd. I've never known a sailors' bar that wasn't heaving with maids and matelots.

'I won't wait all day,' Monique said. A cryptic lady, of very little patience.

Blankly I smiled at Troude. He looked at me. She drummed her fingers prettily. I yawned a bit, started watching the boats. One was fluttering its sails, having difficulty braking or something coming into its moorings. Monique was slim, but she'd had to work at it. A calorie job, no mistake. Her figure gave her away, in spite of the minions who'd slogged to make her appear less

71

voluptuous than she was. She belonged among those fashionables who think a woman's got to look cachectic to be attractive. She'd not quite made it. Her hair was dark, lank but with sheen. Her face hadn't enough make-up on for me, but then I'm a magpie, want them to wear tons of it. They rarely do.

'Make him, Philippe.' She'd lost patience.

'Pick it out, Lovejoy,' Philippe Troude said.

They meant the miniature model lifeboats on the glass-fronted mahogany cabinet against the wall by the door. Two of them, each made by a man who hated the other in the frightening days before there were any such things as modern lifeboats. Historical models are all the rage these days.

'What silly sod spoiled the oars?' I asked. Troude gave a swift give-away glance of triumph at the woman, almost wagging for praise. He was crazy about her, and she didn't give a damn.

'The oars are exactly level,' La Monique said, coming to.

'They shouldn't be. Willie Wouldhave made that model. He cut them different lengths in 1789.'

It was a scandal that led to the most terrible row, back when those events could ruin a man for ever. As always, the wrong man got fame and fortune. The honest man starved to death.

That year, a fearsome gale ripped across the River Tyne driving the brig *Adventure* onto Herd Sands. Ashore, Tynesiders watched appalled as the crew drowned. A prominent local tycoon called Nicholas Fairles offered a money prize to anyone who could create a rescue boat able to withstand the ferocious local seas.

Enter the goodie, one William Wouldhave, honest genius of that parish. He was a dour, morose, barbary bloke who didn't make friends and influence people. In a dazzling fit of intuition, he abandoned design, and opted for buoyancy. Against all contemporary notions, he built a strange-looking boat with a cork layer actually sheathing the boat's sides. Greenland style, in shape. The ten oars were strangely of different lengths, but did the job. It seemed ingenious, clever, even brilliant. Willie cooled his famous temper, and basked in the glow of being, for once in his heated life, odds-on favourite in the great rescue-boat competition.

Enter the baddie, one Henry Greathead, who made a duff, mundane boat – sail, mast, no special buoyancy to speak of. A really average plain boat without much to commend it. Very long odds, Henry Greathead's nowt-new rescue boat.

Except his best friend was none other than Nicolas Fairles, head of the South Shields committee. Who naturally awarded Henry the award, prize money, the accolade that would guarantee him fame, fortune and honour.

And poor hot-tempered honest Willie Wouldhave? The committee invited him in, and gave him a guinea as consolation, 'second prize' they called it. Angrily he flung the guinea back in their faces and stormed out, to die in the poverty that bitterness always seems to bring.

And the rescue-boat committee? *They let Henry Greathead pinch Willie's superb design*. He received a fortune from Parliament. The first modern 'lifeboat' was made, and did its first famous rescue the following year. And Henry Greathead was given medals, prominence, did lauded lecture tours, got gold medals from Royal Societies . . . I won't go on, if you don't mind. It makes my blood boil. Lifeboat men still call the brilliant design 'Willie's Corkie'. The inevitable monument is to both men, the extolled gainer and the sore but honest loser.

'I don't know,' Troude was apologizing to the gorgeous lady.

'The other one, then.' She spoke dismissively. No tea and crumpet for poor old Philippe tonight.

'It's dud, lady.' I was narked. I wanted to go and see where Baff got topped, not play her silly game. 'Move your pins.'

'Pins?' For the first time she lost composure. Her accent intensified slightly.

'Legs. The chair you're on's supposed to be provincial Continental, with a French mortice-and-tenon joint. The pin's like a dowel, to hold the joint. The French', I added to nark her, 'say *goujon*. Sorry I can't say it proper. It stands proud from the wood, in time. Fakers construct it the same, but have to dye the protruding end to get the shade right. It's darker.'

She moved as if to inspect the chair beneath her, pinked slightly and didn't. 'We paid . . .'

'Aye, well you've been done.' I rose, said thanks and started to go. She'd thought I'd been lusting after her legs all the interview. I had, of course, but only after I'd seen the too-revealing darkened shiny *goujon* head on the joined chair she adorned.

'Wait, Lovejoy, if you please.' Troude came hurrying after, now more of a go-between. He'd been a god at the Nouvello. 'Please inspect the Sheraton table – '

'Fake, Mr Troude.' I'd given the small table a glance on the way in. No gongs sounded in my chest. It was a fake no older than last Easter. But the surface worried me. Beautiful, made with endless unrelenting slog. I didn't know any faker still did wood finishes that perfect, not since old Trinkaloo died last Candlemas. But still a fake, if an excellent one. How odd to see one this excellent at Sir Edward's Event, and now another so soon. Dunno why, but I felt sickened. Something I'd eaten? 'Inspect? No, I won't,' I told him, still going. I could see a couple of boats dipping into the wind as they tacked to make the harbour. 'You've mucked me about once too often. I'm sick of you planting stuff in the Arcade, switching stuff with Frederico in case he was more of a crook than you suspected. It was pathetic. I resign.'

'That is impossible, Lovejoy.' He tried to get ominous. 'You are an integral part of the grand design.'

Even I had to grin at that. Grand design? Was he about to march on Moscow, for God's sake? I sighed, and pushed through the doors shaking my head. The most depressing thing about people these days is that they all talk as if they're deciding on global nukes when instead they're merely wondering if they should go down the pub or watch the match instead.

Jodie Danglass fell in with me as I reached the north shore after twenty minutes' fast walking. I was at the ice-creamio.

'Can I have a lick, Lovejoy?' She wasn't smiling, but women laughing at you never are. I know.

'No,' I told her, narked. 'Get your own.'

She bought one, raising her lovely eyebrows as the ice-cream man laughed out loud. She put her arm through mine. We went to watch the sea, leaning on the railings. I like seaside, as long as it's like this, with boats and plenty of folk on the sands and all the dross of the fair. The trouble is there's too much of our coastline left undeveloped: secretive, dark, silent, tree-lined, remote, where hardly anybody goes and nothing happens except un-controllables like Nature's cannibal act.

'How come you're their dogsbody, Jodie?'

'Happened by, Lovejoy.' She spoke too casually.

'Pay good, is it?' A little lad on a donkey was frightened. His dad pelted up, did a rescue. The little lad fell about with hilarity. It had been an act. The dad scolded, started laughing. The mum was furious. Even the donkeyman laughed, shaking his head. Lots of acting today at Mentle Sands.

'Not bad.'

I watched her tongue on the cornet. The white ice-cream seemed to like going in, sweep by sweep. I found my throat had gone dry. She was amused.

'When do we move on, Lovejoy? As soon as you are sure I'm getting less money than you? Or when you've decided you might stand a chance with Monique Delebarre?'

Move to where? She hadn't guessed yet that I'd resigned from Troude's brood. She detested Monique. I went along with her misunderstanding. Maybe she couldn't believe that somebody would actually refuse Troude and the lovely Monique. 'Dunno. I expect we'll know soon enough. That the stall?'

'As Baff was on? No. The police took it away as evidence. It was hard luck. Poor Baff. He just drew the wrong lot. Accidents happen, Lovejoy.'

Yes, well. Except a yobbo mob picking on a seaside vendor can sometimes be directed. Then it's no accident.

'Ta for the company, Jodie. And the intro. I appreciate it.'

'No time for solace, Lovejoy?'

She'd finished her ice-cream. I watched her lovely mouth assimilate the tip of the cornet, and listened to the faint crunch as it achieved total bliss on entry. My ice-cream was running in a hot melt down my wrist. I had to chuck it in a waste-bin. Seagulls swooped, shrieking deprivation.

'If you like. La Delebarre's antique chair was a fake, Jodie. And somebody'd "improved" the oars on Willie Wouldhave's model. Thought that was still in South Shields. How did they get it? Must have money to throw away.'

We walked to the Ruby, me dawdling to see her legs.

'They wanted some you couldn't have seen, of course, Lovejoy. Taking no chances. One thing.'

'Mmmh? Get in.' I got the crank handle.

'Since we left the marina all of a sudden I'm Jodie. Until then you drove me mad calling me Jode. Why?'

75

She didn't like it. I could have kicked myself. I give me away to women all the bloody time. I'm pathetic.

'Shut your teeth.' I swung the handle. The Ruby groaned awake, started a reluctant muttering, rocking side to side. 'You women are obsessed with your own image.'

Lovely teeth, beautiful shape, and a complicitor in Baff's murder. I watched her laugh at me. I had to explore further, with whatever means I had.

'That's more like the Lovejoy we all know and love.' She actually said that.

One of Galileo's girlfriends was a corker. A real stunner, Artemisia Gentileschi was. The reason we know so much about her is that she strolled about her dad Orazio's studio naked, driving his apprentices crazy with lust. One apprentice, Tassi, couldn't stand it. He raped the gorgeous Artemisia, and history – with the vicious impartiality history sometimes achieves – recorded the horrendous consequences.

Poor Artemisia's dad Orazio (pal of Caravaggio, his only other claim to fame) sued Tassi. The court scene was enough to scar you for life. It certainly scarred Orazio's lovely daughter. The law saw to that. In a variation of today's courtroom tortures, the Roman court insisted on thumbscrewing poor Artemisia – presumably on the logic that truth needs forcible encouragement from females. A doctor's examination of her pudenda was conducted in front of the goggling courtroom rabble. The apprentice was found guilty. Artemisia was justified, her honour restored.

Not enough. She went ape. Can you blame her?

An artist's daughter to her very soul, she revenged herself with exquisite talent. Before, her paintings depicted nudes and more or less holy scenes, all grottoes and haloes. Now, they showed stark vengeance in the bluntest and most aggressive way possible. Her *Jael and Sisara* – that event which the Bible tries to persuade us was God-approved, where a bird drives a nail through the skull of her kipping cousin – isn't quite as gruesome as her *Judith Decapitating Holofernes*, but neither's a laugh a minute. The rest of her post-courtroom period's the same. Message: some nerk ruined Artemisia's self-image, so look out, world. The two dozen or so of her paintings on show in Florence were the only exhibition

I've ever seen where the crowds stayed totally silent as they shuffled from one macabre painting to the next. Superb artistry, yes. One thing got to me. It was the serenity on the face of the decapitating, hacking, sawing, nail-toting, hammering, skull-piercing birds. And all of them were Artemisia. Revenge is sweeter for outlasting the revengee, eh?

See what I mean? Muck about with a bird's self-esteem at your peril, or wear a parachute. As I drove from Mentle Marina I realized I'd been careless. My galling diminutive for Jodie had vanished as soon as I'd realized she was one of Troude's people, hook, line and sinker. Quick as women always are, she'd spotted something in my manner. Lucky she'd guessed wrong about my staying hired, or she'd have guessed I'd rumbled her.

Nothing for it but to accept Jodie's company. We drove to my cottage. I thought of ice-creamio stalls, and composed firm decisions about not going to France. I didn't want to go. But why were so many people determined I should? Jodie made such life-or-death problems vanish into ecstasy.

10

There *is* no battle of the sexes. No such thing.

Never mind that everybody talks about it, says it rages all the time. It doesn't exist. Reason? Everybody's on sex's side. And it wins hands down.

Of course, we pretend like mad that there is. What utter hypocrisy. What a hoot. Women, like sex, won any conflict long before the starting whistle blew. They knew so. And why? Because they're the only supply.

Mind you, sometimes sex can resemble all-out ground war. It did that afternoon with me and Jodie. I actually found myself staring at the bruises on her, in horror that I must have done those. She laughed, called me stupid, asked if I offered the same service to all birds or was it just her, light chit-chat the way they do when they've proved you're an animal in infant's clothing. Nothing we can do about that, either. I wondered why a woman like her would put up with an oaf like me.

'You know something, Lovejoy?' She was almost purring, while I cursed and tried to find the kettle and swore blind somebody'd nicked my tea bags. 'I could go for you.'

'Like we've been holding a novena?'

'Who's the latest bitch?' She tutted when I glared round at her. 'I don't mean your popsies. Or that whore you drove for Gazza the other night. I mean *the* latest.'

'What've you done with my sodding milk?'

It was curdled in its bottle. Astonishing. The weather must have been thundery. Or was it simply old? I could remember buying it . . . whoops, a *week* ago? God, time flies. I looked hopefully at her, lying in that recumbent dreamy posture that brings back the ache.

'Fancy nipping up to the bungalow shop for some milk, er, love?' I'd tried for Jode a few times during, but passion had interfered with reason and Jode hadn't quite made it. I vaguely wondered if Jodie had.

78

Well, that really set her laughing, shaking so her breasts came to be the only thing in the world. She was still laughing when I chucked in all thoughts of brewing up and waves on the seashore went dot dot dot. It was only afterwards, on the way to see Gobbie, who'd know about Leon the French divvy if anybody would, that I started wondering if she was so badly hooked on Troude that she would willingly go with a scruff like me on his orders. To keep me on the chain?

I've no illusions about love. I believe, honestly do believe, that women do what they can get away with. I mean, take any staid reliable lady. Supposing she meets Handsome Jack; he says, Come, dwoorlink to some resort – safe from prying eyes, cast-iron excuses for her family and loved ones. He's rich, romantically unattached, excellent company, amusing. What does she do? Spurn this upstart with a Victorian avast-ye-Satan? No. I honestly think ninety-nine point nine recurring per cent of respectable matrons would say yes, and go for that hidden lust, only they'd call it secret romance.

I'm not being cynical. I'm being sad, realistic. Nothing against it. It's just that we're somehow compelled to act as if we all believe that morality wins hands down. It doesn't. We know so.

Gobbie, know-all and undeceived. That is to say, he's old as the hills and seen it all. He even knows – knew – Leon.

I found him at a boot sale. For those unacquainted with East Anglia's pastoral pastimes, this isn't selling footwear. You fill your car boot (trunk in Americese) with any old dross, take it to the appointed place – playing-field between matches, schoolyard, village green – and pay to park your gunge-stuffed vehicle among other GSVs. Then you sell your rubbish to anyone who'll take it, and buy everybody else's rubbish to take home in your poor groaning old motor. It's recycling at its best. If it wasn't for boot sales, the world'd be nipple-deep in tat. Gobbie was there, staring morosely at the teeming field.

'Wotch, Gobbie.'

'Hello, Lovejoy.'

This sale was in aid of scouts and guides and brownies. Novelty yodellers did their stuff on a mock-up bandstand. Tambourine singers competed. A youthful morris team wore itself out ruining the village cricket pitch. Brownies served tea and crumpets heavy as lead. Fathers shifted crud from one car to another. A gaggle of antique dealers scavenged and prowled. I recognized a few, Liz Sandwell, Merry Halliday, Rhea who gives sexual favours for genuine Georgian furniture, Capability Forster who designs your garden then sends his lads to nick valuable antiques from your home. Harry Bateman too, I saw with surprise. His wife Jenny's hooked on some non-starter, but doesn't care. Big Frank from Suffolk, silver-mad and on his umpteenth wife.

'Gaiety gone mad, eh, Gobbie?'

Gobbie's so named from his long-range spitting prowess. A true cockney old-time dealer, Gobbie. And a veteran of the Continental night runs for the antique trade. Retired.

'Riot, son, innit?' he said drily. 'Got a prile of ointment pots, though.' He tapped his bulging coat pocket. He only deals in secret now he lives with his daughter. She thinks antiques degrading.

'Goo' lad you, Gobbie.' I eyed him speculatively. 'Any Singleton's?'

Singleton's Eye Ointment has been on sale within living memory. It was orignally Dr Johnson's (not *that* one) of 1596. Singleton took over three centuries back, selling the stuff in parchment. These pots had a few name changes over the years, but after about 1858 became Singleton again. Look for early unglazed examples, the rarest. You still find ointment pots pretty cheaply – a day's wage on average. Boot sales rarely charge more than a few pence for anything, so Gobbie'd done well.

'Here!' Some bloke rushed up, pointing, furious. 'You in charge? Those little bastards are dancing on the cricket pitch, for Christ's sake!'

I knew there'd be trouble. A leaf blowing across the hallowed turf can cause heart failure in village cricketers. I saw a dog shot once for wandering on our village's.

'Leave it with me, sir,' Gobbie intoned, to my astonishment. 'I'll move them directly.'

'I should flaming well think so!' The bloke tore off to be furious elsewhere.

Gobbie resumed as if nothing had happened. 'No Singleton's, but still not bad.' We watched the parades, the turmoil of milling folk. Then, 'You in with that Frog, son?'

'Resigned, unpaid. Glad to be out of it.' I was relieved he'd spoken first. An astute old bird is Gobbie. He'd probably guessed why I'd come the instant he saw me wander in.

'Best is not to be noticed at all.' Gobbie looked about the field. 'Know what, Lovejoy? The old antique game's coming apart. Looks safe, ordinary. Feels corrupt, horrible.'

'Shouldn't you be doing something about them dancers?' I was worried the kiddies'd catch it from that cricket goon.

'Eh? Nowt to do with me, son.'

Blokes like Gobbie make me smile. I can't help it. He'd sounded like our bishop, telling the cricketer he'd handle it. Now there was a disturbance out there, three adults arguing, the furious gent pointing angrily towards us, the morris dancers faltering, handkerchiefs fluttering slowly to a stop.

'Leon was something to do with Troude. Right, Gobbie?' There are so few divvies around, each of us had heard countless stories of the others. It's pub gossip in the trade. Troude the high-flyer wouldn't know that.

'Leon snuffed it.' Gobbie's old eyes took me in. 'You sub?'

'Aye, substitute. Silver imports, Troude said.'

Gobbie snorted. Folk came hurrying our way, all furious. I was sick of their bloody cricket pitch.

'Much he'd know, silver or owt else.'

'Is he not an antiques roller?' I was astonished. Why did Troude need me, then? 'Or a dealer?'

Gobbie's laugh of derision set him coughing, a gentle ack-ack-ack. 'Him? There's no such thing, Lovejoy. Not no more.' His bleary stare raked the approaching mob, but he spoke only of the antique dealers, now arguing over some fake. 'Just look at those buggers. Nobody knows naffink no more. Twenty antique dealers, not one has a clue. All they want is a few quid. Wouldn't know an antique if one bit them in the arse. Troude neither.'

People talk truth, you listen.

'You distinctly said – ' the cricketer started heatedly, while organizers and brownies surrounded us, all yammering.

'You didn't rope them a different square,' Gobbie said, pontifical in reprimand. Lies didn't alter his tone one jot. I marvelled. 'I wrote to your secretary last week telling him to rope them off a separate square. Avoid misunderstanding. Not the kiddies' fault. They were told, dance in the roped-off square.'

'I got no letter!' the cricketer cried.

'See?' the brownie mob cried righteously. 'See? *Inside* the roped-off *square*!'

Gobbie announced, 'Rope off a different square. They got permission. You didn't do your bit.'

They all left, still arguing, the cricketer scurrying for some rope. I looked curiously at Gobbie. Some blokes simply exude status. You have to admire fraud, wherever it walks with style.

'Know when antiques wus, Lovejoy?' The old visage cracked into a dozen little smiles. 'Fifty year since. I played the violin, dance bands in the Smoke. Then the talkies came, fiddlers out of work everywhere. Became an antiques runner. You should've been there. Running down Aldgate, three o'clock of a rainy morning. Hauling trestles up Cutler Street silver market – not that frigging shed they got now, the real one. The barrers in Petticoat Lane, iron wheels sounding like tumbling coal on the street stones. Old Tubby Isaacs singing on his whelk stall – real live eels – top end, where you could look at Gardner's Corner or Aldgate Pump. Nobody about in the shiny black morning 'cept real folk.'

'What happened, Gobbie?'

He came to, bemused, astonished I was still there. 'Gawd knows, son. Everybody became a great greedy herd, just feeding and fucking, never lifting their heads to look. See Maisie?'

'Mmmmh?' I knew Maisie, fair, fat, forty, fly-by-night with the reliability of a weather forecast.

'Says she's been antique dealing six year. I told her, "No you not, ducks." She got narked. You're the only one who knows what I mean, Lovejoy.' He paused. The antique dealers drifted. Their argument would linger through several nights' drink-up times at the pubs. 'Nice here in the country, though. Daughter, grandkids, her bloke good-hearted. No telling anybody what I seen.'

He has bad feet, did a practice shift of weight, wanting me to ask.

'What've you seen, Gobbie?'

His smiles coalesced. It was strangely beautiful. 'I seen a Thomas Tompion clock on a street barrer, Lovejoy. Seen a Hester Bateman inkstandish pledged for a half-a-crown Derby roll-up bet.'

He made to go, with that I'm-hurrying gait of the arthritic.

'Ain't no antique trade no more, Lovejoy. Nor no dealers.'

'Leon the last, eh?'

He halted, staring at the dancers being triumphantly roped off by the cricket-club man.

'Last but for you, Lovejoy. Watch out, son. They did for him in a loading accident. Some roadside in France. Heard from a box shipper. Me mate, 'fore the London docks went posh.'

Well, old matelots tell each other things.

'But why did they top Leon, Gobbie?'

'Dunno that, Lovejoy. Word is, he wouldn't play along.'

'With what?'

'Gawd alone knows.'

'Here, Gobbie. You really running this lot?' I couldn't help asking.

His face parted in a great grin round one tooth. 'Nar, son. Dunno what they're all on about.'

And off he shuffled. Box shipper, one who exports container loads by sea. Mate, a Cockney's drinking partner, trustworthy to the hilt. To do for, to kill seemingly by accident so there's no fallout.

'What can I do, Gobbie?' I called after him. I meant to repay the favour.

He didn't stop, laughed ack-ack-ack. 'Bring times back, Lovejoy. I'd give everything for just one last scam.'

The old soldier's laugh. You used to hear a lot of it, old sweats who'd been in the trenches. Inaudible beyond eight yards.

'Look.' The cricket secretary came, sweating heavily, pointing in an aggrieved manner. He'd seized on me, authority by association with the old magic man. 'Look. I can't have those children dancing on the bowler's approach run.'

'Sod off,' I said sourly, and left through the hedge. People get my goat. Everybody wants solutions for their problems. Who helps me with mine. Bloody nerve.

Falsehood may be the bride of truth, but in murder and antiques it's legend is her lover. Old Gobbie meant that Leon had been topped. Like Baff, though the means of killing was different. Two deaths, Troude the common factor.

Stopping off before I reached town, I went to sit in a tavern yard. They rig up pot plants, swings, a children's zoo – rabbits, a guinea-pig, hamsters, smug chickens – with trestle-tables for you to swig ale on. It encourages families to come.

Troude hadn't mentioned Leon the French divvy, not by name, so I was guessing. I knew little of the bloke, except he was famed in subterranean antique lore. He's supposed to have helped the Louvre, in its multitude of nefarious dealings among Continental antique dealers. Just as a roving football scout spots schoolboy talent in a Sunday park then clandestinely phones a First Division club, so Leon – no surname ever whispered – would spot that staggering convent altarpiece, let's say a Lorenzo Lotto painting, and for a consideration contact some Louvre stringer. The convent delightedly accepts a pittance (less than a hundred dollars) for their old daub, whereupon the Louvre then announces the discovery of a priceless old Lorenzo Lotto painting, got for a song! (Well, a song plus Leon's cut.) Imagine how sweetly ye heavenly choirs do singen over such a triumph! Lawyers join in, soon as the courtroom opens. Incidentally, if you think I'm making up this Lorenzo Lotto story, don't ever go into the antiques business.

Leon was a power, made a good living. Except suddenly I was uneasy. How much of all this was fact, and how much lies or legend? Troude, posh in his richdom, lived remote from my level. I mean, I'd never heard of him a little ago. This is the trouble: penthouse princes see us from a height, as eagles see ants. And I'll bet one thing for absolute sure – those eagles don't know one single ant, whereas we ants can identify every individual eagle down to the feathers on the tail.

The pub was quiet, hardly a soul in. Almira's motor arrived, it came like a military band. Two old soaks on the bench lusted at her stridey figure as she advanced on me to stand akimbo, glaring.

'Are you avoiding me, Lovejoy? And who's that mare in your cottage?'

Who indeed? Two children stopped admiring the little zoo to stare at this aggressive newcomer.

Better look downcast, I decided. I hung my head in sorrow. 'Still there, is she, dwooerlink? She's haunting me. I had to escape.' I shrugged, all pent-up emotion. 'It's not her fault, Almira. She's going through some crisis.'

She blazed on. 'That doesn't explain – '

'Why the hell does she come to me, though?' I paraphrased her forthcoming sentence. 'I can't solve her frigging love life.' I gestured her to sit down. She did so, reluctantly. I eyed her. Yes, time to give her a gentle reprimand. 'Your phone, love. Is your husband having it tapped? Makes some funny noises.'

'My phone?' New thoughts for old, I saw in her face. 'There were no messages, Lovejoy.'

'That proves it. Somebody wiped them both off. Is he back?'

'Who?' She looked at the two children, now standing listening beside us. 'Go away!'

They didn't move. 'Why's your mummy cross, Lovejoy?' Peggy, the taller girl, asked me gravely.

'Because I won't do as I'm told,' I said. They were shocked. So also, I saw, was Almira. She tried to smile, to show she detected no double meaning.

'Run along, children,' she said tightly. She wasn't used to brats. She'd say that, soon as they were out of earshot.

'You have to do as you're told,' the titch Justine said sadly. 'I've to wipe my own button. I can't wee on the tortoise.'

Lucky old tortoise. 'That's not fair, chuckie,' I said. Somebody called them and they went disconsolately towards the tavern's side door.

'No, Lovejoy. Jay isn't home for several more days yet.' She'd had time to think. Now, Jervis isn't all that common a name. But it definitely does start with a jay. She tried to be seductive. 'I'd like us to take a run out tonight, Lovejoy. Stay over somewhere. London, perhaps? I've a friend who says her cottage will be free for us to have a week or so on the Continent. Will you come?' Lips wet and luscious, seduction at its most powerful.

Drawing breath, I prepared to say no, resist her. She was offering unrestrained passion, but it was me who'd be walking into danger now the moment had come. 'Course, love,' I said. My mind complained she'd baulked at France a short while ago. Now it was the Continent at all costs. Why?

As I went towards my Ruby she actually came out with it. 'I'm not used to brats, Lovejoy. You have such odd patience.'

See what I mean? Sometimes you can guess what women'll say,

or even do, but you're no nearer. I'd have to do an exploratory stint on Gazza Gaunt's Tryste waggons.

'Good heavens!' I patted my pockets. 'Forgot to pay! My cottage, half-five. You will come, dwoorlink?' I looked anxious.

Almira hesitated, but didn't want a row on a pub forecourt. 'Half-past five, Lovejoy. Shall I tell Claudine?' She tutted at my uncomprehending stare. 'About her cottage in France, Lovejoy.'

'The sooner the better, dwoorlink!' Like hell, I thought.

I hurried inside, paused long enough in the taproom to hear Almira's great motor start and pull out, relaxed and went to the off-licence bit, tapped on the hatch. There was hardly anybody in the bar, all unfamiliar faces.

'Wotch, Tone.'

Tony grinned through his window. 'Mummy ballocked you, Lovejoy?' So Peggy'd blabbed. He gave me a glass like an undine, his cruddy special welcome. To me most drinks are unfathomable.

'Who's making Justine wipe her own bum? And why can't she pee on the tortoise?' I'm her godfather. Much good it does either of us. I've to drink Tony Crookham's poisonous liqueurs and Justine gets oppressed.

He fell about, sobered. 'Good to see you, Lovejoy. Hear about Baff?' Tone was always quick on the uptake. It was the real reason I'd stopped by.

'Whatever was Baff thinking of, taking a part-time job? He wasn't so badly off as all that. I saw his missus.'

'Hasn't everyone?' Which gave me food for thought.

'Who especially, Tone?' I'd asked the question outright like an idiot before the penny dropped. Tony was uncomfortable, leaning back to check along the bars for ears.

'Word is Baff did the breakdowner on some foreigner's place.' I almost said it with him. 'On the outskirts of Mentle Marina.'

'How did you hear, Tone?' The one question no publican ever wants to answer, or have friends ask.

'Sherry mentioned something about it,' he said, all on edge, speaking quieter still, looking round. 'Only in passing.'

Well, well. Still, we godfathers are responsible only for the morals of our goddaughters, not of their parents. 'Course, Tone,' I said, and took my leave.

Nothing to do with me, I told myself as I cranked my Ruby and leapt in while the engine still cared. Tony's wife Georgina's a lovely Irish redhead, tall and slender with the air and breeding of the aristocrat. And she's sexually superb. I meant to say I think she looks as if she probably is.

So somebody in Troude's syndicate had had Baff murdered. A rum world.

Chugging out and on the town road, I wondered about people. Look at Tony and Georgina. Nice people, known them for years. I'd stayed in their tavern during a spell of homelessness, and we'd stayed friends. Yet Tony slopes off from Georgina, who'd make any bloke's breathing go funny, to Sherry, a bird of great sexpertise but minimal other attributes. A frosty old lady I know once told me her mother preached, 'It's for the man to try/ And the woman to deny.' Well, more marriages founder on that reef than any other. Maybe Georgina was busy denying, so Tony sailed elsewhere? You never know what goes on between a bird and her bonny, do you. I clattered the Ruby to Gazza's garage. I'd never thought of his shag waggons as a form of marital breakdown service before.

11

Everything's luck. Who you end up loving, finding that priceless Old Master painting, getting away with murder. And you get no help. I mean, set up infallible rules to guide you in life, and you're still as baffled. There's a group of nations called G7 – they do things with international money. They met in England a bit since. Would you believe, a Japanese collector paid a fortune for the blinking crappy modern chairs they sat on? I understand less and less as time goes by. They could have bought some antique chairs for half the price.

It's my own fault. I'm a mine of pointless fact. Like, Queen Victoria and Prince Albert's wedding cake was 9 feet 4½ inches tall (can't help you into centimetres if you're a decimal nut). Also, Equatorial Guinea hasn't a single cinema, tough on local film buffs. Furthermore, Engels, Marx friend-of-all-mankind's side-kick, wanted 'ethnic trash' exterminated – he included Basques, Scots Highlanders, South Slavs, anybody he called 'backward'. Aristotle was first translated into English in 1620 . . . See? Mind like a ragbag, all contents useless – except, when some bit's oddly not.

There's one old dear in our village says we all know what's coming, that we prepare for it the whole of our lives. I tell her she's a daft old coot. She says I'm unwilling to believe the obvious, which is ridiculous because my mind's always crystal clear. It's just that occasional flukes sometimes make you think, good gracious, how lucky I knew that odd scrap about Mrs Hannah Glasse's cookery book being worth well over a hundred times more than its look-alike contemporary pirated edition! Or when you've just looked up the measurements of a loo table – nothing to do with lavatories; for the Georgian game of lanterloo – only to land on one the very next day. The trouble is, sometimes you discover which bit's the important one in the most unpleasant way, or when it's too late.

*

Sandy was all over the front page, I saw from the evening edition. I was in Gazza Gaunt's yard, having some grotty machine coffee, when I caught sight of the headline in Mercy Mallock's paper. I asked for a look.

'Sandy's invented a new political party, Lovejoy,' she said. I read, gave it back. 'Europe Time, it's called.'

'What's up?' she wasn't smiling.

'My bloke's left me, Lovejoy.'

'Barmy sod.'

Mercy Mallock's the only woman driver Gazza employs, presumably on the grounds that blokes are macho tough and can defend his clients should the need arise. It's a laugh. I'm off like a hare at the first hint of trouble – to call on somebody like Mercy, truth to tell. She used to be some notable's bodyguard, believe it or not. Her hobbies are kendo, karate, all those martial arts that sound like food additives and consist of kicking people in white pyjamas. She is of surprising daintiness for all that, graceful and always groomed, looks a stunner dolled up. Now, she was in some sort of boiler suit.

'He was never satisfied, Lovejoy.' She was sitting on the running board of her van. 'Not that,' she added quickly at my look. 'I was area champion two years running, trained with him every night. He left me for a woman shot-putter from Stourbridge, built like a sumo. How can I compete?'

Impossible. 'He's a nerk, love. Any bloke'd give his eye-teeth.' I didn't run him down too much, because women are odd. I didn't want her rounding on me in his defence. 'Want the night off?' Mercy's passion waggon was the last in the yard, waiting to go. I was the only driver without a van.

'No, Lovejoy. I'd better keep going.' She gave a wan smile in the yard's lights, fluorescents of ghastly pallor. 'Is it this hard for a man who gets rejected?'

'Dunno yet,' I said, to give her a smile. Didn't work.

Ten months since, I hired her – nothing illicit; Mercy's honest – to eavesdrop on some antiquarians at the London Antiques Fair. It was really disappointing. They were meeting to decide what antique books they'd bid a million dollars for (surprisingly only six: Shakespeare's First Folio, 1623; the American Declaration of Independence, 1776; Audubon's *Birds of America*, 1827–38; *Don*

Quixote's First, 1605; the Gutenberg Bible, 1455 or so; the *Bay Psalm Book*, 1640). They commissioned a counterfeiter, Litho from Saxmundham, to forge the twenty-pound notes to buy the books with. Litho forges by lithography, a printing process using stone developed two centuries ago by Aloys Senefelder, a mediocre playwright wanting to facsimile his plays on the cheap. I made nothing of it, but it drew me and an excited Mercy together for the one time we ever made smiles.

Gazza came over, the big business. 'Nothing for you, Lovejoy. Mercy, here's your ticket. Pick up at the moorings by the Black Boy, code word Heaven. Forty minutes.'

'Thanks, Gazza.' She gave me an apologetic look. Her van was the newest and most luxuriously appointed of the lot.

I sulked, to get Gazza's mood right, then left dejectedly, but not as dejectedly as all that because it was all working out just as I wanted. I flagged Mercy down at the intersection to cadge a lift. It's not allowed – Gazza sacks you for less – but I'd once been especially kind to Mercy and it worked.

'Did Gazza say the Black Boy, love?'

'Yes, Fremmersham.'

'Give us a lift, love?' I climbed in quickly, not giving her a chance to refuse. 'Console each other.'

'You too?' She gave me a glance, pulled away. A cracking driver, million times better than me. I find almost all women are. London bus drivers rattle you round like peas in a drum, unless they're women. Birds drive smoother, and just as fast.

'Getting over it, Mercy,' I said, all brave. 'Her family's titled, rich, Oxford. You can imagine the reception I got.'

She squeezed my arm. 'Poor Lovejoy. That the blonde, Jocasta, who has the racing-driver brother?'

I was startled. I'd been making up my heartfelt sadness, or so I'd thought. I couldn't even remember a Jocasta. 'Don't, love,' I said, almost in tears. 'It hurts too much. Let's talk about something different. I might go on a Continental holiday soon. Play my cards right.'

'Where?' She glided through the gears. I wish I could do that. 'I love the Continent, Lovejoy. Beautiful weather, lovely scenery. They take an interest in their food, real life, art.'

Honest surprise lit my countenance, I hoped. 'Didn't know you felt like that, love. France, I think.'

'Lucky you, Lovejoy.' She sighed, patiently allowed a cyclist to pedal over the level crossing before the barrier descended. Most drivers I know would have shot the amber and terrified the cyclist out of his pants. 'I lived there so long.'

'You did?' More raised eyebrows. I should have gone on the stage. 'Oh, aye. Weren't you a courier or something. . . ?'

'Bodyguard, actually. Didn't you know, Lovejoy?' She smiled, gave a rather shy titter. 'I know I don't look like one. That was the trouble with Gay.' The cloud settled again. Gay's her karate feller, but nobody jokes about *his* name.

'Fancy!' I said, yanking the subject back where I wanted. 'I've never met a bodyguard before. What did you actually do?'

'They hired me after I became pentathlon champion.'

'Didn't it feel . . . odd?'

'Because I'm a woman, Lovejoy?' she demanded, stung.

'Eh? No. I hardly noticed that. I mean, being responsible for some politicians you'd never heard of.'

'Bankers, actually.' We reached the town bypass and pulled out coastwards. Fremmersham's on an estuary some five miles out. I looked at her face in the dashboard glow. Pretty, composed. Barmy old Gay, that's all. Swapping shapely Mercy, for a weight-lifter. There's nowt as daft as folk. 'I spent my life at airports, shepherding stout men with briefcases.'

'Can't imagine you doing that, Mercy.'

'They asked me to stay on. Mostly they're Dutch girls, on account of their languages and because they look the part. I was lucky, on account of Dad.'

'Got you the job, eh? Influence counts in banking.'

She glared at me, touchy. 'I got the job entirely on my own merits, Lovejoy! My languages. Just because my hobby's sport doesn't mean I have to be thick.'

'Right, right.' I lapse into a modern vernacular when I want to placate folk, trying to sound like I'm just from a disco and full of fast junk food. The rest of the journey was uneventful, because I made it so. We chatted about her loss of confidence now her Gay had given her the sailor's elbow, her hopes, her sports, her having to give up the flat. Routine incidentals, you might say, that make up life's plenteous pageant.

At the pick-up, I stayed well out of sight, just watched her lights dwindle from the taproom bar, then merrily tried to get a lift back to civilization, away from the lonely estuary and its one tavern and boats swinging in the night breeze. Mercy Mallock was in my mind. I felt more cheery than I'd done since hearing about Baff getting topped.

Lucky enough to get a lift from Spange, a dealer without portfolio – meaning not an idea in his head – I made it to my Ruby and thence the White Hart, and organized a whip-round for Baff's missus. A paltry sum, but plenty of IOUs made it seem more. Enough excuse to see Sherry, anyway. So I left smiling. Quite a good evening, really. I'd covered some ground. Oh, and I'd made arrangements to see Mercy again, the point of it all. If France loomed as ominously as it seemed, I wanted allies.

But just how far things had gone was brought home to me as I was leaving for home. Donk came hurtling in just as I made the outer door. He had an envelope. Reluctantly I paid him his message money out of Sherry's whip-round. Only borrowing. I'd owe.

'Urgent, Lovejoy. Meeting's in an hour.'

'Eh? It's bedtime, for God's sake.'

'You heard.' And off he thundered. I glanced guiltily about, in case any of the antique-dealer mob had seen me misuse their donations, brightened at the good omen when I saw they hadn't, and opened the envelope. In the solitary light of the forecourt I read Jodie's rounded scrawl. The meeting with Troude and one other would be tonight, quarter before midnight, outside the George.

Some hopes. I wasn't their hireling. They could take a running jump. So I lammed it down the dark country road to my cottage, brewed up, sat and read a couple of antique auction catalogues that had come, generally faffed about doing nothing, and settled down by about one o'clock.

Which was how I came to be heading for France. Not quite instantly, but in circumstances definitely beyond my control.

12

A book was published in 1869 entitled, *Autograph of William Shakespeare . . . together with 4,000 ways of spelling his name*. Which may sound loony, but represents some bloke's unstinted endeavours. You have to respect it. Some other bloke wrote the longest poem in the language, five ponderous volumes on Alfred the Great – as unreadable as it sounds, as neglected as it ought to be. Pure endeavour. The Eastern Hundreds has more than a fair share of endeavouring eccentrics – this in a nation of eccentrics –so we're belly-deep in weirdos. It was therefore no problem to find the world's greatest sexponent, at one-thirty on a sleepless frosty morning. I wasn't surprised to find Forna Lux wide awake and lusting. Everybody knows Forna Lux, but is especially wary of her because she knows everybody back, which isn't good news if you pretend holiness.

'Lovejoy, babbikins!' she screamed into the phone. I held it a mile from my ear, but was still deafened. 'What've you got?'

Forna is her own invention – I mean her name. She denies ever having received any cognomen. I don't believe her. Obscure of background, indeterminate of accent, no known family, Forna has a serene individuality that defies pinning down. She lives alone, on information culled from anywhere. She says she's written seventy-nine books under that name, all on sex and ways of doing it. I like her. She's a slender yet blowsy middle-ager with glittering teeth, peroxide hair, and wears more gold than a jaunting gypsy.

'I need your help, Forn,' I said into her screech. 'Sorry about the late hour.'

'It's early, babbikins!' Her voice is that shrill noise chalk makes on a school blackboard, if you remember that far back. Sets your molars tingling. 'You know me, always at it!'

The laughter almost melted the receiver. I waited it out. Forna works harder at her records – perversions, lists of clients seeking ecstasies of a hitherto unpublished kind – than most antique dealers do theirs. I like a professional. No, honest. Standards mustn't be allowed to fall.

'A certain bloke, Forna.'

'Can't be done on the telephone, babbikins,' she cried. Come round if you're desperate. Same position, same old place!'

She has a knack of making the most mundane phrase suggestive. I sighed, got dressed, found matches for the Ruby's headlights. Twenty-past two I was chuntering into Forna's Furnace.

Lest I give the impression that all the Eastern Hundreds are mad on surreptitious goings-on, what with Gazza's outfit and all, I ought to explain that Forna runs her own publishing house. It's respectable, as such places go, with a logo, two secretaries and a small printing works near Aldeborough. She's the dynamo and prime mover, though, and runs it from her cottage in Sumring, a hamlet trying hard to be noticed for something else besides Forna. She has automatic locks on the doors, successive stages of entry under banks of hidden cameras.

'Enter my inner sanctum, babbikins,' she screamed.

Several locks later, I passed through the last of the reinforced doors. A sitting room, with one Turner seascape, watercolour, testifying to her taste among a load of Art Deco nymphets and erotica statuettes you can't keep your eyes off. Forna wore pink satins, impossible pink lace flounces, synthetic pink furs. She always wears a ton of make-up, which I admire. I chose a chair at a distance, got nowhere. She cuddled me on the sofa, poured me a drink I didn't want.

'Wants, babbikins?' she shrilled in my ear. 'Every man's got those. I want yours, that's all!'

'Ha ha, Forn,' I said gravely, hoping for fewer decibels so I could at least hear the answer. 'Any news about a bloke called Jervis, or Jay, related to Mrs Almira Galloway?'

'Cost you, Lovejoy.' A trace harder now, but still octaves above top C.

'What?'

She contemplated that for a full five minutes. When I first knew her she was quite soft-hearted and had a dog called Frobisher, but it got killed when somebody ran over it. She abandoned business for a six-month, then resumed with a heart of flint and a disguise to match.

'There's a young artist I know, Lovejoy,' she shrilled. I leaned away, hoping my auditory acuity would survive. 'Has an old bike. My cousin, actually. He needs money for art school. Is there much of an antiques market in old bikes, Lovejoy?'

This was the squeeze. Forna always wants to help her cousin's lad who's always manfully striving to better himself. Her bloody cousin must breed like a frog, the number of times I've helped him with antiques. Were there other clients, bankers helping this same unfortunate striver with fiscal problems, clerics helping him over theological humps, engineers giving useful tips about his gas turbines?

'Bike? Tell me, and I'll tell you, Forn.'

'No, dear,' she screamed. 'You run down the different sorts. I'll stop you when you get to the one he wants to sell.'

'A German baron produced the first bicycle, a walking machine with a steerable front wheel, back in 1817. Your, er, cousin can't have one of those, just on probability,' I began. Give her her due, Forna listens intently, takes it all in.

'Wood, were they?'

'Mostly, but very popular. A Dumfrieshire bloke invented workable levers to drive these walking machines about 1840,' I said, watching for a glimmer of recognition in her eyes. Nothing. 'You'll know the velocipede, Forn. Pierre Michot made about two hundred a day in the 1860s, but sold out for filthy lucre. They're not too rare, but cost.'

Her eyes sparked. 'Maybe it was one of those, babbikins?'

'The penny-farthings are the best known,' I went on, heart sinking at the price I'd have to pay, but I desperately needed to know more, and I'd scraped the barrel for information. 'James Stanley was the genius, a little Coventry chap who made fixed pedals for the front wheel.' I got carried away. 'Posh bicycle clubs became all the rage, with bright uniforms and personalized bugle calls. Labourers were barred – muscular strength was unfair, you see, to effete aristocrats in the team.'

'I think maybe it was one of those,' Forna said, eyes now brilliant with pleasure. For pleasure read financial relish.

'His brother's son, John Stanley, made the one you'd recognize today, Forna. Equal wheels, chain drive, brake and bells. These Safety Bicycles were a terrific advance, highly sought among modern collectors. The Rover design was the pattern . . .'

'That's it!' Forna cried. I heard no more until I'd watched the midnight cops-and-robbers film while she searched her records in some secret cupboard with a whirring door. I kept wondering where I'd get the price of one of John Stanley's original Rover bikes from. Of course, the bike itself wouldn't show up. I'd pay for it, then she'd promise it, promise it, promise . . . Then, by mutual agreement, the antique bicycle and her artistic protégé would turn into slush and vanish down the gutters of time. For a bird who lived on hard news, Forna's income fed on fiction.

'Here, babbikins!' She emerged and sat, pouring a new drink. 'Jay for Jervis Galloway, Lovejoy,' she shrilled. 'A Parliamentarian, not going to stand at the next election – an expected large windfall from some unspecified new business. Politician of mediocrity. Turncoat. Conservative to Social Democrat to Labour. Wealthy by his missus, a dick-struck cow who fox-hunts.'

'That it?' Almira would love her description.

'No.' Her voice sank a little. 'Heavy money into coastal development, Lovejoy. A syndicate of antique dealers funnels money through him into Mentle Marina. Philippe Troude I know.' She smiled. 'He buys more love potions than a wizard. Struck on some French woman with high connections.'

It matched, but added a little. 'He your client, Forna?'

'Did I say one bike, Lovejoy?' she cried. 'I meant one of those velocipede things as well!'

'Good heavens,' I said evenly. 'What a lucky lad your cousin is! Troude your client?'

'Has been since he opened his marina complex, Lovejoy. No harm in the man, not really. Pays on the nail, pleasant with it.'

She told me his foibles, bedtime idiosyncrasies, tame stuff really. I hardly listened. Four in the morning she was still wide awake, answering some incoming call. I left knackered, wanting to kip.

Yet back at my cottage I couldn't rest. The parcel delivered by a relenting Michelle was inside the door. I'd passed it a couple of times, reeling from the bonging but too worried to've taken up its challenge. Now, I opened it with care. Very small, an ovalish velvet box that barely covered my palm. And a note saying sell it on commission in London, not anywhere local. It was from Baff, RIP. *Anywhere else but the eastern hundreds, Lovejoy, you have the connections, I have not any more you see how about a 3/7 is that okay with you good luck no questions asked mate, never seen playin cards like these, they seem complete set as far as I can tell, regards, Baff*, he wrote with Elizabethan disregard for scriptural refinement.

The velvet case contained fifty mica (thus transparent) oval slivers. At first, I couldn't work out what the parts of faces and bits of apparel and hats and wigs were painted on them for. Then I saw on the bottom one, painted on solid heavy copper, a Cavalier-like gentleman looking at me, dated 1641. It bonged me stupid. A spy-master's set of disguises! I'd never seen a complete set before. I picked one mica slice at random, superimposed it on the oval miniature portrait, and the Cavalier had changed into a swarthy turbanned Turk. Replace it with another mica oval, the miniature became an exotic bewigged blonde lady with exquisitely huge breasts tumbling from her bodice. No playing cards these. My hands trembled so badly I had to set them down.

In troubled yore, disguise mattered. A spy-master – like Mrs Aphra Benn, the heroine I keep on about – wants to send, say, a message to a secret ally. But letters could be opened, like Mary Queen of Scots', and you'd be for it. Carrier pigeons could be hawked on arrival, then all was lost. Messengers were intercepted, bribed, waylaid. A problem, no? So your spy-master has an innocent parlour game distributed to secret sympathizers. They look like partially painted mica slices sort of, with roman numerals on each transparency. The secret sympathizers – Royalist, Parliamentarian, whatever – going about their daily business would receive an innocent letter for birthday greetings, some such, bearing a date or some numeral. The sympathizer hastens to the children's nursery for a merry game of Appearances, and casually notes the matching numbered slice. He superimposes it on the miniature portrait, and finds himself now staring at . . . at a middle-aged woman pedlar! Get it? He now knows that the next secret messenger *must* be of that description. They were Flemishmade, usually, and are unbelievably rare. I'd only ever seen one complete set before, and that was on a BBC *Antiques*

Roadshow, where the expert didn't know what they were for and thought them a simple entertainment. Some entertainment!

But.

This pack I'd actually heard of before. They'd been sold at a local auction a year since. I'd missed them by a whisker, arrived too late to bid. Tinker told me they'd gone to some French bloke who lived near Ladyham. For a fortune.

Had Baff pulled the breakdowner on Troude? And been exterminated for his pains? From then till six o'clock in the morning I sat and thought. And thought.

Then I cast caution to the winds, walked up the lane to the phone by the chapel and phoned Almira.

'It's me, love,' I told her. 'Let's go.'

'Oh!' she said, brightly gathering her wits. Somebody was with her. 'Very well, ah, Claudine. I'll come right over.'

Two hours later, I was shivering in the minutest aerodrome you ever did see, at Earls Colne. We flew in a thing called a Piper Saratogo, which looked like a sparrow that had swallowed a watch. I closed my eyes, and dozed through a flight, a landing, an interminable drive, and finally came to a rest where oblivion awaited between clean white sheets. It was broad daylight everywhere except in my head.

13

Opposites aren't. I always find this. Murder, when you go into it, tries to be something else, like unwonted killing, not quite murder as such. Motive's the same; it isn't anything like an explanation. The only two things that stay what they start out are love and hate. They're white-hot hundred-per-centers, complete of themselves. Idyll therefore is not idyllic. I could have told Almira that, if she wasn't a woman and therefore likely to laugh at whatever I said. It's the way they are.

So, in lovely France, in a pleasant house miles from anywhere, with two lovely ponds in the lovely garden, not another building to be seen from the lovely stone terrace, lovely herbaceous borders to gladden the eye, lovely exciting Almira for the one lovely exciting essential, and lovely food baked or whatever by unseen hands below stairs, I was utterly bored sick. If heaven's like this, I thought, screaming inside.

That fourth day in France was the real landmark. I woke up, came to. Almira was lying beside me on the bed. The house was an odd shape. The main bedroom had the disconcerting feature of being open to the rest of the house, so when you turned on your side you could see down into the hallway and part of the living room. If a door to the left was ajar you could also see the feet of an elderly lady called Madame Raybaud who cooked and gave instructions about where things had to be left. She went berserk when I moved a bag of groceries half an inch. Centimetre.

The place was silent, except for Almira's gentle breaths whoofing on my shoulder. It was early afternoon. You've to go to sleep after noon grub for about an hour. You get used to it, but it's a terrible waste of effort. I lay on my back, sweating from the heat, and gazed at the ceiling. Shadows on the plaster walls, a portrait of the Madonna, a crucifix, not much furniture, though some quite old, of local rusticity that I liked.

Almira turned over. The thick fluffy mattress clung to you for dear life whatever you did, but me and Almira had conquered that by compelling passion. She was good, vibrant, desirous, didn't simply lie there waiting for you to get active. She joined in with an eagerness I'd come to relish. Mind you, I relish inert birds too, so there's no means of telling which is best. I looked at her sleeping form, and felt a warmth that shouldn't be there. Birds get into you, and then you're helpless. I'm not afraid of commitment, no. How could a bloke like me be scared of loving one bird for life, to the exclusion? I'm decisive, sure, definite. It's my character.

The window shutters looked simple but had a folklore all their own. Simple hooks got you mad by staying hooked just as you thought, here comes daylight and a vision of the valley. I wrestled silently with the damned things, finally got them open enough to see out. Windows are for looking from, not blocking up.

Our house was a size, on the shoulder of a vale with a river coursing below. No anglers that I could see. Back home they'd be out in droves with coloured umbrellas and odd hats and flasks, murdering minnows. No other farmhouses. Small fields, I noticed, no cattle in them to speak of. Where the hell did Madame Raybaud hail from? She came on a bike. It made me smile, thinking of Forna's cousin. She'd have to wait for her fee now.

There's nothing to see in countryside, is there, so I leaned on the sill, thinking of Baff. East Anglia was as depressingly rural as this, so possibly not far away out there an assortment of strange characters lurked possibly as exotic as ours. Was there a Dicko Chave, perfect gentleman, proposing to any bird who stood still long enough? A Sherry, giving exciting welcomes to hotel guests for a consideration? Glass faker-makers like Phoebe Colonna and Steve Yelbard? Did Gallic versions of Gazza's Tryste Service trundle these dusty lanes, bearing Dianas to some costly nocturnal lust? I found myself shivering, don't know why, chucked trousers on and padded downstairs.

The terrace was a longish paved area under vines and clematis, between foliage that fell away down the hillside. No definite edge to the garden that I could see. It blended with scrub. Lazy smoke rose from the greenery. Did we have beavering gardeners as well as a cook? We were complete, a nuclear family or something. I looked at my feet. Very odd, but the strangely new slippers fit me. I'd tugged them on without thought. These trousers weren't mine. They were new. I'd brought nothing except what I'd worn when, practically walking in my sleep, I'd stepped out of Almira's motor. She'd brought none of my things, silly cow. That's the trouble with women, never . . . never . . .

Some fault in the logic halted me. I sat on the wall at the end of the terrace. Nobody'd know I was here. No phone, no nearby village. I'd walked along the lane for a couple of miles, finding only a couple of cottages set back from the verge, orchards, a field or two, woods. It was picturesque rural tranquillity at its most poisonously repellent.

Almira's motor vanished some time during the first night. I'd heard it go, but not been in a condition to look. I mentioned it to Almira but she said it was going for a service, so that was all right. I find preconceptions go wrong on me, especially about countries. That's what I meant about opposites. Maybe some old snippet from history was making me uneasy about being in France? Like, Richard the Lionheart got shot while besieging some local town here. With gentle nobility, he died lingeringly, forgiving the enemy archer – who was then literally skinned alive for daring to kill a king. See what I mean? France is gentle, noble. Or France is lies and cruelty. Preconceptions. I'm the same about women, always wrong. Men are easier.

My logic started to niggle. I've had one or two birds – well, all right, maybe more than that. Experience has got me nowhere but, all the same, women do stick to certain patterns. Like, this holiday was never on Almira's impulse. It was planned, down to the last detail. And – the vital bit – women are obsessional packers. Go away for two days with a bird, she brings the kitchen sink and eleven suitcases of superfluous tat. Not only that, I thought, watching a bee rummage in some flower, but a woman packs like a maniac. It's her nature. Agree a weekend away next Easter, she'll strew luggage all over the bed that very day with seven months still to go. And if you're slack about your own packing, they'll furiously start on it for you. I don't know why. Probably they've not got enough to do. You just have to ignore it, like Wimbledon Fortnight. I haven't got much in the way of clothes, never have. Almira'd brought in a selection of clothes the first day – or had they already been here, waiting? I'd been too knackered to observe. She'd had a thrilling time, kitting me out in new trousers, shirts, a selection of shoes. She said it was a French door-to-door service. I hadn't found my old crud. Almira had chucked it. 'You look smart, Lovejoy,' she said, delighted. Four days . . . *I was now anonymous.*

There was a path down the hillside garden. I'd been down it before. It went past one of the pools and finally an old well. That seemed to be it but for a copse further down where the path petered out. I found myself walking down it, for nothing. I was suffering badly from withdrawal symptoms – not an antique shop for a million miles. See what I meant, what's wrong with Paradise?

Wood smoke drew me among the trees. It was surprisingly near. A smouldering garden fire, a brick cottage, two oddly silent dogs chained to a stake, both looking at me with mistrust, and music trying to suggest Spain concealed beyond the doorway.

'Monsieur?'

I jumped a mile, but it was only a grave-looking, stocky man, clearly some gardener. He held a hoe, was quite pleasant. School French always lets you down, but you're sometimes forced to give it a go. I tried. His face took on a surly what's-this-gunge expression. I came to recognize it as a hallmark admix of French scorn and impatience, reserved mainly for me.

'Hello. *Je suis* Lovejoy,' I said. *'Je visite avec Madame, dans le maison.'*

We talked similar stuff for a few breaths. He invited me in, gave me some drink that produced an instant headache. He was Monsieur Marc. He was a gardener, I understood. I was not a gardener. What is it that you make like *métier*, Monsieur Lovejoy? I buy of chairs and of tables, Monsieur Marc, especially *plus vieux*. French wears you out. I could ask him if he liked apples or *poires* and how old was his Mum, but replying to counter-questions, ever my bane, was hopeless. I thanked him a million times, because thanks is easy. He saw me off after I'd told him the flowers were much more better *comme* the *fleurs dans* England, not is this not? I tottered past his dogs – weird; I thought dogs did nowt else but bark. Maybe stunned at my syntax.

His hoe hadn't been a hoe at all, I saw as I left. It was a sickle, slotted bayonet-fashion underneath a longarm. But that was all right, wasn't it? I mean, out here in this rural peace a gardener'd need a weapon, *il* practically *faut*, right? Foxes, heaven knows what. Did France still have boars, wildcats, worse? I felt

protected, snug even. Good thinking, Monsieur Marc. I returned to
the terrace, where Madame Raybaud was setting out tea. She had
her own idea of what English afternoon tea was – heavy scones,
butter and jam, Earl Grey and a kind of clotted cream in small
ramekin pot things. Lovely, but so far we'd not had a single pasty.
Almira came down looking a picture in a summery saffron linen and
matching shoes, good enough to eat. No problems with her
declensions, I noticed. She and Madame Raybaud prattled on about
Monsieur and talked laughingly of groceries. Clearly old pals. I had
the notion that Monsieur was not me, but how would I know?

Often I wonder if there's all that much to do in heaven except
look out. Oh, Almira and I were really enjoying ourselves, I
thought over mouthfuls of Madame's thick scone. How could it be
otherwise? Gorgeous bird, no worries, fine weather – though I'm
the rare sort who actually likes rain – pretty garden, passion on
demand with a lovely compliant woman, watching her sunbathe
and occasionally swimming in the larger of the two ponds.
People'd pay fortunes. It was just my festering discontent. Most of
it, I decided, smiling across the terrace table at Almira's lovely
face, was simply withdrawal from antiques. I get symptoms worse
than any addict. I just can't help it. Women tend to get narked if
you own up, tell them you're dreaming of some sordid antiques
auction. They think you're criticizing them for making you bored.
It's because women love holidays. I don't. Holidays, like a
number of other things I mentioned a bit ago, aren't. To me,
they're hard work.

Sorry to go on about holidays being truly boring gaps in life, but
I'd noticed a few features of Almira's behaviour. I knew this place
was owned by her schoolfriend – I'd forgotten her name – and
guessed that probably Almira had visited before. But a woman
walking about her own garden behaves very differently from one
who's merely coming through, so to speak. Even if she's shacked
up with her very own lover with hubby safely slogging elsewhere,
she looks totally different. She touches this bougainvillea, that
oleander, with possession somehow. Women do it to men as well,
so you can tell what's going on before it hits the newspapers if you
keep your eyes skinned. Even if you don't want to spot unpleasant
truths, sometimes you can't help but see the obvious.

This house was hers.

Certain conclusions are inescapable, once a fact hits home. The Almiras of this world can't live without a phone. No wires proved nothing nowadays, in the cellular-phone aeon, so there was communication about. Yet I'd been told otherwise. If this was Almira's secret love-nest, she'd still have electronic wizardry. If it was her husband's family nook, he'd be even more likely to have wires humming between here and political headquarters.

Once a lie creeps on to a tea table, you're done for. The scale of the deception scarcely matters. Like contamination defiles a feast, or a stain ruins a dress, it's spoilage city. Okay, Almira might want to keep me away from contacts, the way a holidaying bird excludes all those clamouring duties she's left behind. But one fib compounds another. The keys to Almira's motor had been hanging on the wall of Monsieur Marc's cottage. She'd only one set. The keyring's fancy, with one of those dotted inbuilt lights they give you at Sandor Motors. I knew its logo. I'd asked them for one when they mended my Ruby once. They'd told me to sod off. I'd not said anything. So Monsieur Marc was more than a full-time gardener. So what?

'Look, love,' I said brightly as we finished nosh. 'How about we have supper out tonight? Maybe see a nearby town?'

She smiled, fond with possession. 'As soon as the car's back, darling, we shall. I want to walk through to the river down below. Madame's just been telling me there's a lovely lake somewhere near. I'll get directions from her, shall I?'

'Lovely, dwoorlink,' I replied, most sincerely.

One more lovely and I'd go mental. But I smiled, and wondered when they'd come. Our holiday was only supposed to be ten days. If they delayed much longer there'd be hardly any time to shift their antiques. If any. I felt pretty sure I knew who we were waiting for. I wasn't quite correct, as it happened, in fact not even near.

Incidentally, don't hide from fraud. Hiding from it's the easiest thing to do, and always brings disaster. Yet we do it, every single day. The fact is, fraud is always – for always read but *always* – clearly recognizable. You sense that your husband is deceiving you with another woman? You tell yourself, heavens, no! Can't be! He's merely edgy because of things at work . . . The checkout girl is doubling up your grocery prices? No! She's a pleasant lass, always smiles . . . We trick ourselves. Complacency's so cheery. Facing reality is hell.

Once, I went to a night lift in Cambridgeshire. I'd been in a Cheesefoot Head pub when this maniac wandered in and surreptitiously showed a fragment of shredded silver. My chest bonged like Great Tom's clapper and I was across the taproom like a ferret. The bloke let me touch it. Honest Early Christian silver, seventh century. I almost wept.

'Look, mate,' I told him. 'You a moonspender? Give me three days. Name's Lovejoy. I'll have a syndicate together, honest to God. Money up front.'

A massive aggressive hulk shoved me aside and showed me his craggy yellow teeth. The pub went quiet.

'You're off your patch. I've heard of you, Lovejoy. This be local business, boy.' He had two enormous goons for help he didn't need. It's always like this, because field finds of Dark Age silver can bring in nearly enough to settle the National Debt. East Anglia's taverns have this illicit trade sewn up. (You're supposed to tell the Coroner, who on a good day promises you maybe perhaps some reward money, possibly, with any luck. Whereas illegal syndicates pay cash on the nail, the night your little electronic detector goes bleep. Guess who wins?)

'Okay,' I said. I didn't want to get left in a dark ditch. 'You called Poncho? You'll know I'm a divvy. Want me along?'

Which did it. Poncho hired me for a few quid and a free look at the treasure as it was dug up. We drove out in tractors – tractors, for God's sake, on an illicit night steal of pre-mediaeval buried silver. All the stealth of a romp. Cambridgeshire wallies – antique dealers working the bent side – are like this, half business acumen and half gormless oblivion.

We were dropped in some remote place. I'm clumsy at the best of times and kept falling over in the pitch. Countryfolk go quiet after dusk, except when they're cursing me for being a noisy sod. Just the five of us, including the moonspender with his detector and earphones. No moon. I wanted to go straight to the spot and get digging, but away from civilization rural people suddenly acquire a terrible patience, think nothing of standing still for an hour so's not to disturb an owl or a stray yak. I can't see the problem. They made me sit down on the ground so's not to make a din, bloody nerve. All I'd done was stay still. I was excited at what we'd dig up.

The field was standing grain. I'd asked a few times why didn't we get going. Nobody was about. Poncho growled that he'd thump me silent if I didn't shut up. After a whole hour, I drew breath to ask if there were rival moonspenders bleeping their discs at our treasure out there but Poncho's hand clamped over my mouth. His two goons were suddenly gone. They returned twenty minutes later, suddenly four instead of two. We all ducked out then, and finished up in a barn two miles away interrogating two sheepish oldish chaps. Poncho was furious, but our moonspender laughed all over his face when the goons lit their cigarette lighters as the barn door clamped to.

'It's only Chas and Dougie!' he exclaimed.

'Hello, Lol.'

They stood there crestfallen, blinking. We should have had Joseph Wright of Derby to paint the scene for posterity, intriguing faces illuminated by the stubby glims. Two more innocuous gents you never did see. Thinnish, grey of hair, meek of mien. No trouble here. I walked round them, curious. I'd never seen gear like it. They carried a short plank, a huge ball of string. The one called Dougie wore a flat cap with wire hanging from the neb, like a threadbare visor.

'You were in my field,' Poncho growled.

'No, we were just making a pattern. Honest.' They were scared. They'd realized we weren't police.

'It's all right,' the moonspender said, still grinning. 'It's what they do.'

'They'm grain-burners,' a goon mumbled. The barn chilled at least twenty degrees. The two blokes went grey with fear and started vigorous denials. Countryfolk are vicious if they think you'd dare damage crops, haystacks, farm gates. Really barmy, when there's so much rurality to spare.

'No,' Lol scoffed, laughing. 'They're artists, loike.'

And suddenly I twigged. 'You two from Outer Space?'

They looked even more embarrassed. 'We do no harm.'

Poncho wasn't satisfied. His illegal night lift had been spoiled.

He wanted blood. Lol explained that Doug and Chas were the crop circlers.

'They make rings in the grain. Bend the wheat down – '

More growls from the goons. Farm people, they hated this.

'What for?' Poncho had to know.

I joined in, to spare a couple of lives from Planet Mongo. 'It's in *Nature*,' I told him. 'There's whole books now on crop markings. There's even an institute – right, Chas?' And got eager but terrified nods. 'They're flying saucers. Some say.' I had to smile, using the old expression. Some say – *and others tell the truth*.

'It's only you two bleeders?' Poncho said, amazed.

Chas said yes. 'I like wheat fields, but Doug here likes making patterns in barley because the grain heads hang – '

'We don't spoil any crop, honest!' Doug put in, nervy at the countrymen's hatred.

'It's just a fraud,' I told Poncho. 'They're famous, but unknown. Studying the crop markings is a new science, cereology.'

Poncho took some convincing. 'You', he finally sentenced the shaking pair, 'are banned the Hundreds. You hear?'

They agreed, and were let go – but only after the night lift was accomplished: a silver platter and a chalice, sold on to a Continental dealer two years later, I heard down the vine, and miraculously 'discovered' in a Belgian attic when an old house was being demolished. Thus authenticated, the precious silvers joined the 'legitimated' mass of ancient treasures given wrong attributions in the museum collections of the world.

Fraud. When speaking straight off to the moonie in that Cambridgeshire pub, I'd forgotten one of my own laws of antiques: Fraud is everywhere, *so never ignore it*. See? One fraud compounds another, spawns off a third, a fourth, for greed feeds off the whole evolving mass of deception. Meanwhile, the brave new science of cereology goes on, as more and more mysterious crop markings show up everywhere . . .

And I dursn't hide from Almira's fraud any longer.

14

The lake was quite a size, as jumped-up ponds go. We walked along a little shore among trees that tried to get their feet wet but couldn't make it. Pretty. There are quite a lot of flowers in the woods in France. That's all I wish to say on the subject of their countryside. Rural lovers can keep it. They can have ours too, as far as I'm concerned.

'It hasn't rained for days, Lovejoy!' Almira was like a young girl, running ahead, pointing. 'The ground's lovely!'

Ground? Lovely too? Jesus. Mind you, a woman's alluring shape makes you think of possible ways to counter yawnsome nature rambles, so I smiled, but she skipped away, enticing.

'Not here, Lovejoy. Wait till the summerhouse . . .' She caught herself quickly. 'Madame Raybaud said there's one along here.'

Well, deception is as does. I cooled, looked across the lake. Nobody was about. We weren't being seen and it all seemed private, so why suddenly the reserve?

'Lovejoy!' she exclaimed, flushed. 'I said no! Wait. It's just along here . . .'

We managed to get her breast off my hand and make it round a small promontory to where a logwood cabin stood. It seemed mostly windows. A boathouse, a rough track leading into the trees. Nice – sorry, *lovely* – if you like being remote. It was locked, but – surprise! – Almira guessed exactly where the key would be on the lintel. More clues to ownership: she didn't have to look for door-handles. I felt that same sense of a woman *in situ*.

It was getting on for four o'clock when we came to and donned enough clothes to show respectability if a passing racoon or whatever happened by. She decided to brew up when I moaned neglect, and laughingly went to clatter in the kitchen. Big kitchens in France, but no ovens to speak of. Stoves by the score, though. I stood on the verandah to look over the lake.

Sunshine's not all that bad, when it's the golden ambery kind you get in late autumn. It's the straight up-down stuff of broiling summer I hate. I stand in shade wherever it lurks. So, to one side of the sheltered projection over the boathouse slipway, I watched the lake and the weather and what a load of crap countryside is. Then I heard Almira lal-lalling to a tune, and smiled as the light came on. I had an Auntie Alice once who lal-lalled to any tune on earth. She could turn Vaughan William's Sea Sympathy into lallal. I edged nearer the corner to listen, smiling. Which was how I came to see him.

It was Marc, leaning on a tree. That sickle thing hung in his belt. He carried a shotgun the way countryfolk do, broken over the crook of an arm, barrel down, stock under his elbow. Hands in pockets. Plus-fours, thick jacket, small hat with feathers around the band. Slowly I drew back. It's movement gives spies away. That and, I thought sardonically, being too sloppy when you think the opponent's a duckegg. Like Marc did me.

Quickly I made the kitchen, demonstrating affection to see what happened. She pouted, glanced at the window, shoved me aside, did that playtime mockery women engage in to promise passion when they've got a minute. Which meant she knew Marc was trailing us. Hence the absence of sex on the sunshine shore.

'Dwoorlink,' I said, all misty, when we were sipping in the bay window. 'I've an idea! Let's sleep here tonight!'

'Oh, Lovejoy.' She smiled, but close to tears. 'You're such a romantic. But it's impossible.'

'Why?' I was bright as a button. 'Can't you see? Nobody near us, to see us or hear us . . .' I halted, uneasy at the words' familiarity. I'm no wooer. Women see through me.

'Because,' she said. It was meant to sound light-hearted, but came out unutterably sad.

'Because what?' I took her hand. 'I've never said this to any other woman, love. But I honestly wish you were the very first woman I'd ever met. I want us to – '

'No, Lovejoy. Don't say it.'

She turned away, real tears flowing. I was uncomfortable, more upset than she was, because I'd almost nearly virtually honestly been about to say something unspeakably dangerous. I felt myself go white inside, if that's possible. Why had she stopped me? Usually women go crazy to hear such daftness from a bloke. Was she acting, then? Or even more chained than me?

109

We spent the rest of the time proving merriment to each other, that this was a holiday affair of the very best kind. We made it home at the very edge of light.

And saw a Jaguar making its throbbing approach towards our very own front door. Like I said, I almost got everything nearly right – another way of saying everything wrong.

'Good heavens!' Almira exclaimed in a way that told me she was furious we'd not returned earlier. Probably planned how we'd be sipping aperitifs or something clearly innocent when he arrived. 'Look who's here! How ever did you manage to find us, Paul?'

With a man of vigour, you'd say uncoiled from the car. Paulie unravelled.

'Good evening, Almira.' He'd been ordered to sound portentous. 'Lovejoy.'

'Wotcher, Paulie. Alone, I see.'

'Afraid so. It's Cissie.'

'Oh, aye.' When was it ever not? I didn't say it.

'She's ill, Lovejoy. She wants you to come. I phoned home to find you, Lovejoy. And heard you were here, at your friend Claudine's chateau, Almira.'

Suspicious, but maybe true.

'What are you doing in France, Paulie?' I asked, eyes narrowing, ready to disbelieve.

'We were on our way to Marseilles, a clinic there. Cissie's been ill, took a turn for the worse on the journey. I got her seen at the local hospital. She's there now, Lovejoy.'

It might just be true. I looked at Almira, who was being all concerned. 'Oh, poor thing,' and all that. I wondered how genuine we three were all being. He honestly did look distressed. But was Cissie truly honestly ill, or had Paulie merely been ordered to do King Lear?

'Come where?' I gave back, wary. Coming on Cissie's orders was no simple matter.

'The general hospital, Lovejoy. It's about forty miles. I'll drive as soon as I've got myself together.'

Madame Raybaud hove into view, sombre of mien. Old women everywhere have this knack of sensing morbidity. They're drawn to it like motorists to an accident.

110

'Poor thing!' et sympathetic cetera from Almira. 'I hope it's nothing serious. . . ?'

His eyes wavered. 'I . . . I'd better let them tell you there,' he said. 'She wants to see Lovejoy. For his help.'

If he was acting, it wasn't bad. If it was genuine, it was, well, a totally different game. Maybe not even a game at all.

'How come you know Almira?' I asked, still wary.

'Know each other?' She gave me her huge eyes, a half-incredulous laugh. 'This is no time for silly jealousy, Lovejoy!' She coloured slightly. 'Paul has been my investment counsellor for over six years!'

So the party line was that she knew about Cissie and, formerly, me. And about Cissie and, now, good old Paulie. Therefore Cissie knew about Almira and me, and wouldn't blab to Jay. One thing rankled, though. I'd never known Cissie pass up a chance to stab an orphan kitten, let alone make a cutting remark about my indiscretions. Cissie would have slashed me with some remark about consorting with rich married women. Apart from that little flaw, their combined story could just be true.

'Why does she want me?' I asked. She never had before.

'She wants to tell you herself, Lovejoy.' He looked at me, then away. 'We've not got all that long.'

'Oh, my *God*!' from Almira, starting indoors to find some packing to burden us with. 'Come *on*, Lovejoy! Get *ready*!'

An hour later, we hit the road in Paulie's Jag. I looked back several times, but we weren't followed, far as I could tell. I perked up. Maybe the hospital had some antique medical instruments for sale. I know a collector in the Midlands gives good prices for mint surgical stuff. I'd ask Cissie, if we were on speaking terms. I wondered if she knew the word for charades in French.

15

Maybe it's the ambience – or one of those other words that sound full of the ineffable – but foreign hospitals seem more scary. Our own always smell of overboiled cabbage, resound to the clash of instruments and lifts whirring down to green-painted underground corridors with lagged pipes chugging overhead. Hideous but knowable. Hideous and unknowable is worse.

The day slid into dusk as we drove. What little I could see of the countryside was sculptured. Quite classic, really. From a prominence in a small lane you could see the line of sea with a small ship, though I'm bad on direction. Almira sat in the back, talking Poor Cissie's Ordeal and occasionally sobbing, though women's tears are often not. I dithered between doubt and doom. I mean, I didn't even want to be here. I wanted home.

'How come you're here really, Paulie?' I asked in a straightish bit. Don't distract the driver.

'Ah,' he said. He hadn't been told what to say when cross-questioned. But it still didn't mean fraud. Like I said, he's thick.

'In France,' I said. 'If we are in France,' I added to rub it in. Then I thought, hey, hang on. What had I just said? *If we were in France and not in some other country!* But once you're out of your home, you're roaming, right? What did it matter? I wish I could remember details of the flight in with Almira.

'Well, ah, you see, Lovejoy,' Paulie was saying, lost, when Almira put her oar in.

'Didn't you mention you were coming over for Cissie's health, Paul? That clinic, Marseilles?'

'Indeed I did!' with a shade too much relief for my liking.

'What sort of clinic? What *is* wrong with her, anyway?'

'She'll tell you, Lovejoy,' Almira reprimanded. 'It's lucky we were so near! Don't pry.'

The motor-car numberplates had that cramped French look. Or Belgian? Dutch? German? Why was I worrying where exactly we were? Nothing I could do about it. I couldn't read the road signs.

We hit no motorways. We must have been somewhere pretty rural because I didn't see a major road. The villages we passed were memorable for postcard-style fetchingness and unmemorable names.

'Anyway, nothing wrong with a holiday,' Almira added.

No money, clothes only what I stood up in. I could hardly make a run for it.

'Very little,' I said, to show how good I felt except for my deep nagging concern over poor old Cissie.

As we drove into this small town, I glanced at Paul, under cover of turning round to say inconsequentials to Almira. I'd never really seen him this close, never to take a real shufti. He was a worried man. I could tell. His posh sort never really sweats, just becomes behaviourally focused. Were he a man of action, he'd be taut, lantern-jawed, keen of eye. But he wasn't, kept looking at his watch, other cars. And even once let his speed slacken a few miles. Making time a shade too good? He'd been ordered to arrive dead on. I wondered who by.

The hospital was small but genuine. Nurses, people waiting, an ambulance or two, some poor soul in blankets being trundled between the devil and the deep blue sea. Pain in any amount's really authentic, isn't it? I waited with Almira while he did the *bonsoir* bit with a starched clerical lady at the longest desk I'd ever seen in my life.

'We can go up,' he said. An audience with the Pope. I felt quite cheered up because his drone had come back. Until now his voice had taken on a near-human quality, really strange.

It's hard to walk along hospital corridors. Not because they're uneven but because your feet feel guilty all of a sudden, as if they'd no right to defile the shining surface. I hung back, letting Paul and Almira go first. Genuine all right.

The wing we reached – two floors up and a nurse with a mortician's look – was quiet to the point of stealth. No din. No rattles of equipment. Doors closed, frosted glass, charts looking pessimistic as charts always do. Along three corridor doors, no less, and me finally really apprehensive. With this degree of care, Cissie was for it. No bonny Lysette, like you get in the Whittington at Archway, I felt with a pang.

113

'Please wait,' we were told. Paul was admitted. Then I was beckoned, and in I went.

It chilled me. Why every grim hospital interior has to be aquarium-lit I don't know, but it scares the hell out of me. The room held one bed, Cissie inside it, pale, her legs under a blanket. Nearby, but mercifully unconnected, were those bleep screens, gasp machines with paired cylindrical concertinas poised to squeeze, tubular glass valves, silvery switches. It looked like a rocket launch. The one honest light barely made a single candlepower. She seemed asleep.

Paul wakened her, after asking the nurse if it was all right. Cissie opened her eyes.

'Hello, er, love,' I said. Nowhere to sit. Doc Lancaster once told me that hospital telly soaps always go wrong in making their actor doctors sit on the edge of the bed, and approach the wrong side of the bed. I crouched to peer at her, trying to work out what I was for.

The nurse warned, 'One minute.'

Cissie's eyes opened, surprisingly clear. 'Lovejoy,' she whispered. I was shaken. I didn't know she could whisper. I must have recoiled, expecting her honing voice. 'Paulie,' she whispered. 'I want to speak to Lovejoy alone.'

'Right, right, dear.'

'The nurse too,' Cissie ordered, with a trace of her old asperity. She groaned, shifted slightly with the nurse's help.

The nurse left too, glaring as if this was all my fault.

Five minus three left me and Cissie. Her eyes closed for a little while, some sort of pain.

We'd lived marital a fortnight, then six weeks for intermittent skirmishing before the separation. It was the fastest divorce on record. She'd married Paul on the first permitted legal morn.

'Lovejoy,' she whispered. 'I wanted to say I'm sorry.'

'Eh?' I straightened, honestly found myself edging away. Abuse, yes. Hatred, aye, sure. But an apology? I felt I'd walked onstage in the middle of *The Quaker Girl*. That unreal.

'I know you must hate me, Lovejoy,' this whispering stranger said. She seemed to sleep a few seconds, blearily came to with appalling effort.

'No, er, Cissie,' I whispered along.

114

'Yes.' She fixed me with unnaturally bright eyes. 'I was cruel. I was wrong.'

Wrong? Cruel? Sorry? It was beyond my experience. 'No, er, don't worry. It's all . . .' In the past? Did one say things like that, times like this? 'It's okay.' When of course it wasn't. Okay for Lovejoy, not quite okay for somebody dying.

'I want you to do something, Lovejoy. If it's too much, then please say no. I won't bear any grudge.'

Please too? 'What?'

She wanted to move on to her side a little, and signed for me to move her round a little.

'I'll get the nurse,' I said, worried sick.

'No, Lovejoy. I don't want her to hear this.'

I held her, found myself cradling her body in an embrace that would have seemed like old times, except we'd never done this before, not with each other anyhow. Her face was close to mine, her eyes huge.

'What is it, love?'

'Paulie's a fool. Not a patch on you, Lovejoy.'

Not exactly the time to say I'd always known he was a pillock. 'Oh, well,' I managed.

'Please. I want you to help him, Lovejoy. Is it too much to ask, Lovejoy?' She coughed a bit. I tried to cough for her like a fool, holding myself stiff at an awkward angle.

'I don't know what it is I'm to do. Nobody's told me anything. Is it this Troude thing, something about silver shipments?'

'Paulie's in too deep with Troude. He's so desperate for it to succeed. All it is, they are storing some antiques, for export somewhere. It needs a divvy. Say you will.'

'Maybe,' I said, instinct keeping it so I could escape moral bonds should I want to off out. Gentleman to the last.

'I can't blame you, Lovejoy. It was all my fault.' She slipped away then a while, came too after an inward struggle. 'I'm frightened, Lovejoy. And leaving things in such a mess for Paul makes it worse.'

'I'll do it, Cissie,' I said. Instinct yelled to steer clear of the phrase at the last second, failed.

She drove it home. 'You promise, Lovejoy?'

'Promise, love.'

She sank back with a profound sigh. I was just taking my arms away when the nurse came in to say I had to leave, it was time for Mrs Anstruther to rest.

'Blood transfusion due in ten minutes.'

'Right, right.' I looked at the still figure breathing so shallowly, thinking of her in a plastic tent, the mask going over her face, drips being adjusted. 'Bye, Cissie love.'

Her eyelids fluttered. She said nothing. Paul came. And Almira, who said she wanted to say goodbye to Cissie. She was in tears. Paul was silent. I went along the corridor and watched the night outside with its strings of lights along distant roads through the darkness. It had come on to rain.

The way out was hard to find. I managed it third go. Only once did I discover something strange, and that was more by misjudgement than anything. It gave me pause. I stayed among a crowd of visitors getting something to eat down a corridor off a sort of out-patients' place. I heard an odd laugh, odd because it was familiar and shouldn't have been there. I sidled out and stood under the canopy thing looking at the rain.

An ambulance bloke came past, smoking to advertise the benefits of sickness.

'*Pardonez-moi, Monsieur,*' I got out. 'What is this that is this country, silver plate?' My French just made it.

'France.' His voice mocked my sanity. He strolled on, adding a critical suffix about foreigners, especially me.

As if it mattered, like I said. Except that Cissie was going to die in France. I'd seen the terrible diagnosis written plain as day on her chart. Diseases strike terror into me. Pathetically, I wondered guiltily if it was catching. How long ago had it been? I tried to work out. Could a disease lurk, only to spring out. . . ? Gulp. I'd been pretty tired lately. But coping with the rapacious Almira would have weakened a randy regiment, so there was no telling. Three silhouette nurses talked inside the porch across the forecourt. A tubby girl gave an odd whoopy laugh, cut it for professional reasons. Matron would scold.

'All right, Lovejoy?' Almira, at her most sympathetic.

'Aye, love.'

'Lovejoy,' from Paul. 'I'm sorry. I . . .'

He looked so lost I even felt sorry for him. 'It's all right,' I said, wondering what the hell I was saying. I was reassuring him that I was fine. 'I mean I'm sorry.' Even that didn't sound right.

'We should get back, Lovejoy,' from Almira. Paul said he'd drive us.

We finished the journey in almost total silence, except for Almira saying if there was anything we could do, Paulie, just get in touch, not to bother giving any notice. How, without a phone? I didn't ask. He nodded, kept glancing at me as if I was somehow more injured than him. I tried to force myself, but couldn't reach out and shake his hand. He didn't offer, either, so that was all right.

'Cheers, Paul,' I said as we did that silly look-at-the-floor shuffle folk do at such times. 'Be seeing you.' Would I?

'Yes,' he said, brightening. He went downcast, probably realizing that it was Cissie's dying wish that was possibly going to get him out of some scrape.

'Not coming in for a nightcap, Paulie?' Almira asked.

He seemed to lighten in hope for a second, then something in her expression clicked and he shook his head with the nearest he could manage to resolve, and dutifully got back in the Jag. Once a serf, nowt but. A night bird did its barmy whoop noise. It sounded so like a girl with a funny laugh.

'Better get back,' he said. 'Thanks.'

Almira bussed him farewell. 'Give our fondest love to Cissie.'

'Lovejoy.' He was trying to say something as he fired the engine. 'Thanks, old chap. I really do mean it, you know.'

'That's okay,' I said.

Me and Almira waved him off. He had the radio on as he turned up among the trees, headlights a cone of light dragging him swiftly away. It was that clarinet tune that hit the charts practically in the Dark Ages, something about a carnival.

'Poor Paul.' Almira said. 'Poor Cissie.'

'Yes.' Something felt very odd. That night bird whooped.

'Lovejoy.' She stood close, under a night sky fast clearing of scudding cloud. Stars were showing, and a moon they call a night moon where I come from, thin as a rind and reddish-tinged.

'Yes?'

'Cissie . . . It's no reason for us to be any different, is it? She'd want us to live exactly as we are.'

'Would she?' Odd, strange, queer, weird.

'Yes.' Very vehement. 'There's very little holiday time left. Just let's remember that, darling.'

There is something in this relief theory, that the misfortune of others shoots us so full of relieved thank-God-it's-not-me sensations that we instantly go ape. That night Almira and me really did go over the top, cruelty melding passion and desire in a frenzy so near to madness there was no telling where lust began and delirium ended.

The night seemed to last a week. Which was just as well, because holiday time was over, and fighting time was come.

16

'Good heavens! At last!' Almira cried from the terrace after breakfast.

I too expressed pleased surprise, the sort you see in those terrible old 1950s B films where rep-theatre acting glossed all emotions into mannerism. Being a genuine phoney's easy.

Marc drove Almira's motor up to the house and alighted with a flourish. He prattled something about having fought the garage to a standstill, demanding Madame's *voiture* back *immédiatement*. She was thrilled. I pretended I genuinely thought it had been driven from a nearby town instead of from Marc's cottage two hundred yards off. Marc retired, proud with achievement.

We beamed assurance across the coffee cups. I played along. I mean we said practically everything. Almira had already wondered sadly how dear Cissie was this morning, and how Paulie was bearing up. What a pity there was no telephone! This odd nagging feeling returned, that I was being led towards a distant but quite safe destination. Everything above board, nothing hidden. Great, eh? Lucrative, with Troude's assurances that money would flow in.

'Cissie told me about Paulie's investments in an antiques project, darling,' she finally said, doing her bit. 'You promised to help.'

'Mmmmh,' I concurred, doing mine.

She was ravishing, today in lemon yellow. 'It's Philippe Troude's project, isn't it?' She gave a half-laugh. 'Well, with Monsieur Troude arranging everything, nothing can possibly go wrong. He's a billionaire, Lovejoy!'

Over those curly bread things Madame Raybaud seemed to think were breakfast Almira seemed excited, under her thin disguise of transitory grief for Cissie. It'd be today. No woman can hide the delight of anticipation. It was there in her eyes, her moist lips, her showy manner. I've already told you about fraud. Remember the crop markings? And how *that* little fraud had become legitimate, even founded a whole new science? The only hassle came when it intruded into Poncho's fraud, which had itself spawned other new frauds . . .

And guess what! A message came! A messenger on a Donk-type bike rode up, solemnly handed Almira an envelope, got his chit signed and offed.

'Not bad news I hope, dwoorlink?' I said anxiously as I could on half a grotty bun and a swig.

Almira read the note. 'It's from Paulie, darling. Philippe Troude is here. Can we meet them today, talk over the arrangements. Thank goodness it's not bad news about Cissie!'

'Thank goodness!' I agreed. How lucky Almira's motor was back in time, I thought but did not say. But as long as antiques loomed I'd be happy. You can trust antiques, the crossroads of loving, murder, deceit, forgery and corruption.

'Now that we have the motor, dwoorlink,' I suggested, knowing the answer, 'have we time to look for an antique shop?'

'What a good idea!' she said brightly, telling herself she thought I'd never ask.

We hit the road. The keys were in the ignition. No concealment of direction, no angst over questions. Lovely chatter, pleasant talk about how she really admired the views, how much land France seemed to have, how much prettier France was than the Low Countries, don't you think, darling? Which told me I wasn't ever coming back to Madame Raybaud's domain, or the shack by the waterside with the hunter in the woods.

Through quite mountainous countryside – though goose-pimples look hilly if you live in East Anglia – Almira drove with ease and accomplishment. Driving on the Continent you have to think hard every inch because they drive there on the wrong side of the road. Nothing wrong in that; it's just their way. But Almira's expertise showed she wasn't new to these cack-handed roads. Nor did she need to inspect the signs, just casually notched them off.

Almira was quite at home here, thank you.

We avoided the big national highways. It seemed to me there'd only to come some sign promising a D, A or N road for Almira to cruise off down some rural snaker. I didn't mind. Nice to see open air, towns and that. I felt the odd familiarity of a newcomer to

France. Maybe it's the names. Villiers I remember, because there was once a Villiers engine, now highly collectible on old motorbikes. And a river called Anglin, very appropriate unless I've got it wrong. We drove forty miles, then stopped for coffee at a tavern. Hills rose in the distance. No, Almira couldn't tell me which they were, but there was a map somewhere in the glove compartment, darling . . .

See? No secrecy, no possible subterfuge. Mrs Almira Galloway was clearly nothing to do with the Troude scheme financed by Paulie et al. She was just along for the ride, so to speak.

As we talked and saw people roll up, stop for a chat, smoke and coffee, then trundle off, I prepared my sentence. And asked the serving lass if there was a *ville* nearby *avec un* antiques *magasin*. I'd have been quarter of an hour disentangling her swift joyous reply but for Almira, who cooed why didn't I ask, for heaven's sake? And drove me six more miles. To heaven.

'There's always one antique shop, Lovejoy,' Almira was pacifying me for the eleventh time, getting narked like they do when you ask quite a reasonable question. 'Don't keep on.'

'We should drive to the next town,' I grumbled. 'Happen the bird got her wires crossed.'

'We've hardly looked!' she was saying, when I stopped and felt a bit odd.

The town was hardly that. Set among small fields, it was on a little plain, a river not far off. It seemed amateur, somehow, but didn't care. Houses of that peculiar Frenchness, dry ground, trees indolent, unlike our busy East Anglian trees that are always hard at it – God knows what 'it' is, but they always seem to be giving it a go, stirring the air to a brisk breeze. Maybe it's our skies, never still. A few cars, a horse and trap, a lone flag proclaiming nationality. The windows of houses always look strangest to me in a new country. Flowers competing on opposite sides of the main street.

'This way, love.'

We crossed the main street. Three or four shops, a small restaurant, some men drinking outside at tables under an awning. A lane led up from the thoroughfare. I felt the oddness from that direction, towards the church. Less than a score yards along stood a yard, with a bow-fronted shop boasting antiques.

121

Remember this, for money's sake.

French furniture either goes ape in fashions so distinct from ours that your mind boggles – rococo chairs so ornate you sometimes have to work out where your bum goes. Like the fashion to implant floral decorative Sèvres porcelain plaques in the surfaces of cabinets about 1774 on, glorious but overwhelming unless you care for those horrendously smiling masks of women and lions that ornament the corners and frieze. Or it does the other thing, goes individual with a strange elegance that I love more. Oddly, the great furniture-makers were often not French at all, though they sometimes learned their craft there. Like David Roentgen, who sold in Paris but worked in Neuwied.

I stared. In the yard was a small converted Citroën truck. I reached to uncover the bureau more, but the odd feeling died. I let go, and turned in disappointment to find a diminutive bloke standing next to me. Gave me a jolt.

'Er, *bonjour, Monsieur*,' I said. '*Je désire pour regarder votre antiques.*'

He sighed a long French sigh and shot a mouthful of exasperation at Almira, who explained while I wandered to where my sensation grew stronger. It's exactly like that hot-cold game of children's parties. You *know* when you're standing next to the real thing, even if it's only a mildewed crate.

' . . . need, Lovejoy,' Almira was saying.

'How much? *Combien pour acheter*?' I told him.

He gauged me. He was the slyest man I'd ever seen. Even his direct appraisal was an oblique squint-eyed effort that never quite made your face. Then, when you'd finally given up and turned aside, you'd find his quizzical shifty eyes trawling after you, taking you in. He'd have made a cracking spy.

'This is not for sale,' Almira said after a voluble interrogation. 'The bureau on the car is.'

'*Je désire acheter le* contents *à l'interieur.*'

'?' he asked Almira.

'*Non*,' I said. I knew that *flic* and *agent* were police-laden words, and he'd gone even shiftier. '*Mais je . . . aime beaucoup* what is inside, Monsieur.' I remembered I hadn't a bean.

Almira told him I was an antiques collector. He brightened shiftily, and tried to pull me back to the piece on the truck.

'*Pas* the *tromperie* fake,' I said. '*Mais le vrai un.*' Just in case he managed to sly his way round this syntax, I added, '*Le vrai un. Dans votre* box.'

He tried telling me all sorts about the priceless magnificent late eighteenth-century bureau, just arrived on his truck, but I wouldn't have it. At last, slyly he undid his crate – already the screws were out – and slyly exposed a fire screen laid in the bottom. I went weak with delight.

Sometimes, mixing styles can be so dazzling that even the simplest object becomes glorious. I mean, can anything be simpler than a fire screen? Anything rectangular that stands up will more or less do the job, right? But Georges Jacob in the last quarter of the eighteenth century made a meal of rectangles. He married the new classical style with the older natural period. Another foreigner – Burgundian – he was a riot with the Parisians, and even did a brisk export trade to posh gentry in England. It was good enough to eat. The screen itself was slightly arched gilded wood, carved with sphinxes, arrows, twists on the support columns, cornucopias on the feet. Little garlands and ribboned top, all carved with unbelievable skill, showed just what they could do in those hellish workshops.

'*Est-ce-que à vous, Monsieur?*' I asked as best I could when breath let me.

He was ruminating slyly at my response, said something shifty to Almira.

'He owns it, Lovejoy,' she said, staring. 'But it's not for sale.'

'Everything else on the planet is,' I countered. 'Ask him.'

The piece smiled up at me from its bed of polystyrene grot in the crate. The screen's panel was a wonder, embroidery pristine as the day it was finished, florets in plum on a beige ground. Lovely. Some people say antiques are just inert materials. They're not. Antiques know what we think of them. Forgeries don't have feelings, but sure as God the real things do.

'. . . Lovejoy.'

Almira interrupting. 'Eh?'

'He says no deal. Buy the bureau on the truck, or nothing.'

'Tell him to stuff it.'

And I went outside to the car. She stayed behind to say no ta to Sly. We left, me burned up at having to part from that wonder. I could hardly speak until we'd driven out of the place.

'That fire screen was magic,' I told her, courageously not weeping. 'The bureau on the truck was a copy, modern, of Roentgen's work. He was famous for his stupendous gliding parts – drawers, doors, rests – and marquetry. He's become more faked than most Old Masters, especially here on the Continent.'

'What *is* the attraction, Lovejoy?' She was driving, perplexed. I sighed. You can't tell some folk, even if you're crazy about them.

'Roentgen's skill was so terrific that even the makers of automata – you know those little working models? – got him to make their models.'

'So? Couldn't you buy that fake bureau, and make more money on it than the genuine fire screen?'

'Of course.' You have to be patient. 'But the antique is alive and beautiful. The other's a load of dead planks.'

She was exasperated. 'But *profit*, Lovejoy!' Like I'd never heard of that old thing.

'Bugger profit,' I said crudely.

It was several miles before she spoke. We were pulling in to a town car park, quite a sizeable place with Paulie and Philippe Troude just arriving at a café and the lovely Monique preceding them in.

Almira said, 'Lovejoy. Are antiques, well, real people?'

Women can surprise you, even when you think they've run out of ideas. 'That's right, dwoorlink. I only wish that real people were real people.'

I made it sound a joke. But I was only thinking how curious it was that a rare genuine antique like that Georges Jacob screen had turned up in a dump like that village shop, with a superb valuable fake like the Roentgen bureau in the same yard. So I smiled and said I loved her. She smiled back and said she loved me. We were sickeningly sweet.

'Paulie and Cissie will be so grateful, Lovejoy,' she told me. 'I'll go across with you.'

Carefully not holding hands, we crossed briskly. No antique shops in sight, so I didn't care. I wish I'd been more discriminating. It's foolish to obey women, because they're usually wrong, but what can you do?

Paul emerged as we went in. He tried to reach for my hand to say so long. I passed him with an out-of-my-way look. A wimp's a wimp because he's determined to stay one. I'd no patience.

'Where to?' I asked Almira. Except that she was no longer with me. I looked round. She'd gone. And Paul.

'Monsieur.' A waiter ushered me through a scatter of diners, and from then on it was no game. Couldn't expect it to be, because antiques never are. But I felt utterly at peace, so serene. Antiques, even if they aren't mine, are the breath of life. I had to be near them at any price, and felt close.

17

There was a lunatic survey not long since. I read it in Doc Lancaster's waiting room midst ponging infants and wheezing geriatrics. Two things Make the Heart Sink, the magazine shrieked, 'Parting After Sex' and 'Meeting Somebody You Want to Avoid'. Well I'm sure the first is wrong; parting after sex is a pretty good idea. But the second is dead on. Bingo-time.

I entered this little nooky room above the café. The Heart Sank as I recognized the bloke seated at a polished table. That is to say, I'd never clapped eyes on him before in my life, but I recognized him all right. He was Superior Officer, fresh from military command of the most exacting kind. I hated him instantly, his ideals, his purity of vision. Nothing wrong with being a soldier, but there's one sort that chills the blood. They have the light of eagles in their eyes, and smell cannonfire sipping yoghurt with the bishop. They are patriotic, loyal, unyielding. They cost lives – hundreds, thousands of lives. And I'd only one – none to spare for the likes of him.

'This is Lovejoy, Monsieur.'

Troude was pleasant as ever – in fact, I instantly saw Troude in a kindlier light. Beside Monique's lacquered delectable hardness and the colonel's crew-cut ramrod stiffness, Troude was almost pally.

'Monsieur Marimee will control the process,' Monique said, *ex cathedra*.

Marimee fixed me with a gimlet eye. Clean-shaven, steel-grey hair, slightly sallow, lean as a whippet, he looked ready to jump from the plane at a cool eight thousand feet. Odd, but the table – a humdrum modern folding job straight from the nosh bar below – instantly took on a desperate polishy appearance, like it was on parade. It's the effect these blokes have. Of course he had a file. He opened it, threatening me with his eyeballs.

'You are a criminal.' The English was a bit slidey, but clear with meaning.

126

'Not much of one.'

'You are an *ineffectual* criminal.' He flipped a page, gave it no glance. I was getting the treatment. Authority ruled; his, nobody else's. My silence riled him. He rapped, 'Answer!'

'The question. . . ?' I wanted to obey in the meekest manner possible, do his job and exit smiling. Not much to ask.

Stupid to needle him but I couldn't help it. He appraised me from under eyebrows borrowed off an albino beetle. Troude fidgeted. He wanted us all to go forward in harmony. Monique was impatient with the entire world. Some women give the impression that an execution is the only way out.

'Insubordination will not be permitted, Lovejoy.' He got the name right, so his English was wellnigh perfect. 'This project requires absolute compliance. No discretion is permitted.'

He'd nearly said or else. I slipped it in to complete his meaning. Or else he'd shoot me? Then they'd lack a divvy, and they needed one.

'Very well.' And I added, 'Sir.' I saw he said it inwardly with me, satisfaction easing his stalwart frame for a second. His military mind wanted only to talk to chalk, like a superannuated teacher. 'What project?'

'Recovery of items from a location to be specified.'

'Very well.' The scent of fraud trickled in about here, ponging the nostrils. For recovery read robbery. 'Sir.'

'You are not curious about the items? The location?'

'I know you will inform me when the times comes, sir.'

His eye glinted. 'You have served?'

'In an army? Once. I was a famous coward. And ineffectual.'

No curled lip, but he hated the levity. 'Ineffectual criminal *and* soldier!'

Troude's sudden agitation warned me not to reply that maybe the two occupations shared lifestyles. I swallowed it.

'Is it the Commandant's wish for me to leave the project?'

Monique started. Troude almost fainted. Marimee found himself in a quandary. Gratified at the title, narked by having to admit I was valuable, he found refuge in an order.

'You will continue until the mission is completed.'

His project had become a mission in half a breath. I sighed. My famous instinct was yowling for me to get the hell out, run like a hare, swim back across the Channel. Cissie was dying in the hospital, believing in my promise.

'Very well, Commandant.'

'There will be two phases. The first will be in Paris and possibly London. The second will take place in a certain location to be notified. Time-scale: immediate, and within three weeks respectively.' He leaned back. The room relaxed slightly. He looked at me hard, hands behind his head. Immediate did not mean instant, it seemed. 'Questions are permitted.'

'I work alone?'

'No. You will have two assistants in Phase One. Phase Two is not for your ears until One is accomplished.'

'I will receive enough, ah, tools to carry it out?'

'Planning has been exemplary for both phases.' He shot to his feet, abruptly showing a non-punitive emotion for the first time. Troude looked wary, Monique irritated at some coming digression. I shrugged mentally. Okay, so I was not to query the perfection of his military mind. I'd not argue.

'Your nation, Lovejoy, is *despicable*!' he shouted.

Eh? Another mental shrug got me through that, but he was boss and implacable threats lay thick all about. I know when to bend with the gale. Marimee marched to the window, clear eyes seeking snipers out there on some distant hill. My whole *nation*? Maybe France'd just lost to us at cricket, whatever.

'Your tabloids speak of *losing* your empire, as if it was mislaid on your London buses! The truth?' He swivelled, fixed me, swivelled back, an animaloid gun turret. 'The truth is you *gave it away*! You proved spineless in the crunch!'

This sort of stuff bores me to tears. Who the hell cares? So obsessional historians score points off one another. It's no big deal.

'Your immigrants retain their national identities, *n'est-ce-pas*? Each group as distinctive as they were in Hong Kong, Kenya, India. Like', he sneered without showing whether his lip was really curled or not, 'the so-wonderful Americans.'

'I think it's what they want to do,' I said lamely. He'd seemed to be waiting for an answer.

'It is behaviour without *soul*, Lovejoy! In France, we *blend* immigrants! They become French. We fight for principle! As we

128

fight for our language. English is barbaric, a degraded hybrid! India alone claims six thousand of your "English" words. Your music is bastardized, assimilating Trinidadian . . .' I won't give the rest, if that's all right. It's a real yawn. For God's sake, I thought as my mind switched off his claptrap, if a tune's nice, sing. If it's not, don't. It's not exactly a proposition by Wittgenstein, for Christ's sake.

His assault when it came frightened me off my chair. He leaned at me, yelling, '*And you don't care!*'

'Er,' I said, returning. I'd almost shot out of the door. 'Well, I know some folk do. There's a lot of interest in ethnic dances and whatnot . . .'

'You surrender your national heritage!'

What the hell was he on about? I was here to shift some antique silver, and the nutter earaches me over reggae and steel bands? Troude caught my despair, shot Monique an appealing glance. She intervened. Her luscious mouth moved.

'Lovejoy. You will receive daily orders from the assistants of whom Monsieur Marimee spoke. Depart for Paris immediately.'

'Very well.' Assistants who rule? If her mouth said so. I'd do anything for it.

Marimee controlled himself. His outburst done, he sat with fixed calm. I didn't like this. Serenity's not that sudden. It comes like a slow glow from a candle. His tranquillity burned up like an epidemic. Wrong, wrong. The bugger was barmy. 'Immediately now or eventually now?'

She almost smiled, but didn't. '*Maintenant*, Lovejoy.'

'Very well. Good day, Commandant.'

As I reached the door Marimee spoke with clipped precision. 'I regret to inform you that Madame Anstruther died at twenty-three hours precisely.'

'Eh?' I halted. I didn't know any Anstruthers. Except I did. Paul Anstruther. And of course Mrs Cissie Anstruther. I looked back at them, hand on the knob. Waiting stupidly for some sort of qualification, perhaps. Like, well, Lovejoy, not quite as in *dead* dead.

Troude was looking at the threadbare carpet. Marimee's eyes were opaque, done this a thousand times before along established lines, no need for any kind of display. Monique was looking at me curiously. Every time she stared it was as if I was seeing her for the very first time, a kaleidoscopic woman. This time's look was quizzical: how will you react?

'Very well, *mon commandant*,' I said, and left. Useful old phrase, very well. Stands for a million different things. I've often found that.

When I got to the car park, Almira's motor had gone, of course. And Troude, Marimee, Monique Delebarre, were already motoring away from the café into the thin traffic. I'd lost an ex-wife, my wealthy mistress, any means of transport, finance, and I was alone in a strange land. I felt a desperate need of two assistants, with orders. They were to be here *immédiatement*, for Phase One had begun, according to Colonel Marimee.

They arrived about ten minutes later. Life went downhill, with variations.

18

You never know with new people. You meet them, and form instantaneous judgements. Mine are always wrong. I'm truly gormless. If I met Rasputin I'd think him St Cuthbert and only clue in when the body count increased. Like my assistants, when finally they arrived. Nobody can be as wrong as me. They proved it.

Standing idly by the traffic lights, I wondered if Colonel Marimee was as militarily superefficient as all that. I mean, I was here, poised like a greyhound in the slips, ready for this phoney antiques scam, and where were my two assistants? Luckily, French drivers don't let you cross, so I didn't feel out of place waiting. I reasoned that ice-cold Marimee had planned this little interlude as a kind of initiative test. These military minds think straight lines. The last time I'd done one of these what-nexters they'd put me down in the Yorkshire moors in the deep midwinter so I'd die. I'd saved myself by kipping with some cows in a byre until daylight. The sergeant put me on jankers a fortnight for cheating. See what I mean? But here, lacking cows and initiative, I loitered, hoping my assistants would finally get fed up and come for me.

Their motor was a mundane thing. It passed, dithered, pulled in. Two roaring forties, him balding and specky; she smiley and talkative. They had a dozen maps out. I barely gave them a look, then a faint chime bonged deep in me. I bent down to peer inside their car. On the back seat was a very, very interesting chair, tall, thin, with six cross-struts for back support. Genuine Astley Cooper! I knocked on the window. I must say, they put on a good act.

'Yes?' the driver asked. His wife nudged him. '*Oui*?'

Scotch, thank God. Out of the declension jungle! 'Hello,' I said. 'Lovejoy.'

He glanced at his wife, probably checking that I was the right bloke. They probably had photographs of me in the glove

131

compartment. Sensible to make sure, really. I could be anybody. 'Could you please guide me to the Paris road?'

'We never get the maps right,' his missus said, smiling.

Good cover! Shrewd. I beamed. 'I could show you,' I said loudly, to show the world this wasn't prearranged. A really accidental encounter, *tout le monde*! 'If you'd give me a lift.'

'I'm not sure . . .' he said, doubtful. I thought that was overdoing it, but the bird shoved him affectionately.

'Och, away, Gerald! Simplest thing to do!' He undid the rear door and I climbed in. 'Mind that crofter's chair, Lovejoy. It's very valuable.'

'Lilian,' Gerald reproved as we pulled away. Why did he want her to be so circumspect? The antique was his signal, after all. Well, we all were treble secret I supposed.

'Och, he's all right!' Lilian said of me, warm.

'Astley Cooper,' I said, smiling my thanks. She was bonny, as well as a superb judge of character. 'Not a crofter's chair. Not a farthingale chair.'

'It's a Regency spinning chair,' Lilian said. She adjusted her vanity mirror to see my face.

'Nor that, love. Sir Astley Cooper was a surgeon, knighted for operating on the Prince Regent. He designed this chair to teach little children to sit upright.' They went silent. An odd pair, these, seeing we were on the same side. Had I missed some code word? 'The other names are daft. Nice to see one of Astley Cooper's chairs left plain. Goons nowadays decorate them with everything but Christmas lights.' I chuckled, but on my own.

The motor swerved violently. An open tourer shot close to us, horn blaring. A girl shook a fist at us, furious, blonde hair streaming. The young bloke with her was straight off some telly advert for South Seas surfing.

'Bloody idiot,' I muttered. The tourer's lights were flashing. Both youngsters seemed angry, though Gerald was driving with a Briton's usual guarded suspicion. 'That was their fault.' Criticize other motorists, you're in.

'I'm obeying the rule of the road,' Gerald said anxiously.

'Course you are,' Lilian said, her pride stung. 'Always impatient. Same as at home.'

The tourer dwindled ahead. In newfound comradeship we

relaxed into those where're-you-from and heavens-my-auntie's-from-there conversations that substitute for instant friendship.

'We're looking at places,' Lilian said, too smooth by far as Gerald reasserted his motor's rights. 'For time-share holidays.' Aha. Their cover story.

'Good idea, time-share,' I said, thinking pretence the party line. Maybe the car was bugged? 'I'm hitchhiking.'

The journey was pleasant, they eventually relaxed. Banter-time as we rolled – Gerald never raced – towards Paris. Luckily, I saw a Paris sign before they did, pointed it out as if I'd known all the time. They'd started up a small travel business. 'Everything will be leisure, hen, in ten years.' Lilian was emphatic, but in a practised kind of way I couldn't quite accept somehow. Still arguing about prices, the cost of renting a shop front in Glasgow . . .

'Dearer in East Anglia,' I challenged, to get her going. Women hate admitting that other people suffer more expense.

'You live there? And you think that's dear? You come up to Clydebank, you wouldn't know what'd hit you for prices! Gerald bought a . . .' The motor straightened after a small swerve, with this time no flashy youngsters cutting us up while overtaking. '. . . a share in a tour operator's. It cost the *earth* . . .'

Gerald and Lilian Sweet, of Glasgow. Travel concessionaires. I listened, prattled, watched the scenery drift by. Marimee would have been proud of the three of us. Not a word passed our lips about the mission we were all on.

We stopped for nosh twenty kilometres short of the capital. I grinned, said I'd stretch my legs. As Gerald locked the motor with meticulous precision, Lilian took me in properly for the first time.

'Are you short, hen?'

'Had my stuff nicked, love. Pickpockets.' Stick to the pattern. Plenty of traffic about now, people have directional microphones these days. I could hear Marimee bark orders.

'We'll stand you a bite, won't we, Gerald?'

'Oh, aye.' He didn't seem keen, though. Maybe Marimee checked their expenses. Lilian got her dander up and he surrendered. We went in this Disney-Gothic self-service for the loos. I was first out, and got collared by a flaxen-haired aggropath. He slammed me against the wall. My breath went shoosh! It was the sports-car maniac who'd bawled Gerald out on the road.

133

'What's the game?' he said, through gritted teeth as they used to say in boys' comics.

'Game?' I gasped, going puce. 'Let me breathe for Christ's sake! I wasn't even driving!' Bog-eyed, I tried to point into the self-service. Let him throttle Gerald or Lilian. But not me.

'Drop your two friends. Wait by my Alfa. Thirty minutes!'

'Right! Right!' Quite mad.

'An' if you don't . . .' His eyes were so near, so pale, watery yet clear. The opposition hired madmen. You humour madmen, then scarper. I tried to nod, managed a weak smile.

'Kee!' The delectable blonde bird slipped up, nudged him.

And they were gone, into a murky-lit grotto place with slot machines and winking screens. I went jauntily towards my own couple, smiling at the prospect of grub looming. Henceforth, I would stick to the Sweets like glue. That Marimee should have told me there'd be dastardly foes on route. Typical. Always half a story. No wonder Gerald Sweet was ultra-cautious.

'Let's see what sort of food they have, hen!' Lilian led the way in. 'I hope they have a nice hot pasty!'

Love flooded my heart for the dear beautiful woman. A pasty! She knew my desperate need. I caught her eye in the mirrors. She coloured slightly, but it may only have been the steam from the cooking. Gerald was anxiously checking his pockets, craning to see his motor wasn't stolen. Lilian laughed self-consciously.

'Gerald's a real worrier, Lovejoy!' she told me. 'Up all night phoning home to see the . . . the business hasn't folded while we're away!' Good. She was careful too.

I cleared my throat. 'Really,' I said. Then as Gerald turned at my tone, 'Nothing wrong with being careful, is there?'

'No, Lovejoy,' he agreed, and for half an hour gave me a lecture on how easy it was to get caught out in business. I noshed like a trooper, listening with half an ear. He was becoming more like Marimee every second. I promised to owe them the cost of the meal, got their phone number and address. They had it ready, to my surprise. Real pros, excellent cover.

As soon as we hit the road, I showed true military-style initiative. I deflected us down a road soon after leaving the service station. We shook off the two gorgeous loons in their Alfa Romeo. I was so thrilled.

134

The hotel was quite small, on the southern outskirts of Paris. I liked it, but maybe it was the relief of being back in a town, free of that terrible pretty countryside everywhere. There was a garden, a fountain thing, lights and tables outside. I've a theory that it's the Continent's weather that permits folk to be so laid back. In East Anglia you could never put awning umbrellas out, scatter romantic candlelit tables round an ornamental grove unless the weather gods freak out into a spell of sun. You've only to step outside for it to teem down.

They said I should stay for the evening meal. Then, as Gerald was about to start on his phone marathon, Lilian suggested they lend me some money. They were only sticking to the pattern laid down by Marimee but I felt really touched. I accepted, with great anxiety and swapping of bank-account guarantors, and got a small room in the garret. A lot cheaper than our own hotels, I was astonished to learn.

Supper, Gerald finally wedded himself to the phone, and I was left with Lilian. It was getting on for ten o'clock. It crossed my mind to tell her how I'd cunningly outwitted the opposition back at the pit stop but thought better of it. Was I expected to chat about everything that happened? Probably not.

'He'll be telephoning now until midnight,' Lilian said.

She looked bonny. No specs now, earrings, a lace shawl that should have been Edwardian but was disappointingly repro. We were in the garden, looking down into the rock pool. Only three other couples remained, talking softly.

'He works hard,' I said. I meant it as praise.

'Och, nobody more than Gerald!'

Well, I suppose Marimee was giving orders for tomorrow. Was the silver lift to be done in Paris, then? Or was that tale now to be discarded, as the cover story it undoubtedly was? I felt things were imminent, brewing up to action. Maybe Gerald had better be warned about the two aggressive enemy.

'Look, love.' I glanced about. Any of these diners could be the opposition. 'This is a bit public.'

'Public?' She seemed to colour slightly, but I couldn't really tell in the low glim. 'What. . . ?'

'They'll hear.' Through the lounge window Gerald was visible, nodding, reporting in, taking notes. 'Even from inside the bar.'

She looked towards the hotel, seemed a little breathless. 'It's risky, Lovejoy. I'm not sure if I know what – '

'My room,' I suggested quietly. It was quite logical after all, the one place that had not been prearranged. They'd had difficulty finding me a nook.

'Oh, Lovejoy.' She was worried, glancing at the building, the other diners, two waiters. 'I've never . . . I mean, what if Gerald – ?'

Typical woman. A bloke's got to take charge some time, hasn't he? I had my arm through hers.

'We've got time before Gerald's done, love. It'll be safe.'

Which was how we entered my small single-bedded room together, in an ostentatiously non-clandestine way that probably announced skulduggery louder than a tannoy. Inside as I closed the door, she paused.

'Lovejoy.' She was all quiet. I bent my head to hear. Very sensible in the circumstances. In those spy pictures a transmitting bug's small as a farthing. The hotel could be riddled.

'Yes, love?'

'I . . . I don't do this sort of thing.'

What sort of thing? 'I don't either,' I whispered encouragingly. 'We're in this together, love. I'm discretion itself.' I decided to prove it. 'I had a tussle with that blond motorist at the service station. I saw him off.' Well, it was nearly the way it happened.

'You did, hen?' Her eyes grew even larger. 'Oh, that's wonderful! Gerald isn't really very . . .' More colour. 'Well, physical, Lovejoy.'

'Doesn't matter.' I glowed in her admiration. Not much comes my way, so I have to glow where I can. 'I can cope, love.'

'Lovejoy.' Quieter still. I was stooped over her now, both of us standing there. We hadn't yet put on the light. 'I'm not quite as young as I was. I'd hate to disappoint you.'

It's one of my observations that women are more practical than us. But that only holds true for ninety-nine per cent of the time. Once in a hundred, their minds go aslant. They talk tangents. Here we were, spies doing our surreptitious best, and she starts on about age. Women's tangents mostly concern numbers, I find.

Years, hours, fractions of a penny for mandarin oranges, when little Aurora was actually born to the split second. Daft.

'It's the way I want it, love,' I whispered, all reassuring. 'You're exactly right.'

'Oh, darling.' Her shawl fell as she put her arms round me. It's not often my mouth gets taken by surprise, but this time it was startled. Her breast was beautiful, though I stabbed myself on a brooch that made me yelp. Just shows how thoughtless modern women are. Edwardian ladies had amber beads to cap the points of their brooch pins, so that marauding mitts of amorous gentlemen didn't get transfixed in a ration of passion – cunning, this, because a dot of blood on a white-gloved finger when re-entering the ballroom meant suicides in the regiment.

'Shhh!' she said, breathless still. I joined in the breathlessness as we made the bed and still I hadn't managed to reveal my doubts about Colonel Marimee's mission.

'Dwoorlink,' I managed, as nature started to decide the sequence of events.

'No, Lovejoy. Please. Say nothing . . .'

I did as I was told. It's my usual way. Sometimes it works out for the best, as now. She was lovely. And it's any port in a storm, isn't it.

Love never comes without problems, but sometimes they come in a way that shows you've had no right to stay thinking. I mean, I ought to have said how attractive she was, this lovely woman. Maybe, it seemed to me in the instant before ecstasy engulfed the universe, I should have admitted I wasn't much, just a bum wondering what the hell everything was all about, give her the option to pull her dress on and light out leaving me, as it were, standing. But I obeyed, said nothing, learned nil, and managed only bliss. If anybody from the opposition was actually listening, we fooled them. She was superb.

An hour later I took her to her door, two floors down. She unlocked it. Gerald wasn't in yet. She pulled me in, just far enough for a parting snog before shoving me gently away.

'Will I see you again, Lovejoy?'

'Eh?' Blank for a second, but she was right to stay in character. We were travellers with the hotel hots. 'I couldn't go on without that, love.' It was easier to say than usual. Her eyes filled. 'It's true, Lilian. You were magic.'

We whispered a few more phrases, enough to convince any eavesdropper, then I stepped reluctantly into the corridor as somebody came upstairs.

And I glimpsed something round Lilian's neck that made my blood run cold. But I managed to keep smiling, nodding good-night, as she put the door to and I went for a well-earned kip.

God knows how I'd failed to notice it. Heat of the moment, I suppose. Only a small gold medallion, with a monogram. Its initials, SAPAR, round the periphery, struck into my brain and set my two lonely nerve cells clanging like clappers in a bell. Stolen Art and Purloined Antiques Rescue.

But quite the most frightening was a single gold letter stencilled in the centre, larger than the others Letter H. Lying on my crumpled bed, I found myself shivering like in a malarial rigor, except this was much, much worse. I wondered for the first time who Lilian and Gerald really were. And the gorgeous golden maniacs in the posh racer. The world had unglued, to clatter all about me. Marimee would have me shot twice a day for a week. Paul, Almira, Troude, Monique, were on a dead loser. And me? I was in the worst-ever trouble of all.

H stands for Hunter.

Time to run.

19

About sexual emblems.

They have a fascinating history. The antiques that have filtered down to us oftener than not go unnoticed. In fact, I'd go so far as to say that sexual antiques get shunned. Women, as with everything else on earth, hold the key.

In every age, every fashion, sexual artefacts flourished. They do now, except we won't admit it. My favourites are nipple jewels. Not merely studs in the nipple's eye, but lovely pendants with question-mark supports for pierced nipples. All the rage late in Victoria's reign, the ancient world's fashion came round again. Breast tassles, some with erotic tails of hair, tiny whips, even fine blades, offered all kinds of fetishes for the women who preferred to mount her own performance, so to speak. Merkins were natural, in an age of wigs, though very few survive. These flattish wigs made for the pubis – smallpox tended to denude your genital hair – mostly human hair in kid leather, were desirable enhancers. They came adorned with every kind of jewellery, including gold stitchery. Belly jewels, implanted precious stones actually surfacing through the skin, spectacular ornaments for the genitalia, they've all had their day.

Because more boy babes died than girls in those past days, women outnumbered us. Superstitions ran rife about conception, a must for a woman to hold up her head. The more she produced, the better. With ineffable logic, they decided that the greater the arousal, the more certain the chance of fruition. They invented with ingenuity and skill. They called in seductive lady helpers of great beauty, who'd excite to passion – using any devices they could think up – then escape from between as husband and wife came together, to coin a phrase, with an almost audible clang. Hence the toy phalluses, images, statuettes, paintings, erotic prints from the Far East, precious gems (of course of the right birthstone significance, because you wouldn't want your rival to benefit simply because you'd used emerald instead of ruby, right?). I've even seen one locket, made for some Victorian lady, which contained the beautifully carved miniature male genitalia of sapphire on one leaf, and the female sculpted of amethyst on the other. Conjures up the charming image of a demure lady praying in church, fingering her locket, which, being firmly closed, made the male and female jewels inside the locket unite in the most intimate manner. Presumably she was born in February, her lover in September – and note that astrological stones aren't quite those of the calendar months. Semiprecious stones became a means of communication. Diamond, emerald, amethyst and ruby look rather rum in a linear gold mount, but they spell DEAR to the observant swain. I've seen a fairly modern platinum-mounted one of feldspar, a gap, then chrysoberyl, then kunzite – the gap standing for 'unknown'. Incidentally, if you see kunzite – violet pink of different colour depths as you rotate it – in a brooch for its name, then the gem's really not a genuine antique, for G. F. Kunz was an American at the end of Victoria's reign . . .

Where was I? The gold-lettered pendant on Lilian's gold chain. Husbands give their ladies depictive jewellery showing occupations. Gerald was a SAPAR man. There's only two grades in SAPAR's organization: A for the admin, legal, research lot; H for the self-effacing, but ruthless, hunters.

Escaping, that's where I was. On the run from H for Hunter Gerald, the clever swine.

First, nick a motor. Fifth car I tried, I got in, started up with ease. Reasonably modern, so it wouldn't conk out and embarrass me. Hot-wiring a motor at a somnolent night town's traffic lights attracts attention.

Knowing what theft is exactly, is Man's dilemma. I thought this abstruse quandary as I guided my new possession from the hotel car park and zoomed back the way we'd come.

Stealing a car, possibly to save my life, was not theological or moral theft. The Church teaches that stealing bread to save your starving children isn't. As the lights on the south-east road lit my reflection in the windscreen, I worried in case the Church didn't teach any such thing. If it doesn't, it ought. Naturally I felt sorry for the lady whose dawn would be clouded by her missing Peugeot, but I didn't choose to be here, driving wrong-handed into gathering night rain. Everything simply wasn't my fault. She looked quite smart, did Madame Jeanne Deheque in her photo snap, with her deliberate hair and long eyelashes. No credit cards, maps, nothing to help a stray escaper, the thoughtless cow. Typical woman.

The memory of the service station on the main road was fresh in my mind. No passport, no knowing where I could find refuge. But I was pretty sure I could find the town, the car park, the café where Marimee had grilled me. From there, it would be easy to trek back to Almira's house and the chalet by the lake. Thence filch my passport, and home. No speeding – French cops are death to dashers. I was the sedate motorist. Enough petrol to last a lifetime. I settled down to a steady night drive.

Gerald had been pretty cool, all right. His cover, a travel agent looking for time-share accommodation, bonny homely wife along picking up the odd antique for the business premises. No wonder he spent hours on the phone. No wonder they exchanged glances when their casual hitchhiker knew an Astley Cooper chair and all of its off-key names. But a SAPAR hunter? Gulp.

The Mounties get their man. Sherlock Holmes wins out. In antiques scammery, the SAPAR hunter's the one to avoid. Whispers tell how two or three of them – there's only ten, would you believe – have actually killed thieves who proved reluctant to disgorge the booty, before politely restoring the stolen antique to its grateful legitimate owners.

Nowadays, antiques are the big – read mega-galactic – new currency. Drugs and arms sales are still joint leaders, but only just. Antique fraud is closing fast on the rails. Greed is powered by everybody – terrorists, politicians, Customs and Excise, Inland Revenue taxmen, governments, international auction houses, you, me. Most of all, though, it's the absence of honesty. We all have eyes to love the delectable antiques they see, but they're paid eyes. Paid but loving. And that means hired, because money cancels love. We pretend it can't, but it does.

Since every antique worth the name's on the hit list, the world clearly needs seekers after stolen antiques. Scotland Yard's Fine Art and Antiques Squad is largely impotent. Oh, statistics emerge now and then, to claim that three per cent of stolen antiques get recovered, but who knows? Answer: nobody. Even I get blamed for the world's pandemic of antiques theft, for God's sake. That's *really* scraping the barrel for the lees of logic. You want the truth? Great Britain alone has 16,000 lovely Anglican churches – and lets one get battered, robbed, pillaged, *every four hours*! It can't be me alone, right? You see, crime pays. Less than twenty per cent of our police forces have art and antiques fraud squads, so what chance has holiness? (Incidentally, that 'squads' is a laugh – they're mostly one bloke each in a dusty nook; Scotland Yard's entire mob is two.)

People place some reliance (note how carefully I worded that?) on the Art Loss Register. Others swear by LaserNet. I swear *at* both. You pay a fee to see if anybody's reported as stolen that antique you want to buy. They collect records of antique thefts. Auction houses joke along with their Thesaurus system. Why joke? Well, you just try matching any ten catalogue descriptions with the objects they purport to describe, and you'll finish up in tears of laughter, or worse. It's hit or miss. Like the Council for the Prevention of Art Theft, they're new and blundersome losers against impossible odds.

But SAPAR is different. For a start, it's not listed in any antiques glossy. No list of subscribers, in no phone book. Its employees are practically ghosts. I know antique dealers who've been in the business quarter of a century who believe there's no such incognito mob. If it hadn't been for an utter fluke – making love to a SAPAR hunter's missus on the hoof – I'd never have spotted Gerald. Having his wife along with him for cover, and giving me a lucky lift, was possibly the one mistake he'd made in his life as a hunter. I just hoped I'd shaken him off.

Three-forty in the morning, I made the lane past Almira's country house. I drove on, collected my wits, had a prophylactic pee against a tree, put the car off the verge in the wood, and walked silently to the gate and down towards the house.

You can never return. Nobody ever can. It's one of my infallible rules. Call in at your old school, see the playing fields where you scored that super goal . . . Mistake: the place is a housing estate. Visit your old church? Hopeless: it's derelict, tramps lighting fires in the vestry. Detour through your old neighbourhood, all heartaching nostalgia? Don't: it's a biscuit factory. Slink, like now, through a French grove towards the holiday home of a lady you awoke night after day for yet more unbridled lust? Error cubed. Even if it's to nick your own passport, get the hell out. Returning is wrong.

My other infallible mistake is to disregard my own rules.

The house seemed still. A high-powered motor stood on the moonlit forecourt. So good old Paulie was here, doubtless boring somebody stiff as usual. No other cars. Was Almira's at Marc the Nark's cottage, watched over by his pair of hounds? I stared at the place for a few minutes, dithering.

The way in, which I'd planned during my drive, was through the rear. The ground sloped up towards the road above at quite a steep angle. It was as if the house was sunk into the earth that side, leaving the front standing free. Split levels always help burglars. They're easier to climb, which means less of a drop if you have to escape fast.

No balconies, though, except one looking south towards the lake, so it wasn't all beer and skittles. Drainpipes, rough stone with crevices. I used the old drainpiper's trick of filling my pockets with a variety of stones from the ground. Find a space where the mortar's missing, you can slot a stone in to serve as a mini-foothold. I smiled as I started up. 'Swarmers', as the antiques trade calls cat burglars, are mostly slick. Some I know would have already done the job and been at the Dover crossing by now. The roof over the main bedroom was only ten feet up. But being cowardly does no harm.

Quiet, careful, I climbed. My belt I'd removed and tied round my neck for a good handhold if I came across any hooks. I must say, when I'm scared I'm quite good. I honestly think I could have made quite a decent living at burgling.

The roof astonished me by being more of a problem than the wall. Can you credit it? Up there, spread-eagled on a slope of tiles formed like a rough earthenware sea, I found myself baffled, thinking, what the hell do I do now?

Then I remembered the fanlight. It had figured largely in my daring plan. Never closed, it showed the night sky to anyone gazing obliquely up from the bed. I'd learned that. I began edging across towards the moon's reflection that defined the window. Odd, I could smell cigarette smoke. I halted.

Was somebody kipping, or not kipping at all, in Almira's bedroom? Having a smoke? I heard, definitely heard, a man clear his throat. A resounding *yes*! I was stymied.

Choice reared its aggravating head. If the bloke inside was Paul the wimp, it would hardly matter. I could simply walk in, scavenge my passport and off out of it. He was a drink of water, and I'm not. But what if I walked confidently in to find some mauler waiting for me on, say, Marimee's orders? Did Paul smoke? Oh, Christ. I'd forgotten.

Within arm's reach of the louvre window, and nowhere to go. Daft to slither across to silhouette my head against the moonlit sky. Bedrooms? Three others, I knew. What the hell was the bloke doing sleeping in Almira's bed when the other guest bedrooms were all free? Surely they were?

And the light came on, blinding me. I almost yelped with fright and cringed, terrified reflexes trying to shrink me into invisibility on the roof. I could be seen by anyone in the woods above the house.

'Katta.'

Paul's voice. Katta? Who the. . . ? *Katta*? Cissie's Continental maid. No good staying baffled. I had to risk something, or stay treed for good on Almira's damned tiles. Two silent shifts, and I slo-o-o-owly peered over the edge. Obliquely, safer now the bedroom was brighter lit than my heavenly space, I looked down. Onto Paul and Katta.

He was in paradise. I've been there, and knew instantly a million things I'd only ever guessed at. Until now. Katta's vast naked form was kneeling beside him. Him supine, she hugely tumescent, working away, her head raising and lowering like a feeding animal's. His hand was on her nape, his other cupping her pendulously swinging breast. His neck muscles were straining taut as he arched, striving towards the bliss that is oblivion. She was laughing. How she managed to, God knows. Her hands were on his hips, pinning him to the bed. It was a rape, a gift, Katta's enormous fatness rocking flabbily over the recumbent man. I've made it sound repellent, I suppose, but it was beautiful. Poets should have been there. Was it the contrast, her spreading flesh and his lean length? Or the fascinating incongruity of Katta's unbelievable mass seeming to chew him into docility? Or her shaking with laughter while he soared towards detumescence – ?

A car door slammed nearby, and another. Footsteps scrunged gravel, and voices spoke casually down on the forecourt.

And I hadn't heard a thing, so engrossed by the lovely scene on the bed. I froze, couldn't for the life of me look away.

'. . . have six or seven of them staking it out,' a bloke's voice pontificated.

'If that's enough. You know what he's like, Jervis,' Almira countered. 'I have the key.'

'Not really,' Jervis said. A good try at wry humour. 'You two *should* be able to advise!'

'Don't be offensive.' Jingle of keys, sound of a lock. 'Always the politician, Jay.'

'It has its advantages, my dear.'

Katta heard the door, quickly lifted her head, mechanically wiped her mouth using the back of her hand. She rose with the strange nimbleness of the gross, evaded Paul's agonized, stretching hand, and trotted from my sight. Paul groaned, covered himself, put the bedside light off. I ducked away. God, I felt his deprivation, poor sod. Robbed, a second from ecstasy.

And that was everything. I thought for quite a few moments, up there on the moonlit tiles.

You see, I'd glimpsed Katta's face as she'd lifted her mouth, spitting away joy unbounded, and it was wrong. Her face wasn't right. Oh, it was Katta, sure. But her expression should have been anxiety, worry at being discovered, what the neighbours would think, et familiar cetera.

It hadn't been any of those. It had been utter shock, almost fear. The sort of revelation that tells all, especially about whom she's suddenly so scared of walking in through the door.

When she'd heard the last of Almira's sentence and Jervis's rejoinder as they'd opened the front door, she'd been halfway across the carpet. *And her swift fright had instantly evaporated.* She'd even turned, given Paul a charming rueful smile, blowing his tormented features a kiss from a mouth suddenly formed into an exaggerated tantalizing pout. Katta had slipped out of the room much calmer than she'd shot away from their love-bed. So she'd been frightened to death of someone finding her and Paul – then suddenly not given a damn when the intruders were merely Almira and Jervis. How come?

It took me quite a while to escape from there, passportless. I didn't care. I was almost pleased with life, as I made it back to the car and drove back to the trunk-road service station, to wait for the golden pair to come.

They captured me while I was having some grub in the self-service. The swine didn't let me finish it, either.

20

'Lovejoy.'

Here he came, Narval the Throttler, plonking himself down opposite, extermination in mind. God, but he had the most electric eyes you ever did see. Killer's eyes, staring, seeing only their own madness. She stood hands on hips, looking for a surfboard and a beach. Why did she have marks on her arms?

'Kee.' I had a mouthful. 'What sort of a name's that?'

'G.U.Y.' The girl was cool, languid in a warning kind of way. Bored witless. She'd be at least as much trouble as Kee. I spelled the name to myself. Guy. He was Guy, say Kee. 'Guy Solon. S.O.L.O.N.'

'Up and come, Lovejoy. Now.'

'Right.' I seized a fragment of grub, and upped and went.

'You're in trouble,' Guy said conversationally. 'Veronique'll explain.' This made him laugh, a whine interrupted by giggles that never made it. I felt in sore need of allies. Mercy Mallock?

'Trouble,' she said, laughing too. We were so cheery.

'Who from?'

'A high-ranking officer.' Veronique looked at me. I was shocked. Her eyes were a vigorous blue, so bright they seemed illumined from within. Standing beside this pair of clones as Guy unlocked his motor I felt like the coalman. I'm never well turned out at the best of times. After my climbing efforts, no wonder Veronique's gorgeous radiant orbs scored me as a tramp.

'Someone with standards, eh?' I prompted. They only laughed. Their brittle merriment was getting me down. I hoped it wouldn't last. I longed for Lilian's seductibility, even Gerald's anxious friendliness. (No, cancel that. No hunters, please.)

We took off in a Grand Prix start. Whiplash Willie hit the road like he had seconds to live. Veronique yabbered into some phone while I tried to find the seat belt, seemingly a triumphant account of their recapture of some wayward nerk. I tore my eyes off her. She sat in the rear seat. I was lodged perilously beside Guy. No wonder he was on a permanent high, with a bird like her. But how to keep such a creature? You'd have to be the world's greatest powerhouse of excitement, handsome, constant dynamite, rich. I glanced at Guy and sighed. He seemed all of those things. We ripped through France, two deities and a scruff.

And made Troude, and the place we were going to collect the antique silver from. Sometimes, absolutely nothing is true. Ever noticed? This was one of those times.

It was a garden party. I was astonished, then embarrassed, then mortified. Talk about wealth.

'Welcome, Lovejoy!' Troude greeted me with such calm pleasure I could have sworn it was nearly genuine. He advanced across the grass beckoning waitresses and acolytes. 'So glad you could make it!' He did his merry twinkle. 'Your wanderlust is cancelled, Lovejoy. Henceforth, adhere to the schedule.'

'Henceforth I shall, thither,' I promised. He said schedule the English way, 'sh', not the American 'sk'.

The enormous mansion wore lawns like skirts extending in all directions. Groves, garden statues, pools, small summerhouses, it looked a playground. Primary colours everywhere. The house itself was regal, symmetrical, balustrades, wide stone steps up to a magnificent walk. I'd thought Versailles was somewhere else. Or maybe France has a lot of them knocking about.

The guests were even more ornate. They looked as if they'd brought summer with them. No rain on their parade, thank you. Cocktail dresses the norm. From there, every lady zoomed upward in extravagance, Royal Ascot without the horses. I looked at a statue of a discus-thrower. I could have sworn he was breathing, put it down to imagination. I was nervous in case I was going to cop it for going missing.

'Now, Lovejoy! None of your famous bashfulness!' he chirruped. A glass appeared in my hand, cold as charity, moisture on the bowl. Ancient Bohemian glass, too. Beyond belief. (Watch out for modern Bohemian fakes – they are our current epidemic. The best are vases, costing half a year's average wage if genuine, the price of a railway snack if fake. Sixteen inches tall, ornate damson-coloured vases engraved with forests and deer, they're basically a tall lidded cylinder on a stem, such a deep colour it'll look almost black. Sinners buy these fake Bohemians, then sell them at country auctions as genuine.)

'Come and meet some of our visitors!' Troude was saying. 'You've already met Veronique and Guy, I see!' He chuckled, introduced me to a charming couple from Madagascar who had a yacht. 'Lovejoy hates sailing,' Troude told them. 'Though his next movie's about a shipping disaster.' He glanced at me in warning. 'That wasn't confidential information, Lovejoy, was it?'

'No, it wasn't.' It also wasn't information.

'Lovejoy's company has four wholly-owneds in LA,' Troude said, smiling. 'He changes their names on a weekly basis!'

The couple from Madagascar laughed. Troude laughed. God, but I wished we'd jack it in and stop laughing. Even Monique, among a crowd of admirers, was laughing. I looked again. That discus-thrower really had actually breathed. Laughing too? Here came Paulie and Almira. How close were they, really?

'Lovejoy.'

'Wotcher.' God, I hated Paulie's name, the swine. I couldn't help scanning the garden party for Katta. Difficult to hide anybody that fat. 'Almira.'

'Hello, darling,' from Almira, on edge but laughingly. 'Sorry I had to dash. But you got here!' She was exquisite in a stunning flared dress of magnolia, usual among this slender clique. And she was getting away with high heels, when the other women had gone for less rakish footwear. I'd have been proud of her, if I hadn't noticed her husband Jervis Galloway, MP, deep in conversation among a gathering of colourfuls. Nobody introduced me. It was Diana's paramour Jay, all right. When I drifted his way I got deflected. The statue breathed again.

'Come, Lovejoy!' Troude was affability itself, steering me round, introducing me, saying I was here to finance movie deals with Italian money. I kept my wits about me, saying the deal was for five movies and all that. I clammed up when people asked who'd star in them, said that was still being negotiated.

'He's cagey!' Troude laughed. The people laughed. Even I laughed. And now a statue of The Three Graces, naked women embracing, breathed. And a zephyr gently moved their hair.

'The movie industry's crazy,' I laughed, to laughter.

Talk, chatter in the golden sun, Veronique and Guy being

delightedly admired strolling in their magnificent world, everybody loving or lusting after Monique – more sedately dressed than the others, dark green with silver jewellery. And Marimee there, looking not quite at attention. An orchestra played soft airs in a wrought-iron pagoda. Lully? Something that way on. Everything was superficial, no digging deep for motive or disgorging woes. It was so beautiful it troubled me.

I sought out my Madagascar couple. They looked ready for the Olympics. Everybody was gold and gorgeous. I felt sick. They wanted to talk about yachting, sails and motor engines, races I'd never heard of. He was a friend of the Algerian couple, the man explained, brought into this syndicate by the Mexican couple. I wondered, was it one per nation? If no, I was superfluous, seeing Almira'd fetched hubby J for Jervis. They liked the idea, they told me, surreptitiously lowering their voices. I said I did, too. They asked me how long it would take. I asked from what to what. From start to finish, they asked. I liked their intensity – first time anybody had stopped laughing – but said it depended on how soon we got started.

'Can I take him away?' Troude begged, just as I'd noticed that the shadows cast by the sun hadn't moved, though the trees in the distance had glided quite a foot or two along the background of the orchestra's summerhouse. How come?

'See you later,' I smiled, going with him. I looked at the grass. It was non-grass. Pretty good fake, but definitely dud.

We headed for the house. Was this whole dump some sort of film studio? A set? I looked forward to getting inside to see if it was real or just a giant doll's house that turned continually to face the sun just like its garden. A mansion house that stays put while its gardens swivels is in deep trouble.

The house felt real, lovely and genuine. I keep saying how a house responds when you step in through the door. It susses you out and thinks, who's this newcomer? If it likes you, it welcomes you. If not, then you'll never be happy there. It's a person, is a house. Be polite to it. I silently commiserated with it for losing its real garden, in exchange for a look-alike turntable phoney lawn plonked on top. Maybe their antique silver was here.

Marimee was there before us. 'Lovejoy did well with the cover story,' he said. 'Lovejoy will receive sanction for the default.'

Default? Sanction? He meant mistaking my – no, his – assistants. I nodded, received a grateful glance from Troude. Monique came with Guy and Veronique. We reached a conservatory facing a walled yard with roses and trellised arches.

'Nice.' I broke the ice. 'If only it'd stay still.'

Troude smiled. No laughs now, tension in the air. Maybe they too were to be sanctioned for letting me escape?

'Why did you return, Lovejoy?'

'Ah.' Why? I'd got clean away, then come back to find my pursuers. I should have thought this one out, quick. 'I'd no passport. I owed it to the memory . . .' I caught myself, cleared my throat. Start again. 'I promised somebody I'd help.'

Marimee nodded, one curt sharp depression of the chin to signify approval. For him that was a flag day.

'It is safe to speak here,' he said. He stood facing, legs apart, back to the window. 'Here we plan the robbery. Here we decide the fate of the valuables. Here we allocate duties.'

'Here we will say what you're up to?' I put in. Troude did an appealing look, the sort he was now starting to nark me with.

'Silence!' Monique said. It cracked like a whip, shutting me up. What fascinated me was it also clammed Marimee.

She walked to face us. I noticed Marimee made way for her, and it wasn't politeness. She boss, him corporal.

'The brigandage is already decided,' she said. Bland's the nearest I can come to, for her attitude. Nobody could possibly dispute the number of the Number 7 bus, her tone informed us. 'The *projet* is fixed. There will be two rehearsals only.'

'Here?' I asked again, thinking of those statues and the rotating gardens. 'Only, isn't it a simple export job?'

'That silver story was a lie to get you here, Lovejoy.'

Cool. It had worked. I was undeniably here.

'You have objections?' Like asking if I had a coat somewhere.

'Yes. Ignorance, mainly. What do we nick, and where from?' Note that I didn't ask why. 'And who's in the way?'

'Details,' Monique said, with a smile like an ice floe. 'Others see to details, Lovejoy.'

And she walked off. Veronique stepped aside, proving to be in the way, taut, her hatred glinting like distant spears. Not all friends, then, amid this much laughter.

151

Leaving us. 'There will be three stages,' Marimee clipped out. 'Stage Three the robbery. Stage Two rehearsal. That is all.'

'Eh?' I was blank. 'Two from three leaves one. You missed out Stage One.'

Marimee's moustache lifted in what might have been incipient mirth. 'That is you, Lovejoy. You buy.'

'Buy what?'

'Antiques.' He made me sound thick.

The others were looking. Troude was trying to elbow me gently from the conservatory.

'What with? From where? What sort?' I got mad, yelled, 'I've no frigging money!'

Marimee paused, eyed me with utter disgust. 'Imbecilic peasant,' he said scathingly, and strutted grandly on his way.

'Come, Lovejoy,' Troude said gently. 'Let's go.'

'Where to, for Christ's sake?' I was so dispirited. I wanted to go home.

He patted my shoulder. 'You're the antiques divvy, Lovejoy. Wherever you say, but mostly Paris. Guy, Veronique.'

On the way out I saw Katta, demurely waiting on in black waitress garb beneath an awning. I looked her way, waved once. She smiled, I swallowed, thinking of her luscious wet mouth in action, managed to smile back. Paulie and Almira were talking near the orchestra. Pity Cissie wasn't here too, I thought without a single pang. This was the sort of do she always enjoyed, as long as she had somebody to ballock for doing the wrong thing In Company, a terrible crime in her book. Maybe she was here? In spirit, some people might say. Not me.

Jervis looked away when I passed quite near him. As we left the eating-drinking-laughing cheeriness, I glanced back to see if Katta was just watching Paul or actually doing something. And saw the house from a new angle. It stayed in my mind. I've a good memory for pictures. I'd seen it before, or some place very like it. And it wasn't any country mansion, not then. It was heap big business, the sort a low-grader like me would never even get within a mile of. In some advert? Yes, sort of definitely.

Until then, I'd not known what to believe. I mean, soon I've got to tell you about international antiques robbers, and I will. But so far I'd been thinking along the lines of, well, those dozens of St

Augustine's sermons, AD 400 or thereabouts, discovered in the Mainz public library. Priceless, easy to nick, pass them off at any customs border post as boring old committee minutes, and make a mint. Especially apt, since that French historian uncovered them on that dusty German shelving in 1991. Something like that. Now, though? Now I knew it was no bundle of ancient 'crackle', as parchments are known in the trade.

'Shall I drive, Guy?' I said. 'Race you to the scam, eh?'

'*Merde!*' he said rudely. 'I cross the border in one hour! You'd take a week!'

'Only joking.' Which meant Switzerland, of course. I'd been too dim to work it out. We were going to do the Freeport International Repository.

Inside I laughed, and laughed, and laughed. Some jokes are too good to ignore.

21

Paris is beautiful. I mean it. Oh, the traffic's noisy – everybody's water-cooled motor horns on max for no reason – and a city's but a city. Yet it surprised me. Small. I'd expected something massive like, say, New York or London. Paris gets to you by cleverly putting all its bits within reach. Unbelievably, it's a walker's city. And its charm isn't synthetic polyurethane gloss; it's natural. Sweet yet protein, so to speak.

They, my golden pair, booked us in at a small hotel by the simple process of screeching to a heart-in-the-gob stop at the front door and strolling in, ready to remonstrate with whoever came forward to remonstrate. The booking-in process wore me out. Guy remonstrated, Veronique remonstrated in a crosstalk act straight from music hall. I got an upstairs room. There were only about fifteen rooms in the whole place.

Nothing to unpack, I opened the window and was captivated. The famed Paris skyline really truly exists! Jumbled roofs, chimneys, windows with tiny balconies. Church spires here and there, television aerials, wires, a splash of washing, pots flowering on sills, now and again a flat roof, an old man having a sly kip, children skipping to some chant. Beautiful. I turned, smiling, and jumped. Veronique was standing silently behind me. I hoped she wasn't one of those stealthies.

'What do you see, Lovejoy?'

'Eh?' She looked sullen, brittler than usual, narked as hell. 'Never been before, love. Didn't know what to expect – '

'Decadent enough for you, Paris?'

A glance out showed me the same charm. A woman across the way was seeing to her pretty window box. 'Looks fine. I'd thought skyscrapers, black glass boxes filled with bankers – '

'Decadence!' She glared past me. 'It needs thorough cleansing, Lovejoy! Of parasites that drag her down.'

Well, there's not a lot you can say to this gunge. I'd been wondering how far it was to Monet's garden, but didn't risk asking while she was in this black mood. I couldn't see many parasites, but no good arguing with a bird.

'You don't see, do you?' Baffled, I started to edge past her into the room. 'The tourist's vision.' She spoke hate-filled.

'Look, Veronique. We're tired. That hell of a drive – '

She grabbed me and with ominous strength dragged me to stand looking across the street. 'Calm? Tranquil, Lovejoy? Pretty? Can you see Notre Dame from here?'

'Dunno.' I was only trying to be helpful, please the silly cow, but she started to shake.

'You know what I see, Lovejoy? I see unemployment – French jobs stolen by foreigners! They pour in to bleed our money, give nothing back! To France: The Last Land Before the Sea!'

'Really?' Polite, I managed not to yawn. These days it's politically upright to grouse about this kind of thing.

'Unemployment! Misery, resentment! You think you have strikes across the Channel? Not like we have strikes! We have more grievances! Recently, every French port was closed. Nurses on strike this week, all public transport in France next. Farmers riot. Our . . .' She struggled over the word, spat as she said it: '. . . autobahns are blocked by fighting lorry drivers. The airports are in uproar, barricades everywhere. Pretty, the view?'

'Yes,' I said simply, because it was.

'You are determined to be stupid.' She let go, stepped away. I'd been close enough to be intrigued by the faint division across her hairline, but looked away.

'I can't understand,' I suggested lamely, but thinking, what does a girl this lovely want to wear a wig for? 'I think France is bonny. Political things blow over. They always do.'

'We French sink under a morass of foreigners! Frenchness is losing its identity. You know Romanian roulette, Lovejoy?'

'Russian?'

'Fool! Romanian immigrants here market imported Romanian women! Thousands are shipped in each year! It's *obscene*!'

She sounded likely to kill anybody who disagreed. I hesitated. Change the nationality, you can collect a million such moans in any bar anywhere in the world. Every nation's at it, same old grumbles against governments, changes, taxes. It signifies nothing. I can't honestly see the point of shoving the clock back to some Good Old Days. We all know they never existed. What *was* wrong with France? I thought it superb, fetching, full of interest. They even have a Mushroom Museum in the Loire Valley. Ever since Louis the Fourteenth the Sun King ordered mushrooms, France has –

'It's a pity,' I tried soothing. She was still trembling. Was it rage? 'But there's nothing you can do.'

She smiled a crooked smile, oblique with vile meaning. Her hand stroked my face. I didn't like it – unusual, this – and drew away. 'Oh, yes there is, babee,' she said.

Just then Guy called from the next room, and she left. I shivered as the door closed. I never have a watch, so I had to estimate a lapse of five minutes. I went and knocked.

'It's only me,' I said to the handle.

Veronique opened, let the door swing while she returned to the bed. Guy was sprawled out of his skull, warbling incomprehensibly. She was already naked, reeling. On the bedside table, a couple of tinfoils, spilled white powder, a tiny mirror, a syringe. A smarting pong filled the air. She was giggling as she tumbled spread-eagle over Guy, whose hands moved over her. I swallowed, backed out.

'Sorry,' I stammered. '*Excusez-moi, s'il vous plaît.*'

'Come back, Lovejoy!' Veronique carolled. They erupted in laughter as I meekly crept away. 'I can handle two!'

Aye, I thought, shaken. I'd only gone to see if they'd mind if I went for a stroll. Druggies. I had two crazed junkies on my hands. The charming skyline of roofs, all colours and textures, was still there. It was coming dusk. I stood at my window to watch it. The distant roar of traffic reassured me that this aerial stillness was founded on the brisk bustling life of a stunning city below. Just my frigging luck, I thought bitterly. My exquisite assistants were zooming deranged through some stratosphere powered by illegal chemical toxins. The gentle 'antique silver' job had become a major scam, with loony political overtones, and I was no longer a mere courier. I was the main player. Which told me what Colonel Marimee's logic would be if the enterprise plunged to failure – I'd cop it. Guy and Veronique would blame me, of course. The pattern was already established by the Sweet episode. Marimee had promised me sanctions and penalties, all because that golden pair had been late. Hindsight, blindsight.

This scam had a bad odour. I needed a friendly face, the sort I was used to. The kind, in fact, I could depend on for absolute unreliability. I went for a walk on my own authority, to clear the cobwebs and mentally pick my way through a selection of friends back in East Anglia.

Paris has it. Really, honestly has it. Oh, I'd slowly become aware that France looks with a vague – sometimes not so vague – mistrust at its capital, same as Italians regard Rome. But she has a quality to life, and quality's rare. And never cheap.

Bravely risking all, I had a coffee in a small nosh bar. The people chatted, smoked. The traffic snarled away outside. Lights were showing. Rain was coming on. You get a kind of osmosis in such places. Even before you know the layout, nostalgia seeps in and you start remembering things you never even knew, about streets, names of squares, statues and buildings. That you've never seen them before hardly matters. They stroll alive out of your subconscious. God knows how they got there in the first place, but that's unimportant. It's the way civilization is. It pervades, doesn't need highlighting.

With some surprise, I noticed how mixed a folk the Parisians were. And the accents! Becoming attuned to cadence, I was now able to pick out some differences. And the garb! There seemed a number of North Africans about – or was I wrong, and they were older inhabitants than most? I definitely heard a snatch of Arabic. The serving lad sounded Greek, and two artisans covered in a fine dust were Italians. A cosmopolitan city.

Grinning like an ape – smiles are never wasted, when you're a stranger in a strange land – I left, walked down to the corner. Greatly daring, I returned and walked to the other corner. Quite a large square, two trees barely managing, some seats, a couple of cafés. Starry Starry Night, with some minuscule motors occasionally racing through and vehicles parked in improbable spots. I stood a minute, rehearsing school words, then went for it and triumphantly bought some notepaper and envelopes. I was really narked that the serving lady served me without noticing my huge cultural achievement. I sat and scribbled a letter home. A wave of homesickness swamped me, but I stayed firm and finished it.

Then I went out, found a pay phone, painstakingly followed the directory-enquiries saga. The phones are quite good in France, unlike everywhere else except Big Am. I got through the trunk dialling in one, to my utter astonishment. Even phoning the next village is enough to dine out on in East Anglia, and here I was –

'Hello? Can I speak to Jan Fotheringay, please?'

'Who is it?' The same bird, Lysette.

'Lovejoy. It's very urgent. Hurry, please.'

'He's resting.' God, she was on the defensive. I might have been . . . well, whoever.

'Listen, Lysette. I'm on Jan's side. He knows that.'

By the time he came on I was frantic, seconds ticking away. 'Jan? Lovejoy. Jan, if I ask for you to come to France, as translator, adviser, whatever, will you?'

'I'm still not mobile, Lovejoy.' He sounded worn out. Just when I needed the lazy self-pitying malingering sod. Aren't folk selfish?

'Jan. It's serious. You know it is, and getting worse by the hour. You won't be allowed to survive. I won't either. Mania stalks out here, mate.' I gave him a second, and yelled for a decision. The pillock, buggering about when I was . . .'Eh?'

'You're right, Lovejoy. Where?'

The hotel, I told him, but he'd have to come immediately because I'd probably be there for only a day or two more. I'd leave some message if he didn't quite make it in time. Like a fool, I babbled profuse thanks as the line cut. For God's sake, I was trying to save him too, wasn't I? I seethed indignation thinking about it.

My second call took longer, but fewer words. I said there was a letter in the post, containing my best guesses. 'Positively no obligation,' I finished lamely, the salesman's lying assurance. 'Help me, pal.' I tried to limit the pause, but it went on and on until my voice got it together. 'Please,' it managed. What a lousy rotten word that is.

Hoteltime. Maybe by now my golden pair would be unstoned. Did people say destoned, or is that what you do to plums? How long did junkies take to come down? I really needed Mercy Mallock, sort these sods out with her karate.

There are occasional non-French motors around in Paris. So I wasn't at all concerned when a car bearing a striking resemblance to Gerald Sweet's motor trundled out of the square as I moved away from the phone by the two trees. I mean, a car is a car, right? I was so definitely unconcerned that I made a long detour, just proving how casual I was.

Back in the hotel, I showed me and the world that Lovejoy was cool by peering down from the window at the passing cars for at least three hours before turning in. I didn't switch the light off, because I'd not switched it on. Good heavens, can't tourists tour? I'd known the Sweets were heading for Paris, hadn't I? So they were here, exactly as expected. So what? God, but my mind's ridiculous. Sometimes it gets on my nerves, bothering me hour after hour with inessentials. I didn't sleep that night.

Seven o'clock, I was downstairs in a panic having that non-breakfast breakfast they give you, one measly crescentic pastry and a cup of coffee. It was urgent to do something in antiques that looked really legitimate, even if it never is.

Which means auctions. It's practically the definition.

22

Roused, bathed, and having conquered the breakfast charade, I strolled the morning streets until Veronique and Guy came at a run and we embarked on our impending spree.

'Did the Colonel say how much money we had to blue?' I asked, but only got shrieks of laughter.

'We must avoid the Parisian winds,' Veronique said at my look. Her coat was heavy, its high collar surprising. 'Paris has only wind tunnels. London's chaotic streets give protection.'

If she said so. I thought it mild if fresh. Guy thought of nothing but his next tumbleweed and roaring his motor through impossible thoroughfares. I'd never met a bloke like him for getting off the starting grid. We'd no sooner walked round the corner than he was in his motor, revving like the maniac he was.

'Antique shops were sprinkled about the arrondissements, Lovejoy,' Veronique explained, her head wobbling and jerking as she tried to talk against the lunatic's darting accelerations between delivery vans. 'An arrondissement's a Paris district, with a mayor, a town hall as you call it, everything. They're numbered in a spiral on maps, from centre outwards.'

'Which one has the antiques?' There should be a special nook in heaven for the bloke who invented roofs for motor cars. And one in hell for the bloke who took them off.

'Sixth. I think', she added, managing to sound dry, 'near the Luxembourg Gardens.' Women nark me. It was clearly my fault, I'm not French.

'There are true antique shops, Lovejoy, and *brocanteurs*.' Guy screeched a mad screech at the word.

'*Brocanteurs* are what you call junk shops, second-handers.'

'Have you a big flea market, love?' I tried to explain Petticoat Lane, Portobello Road, but she was there ahead of me.

'That's where we're going, not your posh shops. *The Marché aux puces*. On Saturdays to Mondays, bargains galore.' Her dryness reached sarcasm.

'Turn back,' I said after a momentary think, which at Guy's speed meant a least a million miles out of our way. 'The sixth arrondissement, please. No dross today.'

'No, Lovejoy,' Veronique said. 'We've got a planned sequence.'

'Do as you're frigging well told,' I said, all quiet and quite calm. 'And tell your frigging loon to do the same.'

You can't muck about when it's antiques-time, and I'd had enough of her dryth and his mania. I wasn't here by choice. I wanted out of their daft unknowable scam. The only exit was by doing my job, then lam off leaving them to it.

She stared at me over her shoulder. '*What?*' Guy actually shouted in astonishment, so loud that pedestrians turned to look.

'You heard.' We screeched to a stop at some traffic lights. Guy revved his engine, Fangio on song.

'Lovejoy,' Veronique said, tight-lipped in the erotic way women show fury in public. 'You will obey orders.'

'Ta-ra, love.' That's the advantage of a bucket seat. You can spring lightly – or even clumsily – into the churning snarling honking Paris traffic, at risk of life and limb, if you're feeling specially suicidal, or even fed up.

Guy swore incomprehensibly, Veronique shrieked warnings, threats too I daresay. The traffic crescendoed to deafen the city. But I was free, and off down a side street like a ferret. It seemed to have no motors in it, by some extraordinary Parisian oversight. I walked a bit, looked back. No sign of Veronique, nor Guy. Nor his motor, thank God. A bloke passed me trundling a handbarrow, which cheered me. Reality was about.

Without any idea of where exactly I was, I found a nosh bar and tried to negotiate something to eat. The stout man seemed surprised to be asked for a lash-up so early in the morning, but responded well. It's really being served with eagerness. Back home you get a surly uncooperative grunt like in Woody's cafe, but this man seemed really pleased. He did me some scrambled eggs – he'd no real notion about kippers on account of my language barrier – and some hot sliced meat I didn't recognize, some eccentric jam, an astonishing variant of tea, toast by the ton, and some hot cylindrical bread things. After, I asked for some vegetable soup with more of his scalding bread sticks, then some

161

cake (cold; I insisted on *froid*, non *chaud*). He turned out to be good on cakes. I had four small ones, then slices of a big dark monster with embedded fruit. He brought his missus out to see. She tried giving me some red wine, really weird this hour in the morning. She understood with regret that wine, to me, came *après* tea o'clock. She pondered – which you do gesticulating volubly in Paris – then brightened, and brought out some liqueur. I had to accept it, but slung it into my tea to dilute the stuff. I took a few cakes for the road, and paid. We all rejoiced. We even shook hands, more oddity. In East Anglia you shake hands with your new brother-in-law and that's it for life. Still, when in Rome. I felt fit at last. No sign of my helpers, all to the good.

Taxi at the main road, and I was on my way to Antiquaires, wherever that was.

'Louvre des Antiquaires, Monsieur,' the driver explained.

'*C'est* it,' I agreed. '*Merci, Monsieur*.'

He told me more, but I wasn't exactly sure what. If I'd had enough words, I'd have asked him to hang about, take me to the sixth arrondissement later on, but decided to quit while I was winning. I'd escaped from my assistants and had breakfast. No good pushing my luck. It was about eleven o'clock when he dropped me off on the Rue St-Honoré, with warnings about the prices antique dealers charge. I said ta, unworried. I knew all about those.

The building wasn't old as such, and looked restored. Quite a crowd was streaming in. I joined them, milling with increasing optimism. It seemed nothing less than a huge antiques emporium, with some two hundred-plus antique dealers stacked three levels high. I was astonished to see notices advertising afternoon lectures on antiques, illustrated no less. There was an exhibition of French end-of-century dress and jewellery. I'd never seen the like in my life. Did French antique dealers actually *want* their customers to learn, appreciate, the antiques that they had to pay through the nose for? They'd go berserk at this sacrilegious idea back home. What a place!

A beautiful feeling enveloped me. I stood against a wall, eyes closed, savouring the loveliness of antiques to come. How much did Colonel Marimee say I could spend? The thrilling answer: *he hadn't!* So I could go on until Guy and Veronique caught up and stopped me. *That meant as much as I liked!* I went giddy. If it wasn't for antiques, God would have a hard time, same as me. Luckily, faith scrapes it together and forms a quorum, but only just.

'Monsieur?' Some gallant moustachioed custodian touched my arm, asked if I was well.

'*Très bon, Monsieur, merci*,' I said. I was too overcome to explain about Paradise. A doorway instruction sheet promised that all the antique dealers were professionals keen to settle the hash of Customs, give certificates where appropriate, and could arrange shipment to anywhere against a fee.

Hang the cost, I thought, somebody else is paying! And sailed into bliss.

Money has a lot to answer for, but is never really to blame. We're the villain of the piece. Money's merit is its divine right to seduce. Never is it more seductive than when you've got plenty, plus a command to spend, spend, spend. Like being in a harem, with permission to have any bird as takes your fancy. But there's one hitch. All antiques are beautiful, alluring, but only some are honest. The rest are forgeries. See the problem? With a spend-and-be-damned bottomless purse, the urge is to simply buy everything, on the grounds that you're bound to net the genuine pieces. Yet to a purist like me that's the ultimate treachery. Why? Because you're encouraging dross.

Not only that, I thought as I stood inhaling the beeswax and varnish nectar of the first furniture dealer's showroom. Money seduces by its power, fine, but its power is almost irresistible.

Look at Italy, for instance. More funding scandals than the parson preached about, and more famous art than any nation on earth. No scandal so great as the Signorelli shambles, which is a warning about money power. Luca Signorelli was an artist who in 1499 was commissioned for 180 ducats to finish the paintings begun fifty years previously by the immortal Angelico, in the wondrous cathedral at Orvieto. Signorelli was ecstatic – he wanted to stun the authorities into awarding him their next contract, which was frescoing the lower part of the chapel. With exalted vision he stormed on, executing brilliant, dazzling work. He even invented new techniques – like his gold-covered wax-point underlaying to cause the reflected candle glow to shimmer when the congregation looked upwards. In other words, a masterpiece, to be preserved at all costs.

Enter weather, permeating rain, humidity, working over the centuries to despoil and erode. (Also, in 1845, a touring load of Russian nobles, who unbelievably *washed away Signorelli's dry overdrawing* on the frescos, cheerfully convinced they were improving matters.) Then – as if time, decay, and predators were not enough – enter politics.

It's not for me to complain. I'm no better than I ought to be. But honestly, when the Italian Parliament votes a special law, the '545', enabling some 300,000,000,000 lire for the care of Orvieto and Todi, arts lovers everywhere have a right to ask where it all went to, right? Not for me to ring Signora Parrino, Minister of Arts, and ask what the hell possessed her. Why *did* she lend 100 billion to a certain corporation the day *after* she'd left the post? 'Where is it now?' a baffled enthusiast asked the innocent, honest Assessore. We all know the poor bloke's reply: 'Disappeared.' How? Dunno, nobody knows anything . . . And even the sterling, upright, efficient and honest, Soprintendenza is meshed and helpless. A fraction of gelt creeps back from That Company when a fuss is raised, but the rest stays salted.

Politics always bulges the sinister corridor curtains where big money flows. The Soprintendente who raised Cain about the vanishing moneys allotted to Pompei's restoration was replaced with Byzantine alacrity. The lovely and outspoken lady who tried to ginger Venice into honesty has gone. Okay, it's politics. What I want to know is, are the priceless masterpieces stashed away in the Galleria Borghese's (permanently closed!) *quadreria* still there? Reasonable question, because the restoration money isn't, not any more. It's been disappeared, it's politics.

'Buy it, Monsieur,' I said, coming out of the trance.

'The plate, Monsieur?' The dealer was suave, polished. 'Yes. It is genuine Palissy. You observe the carefully worked snakes, and leaves of plants – '

'Not the fake, Monsieur.' His partner, a smart middle-aged lady, wore a genuine Breguet watch on her fitted jacket – you can tell them from their plainness, the matt background and narrow chapter ring showing up the plain hands superbly. 'Breguet et fils, Madame?'

'Yes,' she said, pausing uncertainly. That meant not pre-1816, but still a valuable watch.

Palissy was a Huguenot glass-painter, one of the unlucky ones. Even though the royal family patronized him, he still died in clink. When he turned to pottery, he got good whites without tin oxides. No mean feat, because you have to put on a translucent lead glaze and let the white clay underneath show through. Everybody fakes Palissy, though, except his small plates. And this was a big exotic one, but without a single chime. Fake.

'The Majorelle, Monsieur.' I smiled hello at it.

A water-lily table, little over two feet tall. Called so because it was carved literally to look like a water lily. Not truly an antique, except to avaricious Customs and Excise, who want everything older than fifty years down in their little ledgers. About 1900, Art Nouveau ran riot, basing everything on Mother Nature. It's bonny stuff, if you've the stomach, but I can't honestly take such blunt copying, however polished the tamarind and mahogany, the gilt-bronze lily buds, creepers crawling up furniture legs on to the top of the damned thing. Majorelle was a lone cabinet-maker, who knew wood. Pity he didn't go straight and make proper stuff (apologies if you're an Art Nouveau nut. Wish you better).

'To be shipped, Monsieur?' The lady was sizing me up: non-French, a new buyer, non-haggler and pretty much unconcerned with a few percentage points here and there . . .

'My assistants will tell you, Madame, later today.' I scribbled a note for the price as marked, thanked her profusely, and withdrew. She tried catching my attention but I was off into blissland. I find it really quite easy keeping tabs on the antiques I buy. The difficulty is remembering where. I suppose women have this trouble when they're on a spending spree, except they like to scoop everything up as they go, which saves bother. But I had assistants. What did I pay them for, for heaven's sake, if not to help? I always finish up doing the donkey work. Not today.

A little over an hour, I'd bought forty-seven antiques, almost all furniture and genuine, for a fortune in IOUs. 'My assistants will be along *immédiatement*,' I carolled every time. 'Name of Solon . . .' I'd not seen a single piece of furniture that had made me queasy, in the way that Troude forgery in the Mentle clubhouse had. I felt the serenity that comes when rewakening after love. Love is moreish, same as antiques. I hurtled out from the place, collared a taxi and told him anywhere in the sixth arrondissement, starting with the very best antique shops. He was pleased, warned me darkly against the dealers. I said ta, I'd watch out, and tipped him well. He called out his warning after me. I waved, keeping an eye out for Guy and Veronique.

And plunged into the separate antique shops, not sparing the grottier *brocanteurs*. I must say, the stuff was pretty good. Oh, forgeries abounded, as always, and nothing wrong with that. Fakes provide mirth, where very often there is only weeping and gnashing of teeth. I was happy to see the usual dross of Dutch fake silver – and I *don't* mean fake Dutch silver – with its phoney marks, its duff baroque 'strapwork' so gross and unlike the real thing. You've only to see one genuine piece in any museum to be warned off it for life. Why the Dutch love faking Louis XIV silver, heaven alone knows, because they're no good at it. Electrotyping's more of a difficulty, because you do this by making a mould from an original, say a valuable bronze. You coat the copy with plumbago, as we forgers (sorry, we honest copyists) still call black lead, then sink it in a bath of electrolyte. Wire it to a chunk of copper, give it a little current, and sit back. Copper covers the copy's surface. Clue: it will be beautifully fine, deposited atom by atom, unlike the real bronze, which is rough.

The piece I came across didn't need the test, but I gave it a knuckle tap for old times' sake, and heard the tell-tale clunk instead of the lovely faint singing note of genuine bronzes. I smiled an apology to the dealer, then bought a fake painting. It was a mediaeval Madonna and Child, so say, on solid wood panel, done in the true old style. It would have fooled me but for my chest's stony silence when I touched it.

Still keeping a watch for my two nerks, I asked, 'Can I see the reverse, Monsieur?' (Please – *always* look at the back. Here's why.) It was American hickory of the sort we call pignut: very straight, coarse but lovely smooth grain. It's a beautiful elastic wood, can resist any amount of thumps. In spite of these qualities, it doesn't last, so is highly favoured by forgers for painted panels. This faker had really done his stuff – glued several small panels together to make one large one. And he'd stuck them like Theophilus did in the eleventh century, mixing quicklime and soft cheese (I really do mean cheese). Theophilus thought highly of this method, and so do I.

'I'll buy it as a fake, Monsieur,' I suggested. He was outraged, scandalized, overwhelmed, underwhelmed, and finally whelmed. I gave an IOU. My two assistants would be along . . .

There were plenty of antique shops, a few with two or three proprietors. And still no sign of my golden pair. The rest of the time I concentrated on furniture, with a few other antiques here and there. I bought an especially fine piece of fake Strasbourg faïence, but pretty old. I liked it because Strasbourg faïence was copied right from the off. (You often get the number 39 underneath, because fakers misunderstood the significance of numbering. Once you've seen the original brilliant carmine you'll never get taken in; even modern fakers can't match it.)

An hour I worked, darting quickly in and out of shops, eyes open for Guy and Veronique. Eventually I went down an alley, feeling worn out, and settled to a nosh in a busy restaurant. I sat where I could see the street.

Less than forty minutes later I was back in the shops, buying, testing, looking, sounding pieces out, rejoicing fit to burst in a way I hadn't for days. I could hardly keep myself from choking while examining furniture, on account of the robbery that was going to hit the street come nightfall. I could even pinpoint the exact shops. In fact, I returned to one and bought a Davenport drawing-room desk. I'd passed on it first time round, but saw it would be right in the robbers' firing line and probably get marmalized when the ramraiders struck. It was too bonny to die.

'Can I have it taken out of the window's sunlight, Mademoiselle?' I begged the dealer. 'Only it might fade.'

'In three hours, Monsieur?' I'd promised her my assistants would be along. But she complied.

Captain Davenport's original desk-and-chests had desktops that slid backwards to cover the chest, for use in a narrow ship's cabin. Adapted for a lady's withdrawing room, the desk surface could stay projecting, supported by pillars on a horseshoe platform. Yellow walnut, and lovely even if it was Victorian.

Which gave me time to inspect more closely the bloke pacing the pavement. A fly lad, tough, fit, earring. I hid a smile. He'd been in the Louvre des Antiquaires, then here, consulting a card list and catalogues. A dealer never misses somebody putting ticks on a catalogue. Sign of an innocent, or somebody not innocent at all. One thing about ramraiders, they're the least subtle thieves in creation.

The ramraider's one of Great Britain's exports. Just as we invented most of the world's sports, in order to lose at them in the Olympics, so we're indefatigable inventors of scams. The bluntest, not to say most aggressive, robbery in antiques is the ramraider. It's so simple it's almost beautiful. At least, it would be if it wasn't destructive.

Method: take any van – and I mean steal, nick, thieve. Weld scaffolding poles to the rear bumpers to form a battering ram. Early in the owl hours, you reverse at speed through the window of any convenient antique shop, shattering whatever protection it's got. Spill out, go straight to the antiques your sussers have previously marked on a rough sketch-plan you've learnt by heart. Load up, and be off and out of it in less than ninety seconds. Again, I do mean that quick. The London and Provincial Antiques Dealers' Association has been moaning for years about the eruption of ramraiders in the Thames Valley. The best (for best read worst) thing is that it's thieving to plan. Exactly like the art works – Van Gogh, Old Masters – in France, Holland, Germany, during the 1980s and early 1990s, it's theft by prescription. One place in Leeds got hit three times in as many weeks. I'm against ramraiders, actually, because they're pro hooligans. That is, they go straight for whatever they're told, never mind what's in the way. They'll shred any painting, mash any furniture, to reach the priceless pieces they've been sent to steal.

How did I know the lank lad with the soiled jeans and golden earring was a susser? Well, who else would pace a street of antique shops like a drum major, his lips moving as he did his phoney 'stroll'? Then, unbelievably, pause to mark the distances down! Where I come from these daredevil youths'd starve. The pillock thought himself among a load of dupes. I hadn't known the ramraiders had reached Paris, but here they undoubtedly were.

'Monsieur?'

God. I found myself shaking my head, tut-tutting audibly. I smiled apologetically at the girl. She was smart, really well turned out. I apologized. 'The traffic, Mademoiselle! I admire your Parisian drivers' skill. So fast!'

We prattled a bit. I said what splendid stock she had. She was pleased I liked it, tried to persuade me to buy some more. I told her my name, Lovejoy. Claire Fabien offered me coffee for a *merci beaucoup* and a smile. We talked of the antiques locally. I kept an edgy eye on the window, twice almost starting up as I imagined a couple of blond heads, subsiding to chat some more, false alarm. I was drawn, through no fault of my own. I realized after an hour that I should get on, hoover up more antiques, and rose to go. I hesitated.

'Look, Miss Fabien. Might I give some advice?'

'Indeed. I should be grateful from one so knowledgeable.'

'Please. Tonight, remove your antiques. To a storeroom, any borrowed pantechnicon.'

She looked at me, at the street. 'But why?'

'I have a hunch, that's all.' I said my goodbyes, telling her to be sure to give my tardy assistants a receipt.

And that was that.

I did thirty-one more shops, not counting the *brocanteurs* which had mostly duff stuff except for an orrery I picked up for a song. 'Orrery' after John Rowley made a model of the solar system for the Earl of Orrery in 1713. They look like those mobile hangings that were so popular ten years ago, except stuck on to a small stand. It was cheap, the *brocanteur* told me, because the ivory base was all bent and split to blazes. I pretended hesitation, though I was almost sure it was pre-1781 because that was the year Herschell discovered the planet Uranus and there was no sign of it on this orrery's whirlies. With an actor's reluctance, I paid him four-fifths of his asking price with a scribble. Straightening old ivory's the easiest thing in the world: steep the ivory in dilute nitric acid for some days, judging it as you go. It slowly becomes astonishingly bendable, and translucent. Gently force it into shape, then let it dry. That's all there is to it. An old orrery's worth a fortune.

Congratulating myself, I mentally thanked Paris for a marvellous day. I went and stood at the corner of the oblique X intersection of the Rue de Rennes and the Rue d'Assas. As obvious as a spare tool, it was still a full hour before Guy the Prat leapt on me, snarling. He was shaking badly, teeth a-chatter. He'd missed a dose.

'About frigging time,' I said. 'Here.' I shoved the shoal of promissories at him. 'You've an hour before they close. Better split them with Veronique or you'll miss some. See you at the hotel.'

'Lovejoy!' It was a howl. I've never seen anybody so enraged, so desperate. Across the road Veronique was shrieking abuse at a taxi and some motors trying to cut from the Luxembourg Gardens. Jesus, what a durbar. 'Come back!'

'*Bon chance*, Guy.' I strolled off with a wave, pointed to an imaginary wristwatch.

With the sun setting, shops closing, motors getting madder, the driving crazier, I sought out a restaurant and had a whale of a time noshing everything in sight. The waiters finished up laughing at me for my misunderstandings of the menu, but were thrilled at my hunger. Well, I was starving, hardly eaten a thing all day. I felt restored, made whole again from contact with lovely antiques. I drifted about the darkening city, then retired for the night. Guy and Veronique weren't back yet. Still chasing up my antiques? Or, my smile dying, catching up on their vital dosage somewhere? But the antiques had made up for everything. And not a single one had made me feel ill, though I'd seen hundreds of polished surfaces, fake, genuine, phoney, simulants, look-alikes, copies, filiations, shams, authentics twindled into double, marriages of scores, hundreds of pieces. Which makes you think that something was more than radically wrong with Colonel Marimee's scam, whatever that might be. And with Guy and Veronique's assistance, whatever that might be.

And even with Cissie's death, WTMB?

170

23

'Not *that*?' I heard myself exclaim, swiftly returning to ingratiate,
'Quite, er, splendid!'

The famous Paris auction centre is a mess. Imagine Sotheby's,
Christie's, Bonhams, the rest, together in one new building like a
corny copy of a provincial bank. It tried to emulate the nearby
bourgeois façades. I beamed falsely at Veronique and Guy.

'It's marvellous,' Guy bragged as we approached. 'Space for
four hundred cars, every-hour parking.' He would think of motor
cars.

'We need antique auctions,' I reminded. I didn't want Colonel
Marimee getting on at me. 'I did my bit yesterday.'

'You bastard, Lovejoy. *We* did all the work!'

'Oh, aye.' I went all laconic. 'So why'd you need me?'

He growled, his sign of wanting to land me one.

'I'll show Lovejoy round,' Veronique swiftly told Guy. 'You see
Dreyfus. Fifteen minutes.'

I watched Guy shoot into the building. I didn't like him to be so
zingy, behaving like he had stars round his head, and asked, 'He
okay, love?'

'He's fine.' She halted so I bumped into her. 'No more questions
like that, Lovejoy. Today we begin.'

Like what? I asked myself, narked. All right, maybe I'd
sounded full of mistrust about his crazy stare and dynamite style.
I'd only been trying to help, in a caring sort of way.

'Thank God. Where are they?'

We entered the place. She spoke offhand to three blokes who
accosted us, beckoned me with a tilt of her head. I felt a sneaky
pride in being with somebody so lovely.

'For a start, Lovejoy, this is the Hôtel Drouot.' I nodded I'd
heard of the great focus for Paris's auctioneers. Not a hotel at all.
'Rebuilt in 1980. Sixteen salerooms, each with storage space,
three selling floors from central foyers. Temperature – controlled
storage, bond areas . . .'

'Great.' Only sixteen? Did that explain the grumbles of international dealers? Mind you, I'm prejudiced. There's nothing wrong with auctioneers that retirement wouldn't cure.

'This way.'

Just think of the wasted corridor-miles humanity's logged over the centuries! If it wasn't for flaming corridors we'd have colonized the universe yonks ago. As it is, we're all still plodding down boring corridors, trying to reach our respective launch pads.

Dreyfus was a small pleasant bloke, so respectably dressed he had me notching my own markers of suavity – curling lapel, slanted tie, shirt without a top button, grubby shoes. We greeted each other warmly. He had a partitioned office. No antiques in the inner sanctum. The sofa table by the wall was a dud. Or maybe not so dud? Its luscious surface patina felt right, but the table seriously wrong. It was brilliantly done, looked exactly right. The four feet with their castors gave an authentic bong. But the resonance of it mixed with that terrible fraudulent surface made me nauseous. I looked away.

'Jacques Dreyfus,' he said, twinkling, 'and no relation! Beautiful, isn't it?' He'd be quite at home in any language. 'It will be catalogued soon.'

As a fake, I hoped. The old trick. Its base, castors and all, were nicked from a genuine cheval mirror – 'swing dressers', dealers call them. In Regency days they'd had to make them strong, to take heavy glass. Cheval mirrors are not so valuable, even now, so forgers marry the support to the best flat heartwood. Presto! Your 'genuine 1825 sofa table' – and we challenge anybody to do any tests they like. Your usual patter is, 'No, take your sample for chemical analysis from the feet, please – the tabletop is irreparable, you see . . .' The tests prove exactly right for 1820, and you have your certificate of authenticity. Then you buy some old wood, fake up some feet with castors for the cheval mirror, and sell *that* as completely genuine. Only now your patter goes, 'No, take your sample for chemical analysis from the ebony-inlaid top, please. The base is irreparable . . .'

'The system,' Veronique said. Impatient women aren't new, but there was a new edge to her voice. Social-philosophy time? I'd hated the bit I'd already received.

'Our auction system in France endures,' Jacques said cheerily, 'despite all attempts. We operate a monopoly, though the Common Market lawyers wring their hands in Brussels.'

'I'm ashamed of my ignorance,' I put in. I moved from the chair to sit on a low couch, trying to get away from the distress of that ghastly hybrid.

'The Compagnie de Commissaires-Priseurs de Paris has controlled auctions since the eighteenth century, Lovejoy.' He rippled his fingers like a pianist gathering pace. 'The auction firms – *études* – can have offices wherever they like, but must rent a saleroom in the Hôtel Drouot for a sale.'

'Must?' That would account for the gripes of the non-French antiques traders. '*Il faut*?'

Jacques chuckled at my pronunciation. I began to like him. I was doing my best in a mad mix of French and English.

'*Il*, as you perceive, *faut*, Lovejoy. We are also forbidden to prepare our own sale catalogues. Those are formed up, descriptions of the antiques and all, by a corps of experts certified by our Government.'

'Is there a guarantee?' I asked without thinking. Then I had to struggle so as not to see Veronique tense at my question. I'd have to be even more circumspect. I've the brains of an egg.

'Thirty years.'

'The expert cataloguer is more important than the *étude*, then?'

'That is often the case.' Jacques Dreyfus smiled with guarded apology at Veronique, who was busy pretending she was bored. 'The money is the other, Lovejoy. The Compagnie holds half the sale money until the year's end.'

'And dishes it out when it wants?' I was aghast. 'Don't the big boyos mind? They're subsidizing the small fry, right?'

He shrugged that Gallic shrug. 'The smaller *études* don't have to catalogue each sale.' He looked at Veronique in exasperation, smiley still. 'It's the way things are.'

'No more, Jacques,' Veronique said. Guy came zooming in. 'We must show Lovejoy your collection.'

I brightened. 'Antiques? All as good as your sofa table, Jacques?'

His smile was quite brave, in the circumstances. I had a vague idea he'd sussed me out, but wasn't sure. 'I believe exactly!' He wanted to show me a saleroom. I asked for a loo first, please, and received directions.

There, I was violently sick, retching and leaning gasping against the tiled wall until I could retch no more. I put my forehead against the cold surface a few minutes. Afterwards I rinsed my face in cold water and emerged pretending a kind of I'm-casually-interested-looking-about. Veronique and Jacques Dreyfus were waiting in the foyer. Guy had streaked off somewhere.

'Are you all right, Lovejoy?' Jacques asked. 'You're white.'

'Fine, thanks.' My head was splitting. I grinned like a goon, having remembered where it was I'd been sick like this before, and why. 'Have we far to go?'

'With you along, Lovejoy,' Veronique said through thinned lips, 'the answer's yes.'

Me and Jacques chuckled merrily. In my case – and maybe his? – it wasn't much of a chuckle. But I thought hard of having got my letter off, overloaded with stamps from a tobacconist, and managed something near a jovial croak.

We drove in Dreyfus's motor, a more trundlesome job than Guy's zoomster. I kept sane, and more importantly in a non-puke state, by exclaiming at the Parisian landmarks – the Seine, the Arc de Triomphe, the bigger-than-expected Sacré Coeur – then a double through tangled streets to finish up in an unprepossessing district within sound of trains. It looked the sort of district Paris shouldn't have, grotty, down at heel, soiled.

'This it, Veronique?' I let my surprise show. I was getting fed up with being careful all the bloody time. It's always me gets the headaches.

'Yes, Lovejoy. This is it.' She spoke French with vituperation. I looked about as Jacques parked the motor.

Some darkish children played, stood about. The filthy street wore debris like medals for indignity. The house fronts were frayed, no real paint. The doors looked battered. A couple of windows were patched with cardboard. The aroma of exotic cooking filled the air. It made me hungry as hell, but I had a sour feeling that more sickness lay just around the corner.

'This way, Lovejoy.'

It might have been a church hall, some sort of meeting place, that we found after a few hundred yards. Down steps, with a reinforced door to shut the world of staring children out. Two bulky blokes stood in bulky-bloke attitudes, suited for funerals. They knew Veronique, accepted me without a glance, but listened to Jacques. Paymaster?

We went through an arched doorway. Guy was jangling away, talking non-stop to Colonel Marimee, gesticulating, joking, a riot. The place was crammed with furniture, much covered in sheets. Note that small point: hardly any paintings, ceramics, and no display cases filled with antique jewellery.

The Colonel gave a terse instruction to Guy and stood watching us approach. We signalled our arrival with various degrees of subservience, all except Veronique, who perched provocatively on a polished surface. I swallowed. Montaigne said that however high the throne, we all still sit on our tails.

'Inspect these items and report, Lovejoy,' Marimee commanded. 'You have thirty minutes.'

'*Oui, mon commandant.*'

He meant me. I avoided spewing on his brilliant shoes, and walked down the first line of furniture. The pieces were of a muchness. The larger of the two hulks preceded me unasked, flicking away the dust covers as I went. Jacques Dreyfus followed.

French furniture caught fashions from its neighbours. People say that, yet it's a bit unfair, because France started a number of styles of her own. It's always said that France filched Italian joinery in the Renaissance, Flemish marquetry in the seventeenth century, English mahogany styles in the eighteenth and so on. True, but don't forget France's flair. You have to see the originals – not this load of gunge I was being shown. In skill, France's antique furniture is a front runner.

A tulipwood cabinet stopped me. Supposed to be 1775, it sported four plaques of Sèvres porcelain set into the panels. Small, but a fortune at any auction, if you believed it. I bent down to the plaques. Plants, spring flowers. Carnations, three tulips, lilac, with that lovely apple-green border Méreaud loved. He was the highest paid of Sèvres porcelain decorators, though of course he'd died two hundred or more years before these fake plaques were done. I knelt to look closer. The carnations were exactly right botanically. The tulips, being easier, also were. The lilac was wrong. I've a tree growing in my own unkempt garden, and have tried to imitate Méreaud and his equally skilled pal Léve often enough to know. Somebody had copied as best they could from an imperfect picture of the real thing.

That sickness made me giddy as I rose. I stumbled, fell on a nearby table. I withdrew my hand with an involuntary cry. I'd checked my fall mechanically, touched its surface. It burned me like a chimney from hell.

'Pardon, Lovejoy,' Dreyfus said, helping to steady me. I apologized profusely, saying it was too long since breakfast. Colonel Marimee curled his lip at my offshore weakness. I went with pretence of care, pausing now and then as if thoughtful, but the nausea was almost shaking me.

'Very good, *mon commandant*,' I said to Marimee. Almost all of it was sickening. I still wasn't sure how much of the antiques game he understood. Nor did I know how much he was supposed to know. I could hardly see.

'Adequate? Yes or no?' he demanded.

'Adequate, *mon commandant*.'

'*Bien*.' And left, terse nods all round. There was no relaxation of the atmosphere.

'What about transport?' I asked Veronique. 'I mean, do we have to arrange it, or will they call for it?'

'Who?' she asked back.

'Well.' I was thinking while I was still on my feet, holding the sickness at bay. 'You said we can't auction it here. Hasn't it got to go to the Hôtel Drouot to be sold?'

'Stupid,' she snapped, as I'd hoped she would. 'We aren't selling. We've gone to a great deal of trouble to . . . afford it. And it's a fraction only.'

She was going to say buy, then didn't. My throat cleared itself as I tried to stop it saying, 'Is it all furniture? What else we got?' *Don't say tapestry, upholstery*.

'Wall tapestries, mainly,' Veronique said, starting us off out of the storehouse. 'And of course upholsteries. People say they're more expensive than the furniture itself. True?'

'Always has been, love. Got papper mash stuff?' *Don't say yes*.

'Sure,' she said. 'Thirty papier mâché pieces. Right, Jacques?'

'Good,' I said, meaning bad, bad, bad. They'd have paper filigree too, the bastards. I nodded a nod as good as the

Commandant's, then got driven back to the hotel, where I bade them a smiling so long, and with the relief of the afflicted was spectacularly and constantly sick in the minuscule bathroom. The image of those dark staring children watching us in that shabby street, with their blistered hands and old-young faces and blunted expressions was in my mind. Dr Johnson's crack came at me: 'Remember that all tricks are either knavish or childish.' I thought, please help me. Come soon, pals. You can't leave me to do this alone. My insides were empty, except for this feeling of murder. I saw only the lavatory bowl for half an hour.

The day was waning – all Paris seemed on the wane just then – when I left the hotel. I wandered brimming with nausea into the little square, sat on the seat beneath the tree, looked at the cobbles, put my head back hoping for cool. Clammy head, wet hands. The air felt heavy, muggy, too close to breathe. Somebody sat on the seat. I felt it nudge.

'Where the hell've you been?' I said, not bothering to open my eyes. 'I said come straight away. East Anglia's only forty minutes, for Christ's sake.' But I'd not heard a wheelchair.

'I had to see to Jan first,' she said, which would spring anybody's lids. Lysette, no less. 'He needs special care.'

'You're no use,' I said. This is typical. First time in my life I've ever asked anybody for help, and they send me an ignorant tart. 'Jan give any message?' The least he could do.

'Yes. He said to rely on me, Lovejoy.'

'Get lost, love.' I'd a splitting headache. I made to leave. What she said stopped me.

'I would have waited at your hotel, except for your company.'

What did she know? 'How much do you know, love?'

She was smaller than I thought, pale, composed. I felt a strong urge to tell her to clear off, but bonny women make you lose your gommon.

'Jan was hired to advise on antiques. There's heavy buying in East Anglia, France, all over.' She hesitated. 'He made mistakes. You can't be right all the time, can you?'

Well, yes. 'A divvy can. Antiques are easy, love. It's people queer the pitch every time.' She was trying not to tell me Jan started defrauding the rollers, Big John included.

'You're hateful! I can see what you're thinking, Lovejoy! My brother could no more cheat – '

'*Who*?' My headache belted me across the eyes.

'My brother. Jan's the gentlest, kindest, most honest . . .' Et sisterly cetera.

Wrong again. How was I to know? I'd honestly seen Lysette as Jan Fotheringay's bird. My shimmering vision tried to focus on her anew, without listening to her defensive dross. Jan had pulled the old Nelson, as the trade says. You are supposed to approve a multitude of fakes and genuine antiques – that is, decide if they're good enough to pass most scrutineers, like I'd just done – but he'd then condemned a few beautiful pieces as dross. Secretly, of course, he'd snaffled them, and made a fortune. The problem? It was the rollers' fortune, not his.

'Where's it heading, Lysette? Am I right, Switzerland?'

'Yes. I don't know when.'

That didn't matter. The square seemed clear of familiars still, but for one. I almost got better with relief.

'Look, Lysette. Good of you to come and all, but you're no use. I wanted Jan. He could tell me the backers, whose scam it is. You can't.'

'I can, Lovejoy. Some, anyway.' She named the ones I expected: Jervis, Almira Galloway, Monique Delebarre, Corse, Big John (she didn't call him that) Sheehan, and Paulie of course. And took my breath away by adding, 'Jan told me Mr Anstruther was frightened, but his wife drove him. She's Monsieur Troude's woman, you see, and got her husband's firm to invest everything.'

Cissie and Troude? My headache had only been teasing until now. Across the square, Gobbie spat with laconic skill.

'Got a car, love?'

'I can easily hire one. You want me to help, Lovejoy?'

'Please,' I said, nearly broken. 'Get one, and follow. We leave tomorrow, if I've guessed right. You'll have a travelling companion. An old bloke I know.'

Lysette smiled, suddenly bright and beautiful. 'I'll be there ahead of you, Lovejoy. If *I've* guessed right.'

We made a detailed plan. She left, me watching her edible form move across the cobbles out of the square. I gave her a few minutes, then went to where my real helper sat, thank God.

'Wotcher, Gobbie.'

'Hello, son.' He hawked up phlegm, rheumy old eyes watering. 'Who's the bint?'

'On our side. You'll be travelling with her.' I launched into money, surreptitiously gave him what I had to cover expenses. He'd told his daughter he was going to a regimental reunion, a laugh. I had to ask him, though. 'You sure you want in, Gobbie? It's okay if you duck out. I'll manage.'

'Like hell you will, son,' Gobbie said, grinning. 'You'll squirrel off and hide. I know you. You're a cowardly sod.' I had to laugh. A gappy geriatric grin and a brilliantly beautiful smile, both within a few minutes. Plus a home truth. And allies! Things were looking up.

'It'll be rough, Gobbie.' I paused. What had he said at the boot sale? 'Bring old times back – they were dangerous, remember.'

His smile was as beautiful in its way as Lysette's. 'Them's the times I wants, Lovejoy. One more, worth anything.'

'Remember you said that,' I warned him. I'm glad now I said that, too. 'Here, Gobbie,' I said on impulse. 'Want to brighten your day? Well, night? See a giggle?'

'A robbery? Here?' He was surprised.

'It'll be about two in the morning,' I warned. He fell about at that, guessing what it would be. And he was right.

Well, he would be right, with his million years of experience. He got a motor car, as I'd asked, and we sat there in the darkness looking out at the street. Gone two o'clock, and so far nothing. Odd how some people, especially older ones like Gobbie, seem at home wherever they are. I would have sworn the motor was his own, so familiar did he seem with –

'Watch, son.'

His quiet voice woke me faster than a yell. I'd seen nothing, but then my instinct's for survival. Gobbie's seemed entirely outside himself. Maybe it's because I've so much guilt, that unsleeping guardian of morality.

'Where?'

'Nothing yet.'

Nothing wrong with dropping off, but then I was tired. Old folks seem to nap like babies, in and out of sleep any old time.

'Glad I don't own a Range Rover, or a big Nissan.' They get nicked for robberies like the one we'd come to see.

'There goes one.' A Citroën, innocuous and plain, drove sedately down the night road, clearly somebody late back from the theatre. 'The scout,' Gobbie explained, sussing my wonder at his certainty, 'otherwise he'd have slowed a bit just before the traffic lights. Everybody does, unless he's trying to look casual.'

See what I mean? Only a veteran would think of that.

Mall-mashers, ramraiders, are a particularly English variant of the smash-and-grab. It's a dark-hour job, though of course you can change the batting order, like the most famous one, the 1990 Asprey ramraid that proved the landmark of its type. (They backed a truck through Asprey's window with wonderful precision – just off Piccadilly, would you believe – to snatch diamonds from the stove-in window.) It's a Newcastle-upon-Tyne speciality, averaging one major ramraid a day now, many of them hitting the same retail shops and malls time after time. They're exciting to watch.

'Here it comes, son. Wake up.'

'Which way?' I was asking blearily when it happened.

Two vehicles drove up, glided to a stop in the centre of the road. One reversed gently into position, then accelerated with a roar and simply drove into the antique-shop front. Glass sprayed everywhere, clattering and tinkling around. One or two shards even rattled musically on our roof. While I was watching, astonished and thrilled, the other was already hurtling into the next window. Neither had lights on. They reversed out, tyres crunching glass. Four hooded blokes dived from the motors and leapt through the openings. Each carried a baseball bat. It was a hell of a mess. I moaned at the thought of the antiques within, but what could I do? I'd warned the one girl I'd fallen for, Claire Whatnot.

The motors pulled to wait against the kerb, engines running.

'They got walkie-talkies, son,' Gobbie said quietly. 'See?'

Well, no I didn't. A couple of small vans came round the corner, dousing their headlights as they settled nearby. Two men to a van, I saw. Admirable organization. They ran the scroll gates up. No lights inside save a red direction node borrowed from some theatre stage.

'Christ!' I almost shrieked. Somebody opened our car door. A mask peered in, our courtesy bulb lighting to show his red eyes.

'Just watching, mate,' Gobbie said quickly. 'Good luck.'

'Fuck luck,' the hooded bruiser said. He held a club the size of a tree in his hands. 'Who're you?'

'I'm Gobbie. Lovejoy. Your tyres okay? Don't pull a spud.'

I thought. I don't believe Gobbie. Why didn't the stupid old sod simply gun our engine and scarper? Instead he makes introductions, pulls the ramraider's leg. Spud's the latest slang for a balls-up, after the catastrophe (or success, whichever way you look at it) of Contintental raiders who'd tried to emulate our Geordie rammers in Amsterdam. Hoods nicked twenty Dutch Impressionists worth untold zillions from the Van Gogh – including Vincent's own *The Potato Eaters*, hence 'spud'. The loot sat meekly in the getaway motor which had a flat tyre. I could hear the blokes shouting, things smashing in the antique shops. God knows what heirlooms they were destroying.

'I heard of you bastards,' the bruiser said. 'Clear off when we do, right?'

'Different direction,' Gobbie said amiably.

The bloke disappeared, putting our car door to quite gently. The pandemonium along the parade of antique shops was increasing. The lads were rushing out small antiques. The first wave would snatch tom – jewellery, precious items such as miniatures, handies that could be scooped up. Then furniture, paintings. But only the ones that had been earmarked.

'Why'd he cuss us, Gobbie?' I asked, narked.

'He knows our scam, son. He doesn't like it.'

'He *what*?' A visiting ramraider team *knows our scam*?

'There they go.'

The first van slammed itself shut. The blokes piled in. It roared away, the Range Rover tearing after. The second slammed, the Nissan barelling round to leave the way it had come. The main van raced off, and that was that.

We drove away, taking the first left. I wondered if they'd battered through into the next-door place, which was Claire's, or whether they'd had orders not to.

'Gobbie,' I said, thinking hard as he dropped me off in the night near the square. 'He knew? Really *knew*?'

'Mmmh. You can always tell.' He paused, I paused, everybody paused. 'Son? Is your scam going to finish up with them antiques they just nicked?'

'Eh?' I'd not thought of that. 'You mean, they were pinching them for *us*?' I'd nearly said Troude and Marimee.

'A thought, son. They were older blokes than usual, see? Them touring Geordies are all of seventeen, eighteen as a rule.'

The hooded raider had seemed thickset, maybe forty or so. Gobbie was right. Ramraiding's a youth's game. So why was an older bloke pulling a stroke like that?

'Like', Gobbie continued, gently nursing me into thinking, 'that lot of gorms last month as raided the Metro Centre. Did the wrong stuff, remember? Too young to know the difference between tom and tat. Did a beautiful rammer, got clean away, and found they'd nicked a display of imitation jewellery.'

Yes, I'd heard. It was desperately worrying. Too many variables all of a sudden.

'Any ideas, Gobbie?' I asked. How pathetic. Me supposed to be the leader of this private little side scam, and here I was asking a wrinkly for advice. I disgust me sometimes. I'd have dozed through the whole thing if it hadn't been for him, too. 'Forget it,' I said, and walked away.

'Night, son. See you there.' I swear the old sod was grinning. I was narked. One day I'll get the upper hand, then people'd better watch out, that's all.

24

'Didn't the Commandant say something about London?' I asked hopefully in next morning's flying start.

Guy tore us through the countryside. I wanted some aspirin, but Veronique fell about when I asked. I was really narked. Just my luck to draw the one bird in the world without a ton of paracetamol in her handbag. 'Is this north?'

'He's quick on the uptake!' Guy cried, swerving, sounding his horn. I shrank in my seat as the wind ripped through me. Everything he said sounded copied from American films. Mind you, what's wrong with that? Same as me, really. Birds often tell me so.

Veronique was smiling. I was exposed in the bucket seat, my regular place now. 'He's a servant,' she said, turning to speak directly at me. 'Aren't you, Lovejoy?'

'Aren't we all?' I was worried about my helpers. I meant me.

'No!' she cried. 'You are *dull*! Like all the servile! Show you a sham clubhouse, a seaside toy, call it a marina, and you grovel like a dog.' *Et* withering *cetera*. I'd made a hit.

'I'm no serf,' I fired back. Staying a buffoon never did me any harm.

Not a bad description of Mentle, marina and all. So she – meaning Guy too – had been there? I thought about poor Baff.

From then on, I decided, I'd really try. I shone, talked instead of sulked. I began trying to draw them out, embarked on some funny not-so-funny tales, Auctions I Have Known, scams, robberies (no names, no pack drill as people say), and within a few miles had her smiling. No mean feat, with Guy yippeeing, attacking every vehicle on the road. I slyly timed him, supposing he'd shot his lot before we started out. He'd have to pull in somewhere when his jangles got too much.

'I mean, I really like Alma-Tadema's paintings,' I was giving out when finally Guy started to become quieter, his driving less flamboyant. What, an hour and a half of belting along the motorway? We'd come out of Paris on the A6. 'What's wrong with detail, if it's lovely? He painted all the faces in his enormous crowds. But so what? Easier to fake.' I'd been on about the old 1980s forgeries, still around in some galleries.

'You're a secret luster, Lovejoy,' Veronique gave back in that encouraging reprimand women use. 'We heard.'

'Not a word to anyone, or I'll stand no chance.' I grinned apologetically, innocent Lovejoy, hoping but never really expecting. 'Where do you find anybody to do detail like Alma-Tad nowadays?' I hummed, trying to remember the melody of that old music-hall song. 'Alma-Tad, oh what a cad . . .' My Gran used to sing it in her naughty moods, dreadfully risky. It worked.

'Look in the right place, Lovejoy, you'll find anything.' Veronique's implacability phase returned for a second.

'Not nowadays, love. Forgers don't have the application. And if fakers can't be bothered, who can? You need time, money, love.' I chanced it as Guy, all a-twitch, began looking for exit roads. Veronique darted him a glance, nodded permission. 'Don't annoy me. I've lived like a monk since I arrived. Gelt's all very well, but I'm short on vital necessities.'

She burst out laughing, a beautiful sight, the wind, blonde hair flying, all shape and pattern. 'I *see*, Lovejoy! You're desperate!'

Even though they'd killed Baff, I was narked at her amusement at my expense. 'Look, love. Birds can go years without a bloke. We can't last more than a couple of days without a bird.' I was still fishing, laying groundwork. 'Everybody's . . . well, fixed up, except me.'

She was still rolling in the aisles at my lovelorn state when we halted at a service station. On the way in, I took a gander at the wall map, and realized we were heading east. Reims led to Metz, to Strasbourg. The E35 darted south along the Rhine then, to Zurich. A guess right, for once? No sign of the Sweets, which surprisingly gave me a pang. Lilian had been brilliant, for all that she was the wife of a SAPAR hunter. And none of Gobbie and Lysette.

'How long's this going on, Veronique?' I asked while we waited for Guy. 'I need to know the plan, when, some detail.'

'Why?' We'd collared some superb French coffee. She gazed levelly back, chin resting on her linked fingers.

184

'Good old Suliman-Aga.' I made a show of relishing my first swig though it burnt my mouth. Women can drink scalding, with their asbestos throttles.

'Who?' Very, very guarded.

'Your Turkish ambassador, brought coffeetime to France. About 1666, give or take a yard.'

She didn't say anything. She'd already been to the loo, as I. I realized I couldn't quite see the edges of her pupils, however hard I looked. Funny, that. I'd done my most soulful gaze a number of times, hoping. Though what I'd learn from seeing if the pupils were dilated or pinpoint, God knows. It's supposed to be a clue to drugs, but which size meant what?

Her eyes rose, held me hard with an intensity I didn't like. Lucky that Guy was the mad one, or I'd have suspected the worst.

'We were warned about you, Lovejoy.' She drew a spoony trail in a spillage spot on the table. I was starting to hate surfaces. 'I paid no heed. Now I'm wondering if I underestimated you.'

This is the kind of woman-talk I don't like. Had I been too obvious? I went into a huff. It's quite a good tactic, played with enough misunderstanding.

'Look, love.' I showed how heated I was. 'I'd rather finish this job and get home. If you're narked because I mentioned I'm a bit short of, ah, close company, then tell Marimee and get me sacked – '

'Sacked, shacked, packed?' Guy raced to the table, literally grabbing Veronique's coffee. 'Hacked?' He laughed so loud people looked round. He hovered about four feet above the floor, zingy, fully restored. 'Hacked, then *lacked*? Wracked?' Happy days were here again. I didn't need to look into his pupils.

'Guy,' Veronique reprimanded quietly as we rose to depart. Guy shrilled merriment, streaked off to the motor. We followed. 'You will be told everything, Lovejoy.' She wore a watch that could have afforded me a thousand times over. 'In three hours.'

'Three hours more at Guy's lunatic speeds'll have us in Vladivostok. Will we make it back to Paris? Only, I started fancying that hundred-year-old concierge. She's just my type – breathing.'

That gave her a crinkly half-smile. I felt we were more allies after that short break than before. I tried telling Guy to take his time. He bawled that we were to make Zurich before midnight, and whiplashed us into the traffic with barely a look. Correct, at last. Mind you, the million pointers had helped. Gobbie and Lysette would now meet me as planned.

'Daddy wouldn't buy me a bow-wow,' I sang, explaining to Veronique: 'Alma-Tadema used to play that to visitors on his early phonograph. Real class, eh? Was it the *onzième*?'

'Eleventh?'

'Arrondissement. Your warehouse, the cran. God, I've never seen so much reconstruction. Don't Parisians get fed up? Between the Place de la Bastille and the Boulevard Voltaire, wasn't it? Lovely, once. I'll bet, when it was famous for cabinet-makers.'

Silence. Guy nearly bisected our motor on an oil transporter.

'Mind you, what can you expect?' I said, blathering on. 'The City of Paris's planning department has no conservation section, has it? Cretins. That lets anybody do anything.'

More, but certain, silence. Funny, but now I was sure of their terrible scam my nausea had all gone.

Veronique didn't chat much more during that pacy journey, and I shut up. But I caught her looking at me in a mirror when she did her lipstick. I cheered up. An ally? Or did her languid look mean she was simply on different shotpot than before?

Three more pit stops for Guy to toot his flute and we were across the Swiss border. I felt bright, optimistic. After all, here was lovely Switzerland. Never having seen it, still I knew it was clean, pristine, beautiful, orderly, utterly correct and safe and law-abiding. Veronique seemed to last out on only one kite flight. Except a vein in her left arm was now swollen and bruised. At the border, Guy produced three passports, one mine. They weren't inspected, and we drove on through. I was so excited I nodded off.

'Lovejoy? Wake up.'

We'd arrived, quite dark. I stumbled out, bleary. The hotel seemed plain, almost oppressively compact. Stern warnings abounded in umpteen languages on every wall about baths, water, payment, lights, payment, doors, keys, payment. I didn't read any, but climbed the stairs – stairs were free – thinking that whatever Monique Delebarre's syndicate was spending, little of it went on lodging. Or was this doss-house strategically placed?

186

The microscopic room was dingier even than my cottage. One bulb flogged itself, leaking a paltry candlepower that barely made the walls. The place was freezing. I sprawled on the bed and thought of money.

Now I'm not against the stuff, though I know I do go on. It's really crazy how prices dominate. The UK tries to keep track by teams which examine 130,000 shop-shelf items in 200 towns, compiling the Retail Price Index, but it's all codswallop. Just as comparing antique prices. It's a hard fact that a lovely epergne, a decorative table centrepiece, weighing a colossal 478 ounces 10 pennyweights, was auctioned in 1928 for 12/6d an ounce, which equals 63 pence as this ink dries. Date 1755, by that brilliant master silversmith Edward Wakelin, no less. *And in its original case*, that collectors today would kill for. So where's the sense in comparison? Answer: no sense at all.

The only honest matching is by time. And I knew no forgers, no artisans, who could or would devote time to making furniture exactly as they used to back in the eighteenth century. Except me. Yet Monique Delebarre and Troude and all seemed to have tapped an endless vein of superbs, by the load, by the warehouse.

Even though I'd no pyjamas I decided it was bedtime. Guy and Veronique were rioting and whooping in the next room.

For a while I lay looking at neon on-offs making shadowed patterns on the walls and ceiling. Antiques crept about my mind. Antiques that were laborious, time-consuming the way all creativity is. Like upholstery, tapestry, polishing furniture in a cruel endless method that only the seventeenth and eighteenth centuries ever managed. And, I'd bet, paper filigree, and papier mâché, that took many, many poorly paid hands. I think I dozed, and came to with somebody knocking surreptitiously on the door. I was there in a flash, opening it slowly, lifting as I turned the handle so it couldn't squeak.

Veronique.

My face couldn't have given me away, not in the semi-darkness of the street glow. She came in and stood leaning against the wall by the doorjamb. I was broken, thinking it would be my home team, Lysette and Gobbie.

'We off somewhere?' For all I knew we might have to steal into the night. It seemed the sort of military thing Colonel Marimee would get up to.

'In a manner of speaking, Lovejoy.' She closed the door.

Then I noticed she had a swish jewel-blue silk nightdress on, to the floor. She shelled the cardigan she'd tied round her shoulders, letting it fall. 'Guy's asleep, sort of,' she said quietly. 'Will an hour do? For somebody so deprived?'

My throat swallowed. My question was answered. Guy's bright episodes were sixty minutes, between doses.

'For what?'

She sighed, pulled me to the bed, pushed me gently down. 'You're hardly the Don Juan they threatened us about, Lovejoy.' She propped herself up on one elbow, and smiled down at me. She was hard put not to laugh her head off. 'I come into your bed in the night stripped, shall we say, for action. Does my presence give you any kind of clue as to why?'

. . . they threatened us about, Lovejoy, when we crossed to East Anglia to murder Baff. And silk is the rarest, most labour-intensive textile. Get enough supply, and you could make enough fake antiques to retire on, if you'd a zillion obedient hands . . .

'Get that off,' I said thickly, clawing her nightdress while she hushed me and tried to do it tidily faster than I could rip.

Pride creeps into mind-spaces it shouldn't, I always find. Shame does too, but lasts longer. The trouble is, there's no way to resist, delay. Women have everything, which is why they get the rest. You can't stop them. Veronique got me, and I'm ashamed to say now that she was scintillating, wondrous. What's worse, I had a perverse relish, almost a sadistic glee, knowing that her bloke next door, stoned out of his skull, was the one who'd murdered a mate of mine. And maybe helped to do over Jan Fortheringay? I'd have to work that one out. I behaved even worse than usual.

At the last second I felt her hand fumble and cap my mouth in hope of silence. Women, practical as ever. It wasn't the end, and, shame to say, I was glad. I harvest shame while I've got the chance. Pathetic.

She left after the full hour. When she'd gone I think I hardly slept, wondering about bedbugs in this dive, but finding that antiques marched back in.

There would be others Veronique hadn't mentioned and I

hadn't asked about. Like paper filigree, which the Yanks call 'quilling', the most painstaking antique of all. Ten years ago, you could get a tiny paper-filigree doll's house for a month's wage. Now? Oh, say enough to buy a real-life family house, garden, throw in a new standard model Ford, and you're about right for price. Inflation, the Slump of Black Monday, recession – the antiques made of tiny scraps of paper trounced them all. And their prices soar yet, to this very day. Go to see it done, if there's ever a demonstration in your village hall.

In the 1790s, Georgian ladies invented this pastime. They'd take slivers of paper so small that your breath blows them away if you're not careful. Me being all clumsy thumbs, I've tried faking these objects and they drive you mad. You roll the paper tightly, then colour it (before or after) and stick a minute slice down to a hardwood surface. Make patterns. Surprisingly durable, you can then fashion tea caddies, boxes, even toys, tiny pieces of furniture, whatever.

There are quilling guilds everywhere now, who preach it as one of the most ancient of arts in ancient Crete. Then it was a religious craft, purely decorative, for shrines and churches, only they used vellum. I've seen some on alabaster, to hang in a window so the quilling picture showed in silhouette – translucent alabaster was once used in place of glass, like in some Italian churches. The best quilling examples I've seen are nursery toys like minuscule kitchens, with every small utensil made of these small rolls, twists, cones, cylinders. And entire dolls' houses, rooms fully furnished. 'Quilling', I suppose, because North American ladies used quills of birds and porcupines, though there's a row about the word as always. Inventive ladies used miniature rolls of wax, hair, leather even, and decorated their purses, pouches, even their husband's tobacciana.

Maybe you don't think it's a very manly pursuit, hunting filigree quilling antiques? Let me cure you: take a look in your local museum – they'll have one or two pieces if they're any good – just to get the idea. Then try it. Make a square inch of paper filigree. Go on, I dare you. Know what? You'll give up in ten minutes. If you're like me, you'll get so mad you'll slam the whole load of paper shreds against the wall and storm out sulking to the tavern until you've cooled down.

No. Filigree takes application, skill, endlessly detailed work. Or loads of money, boredom, leisuretime. Or something much, much worse. I sweated, with fear.

As I lay there, hands behind my head and staring at the ceiling, I couldn't help listening to any sounds that might come from the next room. A few mutters, a single shrill scream of dementia from Guy, silence. No chance of sleeping any more tonight. I knew it.

When I next opened my eyes it was breakfast o'clock, the traffic was howling and daylight was pouring in. Shame hadn't really done with me yet. It pointed out that I'd awakened refreshed, you cad Lovejoy. I decided I was now willing to give my newly planned role a go. My jack-the-lad manner seemed to be working with Veronique, and anything that works with women is a must. What's a lifetime's liberal humanism between friends? I'd become the hard-liner, under Veronique's tender loving care.

So to Zurich, in clean, pristine, sterile, hand-rinsed, orderly Switzerland. To rob the biggest repository of saleable untraceable antiques in the world. The easy bit.

25

The meeting was billed, quaintly, as 'Promotion of Exemplary
New Arts'. I wanted to walk there, but Guy, sniffling and having
to blow his nose every minute, objected and we did a murderous
dash-stop-dash roar through the traffic. Zurich was lovely, fresh
and splendid after the sickness of worrisome lovely Paris. It
actually felt seaside, with the Limmit River running down to the
broad sunshiny lake, the Zurichsee. We went down the
Bahnhofstrasse – I was thrilled to notice the main railway station,
because that's where me and Lysette and Gobbie were to meet.
Guy dumped us off near the Rennweg. A sign up and left indicated
the tree-dotted mound.

'Have we time to climb up?' I asked Veronique. God, but she
dazzled this morning. You can understand the ancient Celts giving
up the ghost when tribes of great golden people like her hove in.
'Only, it's the ancient settlement of Zurich. We could see the
whole place!'

'No.' She paused, as near as she'd ever come to a hesitation.
'Lovejoy. What do you think of Guy?'

'For a psychotic murderous junkie he's okay.' I gauged her. The
traffic passed down to the Quaibrücke, that lovely waterside.
'Why?'

'When this is over, Guy and I will finish.' She looked away. 'You
are not spoken for, Lovejoy.'

More evidence that she'd accompanied her killer druggie to
Mentle Marina, otherwise how did she know I wasn't heavily
involved back in merry East Anglia?

'You mean. . . ?' She couldn't mean pair up. Not with me. I'm a
shoddy scruff. She was glorious, rich, attractive.

'You are an animal,' she admitted candidly. 'With an animal's
innocence. It is what I need.'

Why, the silly cow? I'd not even got a motor, nor money, unless
this job paid. Odd, but I noticed that the motors reaching the
traffic lights switched their engines off and sat in tidy silence until

the lights changed. Fantastic, something I'd never seen before. What did they do it for? Save petrol? If I did that to my old Ruby it'd block the traffic for miles, never get anywhere, needing cranking up at every amber-red.

'And do what?'

'Live, Lovejoy.' She nodded at the city. 'Grand, no? Wealthy, no? I want everything, every experience. Guy must go.'

Women have the finality of their convictions, know goodbye when they see it. In fact, that little skill of theirs has caused me a lot of trouble. But the way she spoke sent a shiver down me. It was almost as if –

'Let's go, folkses!' from Guy, practically dancing between us. The district was mostly banking, exclusive and affluent. That Exemplary New Arts notice was a laugh. I avoided Veronique's meaningful side glance, but in the end couldn't resist giving her one. Contact lenses show an oblique rim, only just, round the edge of the iris, don't they? You catch it, if the angle's just so. And coloured contact lenses show it most. I was the only one not in disguise.

The place was a plush room within a hall, a kind of enclosed box inside a larger assembly space. Exhibition? It reminded me of those set-ups railway modelling societies use to create atmosphere for their titchy displays. I'd also seen one used for war games, nearer the mark.

'You come with us, Lovejoy,' Veronique said. Guy was chatting, waving, slapping backs, reaching for swift handshakes. Around the hall, two beefy blokes at each exit, hands folded. Three were in uniform, talking intently into gadgets. Once you got in, there'd be no way out. Nor could anybody outside get close enough to listen. The box occupied the precise centre of the vast hall. Mausoleum? You get the idea, that degree of welcome.

'Morning, Lovejoy.' Troude, a handshake. Lovely Monique, aloof. No sign of Almira, no Paulie, no Jervis Galloway, MP. 'I want to thank you for the work you've done for us. Selecting the antiques we needed to buy at the Paris auctions, your Paris sweep, checking the suitability of the, ah, reproductions. You have earned a bonus.'

'Good morning, Monsieur Troude. Thank you.'

We did that no-after-you-please in the one doorway and

entered the darkened box. The door closed behind us with a thud. Colonel Marimee was on a dais, hands behind his back, facing the dozen or so folk already in. All were standing. Monique was beside him. It was lit with a single strip light. Battery operated, I saw with surprise. Couldn't they afford one from the mains? But a wandering flex breaches a wall, and this was –

'Soundproof, Lovejoy.' Philippe Troude was next to me, smiling. I'd been ogling. 'Swiss security, that they do so well. Banks, you see.'

'Good morning, ladies and gentlemen,' the Commandant rasped in French. This was his scene, everybody listening while he delivered battle plans. Monique translated *sotto voce* into English for the uneducated, mainly me I suppose.

The pair I'd met at that weird mansion-house garden party were standing nearby. I smiled a hello. They nodded back, tense. I felt my belly gripe. If they were worried sick, I ought to have at least a panic or two. Sweat sprang all over me.

The Colonel spoke. 'The event will be perfect. All has gone well.'

At Marimee's barks people looked at each other in relief. Satisfaction ruled. The audience was affluent, smooth, the women elegant. Dressing had cost a fortune. I expected a series of tactical maps to drop from the ceiling, red arrows sweeping around blue ones, but it was only the Colonel, in his element.

'There are two additional steps.' Marimee stared us all down. Drums should have begun, music pounding to a martial crescendo. 'First is financial. Another fourteen per cent is required from each syndicate member. Cash. Investment return will be commensurate. Immediate effect.'

A faint groan rose. I found myself groaning along, like a nerk. I hate that military phrase, as does anyone who's seen a reluctant soldier. This must be my doing, buying up Paris.

'*Mein Herr*,' some stout bespectacled put in. I noticed calculators were surreptitiously in action.

'No questions!' Marimee barked. 'The second step is accomplishment of the objective. Execution will be total effectivity.'

A cluster of three men, almost Marimee look-alikes except less showy, nearly smiled. The executors, if that was the word?

'That is all.'

'*Entschuldigen Sie bitte, Herr Colonel*,' the unhappy stout banker type said. I recognized a money man trying to wriggle out of spending.

'*Non*, Monsieur Tremp,' Marimee said in a muted voice. It shut us all up, groans and all. Except me.

To my alarm, I heard me say, '*Mon commandant*. I take it the items were all correctly bonded in Liechtenstein?'

'*Oui*, Lovejoy,' Monique Delebarre said evenly. But not before Marimee had hesitated. Him, whose first and last dither had been which breast when working up to his first suck. 'Thank you. That will be all,' Monique intoned.

We filed out of the stuffy little room, me asking Veronique if that was it. I'd felt claustrophobic in there.

The Cayman Islands, and little Liechtenstein, let you lob into bond any antique for seven measly days – then you can legally bring it out and legally sell it to anyone. (That's *legally*, got it?) In fact, you may even have sold it while it palely loitered. Our East Anglian antiques robbers love Liechtenstein because that one brief week gives us – sorry again; I meant *them* – time to forge a new provenance history, no more than a brief receipt, however sketchy, for the stolen antiques. Though nowadays everybody likes point-of-sale transfer, like in some Dutch or Belgian places that pay on the nail for any nicked Old Master, so making the sale legit. Zurich's bond currently is five years.

'What else is required, Lovejoy?' Veronique was smiling. 'How do you say, cold feet?'

'Cold feet, warm heart.' The best reply I could give. 'I thought we were going to get our orders, details and all that.'

'We have them, Lovejoy. The meeting confirms that all is on course.'

'For when?'

'For the time of execution. You heard the Commandant.' She smiled. Guy the burk was still chatting, prancing. Folk all around him were amused, in spite of the bad news about the kitty being upped. My belly warned me with an incapacitating gripe that execution has more than one meaning.

The hoods at the exits detained us until Marimee and his three clones left the security room. I was sick of all this cloak-and-dagger malarkey. I mean, why didn't Marimee just whisper his damned orders to us in the street? But pillocks like him feed on this sort of gunge.

They let us go in dribs and drabs, me and my couple last. Guy tried prattling to Marimee, but he ignored him except for one terse command I couldn't hear. It didn't quite bring Guy down through the Heaviside, but forced him into fawning agreement.

'Can I see the exhibition?' I asked Veronique. My plan was to bore Guy, literally, to vanishing point. 'Is it true the Kunsthaus has a Rembrandt? There are four galleries I want to go to. The Swiss National, the Landesmuseum, is a must, eh? It has workshops three centuries old from the Zurich arsenal! And I'm dying to see the Rietberg Museum.' Poisonously cheery, I knew my tactic would work, at least on Guy. Once I got rid of him, losing Veronique would be that much easier. 'Is it true its collection of Chinese art was got from East Berlin in a swap for Lenin's tea strainer? Then there's that other place called the Bührle Foundation. And St Oswald's . . .' I smiled an apology. Their eyes were already glazing. 'After all, one of ours, in a strange land, eh? I'll light a candle for him – if Swiss Lutherans are into ritual!' I chuckled into their shocked faces in the great foyer. 'Which first?'

It took an hour to shake Guy, then another to get rid of Veronique. We'd reached two of Hobbema's landscapes when he finally cracked. He'd been twitching some time when he took Veronique to one side and muttered through his sniffles. She let him go, came back to me with questions in her eyes. I took her arm and kept up my dreadful heartiness, yapping non-stop. She'd wondered if my enthusiasm had been a pretence, a ploy to get her alone. I was repellently obsessional, dragging her round the adjacent gardens to see the Henry Moores and Bourdelles.

'I'm not into Magritte and Ernst, that lot,' I told her, pulling her along. 'We'll leave the new extension, eh? Let's go up to the first floor. There's a Hans Fries, *Adoration of the Magi*. Have you seen it? Only, you just guess how many times the bloody thing's been varnished, and with what sort. Try! I'll give you three goes, but here's a clue: it *isn't* copal varnish. Know why? Because if you stand about four feet away, then look away and quickly look back, you'll see a kind of shimmer – '

She broke, to my relief. 'I'd better go and see how Guy

195

is, Lovejoy,' she said. 'Meet us at the hotel, supper tonight. Okay?'

'Okay,' I cried, giving her a ton of disappointment, riskily saying what if we get sudden orders, where on earth should I find them?

'Today's free, Lovejoy,' she said. 'There's one job for you tomorrow, then you're done.'

Done? my mind screamed as I grinned so long. Done *for*?

Cunningly, and I thought with skilled casualness, I mooched about to see her actually leave. Then I did a series of pretended quick looks in case she doubled back, or one of Marimee's goons was lurking somewhere in the art gallery. No sign. An hour later I walked openly to the main station, where Gobbie would be waiting, and Lysette Fotheringay. Return to normality.

Me and Gobbie were in the station when Lysette arrived. We were so cunning – in Information looking at these tiresome diagrams of railway networks – and simply walked away giving no sign. We went to a nosh bar – expensive, in Zurich – and apologized to each other for having to share a table. That legitimized our speaking together, my daft idea a kid could have seen through. Pathetic.

'Keep your voices down,' I warned them. Foreign languages carry; indigenous speech doesn't. It's always true. 'Say as little as possible. Good coffee.'

'Made proper Swiss style,' Lysette said with pride. 'Through filter papers, none of your French stewing process.'

I sighed. Two minutes, and already we were into national rivalry. 'Look, love. Cut that out, okay? I know we're in the most perfect, orderly, tidy, stable country in the world – '

Her face changed. 'You think so?'

'That's what they say, love.'. Her sudden ferocity made me uneasy, and I'd had enough of being that. 'It's going to be our main ally. Steady police force, trustworthy citizens. The slightest anomaly must stand out like a torch in a tomb – '

'Mr Veriker, would you excuse us, please?' Lysette said to Gobbie. I stared at him. His name was Gobbie, for heaven's sake. Everybody knew that. Well, well. Who'd think Gobbie'd go and grow a surname? Him, of all people. 'It seems that Lovejoy's even stupider than we both could possibly imagine.'

'Watch your frigging gob, Lysette.' I was getting narked. Nowt but birds with hobnailed tongues since I'd left home.

'Come, Lovejoy. Perhaps, Mr Veriker, you'd like to meet us here in an hour?'

We left. I trailed after, sheepish but madder. It would be obvious now to anybody that we knew each other. She went down into a shopping precinct underneath the railway station. It was posh, with splendid boutiques, auto-bank windows, luscious grub, imported knitwear, a veritable Bond Street of superb design. Really Swiss, I thought.

'Your arm, Lovejoy.'

'You sure?' I was still furious. Fair's fair, right? I hadn't asked to come just to help her and her frigging pansified brother . . .

'Change?' An apparition said it in three languages, holding out his hand. Maybe four, five. I wouldn't know.

'Er, aye.' I gave him some. He looked derelict, almost in rags, and filthy.

'Change?' Two more drifted at me from nowhere, hands out. Lysette yanked me aside and we moved on among the people.

They seemed mostly youngsters, huddled in mounds. One or two sprawled. Most sat at a crouch.

'You encourage them to mug you, Lovejoy,' Lysette said, keeping us walking. 'It's a real danger. They sleep here or in doorways up above. I know it happens in all cities – and in lovely neat Zurich.' She sounded bitter.

'Only here, though?' I asked. I knew that in India the railway stations are great social concourses.

She did not laugh, gave me a look of scorn. 'You think you have drug problems, Lovejoy? Nothing like ours. The diseases that accompany it offer the proof.'

'In Switzerland?' I didn't realize I'd spoken aloud.

'Yes, here. The capital.' She drew me to the escalator and we made the open air.

'A few homeless in a whole nation . . .' I faltered.

'How much evidence do you want, Lovejoy? The report from the parliamentary commission which investigated our Ministry of Justice? It found that secret police gangs had records of thirteen per cent of the entire Swiss population on file.' She gave a wintry smile. 'So many Swiss subversives!'

'Your Swiss police?' My plans took another tumble.

'Of course,' she said sweetly, 'the files vanished when the commission report became, shall we say, famous!' She guided me along the pavement. 'Possibly because the secret army we call P26 might have to be unmasked further.'

Either she was off her nut or my plans were even wronger. She hailed a taxi, still talking.

'Economy? All Europe's ills we Swiss have in abundance. Rising unemployment, inflation, poverty, falling home owner-ship . . .'

I won't tell you the rest, if that's all right. I'm not scared of such talk, but there's too much going wrong everywhere, and it shouldn't. A bird I once knew used to say mine was the typical ostrich mentality, but it's not. I just don't want to hear bad things, that's all. What's wrong with that? I didn't look at what she pointed out on that taxi ride, struggled to deafen myself, shut her horrible words out. Lysette went for reprimand.

'It's no good trying not to listén, Lovejoy,' she was telling me as we finally came back. 'Those people in the Platzspitz were mainliners, druggies, pushers, narcos. Needle Park, that place I showed you. It's an open drugs mart, free needles on the State in hopes of lowering the AIDS rate. The suppliers make a billion francs a year . . .'

'Alma-Tad,' my mind sang, 'oh, what a cad . . .'

'We have *Zahfräulein*, tooth ladies,' she was waxing. I tried putting my hands over my ears. She leaned closer, spoke more directly. The taxi driver must have thought us insane. 'Spot checks on children's teeth – so they can start out really healthy derelicts . . .'

Do women never shut up? 'Oh, I wandered today to the hill, Maggie,' my cortex warbled. Thank God, we were back near the Limmatplatz and its massive Migros supermarket with the orange M.

'The Migros?' She'd glimpsed my relieved recognition, rotten cow. 'Our famous store, all things to all men!' She scathed on. 'We Swiss are *so* docile! It is *1984*. Twenty-five per cent of us shop there daily . . .' We stopped at a traffic light, and I got out for air and freedom, leaving her to it.

She caught me up, no getting rid of her. I'd dithered, lost for direction. She took my arm. 'Switzerland has more drug OD deaths in six months than – '

'Love.' I stopped, broken. 'Please. I can't . . . I just, well *can't*. Don't you see? For Christ's sake.'

'You have social and political responsibility, Lovejoy – ' She sounded like Colonel Marimee, in her own mad way.

'Lysette. Let's part, eh? You your way, me mine. Bugger everybody.'

'Community obligations – '

'Aren't, love. They drive me insane. I can't take it. I can only escape. It's all I ever do.'

'He's right, miss,' Gobbie intruded, thank God. How the hell had he got here? 'Lovejoy's a scrounger, has to travel light or not at all. He's a weak reed, wet lettuce, broken straw.'

'Here, Gobbie.' Narked, I straightened from my supplication posture. There's a limit. I'm not that bad. A lady pedestrian spoke sharply to us. We'd been blocking the pavement.

'Lovejoy must be educated, Mr Veriker,' from good old sterling standard Lysette. I could have welted her one. Sociologically minded people once took over ancient Babylon, and we all know what happened then.

'No, Lysette. Educators everywhere ploughed that one.' I reached out and wrung her hand. 'This is it. Fare thee well, lass. Cheers, Gobbie.'

He came with me. I was only half surprised. They'd seemed like a going concern, somehow, and him four times her age.

'You were right, son,' he said consolingly. 'She's too wrapped up in do-goodery. Time for a jar?'

'Well, as long as I'd one ally I'd give it a go. I've been alone in scams often enough. We settled on the nearest thing we could find to a pub. It was the glossiest dearest pub I'd ever seen. We found a quiet corner, away from some blokes with feathers in their hats talking of some shooting club. The thinnest glass of ale I've ever had served. Gobbie tutted, grinned.

'They'd get scragged serving this in my local,' he said. I chuckled obediently, working out how to tell him. 'Pity you and her didn't get on, Lovejoy,' he said. 'Now, son. Where do I come in? She won't give up on you, mark my words.'

'I know, Gobbie. Let's try survival, eh?'

'If you say, Lovejoy.' He grinned, loving every minute of it when things were going wrong, like now. He must have been the greatest antiques runner on earth when younger. I hoped he was still. He was all I'd got. Maybe I should have gone for Mercy Mallock after all.

26

That evening I had supper with Guy and Veronique. I'd been dreading it. We had incomprehensible but superb grub, a wine that didn't give you heartburn, and talk that did. Guy was at his most manic, once having to be fetched down from standing on his chair to give the restaurant a song. Veronique was practised in handling him. Twice during the meal he had to dash out to stoke up on some gunja or other. In the latter of his absences Veronique unbent, spoke freer than she ever had.

'You can see how Guy has outlived his usefulness, Lovejoy. Do you blame me?'

My throat cleared for action. I wish I could think fast near women. 'Well, no.' He was getting on my nerves too, though you never know what goes on between a bird and her bloke.

'You and I will make a killing, Lovejoy,' she urged softly. 'Me: languages, knowing the dealers, the art thefts, the Continent's customs everywhere. You, a divvy.'

'I've not a bean, love.' The waiters fetched some pudding thing that started to dissolve before my eyes. I started on it frantically before its calories vanished altogether. She offered me hers, but only after she'd had the icing surround, selfish bitch. That's no way to start a love partnership.

'I have beans,' she said, smiling. 'Plus, we'll have a small fortune after the share-out.'

That old thing, I thought sardonically, but tried to look gullible. 'To do what?'

'Your job tomorrow's to go with Monique Delebarre, Lovejoy. To the Repository. It'll be simple for you. You'll be told to separately consign the antiques and fakes.'

Now that she'd actually said the word, my heart swelled. Only temporary, but my most reliable symptom of impending terror. It's not uncommon with me, I find. And it always seems to happen when some woman starts projecting her expectations. I wish I wasn't a prat, and had resolve, will-power, determination, things to help life on its merry way.

'Maybe in the next reincarnation,' I said, of her offer.

'No, Lovejoy. This.' She held my gaze quite levelly even though I could hear Guy on his way back, working the tables like a demented politician. 'You have no choice. I've already arranged it with the principal backers.'

A slave? Well, I'd had my careers. 'If I say no?'

'You can't, Lovejoy. And won't want to.' She made some signal to Guy, quite openly. He saw it, promptly seated himself at a small party and instantly had them in fits, ordering wines and clapping his hands at the waiters. 'It's antiques that I'm offering.' She smiled at her plate, up at me. 'And the bliss you need. I'm the one for you, Lovejoy.'

'Antiques?' More grub, this time small dainty sweetmeats laid out round the rim of an oval dish thing.

'Why do you think the syndicate chose furniture, Lovejoy?' I listened with a carefully arranged expression of unenlightenment. 'Think what's happened to paintings, art, and you'll be able to work it out for yourself.'

Bloody cheek, I thought. I drew breath to tell her so. 'Can I have yours?'

She pushed her grub across without breaking step. 'Art theft is done to order. Thieves pierce any gallery, museum – and simply select items like catalogue shopping. Think of the Isabella Stewart Gardner museum in Boston – Rembrandt's *Storm on the Sea of Galilee*, how many millions of dollars? And Vermeer's *The Concert*. They didn't steal cheapos.'

True, what she was saying. Even when museums are supposed to be burglar-proof they still get done. And it's all preselection nowadays, like the ramraiders me and Gobbie'd seen. The robbers know what they've come for.

'We'd be the best pair on the circuit, Lovejoy. You to browse, pinpoint the genuine masterpieces in the galleries, me to organize the thefts. It's my special gift.' Her eyes went dreamy, a lovely sight. Repletion was in the air between us, and so far today we'd not touched each other.

'Did you design this scam?' The words were out before I could think.

'This?' She almost laughed, but derision was dominant. '*This*,

Lovejoy? Do you know how long it has taken? Two *years*! Setting up factories in Marseilles, Birmingham and Bradford, Berlin, Amsterdam, Istanbul, Naples. Ptah!' She almost spat. 'That's your precious *this*, Lovejoy!'

Anywhere with a load of cheap immigrant labour. They'd be terrified out of their wits they'd be hoofed back to their home countries. People galore to work their lives away finishing off fakes with the same terrible effort our craftsmen had used two and three hundred years ago.

'But if it works, love . . .' I needled, for more. I could have killed her. I wish I'd not thought that now. Honest.

'An ox works, Lovejoy,' she said with that quiet intensity. 'A new Jaguar works swifter. I was against this scam from the start. I told them we must rob, instead of creating fakes.'

'Robbery's good,' I conceded, to goad her angry reminiscences further still. 'In East Anglia we finish a deal within forty-eight hours of doing a lift. I did one once – I mean, I knew somebody who did it – where we shipped the Constable painting in two hours flat, money in hand.' Money for Big John Sheehan, not for me, I was too aggrieved to say.

'Of course it's good! It's beautiful!' She almost climbed over the table in her vehemence. She poured me more wine. I drank it for the sake of appearances. 'And churches, galleries, museums – how often do they take stock, do inventories of what they have? Once every thirty years! That's survey-proved! Have you ever seen a private gallery with security worth a damn?'

More truths ripped from her tongue. I know because I was watching it closely. Banks go berserk if a penny is missing. Officers are cashiered for losing a regimental penny. The Exchequer burns the midnight oil over farthings. The Stock Exchange works dividends out to nine decimal places. But she was right. Paris's Notre Dame cathedral once learnt of a priceless sketch missing from its archives only when somebody overheard an American tourist saying he'd seen it in Washington.

'And thieves everywhere are incompetent!' She coursed on while I asked her for some more of that vanishing pudding. Well, you can cook too light, I find. 'Look at your London mob, over that Brueghel. Can you imagine?'

Well, yes. The lads had tried selling their stolen *Christ and the*

Woman taken in Adultery to the Courtauld. The trouble was, it actually belonged to the Courtauld Institute in the first place. But the cracks they came out with in court gave everybody a laugh, some less bitter than others. The ramraider had abused me and Gobbie: *I heard of you bastards*. Nobody's softer-hearted than a crook, and that's a fact. A scam that depended on working immigrants till they drop endears itself to nobody. Except possibly the Moniques and Colonel Marimees of this world. And, dare I say, to the Cissies. And Guys? Veroniques? Almiras? Subject peoples have always been used thus, time immemorial.

It explained why Jan Fotheringay got done. And maybe Baff. And, possibly, the great Leon too. Unwilling to go along with the business once they learned of the cruelty involved? Jan, in on it until he sickened of the whole thing – probably never having known enough of the horrendous manufacturing processes. Baff coming across it by accident when doing one of his breakdowners on Philippe Troude's country residence. His mica Appearances spy-master's kit was proof of that. It all fitted. And Leon because he'd sickened of it, seeing the holocaust by attrition first hand . . .

'. . . fuck, Lovejoy.'

Brought me back. 'Eh?'

'I was saying', she repeated calmly, signalling to Guy, who started a deliriously jokesy farewell from his newfound life-longers, 'that we must celebrate our partnership in the oldest way. In fact I insist, Lovejoy.' Her mouth shaped itself on her lipstick. I stared transfixed as she screwed the red lipstick from its sheath, my throat sphinctering on a spoonful. I hate symbolism. It's never the real thing.

'What about Guy?' I croaked eventually.

'Yesterday's news, Lovejoy.' She continued sweetly as Guy arrived breathlessly, 'Guy. I was just telling Lovejoy . . .' She smiled knowingly into me while I frantically tried to shut her up. '. . . how here in Zurich our newspapers help antiques robbers. No sooner does a theft hit the headlines than adverts appear saying things like *Desperately Seeking Gainsborough*, or *Come Home Spitweg All is Forgiven*. It's the Swiss way of making a blunt offer for the stolen masterwork. In Munich too, of course.'

Looking sideways at Guy, I tried to laugh convincingly for his sake. But it's still pathetic to visit an ancient church expecting to see the *Virgin of the Snows*, and instead see a blank frame. The saddest photograph ever published is *Time*'s, of an Italian pastor with his candle next to a framed photo of that missing masterpiece. She was right. We'd make a formidable partnership, a killing as they say.

We cemented our relationship that night. I allowed a decent interval, four seconds, before deciding to admit her when she tried the door. This is where I should report that I resisted her advances, stood firm against her seductive wiles, but can't. Shame and guilt were trumped in a trice. I relished every moment, and she seemed delighted at my willingness. Passion's nothing going for it except its total ecstasy, paradisical joy unbounded. I have a hundred logics that end up with me forgiven for each sexual transgression; they all depend on it being the woman's fault. Next morning, Veronique was purring, her wig on the pillow beside her. She was a redhead, I saw with shock. Her eyes were dark brown.

'Hello, stranger,' were her first words. 'Going to give me breakfast?'

Guy and Veronique, blond and blue-eyed as ever, delivered me – I almost said delivered me up – to Monique's huge saloon motor at nine-thirty precisely. Veronique seemed chilled, though it was quite mild. She huddled in a swagger jacket, breathing through her teeth the way women do when telling the weather off. Skilled with cosmetics, she'd disguised her neck bruises, thank God. She had kitted me out at an expensive outfitters along Pelikanstrasse. I felt done up like a tuppeny rabbit.

'You know the drill, Lovejoy,' Veronique told me as the limo drew in. 'Say nothing. Agree with Monique whatever she says. Pick out the genuine antiques. A list will be given you at the Repository. Allocate our fakes to storage, and our genuine antiques for forward shipment. That's all you do. Any questions?'

'Then what?'

Veronique smiled. She was worn out, quite on edge. I felt my spirits lifting by the minute now it was starting.

'Then you report to me.' Guy looked worse than the pair of us put together, and he'd had a good night's sleep. I wondered what he looked like without his wig, his coloured contacts, his meticulous make-up. He was beyond hearing, all senses stultified.

'I've planned for us, Lovejoy.'

'Right. How long'll I be?'

'Until Monique says, Lovejoy. We'll be here. Guy.' His name was like an order. Obediently he tried to pay attention, but it was a sorry show. *You see, Lovejoy?* Veronique's eyes asked me.

The driver was one of the hulks who'd guarded Marimee's briefing. He said nothing, flattened me against the upholstery by the force of his acceleration. I felt lonely, odd to relate, legitimately free of my watchdogs for the first time.

'Far to go, have we?' I tried, but got nothing from Suit. His neck was roll upon roll of fat. Underneath would be solid gristle. I'd never tangle with such as he. I sighed, settled back for the ride. Another giver of orders, for immediate compliance.

It was not all that long. Countryside abounds in Switzerland. Mind you, after Lysette's tour of Zurich's grotty grottoes I found that I wasn't as animose to the boring hills as usual. The Alps can be seen from the city, and I was pleased to get glimpses as we drove. Sherlock Holmes, though, said there's more sin in pretty countryside than in any sordid town.

A small village or two out, the motor pulled in and I was transferred to an even huger motor. It contained Monique.

'Morning,' I said. The Suit shoved me. I almost fell in. No reply. I sat as far away from her as possible. Never disturb a wasps' nest. A glamorous nest, though. Bonny hair, with a small hat bordering on insolence. You know that sort of encased, sheathed look some women achieve in a smart suit? Well, Monique achieved exactly that. The despond I'd felt when seeing her the first time, at Mentle Marina, returned in waves. Seeing a brilliant woman you know you'll never have always gets me down.

'Lovejoy,' she said, speaking slowly as if to an idiot. I was surprised. My name had never sounded nice before. Now I quite liked it. 'You have one task this morning.'

'To agree.'

'To obey.' A pause for it to sink in. We were driving along a narrow road. I could glimpse a lake, very beautiful. 'The Repository. You know it?'

'Of it, yes.' Taking the silence as invitation to continue, I went

206

diffidently on. 'The world's great auction houses need a place where antiques can be safely stored. It charges buyers, vendors, antique dealers, so much a month.'

'Yes.'

More silence, so okay. 'It's security city, really. Vast. You buy an antique anywhere in the world, ship it to the Repository, and simply leave it there. Then sell it, raise loans on it, barter it, all without it moving it an inch. The bills of sale are currency among legits and crooks alike, like dollars.' I began to wax eloquent. 'They say that the world's drug money is laundered via antiques in the Repository while the antiques simply remain there under lock and key. Great scheme. And legal! I've seen a possession note change hands for almost half a million pounds, for a George III bureau owned by a SARL – that's a *société à responsibilité limitée* . . .'

Her eyes held me. I managed silence at last. I'm like this, stupidly unable to stop gabbing, a puppy trying to impress its luscious mistress. Pathetic. Plus I was scared.

She looked out of the window. 'Who is the woman, Lovejoy?'

'Woman?' She knew Veronique, because Veronique was her employee. Therefore . . . 'She's a bird – er, a girl I met.' I didn't say where. Lysette, she meant Lysette. And Gobbie?

'Where?' She was indifferent. The motor slowed on a steep incline, turned at the top. Lake, trees, distant snow.

'Actually in Paris. She's moving to Switzerland, with, er, her grandad. She's here in Zurich now.' I felt stripped, started a cringe of evasion. 'Look, Monique. You don't know what it's like. I'm living like a monk. She's the only chance – '

'Veronique.' Flat, bored. 'You've had Veronique.'

'Yes, well.' I tried hard for moral rectitude. 'I don't want to say things about her when she's not here, but I think sometimes . . . I think her bloke Guy's on drugs. It puts me off. Maybe she shares the habit. You understand?'

'Brother.'

'Eh?' That made me draw breath. Then exhale. Then inhale. Then exhale. 'Eh?'

'Her duty was to maintain you.' Was it still mere flat indifference, or was malevolence creeping in?

'Oh, she did! She did!' I chuckled, only it came out octaves wrong. 'Honestly, we've had a whale of a time . . .'

'Stop it, Lovejoy.' I stopped it, listened soberly. 'Today, we are dealers sending in a mass of antiques. They are of course the fakes, reproductions, simulants of the type you approved in Paris. The best of our manufacture. You will mark them for storage. Any that are authentic, genuine antiques, you will mark as requiring shipment. Understand?'

'Forgeries into store, trues for shipment. A bar?' Her eyebrows rose a fraction. I explained, 'Do I cut off the process at a certain number?'

'Gambling term.' Her mind, classifying away. She must find scruffs like me fascinating specimens. No wonder she was bored by everything. I was narked. I'm no arthropod. Time to tell her.

'Because', I found myself giving out nastily, 'we don't want them stealing the wrong lot, do we?'

'Stealing?'

'Your loony colonel's going to pinch the lot, Monique – the forgeries, that is. Plain as the nose – er, as a pikestaff. A kid could see that. Dollop a cran full of fakes. Make sure the Repository catalogues them as genuines. Then get a mad mob to storm the building, pinch the fakes, and claim on the insurance.' It's called a spang in our talk, but telling her so would only set her etymology off again. 'The insurers'll naturally investigate the ones left untouched. Which will of course be the authentic genuine lot I earmark, right?'

She was smiling! Summer radiance covered the motor's interior. I swear she actually emitted light from her eyes like mediaeval saints did. It was really quite dazzling, for somebody evil.

'I'd hoped for something really original,' I went on, though now less shakily. 'The only original thing is the way you've manufactured the fakes. Immigrants, virtual slaves.'

'I did wonder,' she said. It was all so academic. 'You are sympathetic, Lovejoy. You see nothing of what is at stake.'

'I do not care for what is at stake.' I spoke it from an elocution class I'd never attended. I'd got calmer the more amused she'd become. 'Your syndicate are mad. You *imagine* the issue. It is simply not there.'

'We are here, Lovejoy.' The car was pulling in. 'Your name is Henry Getty. No relation.'

Getty? 'And yours?'

She nearly smiled. 'Mrs Monique Getty. We are married six years, are American, and own the collection we are now depositing.'

Three people advanced to meet us, stylish but sober. The Repository serfs, bright with beams of monetary affection.

'Wait for the chauffeur, Lovejoy.'

Mistake. I'd started to get out unassisted. 'Henry, dwoorlink,' I shot back, stung. 'My name's for my friends.'

Best I could manage, as the door opened and we went forward into the great unknown.

27

'Lorela Chevalier,' the woman said, smart as a pin, steady eyes. Not much change out of her, I thought, giving her my innocent millionaire smile and shaking hands. The other two proved mere serfs, oiling ahead to open doors, snapping into squawk-boxes. 'Repository Director.'

A woman of few words? I wasn't too sure I liked such novelties, but showed willing.

'Getty No Relation,' I said, typecast buffoon. 'Trade you Henry for Lorela. Deal?'

'How charming!' she exclaimed, but it was very practised and she kept her eyes on Monique. Women spot where power lies. I was instantly relegated, second-division status.

'Madame Getty,' I said lamely, out of it.

'How do you do,' from Monique, no sudden friendships on offer from Monique, thank you.

'Madame. You received our charges, conditions, prerequisites . . . ?'

'Certainly.' We moved gently towards the house, me depressed because they'd slipped into French. Lorela broke off to spout a command in sideways German before continuing handling us. A lovely scoop of a face, the sort you'd trust instantly if she wasn't in antiques. I was among polyglots, handicapped by being an idiot in my own language let alone everybody else's.

The house was the carousel one we'd had that garden party in. Except it wasn't. I bet myself that this one would stay still. A disturbingly similar mansion house, in unsettlingly similar grounds. Copses, statues, lawns, everything within four hundred yards was uncannily similar. Only the sun was angled differently. I inspected the great pile as we strolled chatting along the terrace. Yes, virtually identical. The Commandant had done his groundwork well, down to the shape of the windows, doors, type of brick, even a stone buttress reinforcing the west wing. Typical military: prepare a model, then a precise life-size mock-up of the objective. Then go to war.

'Lovely house, Lorela,' I interrupted. Monique smiled with woman's complicity at the director. 'Been here long?'

'Twenty years,' from Lorela. 'The building's history, cited you'll recollect on the information we dispatched to you, is rather briefer than first-time visitors usually assume from the exterior.'

'Like many!' I chuckled. 'We've two or three phoneys too. Right, honey?' I gave Monique a squeeze. She didn't have me gunned down, but her stare lasered a hole in my skull. 'In Santa Monica Mountains.' I nudged Monique. 'Neeky here complains it's too near J. Paul Getty – you've heard of that architectural shambles down those foothills? Everybody's laughing at it.'

'They are?' Cool, cool Ms Chevalier. 'Isn't it a breathtaking concept? What did they describe it as, a secular monastery?'

I laughed, putting a sneer in. 'I'm not being critical, 'Rela, when I say that J. Paul G.'s a cardboard cut-out of the real thing – which real thing is *me*! But d'you see any de-light in having to go to Malibu to see the statues, then crawl up a Los Angeles hilltop for one of Cousin P.'s daubs?'

'Henry,' Monique said sweetly. 'Remember what we decided!'

'Right, Moneekee, right!' Buffoon, grinning, winking. I was repellent. 'No relation!'

'Fully understood,' Lorela said in her slightly American accent. Thank God they'd lapsed into English. (Hang on – why did I register that they'd *slipped* into French, but then *lapsed* into English?) 'You have brilliantly covered your origins, if I may say.' To Monique's raised eyebrows she smoothly added, 'Madame Getty will recall the security cover, detailed in the blue appendix to our advice brochures – '

'You excavate all possible approaches.' Monique nodded. 'I'm relieved to hear that our incognito status held up.'

'It's the reason we chose the Repository,' I cut in. 'In spite of your charges. They'm punishment, 'Rela, hon!'

We moved into the grand hall. Balcony, sweeping staircase, hall windows. Identical. Good old Colonel Marimee. His team only needed to stay a week at his country mansion to be able to creep in here at night and move around blindfold. Brilliant. Lorela, her Repository Director's horns out, instantly launched into a spirited defence of her fees.

'There are so many expenses!' she battled. 'You must be aware

211

of the vast intelligence network the Repository must operate? All staff are security cleared. We have sixteen electronic, seven non-electronic auto systems – '

'You come strongly recommended, Ms Chevalier,' Monique said, which got me narked. Here was I getting the whole dump's security details, and she shuts her up. That's women all over. They can't plan. And nothing needs planning like a robbery. Hers or mine.

'Thank you, Madame,' from Lorela, leading us with the career woman's defined walk into a drawing room. She hadn't finished with me. 'You could go to cheaper . . . firms.' She hated having to mention competitors. 'Christie's, Bonhams, or – '

'Sotheby's Freeport Geneva, right? Lucky Number 13, Quai du Mont-Blanc?' I gave a sharp bark, digging Monique in the ribs. 'She hates the enemy, notice that? Trying to sound they's all co*lleagues*! I like it! Commitment! Hustle, hustle, make a buck!'

Lorela gave a glacial nod. Serfs ushered coffee, chocolates, those small sweet things that get your stomach all excited but turn out to be teasing promises. The silver was modern, I noticed, and therefore gunge. Why not go the whole hog, serve plastic from Burger Boss? I scrounged some edibles from habit. The women pretended to taste one. I often wonder if birds think noshing vulgar. 'The difference is that the Repository is *the* Repository, not merely one more imitation.' I whooped in glee at her cool claim to superiority. Lorela Chevalier appraised me levelly. 'We have never, never ever, been burgled, Mr Getty. Other firms have. Which is not to say', she added, critically inspecting a maid's skill pouring coffee, 'that attempts haven't been made.'

'Henry adores the ins and outs of commerce,' Monique said distantly, to effect repair.

'Not me, Mow-Neekee.' I wouldn't leave the subject. 'Hate any kind of work.' I leered grossly at Lorela. 'Except one – know what I mean?'

'Your requirements, Madame,' La Chevalier said, struggling on under my barrage of vulgarity. 'Your possessions are to be in two lots, I understand. One group for shipment to a destination to be notified. One, much larger, group for storage until further notice.'

'Correct.' Monique held a cigarette for villeins to hurl platinum lighters at. 'My husband has decided he will select which antiques will go into which group.' She let her withering scorn for me show, peekaboo.

Lorela smiled, offered me more of the vaporous grub fragments. I took the dish from her, irritated, and had the lot, getting hungrier with each mouthful. What narked me was the cleverness of Monique's ploy. Spring my new identity on me at the last minute, as we enter the Repository, and I'd have no time to devise any alternative ploys. She'd say the play. Me dolt, her the brain – and that's how Lorela was registering us. I'd done exactly as Monique planned. For the first time I really began to wonder how far they were willing to go in all this, and felt truly disturbed. I was on a raft in the rapids.

'Your shipments are already in the motor park, Madame,' Lorela said. 'My apologies for the delay. The Repository insists on a thorough security scan of each vehicle before it can proceed to our unloading bays.'

'Had trouble?' I asked, an oaf trying to be shrewd.

'Over seventy robbery attempts in the past two years, Henry.' No harm in first names now the two women had tacitly agreed on my being a transparent idiot. 'Robbers hiding in bureaux, silence-activated robots sealed in a Sheraton commode.'

I brightened. I'd not heard of a silence-activated robot before. First chance I got, I'd ask Torsion back home if he could knock me one up, have a go at the Ipswich depot. Or had they already tried it in Newcastle? They're very innovative up there. Torsion's a Manchester brain, thinks only electronics.

'How long was its trigger mode?' I tried to work it out. 'They used a robot cable-cutter for that Commercial Street spang. It went wrong. Remote control's overrated, I reckon – '

'Henry.' Monique viciously stabbed a phoney Lalique-style ashtray with the burning point of her cigarette, and rose. 'You don't want to tire Miss Chevalier with your famous stories. We'll get on. Come, Henry.' Like come, Paulie.

And they were off, speaking in German, French, anything but my lingo. I crammed the few remaining petits fours in my pocket to eke out life, and followed. I was right – anybody could do this, any time, anywhere. They didn't need me. Maybe, the intriguing thought came as we descended in a lift, they were making sure I wasn't employed by rival thieves? Now there's a thought . . .

Except, I saw as we went through doors on to a long wide loading platform, there was room for no fewer than six furniture pantechnicons backed up the ramp. Simulated daylight – never quite right to look at antiques by, but next best if rigged by experts. And clerks on old-fashioned high stools at tall Dickensian teller desks, snooping on all they surveyed. A humorous touch: their pens had prominent feathers. I smiled, not fooled. Every pen and pinna would be wired for sight, sound, gunfire.

'Simultaneous, then, Lorela?'

I laughed. A team of blokes in tan overalls were unloading the vans as they went. One queue of whifflers, antiques shifters, nurtured the antiques on to auto-trolleys, forming up at the end of the loading bay. There was no sound except the grunts and murmurs of the men. No fatties, no beer guts. They looked a fit lot. Thirty? With the clerks, about that.

'Queue theory, Henry,' Lorela replied without blanching. 'One line moves more expeditiously than several.' She ushered me and Monique to the head of the column. Two wall vents were already running conveyor walkways, each as wide as the lane leading to my cottage. One exit was painted yellow, one black. 'Here you will select the destinations, and check that your antiques have all arrived undamaged.'

'Well planned, Lorela!' I was starting to dislike this bird. There's such a thing as being too efficient.

'Your antiques for shipment along the yellow conveyor, storage into the black.'

'Excellent,' I said. 'Where do they lead?'

'That information is classified, Henry.' She smiled, indicated the workers. Not in front of the hired help. 'Personnel are not entitled to details that are inessential for their work sector. When you have finished, you shall be shown.'

'And the security?' I asked. 'Can't be too careful!'

Monique could have throttled me, which told me what I wanted to know. 'That I'm sure is also classified, Henry. Hadn't we better get on?'

When a woman says 'we' like that, she means you, not her.

'Sure thang.' I called for bourbon, though I can't stand the stuff, shouting let's get the hell on with it, and shelled my jacket, shoving a clerk off his stool. 'Hey!' I called as the vannies wheeled the first antique on to a disc-shaped area down below and stood waiting in the pool of light. 'Hey, Monique! All I need here's a green eyeshade to be calling the shots in the pool championship! Remember that time in Reno, Nevada?'

'Would Madame like to inspect our display of Japanese art upstairs?' Lorela suggested gracefully, signalling for the work to begin. 'I hope Madame will not be disappointed . . .'

'Thank you.'

There'd be trouble after this. I could tell from the way Monique walked, slightly faster than usual, straight as a die. Women don't walk straight as a rule, unless they're blind with rage. Check it. Watch a woman on any pavement, she proceeds anywhere but directly forward. Women waver, men walk ahead. It drives me mad when I'm in a hurry, always get stuck behind a bird and have to duck into the roadway at peril of losing my life simply to get past. Monique walked straight. Ergo, furious. And who at? I was doing my best, for God's sake. I mean, all this trouble just to case a storage dump was barmy. Mad military overkill.

'Okay, men,' I told the waiting crews of vannies. 'Zoom on.'

'One, Monsieur.' The first pair wheeled their trolley forward into the cone of light, halted.

'Turn it round, please.'

The men stepped aside. The floor revolved slowly, the piece revolving at viewing pace. An inbuilt turntable. Screens on the ceiling announced the piece's weight, the relative humidity, temperature, reflectances, dimensions scanned from a million angles. Equinoctial phases of the moon in Burundi too, I shouldn't wonder. Never seen so much data, and more searchlights than the Edinburgh Tattoo. Even the floor was illuminated, like in coffee dances. Monique and Lorela had gone. I relaxed.

'Look, lads,' I announced. 'I don't want a frigging circus. Just enough light to see the items. Switch off, and for Christ's sake stop everything spinning round.'

In silence, checking that I meant what I said, the clerks made the screens vanish to where good screens go. The lights dimmed to partially blinding.

'No frigging ears in your heads?' I yelled, really getting narked at their hesitancy. I slid off my perch and walked about, pointing. Turn that off, leave that on. Honest, you'd think this lot had never seen an antique in their lives, let alone handled daily intakes of the world's most precious antiques. I wouldn't have got so wild, except the first was a genuine card table, William IV, of the rare kingwood so dark it was almost purple. And not stained with a single dye! Lovely fold-over pattern, plain as King Billy himself always loved furniture to be. Dealers call these 'Adelaide tables', but the Queen had nowt to do with progress except import the Christmas tree to our fair land.

'Right.' I swarmed back up, looked along the clerks similarly perched, down at the whifflers in their tan overalls. Like a Le Mans starting grid, except this was interesting and important, and motor racing never can be. 'Light down to daylight candlepower. Floor still. No information.' And antiques somewhere around. Ready, steady.

Genuine. For a second I let myself bask in its warm glow, then came to. Into the yellow conveyor, right? Wasn't that the way round? Genuine antiques for shipment, fakes into the black for storage? I had to think to make sure.

'Down the yellow chute, lads.'

The pair wheeled the card table up the ramp, and unloaded it through the yellow entrance. A man accompanied it on the conveyor, standing like a moving duck on a fairground shoot, out of sight. You couldn't moan that lovely Lorela Chevalier was disorganized. Her – sorry, *the* – Repository ran like clockwork. No chinks, no loose cogs. I felt myself becoming intrigued. How was Colonel Marimee going to raid this place, get this lot out? Nearly four dozen vanloads, plus what was already here. Beyond belief for size. I felt proud to be in on a scam this big. It'd set them by the ears at the White Hart.

'Two, Monsieur.'

Marble-topped table, Dresden manufacture about 1729, give or take. Hoof feet, 'Indian' masks high on the table's knees to show trendy obsession with the cult of the Americas. Gilt gesso, very flash, beautifully preserved. Dealers would advertise it as mint. Except it was fake. Phoney, false, dud, it was still exquisitely made, by all the same old processes that the ancient craftsmen had used, in their hellish conditions . . .

'Eh? Oh.' Somebody had asked me what I'd muttered. I gave my glittering grin, but mirthless. 'Black. Storage, please. Next.'

And the next. Next. And next. Genuine down the yellow conveyor, false down the black.

An hour or so, I called a halt for a stretch. Clearly, I was here as a double-check, that the vannies hadn't pulled a switch somewhere along the way, right? Otherwise, anybody could have done it. Just sit there, sending our genuine antiques, the ones I'd bought in Paris or ordered Guy and Veronique to arrange bids for through the Hôtel Drouot auctions, down the yellow path, and the zillion fakes – which merely meant any others – down the black. I didn't feel proud, perched there saying 'Yellow', and 'Black' with the blokes sweating and lifting, trolleying the pieces in the viewing area.

Except it got easier when we resumed. The small items started coming sooner than I expected. But there was a mistake. It happened after I ordered a restart. The whifflers placed a plant stand, quite well made but modern and therefore dross, in the circle, and stepped away while the disc rose like an ancient cinema organ from the floor until it reached my eye-level, four feet away. Steps raked alongside so they could reach up. Then they brought in a small box I didn't recognize. By which I mean I really truly did.

It sat there, smiling, mystic, wondrous.

Dilemma-time. I'd not picked this little box out in Paris, at Monsieur Jacques Dreyfus's auction place, at the antique shops when I'd gone ape and bought everything genuine I could see. Therefore it should be fake, right? That was Monique's and Marimee's infallible plan. Me to buy the genuines, the syndicate to manufacture fakes. By separating the genuine antiques from the mass of fakes, I'd earn my percentage of this superb, flawless scam pay-out time. I'd got it right, hadn't I?

Now this box.

Onward shipment, the antiques I'd earmarked in Paris, right? All of which I'd seen, right? Therefore, I should recognize each and every single genuine antique, right? No problem.

The box looked at me. I looked at the box.

And, the Troude-Marimee-Monique scam scenario went, Lovejoy would funnel the fakes one way, and the genuine antiques, all familiar friends, the other. Okay?

The box sat there, waiting.

Now, I had my orders so firm I'd no doubts about what would happen if I disobeyed. Look at poor Baff. Look at poor old Leon. Look at Jan. I didn't want it to be look at poor Lovejoy. The rule was, make no changes. Monique said so. Guy and Veronique had been terrified out of their drug-sozzled wits when I'd bent them ever so slightly. The rule? Genuine antiques, ship; the fakes, storage.

The box smiled.

Genuine, pristine, beautiful, antique – *and I'd never seen it before*. It ought to be fake, so chuted down the black conveyor. Except it was genuine. So down the yellow. Except I'd never clapped eyes on it. So down the black. Except I recognised it. So yellow.

The box beamed. I smiled back. *Wotcher, Jamie* my mind went. 'Monsieur?' a puzzled vannie said.

'Sorry, mate. *Un moment*, please.'

A snuffbox, the colour of old tea, decorated with a simple engraved leaf. Not much to look at, maybe, but the genius that made it was one of the most lovely souls who ever lived. Yonks ago, it was the fashion to go and visit this crippled lad – legs paralysed as a child – in Laurencekirk. He had a great circular bed, and thereon he was stuck, for life. It had shelves, lathes, tool racks, a workbench, all within reach. There, this game youth made these boxes, plus others for tobacco, tea, needles, wools. He even made furniture, and unbelievably cased some clocks, worked in metal and engraved glass. His dander up, he stormed on making violins, flutes, even nautical instruments. A veritable ball of fire, was little crippled lame game James Sandy of Laurencekirk on his circular bed.

Even better, children used to bring him birds' eggs from the surrounding countryside – it's between Montrose and Stonehaven in what I, and others who also haven't yet lost their wits, still call Kincardine. Spectacularly, James Sandy used to hatch these eggs with the warmth of his body, then feed the fledglings and release them to the wild. Can you think of a more beautiful life? Especially considering how oppressed his dauntless spirit must have been?

'Monsieur?'

'Sorry, pardon, *entshooldigan*, er, I've a cold coming. *Un malade*.' I coughed, came to.

Jamie Sandy invented an invisible wooden hinge held by a small transfixing brass pin. Practically airtight, it was highly prized, since your pricey spice or costly snuff never lost its flavour. Eventually, their manufacture centred on Mauchline in Ayr under the Smith brothers during the Napoleonic Wars. Whole societies of collectors now fight over napkin rings, pipes, ring trees, walking sticks, all Mauchline ware in sycamore. But the real gems are these originals, made plain by little James Sandy in Laurencekirk. Okay, so they were only copies of touristy trinkets filched from Spa in Belgium. And okay, so it was a deliberate act of head-hunting when Lord Gardenston enticed a Spa souvenir-carver from the Low Countries to show the Laurencekirk locals how. But what's wrong with that? It produced one of the loveliest geniuses in that age of geniuses. It'd even be worth going to boring old Heaven one day, just to meet James Sandy.

This wasn't one of your machine-mades. Nor one of the Mauchline-ware sycamores with their nicotine-coloured varnished transfer-prints of Skegness. This was exquisite, by the original hand of an immortal. I looked away, uncomfortable. My duty was to stick to Monique's rule: fail to recognize an item, label it a fake and chute it down the black conveyor to storage.

And call James Sandy's work fake? Bloody cheek.

'Yellow,' I heard myself say calmly. Yellow for genuine, authentic, superb. Hang the cost. I could argue the genius's case any day of the week, even with Monique Delebarre and Colonel Marimee, Philippe Troude. And sighed as the bloke nodded and made for the ramp carrying Sandy's wondrous skill. Once a fool, as they say.

'Next, Monsieurs,' my voice went through a great calm. And so signalled the death of somebody I knew, somebody I shouldn't have killed at all, among the rest.

28

We were given a splendid tour. That is, we were finally shown our own stuff *in situ*.

'Vibration-proof,' Lorela Chevalier said, spinning in a doorway. 'Double reinforced glass, triple-access doors, tacky mats against quartz dust.'

'Thermal control a particular reliability?' I asked.

She darted me a hesitant smile, tried to make it genuine. 'Of course, Henry. Barometric pressure . . .' She started a routine prattle, from the Repository catalogue. I could have said most of it with her. Tonto MacIlvenny, our specialist blammer – destructive break-in artist who does over antique dealers' shops throughout East Anglia, but who charges travel expenses from our village – always carries a copy. It's a joke in the Arcade for the dealers to chorus bits from it when Tonto's done over some rival the night previous.

'Walls specially constructed to provide an – '

– effective barrier against any attempted intrusion, whether direct or by undermining, my memory trolled along. God, I could even remember where the catalogue's punctuation went wrong.

' – thus proving the most reliable storage system available.' Lorela got desperately brighter, sensing something amiss. 'These are coupled with a special security staff selected after – '

What would con artists do without the word 'special'? Not quite so well, that's what.

We endured the tour. We saw our genuine antiques being marked *Shipment! To Be Notified!* through milky glass panelling, in a split-level storage compartment, the grimmest half-acre of protection I'd ever seen. I tried to look impressed. We peered through the thickest wobble glass on earth at where our superb fakes were being shrouded, ticketed, arranged, coded.

'Why's the storage separate from the others?' I asked, innocent. We'd come down a mile of corridors.

'The vehicles, Henry,' Lorela answered, having recovered from that twinge of doubt. 'It saves on moving shipment articles twice. Though,' she quickly added, 'the Repository is fully insured at Lloyd's against any kind of . . .'

And so to bed. We were offered nosh, which Monique declined, maddening me. It's all right for them, but no sympathy for a hungry bloke who needs regular stoking.

'No, thank you, Miss Chevalier,' Monique said. 'Henry has other duties today.'

A cat can look at a king, they say. Ballocks, I thought morosely, following Monique meekly out to our Rolls. Monique'd vaporize me if I so much as mentioned lust, love, sex, desire, passion . . . Passion? I watched her, more than the entourage who assembled to wave us off. Passion? Monique must be moved by something akin to it, to go to all this trouble. I made my *merci-beaucoups* and waved absent goodbyes to Lorela.

'How long'd it take you, Monique, setting it up?'

'Two long years, Lovejoy.' She settled back into the plush upholstery, practically purring. Replete? 'Your infantile behaviour in there almost wrecked it.' She turned lazy eyes on me. 'For a moment I wondered what you were up to.'

'Eh?' I gaped. 'I was helping, for Christ's sake! You women. I got all sorts of stuff out of her. You'd never have noticed the infra-reds, heat-activateds, periodic blips – '

She smiled, eclipsing the sun's reflected dazzle from the lake. I swallowed, had to look away. 'You did quite well, I suppose.'

But it wouldn't have mattered if you hadn't done a damned thing, Lovejoy. That's what she was saying. Once I'd divided the wheat from the chaff, my usefulness had ended. For good. The security of the entire Repository was somehow irrelevant. But why? Colonel Marimee and his merry men were going to raid it, steal everything I'd just sorted through. As if divining my worry, she asked, 'Can you remember the security detail, Lovejoy?'

I erupted. 'What the hell d'you think I was winkling them out of her for, silly cow?'

She laughed, and the sun followed its reflection into shade. No wonder poor Philippe Troude was hooked on her for life. But what's the use of living in an orchard if you can only admire the apples, never taste? Except blokes are funny. They'll starve in a prison of their own making rather than walk away to freedom. We have a bloke in our village plays a euphonium, the same musical phrase over and over, hour after hour. People say he's loony, but he's not. I asked him why didn't he learn something else, whereon he instantly played me the loveliest solo I'd ever heard. The phrase he keeps playing – still does – is one he wronged in a band concert ten, twelve years ago. Came in half a bar late. His silver band lost the championship. Ever since, he's played alone in his cottage, sadly getting it perfect, year after punishing year. He explained it all, anxiously bringing out the tattered music, showing me why his calamitous mistake wasn't really his fault. I said why not forget it, and simply join a new band. He looked at me like I was an idiot. See what I mean? Like Troude, languishing in Monique's disinterest instead of reaching out for Jodie Danglass who was crazy for him, or Diana, who was crazy for him. Or Almira WWCFH. Or Cissie, W. *et* eponymous *cetera*.

'Here, Monique. Why don't you let Troude off the hook?'

She stared at me. The Rolls drifted round a bend. 'I beg your pardon?' (No, not like that, more I *beg* your . . .) Meaning I was insolent. Women manage talk better than us. Maybe that's why we don't say as much as they do. Meaning talk as often. The thought lost itself in my labyrinthine mind.

'Jodie'd snap him up any day of the week. I can't honestly see the point.'

'Who?' She was astonished at what I was asking.

'The antique dealer, Jodie. Brought me to Mentle Marina that time. You tried hoodwinking me over that ancient model boat, the chair.'

'The woman?'

'Didn't you ever notice her, you selfish bi– ?' I cut off, humming and hawing my way out to safety. 'She's a friend. Was. Almost was.' And added lamely, 'Once.'

She said nothing, looked. Then clicked an intercom and gave Suit's pendulous nape directions in, what, sort of French.

We drove to a place overlooking a massive lake. Took us an hour to get there, which I could ill afford. I was desperate to meet Gobbie, see how many pantechnicons he'd counted. If Lysette had done her job, she'd have followed them, and I'd know all.

'Where are we?' We alighted at a beautiful vantage point. The restaurant overlooked a promontory, some sort of turrets visible below, a few pretty houses, trees. A tiny steamer drew a dark mathematical wake in the shimmer.

No answer, just a stroll into this expensive place. They swept aside the need for reservation, awarded us the table Monique went to as a matter of course. I followed, wondering if any second I was going to get the elbow. Suit reduced daylight near the doorway, standing motionless. She ordered, offering me the choice but deciding everything, the way they do.

'Lovejoy.' Here it comes, I thought. A duchess doesn't splurge on a serf for nothing. 'Tell me. Why are you not afraid?'

'Why?' Was I asking did I have reason to be scared, or why ask such a barmy question?

She was inspecting me. From nothing I'd been promoted to vaguely interesting specimen, a blundering troglodyte.

'You are a scruff, poor as . . .' Her education came good. 'An habitual criminal.'

Which raised the question of why she was bothering. 'Am I discharged the service, like your Foreign Legionnaires?'

Her expression clouded. 'You disturb me, Lovejoy. Most of what you say is imbecilic, except for certain phrases.'

'Look, Monique.' She was narking me more and more, and the bloody soup was frozen. It even had ice in the damned stuff. I gave it back to the waiter and said to warm it up, please. Even I can work a microwave, for God's sake. He started a distressed harangue with Monique in explosive lingo. She shut him up. He crawled off with my soup. She'd started hers. Too polite to complain, I suppose. I went on, 'I'm having enough trouble with the lingo. If it's declensions you're worried about you should have hired a certified linguist.'

'As you please.' I don't like it when women give in that quick, because they never do unless they're working something out. 'But I find it strange that you often move so surely in areas of which you are supposedly ignorant.'

'Eh?'

'It happened a number of times at the Repository. You detect human fondnesses which others might miss.' That took some saying, but she did it, with pauses. 'I'm unsure of you. Is it a quirk of speech? Or some intuition in your nature?'

My soup came back. The waiter managed not to chuck it at me, and retired rolling his eyes. 'Well,' I told her defiantly, 'he should have got it right in the first place.' Hot, at last.

'You mention the Foreign Legion. Our Red-and-Greens.' She looked at me as I quaffed away, but her eyes were somewhere else. 'Founded in 1831, mainly to sweep up drunken German students bothering our towns. But French in culture, as we are. You can never understand, Lovejoy. Your multiculture society is hopeless. We meld all comers into one entity called France.'

'Or else what?' I'd have had the rest of her soup except the waiter would disintegrate when I told him to hot it up.

'Or else they are superfluous to requirements, Lovejoy.' The main course came steaming, thank God. The waiter was learning. 'Our Legion's desertion rate was never half that of the American forces, though envious nations make much of our discipline.'

Our? I tried to find a resemblance to Marimee in her features. Well, thinking of Veronique and her brother Guy. And Lysette, more platonically related to Jan.

'We French face an onslaught, Lovejoy. On spelling – you'll not have heard of the criminals on Rocard's High Council on the French Language, who want to change the spelling of nearly a tenth of our words. Or the idiot bureaucrats of Brussels who want to change them all! To compel us, by economic force. What is Brussels, but a suburb of a suburb? France is under attack. Washington's population evaluers score Paris – *Paris!* – a mere seventy-two per cent. Our brilliant war record is decried as sham. Our superb wines are ignored – bribery among international judges! So we French now lead the world – in swallowing tranquillizers, twice the German rate! And in counterfeiting, of course. Along the Rue de la Grande Truanderie – the Street of Crooks, in your appalling language, Lovejoy – we excel in laser-printed fifty-franc notes.'

Nice does the best 200-franc notes, though, I'd heard, but wisely did not say. She almost hit two poor approaching waiters, who almost recoiled. She managed to stay silent until they'd poured the wine and retreated. 'Our President learns from the American Secretary of State that France depends on Ami nuclear technology, and has to admit ignorance of this at a public dinner table. Our airports score – '

'Can I start, love?' I was famished.

' – highly. But for what? *Perfume*! Nothing else!' Well I started anyway. 'Our empire is gone, our currency surrenders to the Common Market. We must eat foreign food, as ordered by foreign minnows in Brussels! And our great Marseillaise is to be bowdlerized. No longer *Aux armes, mes citoyens*! It's to be *All one, friends, dance hand in hand. Marchons* becomes *Skip on*.' She was pale, her lips bloodless. 'Rouget de Lisle will turn in his grave.'

'Politics is shifting sand.' I get uncomfortable.

'Once it was only the Americans – with their crass ambassadors. Camelot Country, whose President got the Pulitzer Prize for *Profiles in Courage* written by somebody else.' She became bitter, really vicious, the way all people speak of an envied friend. 'Still, it shows there are advantages to having a President with a father capable of making a fortune from buying up cheap liquor licences during Prohibition.'

'Your art – ' I was sick of her and her bloody whining. So folk have faults. What else is new?

'Is thieved, stolen. You see the headlines, Lovejoy: *Paris: The Empty Frames*! Our honour is shattered everywhere now that any hairy student actor can walk in and steal – '

'He wore a wig to look like a Rasta.' I had a mouthful. 'Pretty clever. Sixteenth arrondissement, wasn't it? Your Banditry Repression Brigade moved pretty sharpish.'

She fell silent. I looked up, waiting.

'You see, Lovejoy?' She'd cooled her ardour. 'You are informed. It happens too often.'

'Don't be daft, love. Everybody goes through a bad patch, even France. You've one of the loveliest countries on earth. Lovely lingo. Look at us. We drop clangers all over the place.'

'Clangers?'

'Faults, make mistakes. Christ, love, the Vatican's own postage stamps got their Latin wrong last year! And C–14 carbon dating's off by 3,500 years – when we thought it infallible!' I grinned. 'Sometimes errors help. Like that statue of Hercules. Second century, right? Its top half's in the Met – didn't they pay to have it smuggled out of, where, Ankara? No wonder the Turks went mental. Where're you from, love?'

'Marseilles.' It was out without thought. She shrugged, a pretty sight. A shoulder lifted, head a little aslant. Beautiful enough to paint, eat, love. Well, maybe not love. You'd never survive. 'Now my city is broke, unemployment rife. Shops close daily. The French population declines, replaced by a tide of immigrants who know nothing of France. The great docks have moved to Barcelona – *Barcelona!* – and Anvers. The influx of Africans is said to number only 56,000, clearly false.'

'So?' I said cheerfully. 'Incomers blend in two generations – '

'The main street was exquisite, Lovejoy.' She was toying wistfully with her food. It was a lovely pie thing, fish and mushrooms with some sauce stuff, vegetables undercooked, best meal on earth. I borrowed a bit from her plate while she talked, to help her. Her eyes were dreamy. 'La Canebière outshone the Champs Élysées for glamour and luxury. Now it's a series of cheap pizza stalls, an Arab souk where no self-respecting Frenchman walks at night unless with guard dogs. And even then you have to climb over filth, piled rubbish.' She focused on me. I was having her spuds. 'You don't think this reasonable, Lovejoy?'

'No, love. Not for self-indulgence. Londoners once petitioned against French immigrants for pinching jobs. Charles the Second had the sense to say no, let the Huguenots come.'

'Liberalism is weakness, Lovejoy.' She said it by rote.

'If you say so, love. Any chance of some more greens?' She signalled, the waiters sprang. 'I don't blame your dockies for demonstrating now the Spanish have abolished their Customs and Excise posts. Wherever there's a border barrier, there's a fortune in fiddles. That's what they're mad at.'

She watched me nosh. 'My lovely Marseilles' major product is now crime, Lovejoy. Gang wars, killings. France has left.'

'Anything I can do, love?' I honestly meant it. But what? Nostalgia's the only untreatable disease.

'You've done it, Lovejoy. Divvying.' She asked a bit more about Jodie Danglass, who she was, what she did, but in malicious tones that gave me goose-pimples. Ten minutes later, me still trying to scoff some profiteroles, she upped and offed without so much as a word of warning. And that was that.

'How many, Gobbie?'

'Fifty-two, Lovejoy.'

'Where to?' Fifty-two pantechnicons? Christ.

'South at first. Hell of a convoy.' He grinned. 'At first.'

'What do you mean at first at first?'

He was falling about, silly old fool. 'They didn't ever form up. They left in dribs and drabs. Know what, Lovejoy?'

'No?' *Every van looked slightly different.*

'They wus every shape and size you ever did see.' I'd counted on it. 'Lysette's chasing after three. She didn't know what she oughter do. They're labelled something about electricity.'

'The vans had different insignia?'

'Far as we could tell, son. We only guessed at fifty-two.' He went apologetic. 'Three entrances, see? Only two of us counting, from hiding . . .'

Pity. If I'd been there, I could have told whether they had been crammed with antiques or not. Instead, I'd been delayed hearing out Monique's Good Old Days saga.

'Right, Gobbie. That's it, then.' We were in a nosh bar near the St Peterskirche. I'd paid a king's ransom for two coffees and a cake. 'They'll hit the Repository in two days.'

'How'll they get the stuff out, Lovejoy? It's a hell of a lot to get in by legitimate means, let alone rob.'

'Wish I knew. Where's Lysette going to meet us?'

We left, me thinking I'd solved nearly everything, talking over old scams. The cafés of Zurich aren't a patch on the Paris ones, which have atmosphere. I know Switzerland pretends to be over seven centuries old, but that's a fib. But Paris really truly has it. I said as much to Gobbie, laughing. He looked at me doubtfully as we walked down a narrow street to the Fraumunster. I was saying what a high old time I'd had in Paris, racing Guy and Veronique round the antique shops, how I'd seen the main fakes' storage area there for the Troude-Monique scam.

Talking to myself. Gobbie had stopped. He was in the gloaming behind me, standing quite still. It was coming dusk.

'Gobbie?' I called back. 'You all right?'

He came on slowly. 'Lovejoy?' he asked. 'You do understand?'

'Eh?' I could have clouted the silly old git. 'Course I do! I'm the one called you in, you burk.' Maybe it was senility.

'Then tell me.' There was hardly anyone about. The Fraumunster was lit. We would have seen eavesdroppers.

'Tell you?' Of all the frigging cheek. Here was this old loon that I'd called out of retirement, accusing me of not sussing an antiques heist? I suppressed my anger, took a breath. I liked the old soldier. He and Lysette got on well. I didn't want her raging at me because of my temper.

So, strolling to the Fraumunster – clever architecture, I'm sure, but somehow threatening – I summarized the entire scam for his thick idiot brain. I mean, I'd only unmothballed him because he knew the Continent, for God's sake.

'Look, Gobbie,' I told him, words of half a syllable for his cretinoidal nut. 'These French raise a syndicate, see? Anglo-French money. They use it to create a zillion superb fakes, mostly furniture.' Christ, I'd given it to the old dolt clear as day. He'd seen the bloody vans filled with the stuff.

'And?' He'd gone all quiet. You can really go off people, even friends. I hated the bastard.

'And, moron,' I sailed on, 'they lodge them into the biggest antiques repository on earth. Got it so far?'

'And?'

One more 'And' and I'd do him. 'Then they nick them, and claim on the insurance – as if they were all genuine!' I chuckled, such gaiety. 'See? Now, the Repository's no innocent about security, so the Commandant will have egg on his face when his robbery team goes in!'

My laughter died away. He'd stopped. We were out into the Fraumunster's famous square, except it's got more side's than even Swiss squares should have. 'And?'

'Well,' I said, trying to recapture the moment. His old whiskery face was staring at me in disbelief. 'I thought me and thee'd hang about for the last act. See Marimee's face when . . .'

'I thought even you'd have spotted the obvious, Lovejoy.' His voice was so quiet I had to strain to hear the old loon.

'*Even* me?' I tapped his chest, choking on rage. 'Listen to me, you silly old sod. I brought you over because you wanted one last go at an all time grandy. What was it you said, at that boot sale? Bring the old times back. And I have! This is the . . . Gobbie?' I almost stepped back in horror. He was crying.

Tears were streaming down his face. I gaped. Men don't weep. We're not allowed. Old soldiers like Gobbie especially don't.

They've seen it all. And why don't these silly old soaks shave proper, for God's sake?

'Gobbie?' I said dully. 'What's up, pal? I'm not really narked. Honest.'

'Lovejoy,' he managed, in a terrible silent voice I'd never heard him use before. I can hear it yet. Close my eyes, and I see him in that floodlit square under the towering Zurich church. 'What about the children?'

29

Needle Park, as they call it, is as unappetizing as, well, the same in any big city these days. The local gesture at liberalism, of a sort. Gobbie dropped me off. I'd told him I'd be an hour or so.

A few of the huddles looked derelicts, but some were astonishingly affluent. Several decent overcoats, a trilby or two, and one bird smartly dressed in a skirt suit of classic career-woman line. It makes you wonder. One group was actually auctioning drugs, the business ethic at play. I finally found Guy and Veronique round a sort of big candle among so-o-o-o happy friends. Guy shouted, some joke. Everybody laughed at me. If it centred on my stupidity, he'd be right.

'Evening, Guy.'

'Kiye!' several chorused my pronunciation. One added in a shrill roar, 'Khow kquaint!'

The laughter died. Somebody coughed, racked and shivering. One drank, offered me a sip. I declined, thanks.

'Chance of a word, please?' I asked. Guy, rolling his eyes, came, Veronique too. She looked in slightly the better shape. I turned after a pace or two and sized them up.

Here stood my two guardians, relaxed, cool. The same custodians, note, who had crumbled in near-terror when I'd gone missing for a few hours among the antique shops of Paris. A decided change, now I'd done my bit. Or now that I was expendable?

'You're not keeping track of me, Veronique.' I hoped for a reasonable reply. Guy seemed beyond it. 'Instead you're shooting the toot, or whatever you people say.'

She swayed, staring through me. Distant traffic stuttered sedately, the Swiss still methodically switching their engines off at a hint of a red. I wondered, is it to save petrol for the fatherland?

'Time off, Lovejoy.'

'Look. I've a problem.' I hesitated, hoping my bad acting wasn't over the top. 'I've the chance', I admitted nobly, 'of, er, seeing a girl. But I've some money coming in from East Anglia. To the hotel, next couple of hours, I think. I need it signed for.'

'Money?' Guy was on Planet Earth after all.

'As a draft. In my name.' I smiled apologetically at Veronique, who'd also momentarily tethered her mind to reality at the mention of gelt. 'I can't be in two places at once.'

'What girl?' Veronique asked.

'Nobody important, love,' I said. 'Not anyone *you* need worry about. But I can see you're busy . . .' That partly mollified her.

'I know!' cried Guy, almost leaping as the notion struck him. '*We'll* accept the money for you, Lovejoy!' I thought the penny'd never drop. 'Sign an authorization with the concierge, and we'll do it!'

'Thanks, pals.' I waved farewell. 'Oh, one thing. How long can I be away? Only, Colonel Marimee said I'd be needed.'

'You should be able to get in enough pokes before tomorrow night, Lovejoy.' Guy leered, fell over. Veronique started to haul him upright. Somebody nearby relieved himself into a small bush. Another vomited. God. Ecstasy, at these prices?

'See you back at the hotel, troops. Sevenish do?'

They called seven'd be ample. So the Repository would be a midnight job. I had twenty-four hours. They could buy a hundred comas with my money, as long as I was free of them for a bit. As it was, I got free of them for much, much longer.

•

Gobbie drove us out of Zurich. I tried telling him the way we'd come, me and my golden pair. I vaguely remember road numbers, but things never look the same returning. The old Italian proverb came dimly from some old Western film, look behind, not before. Fine time to remember good advice when it's pointless. He told me to stop telling him the way. Okay, so he knew the Continent and I didn't. No need to get irascible.

Lysette was along. Never known such a quiet lass. She only spoke at the first Strasbourg sign. I'd dozed off.

'Why is that money necessary, Lovejoy? I have credit cards.'

She smelled nice. She'd been there when I'd phoned the upright, honest Dicko Chave. He'd promised to wire me a load of zlotniks against some antiques I'd found. That story wouldn't have been enough to make him trust me. I'd had to invent a lovely unmarried lass I'd also discovered, as his new possible partner. He'd urged me to propose on his behalf. Poor old Dicko.

'The one commodity my addict custodians need is money. The scent of it winkled the time of the robbery from them.'

'They'll steal it, Lovejoy,' from old Gobbie at the wheel, his face lit by the road lights. 'You should have only pretended there was money coming.'

'No. They'd have guessed, then I'd have been in the soup.' I'd not said how much, but to addicts all money promises bliss.

We drove on. I'd not said anything to Lysette about the terrible truth that Gobbie'd made me face. I couldn't. But I suspected she'd known the true story long since. As I had. And maybe poor Baff Bavington had. And poor Leon, the French divvy. And Jan Fotheringay her brother. Jesus, but I'm thick. That's half my trouble. I'll work something out, then ignore the obvious if it's too horrible to contemplate. Birds are always picking at me for never facing up. Hateful, that they might be right. It's as if I know the words, the tune, but don't understand the song.

'Where did they go, love? Your three vans.'

'Lausanne.'

'Lausanne? Is that still in Switzerl– ?'

'I've made a map with detailed directions, Lovejoy.' She spoke curtly. She meant I wasn't worth talking to. Next breath she told me why. 'I believe you already know the address.'

I hate it. A bloke ought to be allowed one or two tricks, even though they're transparent. I mean, we're not allowed to say when a woman's deceit is obvious, are we? But they can say whatever they like. It galls me. Women have too many blinking privileges for my liking. 'Did other vans turn up?'

'I counted eighteen, in Lausanne.'

So they probably all went there, By one route or another. I'd think of a cutting rejoinder to Lysette any second.

'Lovejoy?' Gobbie said gruffly. 'We're here. Paris. Where was it?'

The nausea rose within me. I'd been sick at my non-thought thoughts for a fortnight, longer even. Now I was back.

'Look,' I tried, surly. 'We'll stop for coffee. It's almost ten o'clock. We've not stopped or anything – '

'*Lovejoy*,' from Lysette. Gobbie said nothing, waited while traffic honked and motorists yelled imprecations.

'Right, Gobbie.' Where had we driven, that night in Dreyfus's trundlesome motor? Seine, Arc de Triomphe, Sacré Coeur, then doubled back to that sordid Paris-shouldn't-have-such-districts near the sound of trains. I managed to direct us through the knitted thoroughfares. We parked, by a fluke, and walked.

Lysette walked with her arm through Gobbie's, I noticed, narked. Gobbie occasionally made as if to glance at me, then avoided my eyes. It took us nearly an hour. We'd actually passed the doorway before I recognized the church-hall-type entrance down a few steps, cardboarded windows opposite, the same smell of cooking. It was wise to walk on by, in case one of those immobile beefy blokes had been left on watch.

'It's here, Gobbie. That's the way in.' Children were playing nearby, calling in foreign dialects. I didn't look at them. It was dark, the street lighting furtive. 'What now?'

'You two off out of it, Lovejoy. I'll look round the district. Be at the corner in an hour, eh?'

Gobbie shuffled away on his quest. Lysette came with me, to a small caff near the Deux Magots. When she did speak it was so unexpected I almost spilled my coffee.

'I should have taken you to the Procope, Rue de l'Ancienne Comédie,' she said quietly. We were at a pavement table. 'Benjamin Franklin went there. But your favourite would have been Voltaire. He also. And Napoleon.'

I would have liked Voltaire? How did she know? I knew I'd look him up sooner or later, be no wiser.

'There are whole books written on Parisian cafés, Lovejoy.' I quite liked my name, first time I could remember since Monique said it. 'Hemingway objected when the proprietors of the Closerie des Lilas – from its lilacs, you know? – made their waiters lose their moustaches. No longer chic, you see?'

'Oh, right.' There isn't a lot you can say to this quiet reflective stuff, especially from a bird like Lysette. You never know whether it's leading up.

'The Coupole has been supplanted by a monstrosity. Beckett, Henry Miller . . .'

My attention wandered. Nobody I recognized around the small

square. Students burst into laughter at a nearby table. Two nurses slumped tiredly on window chairs, smoking. Nurses made me remember that gross but fantastically exuberant Katta. Wouldn't have minded her giving me something she gave Paulie. Isn't it odd how –

'Eh?' An important question had come up.

'. . . kill you, Lovejoy.' Her last words.

'Who?' People looked across with sudden interest. I must have yelped. I quickly smiled for the sake of appearances. I don't know what it looked like, but it felt pretty ghastly from within.

'The syndicate.'

Sweat beaded my forehead, started to trickle down my back. Jodie Danglass was their helper. Surely she wouldn't be party to anything so. . . ? And Paulie? Or his slavish fatty Katta? The suave Troude? The chilling Monique Delebarre might, any day of the week. Guy and Veronique would slay their grannies for a bob, par for their mainline course. Colonel Marimee was deranged; I couldn't count him among the faint-hearts, and who knew how many goons he had to pull the rip? But Sandy, for God's sake? No wonder Mel had cut and run. Had Mel known how terrible the scam was? Worse, did Sandy?

'Why'd you visit Jan, Lovejoy?' Still flat of voice. 'I recognize you from the hospital, coming out of the lift.'

'Dunno. Worried about me getting drawn into something I didn't understand, I suppose.'

'Jan and Sandy have been . . . friends for months.' She shrugged. 'It's difficult. To be sister to a brother with . . .'

'Must be.' Jan and Sandy now? So Mel had good personal reason to scarper, not just money.

'You could leave, Lovejoy.' I wished she'd not fiddle with her spoon. I sometimes wonder if women nark me deliberately.

'Leave?' I said blankly. 'Leave? As in. . . ?'

'Leave. With me. Now, when Gobbie comes, simply drive home.'

That quiet voice, her luscious hair, casual manner, the serene intensity of her Pre-Raphaelite features. All the time cerebrating away like a think-tank.

'*With* you?' She'd made me gape.

'Gobbie will make his own way. He knows the routes.' She

raised her eyes to mine. I'd never seen such deep eyes, though they were at the front, if you follow. Not sunken, I mean. 'You must ask yourself why stay, Lovejoy.'

I really hate that. Asking me why's my business, not hers. 'Why?' I asked her.

'You must learn your own reasons, if you haven't already discovered them for yourself.'

'Look, love,' I said, peeved, frightened. 'This whole thing's made me spew up, drift around foreign lands with – '

'You're ignorant, Lovejoy,' she said softly. 'Ignorance of the simple kind, not malice. But it draws you out of your depth.' She coloured slightly. 'I would care for you, you see.'

Care for how? I nearly said, like you did your brother Jan? Mercifully, Gobbie wheezed into a chair, his eyes rheumy.

'Found one of their factories, Lovejoy. Within a stone's throw of the depot. Next street but three.' He cleared his gruff old throttle. 'I could tell you about it. Save you seeing?'

Lam out? That's what Lysette wanted me to do. 'No, Gobbie. I'll see.' It was me'd been sickened, suffered by avoiding the truth. This served me right. 'Stay here, Lysette.' I rose. She came anyway. I sighed. One word from me, birds do whatever they want. It's their version of loyal co-operation.

Distances in Paris never seem very far, not like London where sequential postal numbers signify districts miles apart. Paris is yards rather than furlongs. We were there in a trice, Gobbie flagging somewhat as we made the last street. I must have been hurrying. Lysette told me to take my time, that Gobbie had already done too much. She didn't mention her prodigious driving, staying on the ball, Lausanne and back, Zurich to Paris. And making mad proposals to a nerk like me.

'See that covered way, son?' There was a kind of projection from a long wall. It resembled one of those ironwork half-cloisters you get over the side entrances of London theatres, for early-evening queues that no longer come.

'Aye?' Several stacked street barrows. Steps, a few sacking-covered windows, some lantern lights, one or two bare bulbs. Rubbish littered the pavements. That scented cooking, metal clanking somewhere, a few shouts in non-French, a background hum. 'Is there a way in?'

235

'The steps go up, but have ones leading to the cellars beside.'

'So I go down?' Nobody along these pavements, not at this hour. I felt my nape prickle.

'No, son. You go up.' With resigned patience, 'Then you can look down into the cellar area, see?'

Now he was deliberately narking me. 'How the hell did I know they'd made it all into one?'

' 'Cos it's a workshop.' He was disgusted by my slowness. Lysette said nothing.

'Wait here.' I left them, eeled down the narrow street. The hum and clanking grew louder. Something thudded, shouts rose, then settled down to a hum. I went softly, looked back. Gobbie and Lysette had vanished. The air felt smoky. The light was only clear at the top of the street now. Here was gloom, foreboding, trouble. I almost started to whistle, like walking past the churchyard coming back from the White Hart.

Some sort of torch would have done me, but I'd not the sense. How had Gobbie managed it? Go up, he'd said, then you can look down. The steps were of the old-fashioned sort you see in North London, iron railings both sides. Some gone, jagged pegs waiting to stab you as you fell.

The door was blowing faintly, sacking, outwards. No lights except some feeble glow – oil lantern? – from within. I shoved. To my surprise it scraped ajar. I stepped in. Somebody calling, others yelling, childish voices answering. A bloke threatening.

Glass, pieces of broken glass, on bare linoleum. Flaking everything, by the light of the oil lamp hung beside the stairs. Oil lamps meant no traceable electricity bill. Up or down? I went where the light glowed most, which was directly ahead beside the staircase. The place stank.

One unbelievable creaking woodwork step down, then a sheen from below. Round a corner, me shuffling inchwise and the hum growing and the shouts louder. If only I could have understood what they were saying. Lots of little voices, the gruff deeper voice yelling abuse. Near silence, then the hum resuming.

And I saw them, suddenly there, children down in the cellars. The floor of what had been the living room had been knocked out, almost ripped, the floorboards scagged at their insertions into the walls near my feet. They had been unceremoniously hacked away.

236

I was near the margin. Another foot or two, I'd have tumbled over and been down among them.

Them? Three or four dozen children, bare-arse naked, working on furniture, planed mahogany, even some walnut. Lovely aroma of fresh heartwood. But it was looking down into hell. Straight out of the seventeenth century, the children were smoothing with their hands, feet. Some were standing on the wooden surfaces, holding on to rods stretched from cellar wall to cellar wall. Oil lanterns shone light.

The children's bodies glistened with sweat. Their hands bled. One little mite was weeping, trying to lick his palms. Another had actually fallen asleep. Even as I looked he got whipped awake with a riding crop.

They were polishing. One boy nudged his pal, keep going, keep going. Some chanted, working in time. One tiny mite went along the rows, casting up handfuls of dust on the worked surfaces.

The man walking down the aisles of furniture – five rows, three or four pieces a row – switched the air. I swear that he lashed a little lass from sheer habit. A couple of men were seated at a deal table beneath two lamps across from where I stood looking down, playing cards. Playing *cards*. Smoking cigarettes. The whipmaster looked at his watch, was downcast at the time and lashed here and there in annoyance.

Two smaller children burst in from the rear cellar door, trying to haul a plastic bowl. I recognized the technique. Brick-dust, doubtless.

The average age? It looked about six, at a guess. The oldest child was about nine, the youngest threeish. They were bloodied, blistered, hands and soles dropping sweat and blister water. They were all scarred, too experienced in life to be scared very much. One's shoulder was a carbuncled, pus-pouring red mass. It took me a while to move away.

Odd, but I walked from there without a single creak of the floorboards. I swear I glided. Odd because when you're desperately trying to avoid making a noise, everything you touch peals like thunder. When you don't give a damn, you don't make a sound. I actually *wanted* that whip-toting flogger to catch me. I'd have . . . I'd have run like a gazelle. I know I would.

'Gobbie?' I called at the corner. 'Where the hell?'

They were watching me come. Lysette said nothing. Gobbie said, 'Awright, son?'

'Stop asking that, stupid old bugger.'

Twice they had to call to me, correct my direction when I'd marched ahead, as if I knew the way and they didn't instead of the other way round. The motor'd had nothing thieved.

'I expected no wheels,' I joked. 'This sort of district.'

'Don't, Lovejoy,' from Lysette as we boarded.

I swung round in the seat, finger raised. 'Not another word from you, love,' I said. My voice was a hoarse whisper, astonishing, because I'd said nowt much. 'Not one.'

'It's not your fault, Lovejoy,' she was saying, when I lashed my hand across her face and she fell back with a cry.

'Now then, son,' Gobbie gave me.

'You too,' that funny whisper said. 'Get us to Zurich.'

'Via where?' Gobbie asked. 'Lausanne – '

I looked at him. It was enough. He fired the engine, and we flew from Paris like angels.

30

'Thanks,' I told them just before they dropped me off. 'You've been pals. See you at home, eh?'

'What're you going to do, Lovejoy?'

'Join the scam.' I gave Lysette a really sound smile. 'Get my chop, live in idle richness.' They didn't roll in the aisles. My jokes always fall flat. I can't even remember ones I'm told.

'You go careful, son.'

'Trust me.' Gobbie was looking at me oddly. Lysette stared at her knees. 'You know my address.' I hate that phrase, keep in touch. It always means farewell.

Darkness had fallen, or what passes for darkness in Zurich. That means lights everywhere, skies filled with sheen, lake reflecting every glim. Our village has an astronomer who keeps suing everybody for light pollution. He'd have a ball here.

'So long. And ta.' I waved from the pavement.

To the hotel. Guy and Veronique weren't in their room. I lay on my bed. Odd, but I no longer felt sick. I felt calm but hot, sort of flu round-the-corner.

Lysette had begun to speak when we were on the trunk road heading east. Steadily, without inflection almost, stating facts rather than wanting to tell anybody anything.

'There's still an anti-slavery society,' she said quietly, of nothing in particular. Nobody had said anything until then. I looked round and asked, 'Eh?' but she ignored me.

'It only scratches the surface. There are more child slaves now than in the whole of history. In leading industrial nations – us Western peoples – just as elsewhere. Nations sign the UN Articles against it, and take no notice – '

'Shut up.' My analytical thought for the day.

'Jan was approached by an illegal immigrant,' Lysette said in that grave non-voice of hers. She might have been reading football results. 'Her children wcre debt-bonded in Whitechapel. She asked his help, because she'd seen him photographed with one of the financiers. Jan was horrified.'

'Debt-bonded?' Gobbie asked it, knowing I'm stubborn.

'There are two forms of child slavery. Chattel slavery – old-fashioned slavery, bought and sold. It exists in North Africa, elsewhere. There are cases reported every year in Western countries, even among diplomats' family servants. In debt bondage children work to pay off parents' debts – India, Pakistan, South America, Africa, the Philippines. I would tell you stories, but you would not bear them, Lovejoy.'

The stupid bitch had gone on and on. I stared at the ceiling, hearing Guy and Veronique arrive next door. They sounded three sheets to the wind, or similar. '. . . Ten thousand little boys were imported from Bihar to make carpets in Mirzapur-Varanasi. They were bought, bonded, simply stolen children. They work from four every morning until two o'clock in the afternoon. Then they are fed one bread *roti* with lentils, and work on to midnight when they're allowed to sleep after another similar meal. I learned this after Jan spoke with the woman.'

'What work?'

'Making nice carpets. Making nice bricks. Making nice polished gems for the elegant West End shops, to please elegant Western ladies. Quarrying stones, making matches, rag-picking, doing *zari* embroidery. And faking – '

'Ta, love.' I meant shut up. Some hopes.

'Plantations, domestics, factories.' Christ, had the stupid bitch never heard of inflexion? She sounded on automatic. 'Thailand's supposed to lead the world, Lovejoy. For exploitation of over three million child slaves, I mean: drug-packers, child prostitutes, leading exporter of bonded or chattelled slaves to the Gulf, Europe. Rongmung Road, near Bangkok's railway station, the children are sold, to be chained workforces, or to baby brothels. Jan was horrified, not knowing, you see. He isn't commercially minded. They told him at the Anti-Slavery place. I think they said ten pounds sterling to buy one child slave, though you can get wholesale deals . . .'

'Excuse me, please. Can you stop half a sec, Gobbie?'

I stared at the ceiling some more. I'd actually uttered the words, remembering, in the privacy of my own hotel doss-house room.

Gobbie'd not stopped, of course. How could he, million miles an hour on some fast roads? I'd grumbled, finally told Gobbie to shut her up. She'd only obeyed when Gobbie gravelled out, 'That'll do, Lysette.' Why did she never do as I said, only that gerontic old sod? It gets my goat.

'Lovejoy?' Veronique opening my door made me leap a mile. She laughed, eyes shining with that unholy thrill that came from within. 'What were you doing? I startle you?'

'Er, no, love, ta.' I was bathed in sweat. 'Time, is it?' *Every one of Great Britain's old manufacturing towns, Glasgow to London, through the industrial North and Midlands, immigrant children are beaten, flogged to labour . . .*

'We've just had word.' She spoke coyly. 'It's tomorrow afternoon. You can get on with your merrymaking.' She paused, hand on the door, provocative. At least, she would have been provocative, except drugs meant she was no longer Veronique. She was a trillion different other folk, people I'd never met and didn't know. Like talking to a chemistry set.

'Off?' I said stupidly, mind cogging slowly into action.

'Postponed.' She smiled over her lie, really more of a leer. Hideous. To think that I'd – 'Worth it, was she?'

Lost. 'Worth it?'

'You look, how d'you say in English, shagged out, Lovejoy.'

Whoops. Forgotten I was supposed to have been wassailing with a local bird. 'Superb, love,' I said weakly. Well, Swiss national honour and all that. 'Beautiful.'

'Good as I?'

'Not quite, no.'

'Tomorrow, Lovejoy, you and I will make sweet music, no?'

'No. I mean yes.'

She smiled. I'd never seen eyes so brilliant. 'It will be such lovely music, Lovejoy. Like never before!' Her sentences were fraying in their chemical heaven.

'Great. See you tomorrow, then. Ah, the money, love?'

She pouted. 'You do not trust little Veronique?'

'Well, I need to, er, take the lady for supper.'

'Guy is sleeping, Lovejoy. He has your money. I shall wake him eventually and bring it to you.'

She left then, me calling a ta, see her later, all that. I let their bedroom whoopee start, heard them sink to silence, then departed that place, taking neither scrip nor purse nor staff to aid me on my way. Well, not exactly. I actually went into their room, stole Guy's car keys from his jacket while they slept their sleep of the dust, and nicked their Porsche. My lies were as good as her lies any day.

The Repository, I worked out as I drove, was model for Colonel Marimee's mock-up. At the garden party, it had slowly swivelled, the way military models do when top brass play tactical planning. That way, the sun, moon, prevailing winds can be controlled, varied to whatever time their plodding minds plan the action. It's called actual simulation, as if there can be such a thing.

No daytime action, so night, with a moon as now, fitful yet businesslike. While admiring Lorela Chevalier's territory, I'd particularly admired the surrounding hillsides. Quite nice mountains, really. Two positions overlooked the Repository mansion house. One was severely wooded, the other somewhat more sparsely. I paused to look at Guy's map. The bloody thing didn't give me phases of the moon. Just typical, I raged. The one time I needed it, they leave it out. Cartographers don't deserve the money we spend on them, that's for sure. I'd been under fire once or twice, and knew that you want to look down on a target. You leave it in light, while staying in shadow. I watched for the moon as I drove. The wretched thing never seemed to stay in one position. Was it always like that? Ours back in East Anglia wasn't. Ours is tranquil, restfully there until it sinks behind some clouds to kip the day out. This Swiss moon rolled about like a puzzle pill, sodding thing. Dishonest.

Odd that I wasn't at all tired. Must be an adrenalin thing. Of the two sharp hills dominating the Repository, I'd already decided the one from which to watch the action. The wooded one, further along the twisting contoured road but more concealment for your actual coward. I felt excited, like going to a film I'd been awaiting. The Repository would be in darkness, leaving me blindly guessing which method Colonel Marimee had chosen to pull the robbery. Or the Repository would be lit like a football field, in which case I'd be the lone spectator at the grandest slickest action ever devised. I had no doubts about Marimee's military genius. He'd

242

scam the stuff out somehow, no problem. I was quivering to see how, though. Tonight I'd have all the excitement, and none of the risks. Like a holiday. I had to stop myself from singing that Vivaldi bit about a hundred sexy maidens.

And after this, home. Please.

Off the road, on the summit among trees. Pity about Swiss trees, really, all pines or pine-lookers. No variation, planted by some maths teacher with a theodolite, growing to order. Snow, surprised me, mainly because some of it was starting to fall thick, unwieldy. A sky glow showed me direction, though I'd already worked that out. Left? I thought about the motor, backed it on a more pronounced part of the slope so I could hop in and release the handbrake to course downhill. If I needed, I could either race off uphill in the direction I'd been heading, or swing back the way I'd come. I'd decide later. If Marimee's men were slick and got the hell out in millisecs, I could simply drive off anywhere I liked, a simple innocent passing motorist. I parked safely.

Up into the trees, a slow climb. From the car clock I worked out I had plenty of time. Two whole hours before the rip happened. It was perishing cold, no wind but those big flakes falling. I was surprised. They seemed to ignore the trees and fall down anyway. Perished, I went back for the car rug. I was in a forest, for Christ's sake. Snow's supposed to hit the trees, lodge in the blinking branches, make pretty for wandering artists, not slip through and land on me. Stupid snow, Switzerland's. No hat, either. I hate getting my head wet. Under the blanket like a squaw, I plodded back up among the monotonous evergreens. Footprints now, I saw uneasily. Well, as long as nobody came by and glimpsed the Porsche, okay.

Fifteen minutes, me blundering into those straight tree trunks every few yards. I was sure the bloody thing moved. And I hated the big snowflakes that came on my eyelashes. I had to keep pulling my hands out and wiping my vision free, damned stuff. Why didn't Swiss snow give warning, like sending different sea winds so you could get ready? I call it basic lack of organization.

Then, of a sudden, the best seat in the house. The Repository was laid out like a toy below, lit by floodlights. Lovely old mansion, with extensions that weren't too bad as modern architecture goes. I could see the smaller separate place where our genuine antiques had gone for shipment. Mustard-coloured sills and doors, I noticed. Nice touch, Lorela. It was a cardboard cut-out copy of Marimee's garden-party mansion. No, the other way round. The Repository was the genuine place, his the one with the copycat garden to practise on.

No real nooks in a Swiss forest, either. Once you stand still, a wind springs up, sends snowflakes swirling round your ankles. I finished up crouched down, close to a bole as I could get, hooded under my blanket. It stank, I noticed. What the hell had they been doing on the thing, for heaven's sake?

Looking down at the great house, I started thinking defensive. I mean, when I was a little lad, bits of those interminable Latin lessons stuck in my mind. Not very well. But it seemed that every time Caesar came across an *oppidum*, a fortified camp, he had to storm it for no other reason than it was there. Like, that's what they're for. The Repository'd had, what, seventy attempted robberies in two years?

All unsuccessful, too, Lorela implied. She exuded confidence: nobody was going to besmirch her reputation. Confidence is daunting. I thought back. I'd never heard of anybody doing the Repository over. Plenty of failures, yes, but that's life. Which was odd, very strange, almost so wrong it must be a fake story in itself. I mean, even the Tower of London's Crown Jewels have been filched in their time. Down below, a small vehicle moved in silence across the snow-covered grounds. Nobody alighted. Another vehicle moved to meet it, disgorging dogs. Six, four huge and two short waddlers puffing along, pausing to stare at the perimeter fence and wall. No men stepped down.

Except the more I looked at the place, the less I believed in it. Surely somebody could get in? Or were the guards in the blacked-out vehicles down there actually Marimee's hoods? Or in his pay? I was sure the Ali Baba must have been tried – hiding a team inside the antiques as they went into storage. Lorela had said as much. And all the rest of the thieves' dodges, the Oliver, the donk, the lep, trackle, bammo, the over-and-over, the shagnast, the burn-out, the Sunday joint, the spang, not forgetting all the electronic scams the lads are at these loony-tune days. Yet there the famous Repository was, being gently snowed upon. Inviolate, pristine, virgin.

The floodlights went out. Plunge, all black. I almost exclaimed aloud.

God, but Swiss hillside forests are dark when you take electricity away. It was suddenly colder. The chill non-wind came that bit faster. I creaked upright to make sure I could still move. Was it the syndicate's first move, a fuse ploy? I peered, saw nothing. Just when I was getting really disgruntled, the floodlights slammed back on, frightening me half to death. Then, within a few seconds, off again. On after a count of forty-nine. After that they settled down to a steady hum. I don't like that abrupt bland crash they make, not even at football matches. It makes me think they're going to take off.

They stayed on, and I thought. A warning device? The Repository computer had programmed erratic switch-offs, and notified the various cop shops and guard depots accordingly. Any variation from the plan meant somebody intruding. You wouldn't need men watching. Police or other security teams' computers would detect any unwonted variance within a split millisec. Clever. Not new, but on this big scale a definite deterrent. I smiled, wondering if the Commandant knew. I'll bet he did. Was he watching even now, ready to go?

But fortified places aren't. Not really. They *all* get done sooner or later, because mankind's ingenuity is tempted to the task. Take that terribly secret Code Black place the Yanks have. You know the one, where the President and his High Command will go the instant nuclear war starts. It's so secret that the Federal Emergency Management Agency – it runs the place – doesn't even mention it in its budget, for heaven's sake. It's even left out of the Classified Secret FEMA's own phone book, except under 'Special Facility'. And nobody knows its name. Between our secret selves, it's called Mount Weather, secret code name SF, and is seven hundred secret acres of prime Virginia wooded land on County Road 601 some eight secret miles from Berryville near Washington. But if it's so secret, how come I know? It can't just be me and the United States President, can it?

Off. Plunge into darkness. I waited, counting. The floods crashed-walloped on after more than two minutes. Erratic, planned to be. Good thinking, Lorela. A game girl –

Engines, faint in the distance. I strained to hear. No vehicle lights that I could see, but then I was looking along the hillside ridge, so naturally wouldn't. Waspish, snarly sorts, two or three, churning and whirring. Jeeps? Something like them, anyhow. No pretence at stealth.

Nearer, savage gear changes, a swathe of headlights now, quickly extinguished, then on from another direction.

The floodlights plunged out with a crash. On in an instant. The vehicles' band-saw engines nearing, no lights now. What the hell? The two security motors in the illuminated grounds below had crawled away, leaving the arena empty. Curious how like a stage set it was, a studio's rig for some shoot-out, brilliant panto lights for the purpose.

The engines slumped. Silence. Me, the snow, the distant mansion elegantly occupying the illuminated terrain in that high perimeter wall –

Something went thump, a couple of miles to my left. I was still looking that way like a fool, so missed the Repository roof falling in with a cloud and shatter. I gaped. Two more thumps, so horribly familiar. The windows imploded, the whole front Repository wall falling in, bricks and dust and snow everywhere. I saw rooms, furniture inside, tumbling upwards into the sky. Flames whooshed out. The explosion felt like a charring oven wind.

Thump, thump. Silence. Thump. And new explosions from the Repository. The main building was being incendiaried. No, that's wrong. Past tense. The engines were already started, churning and snarling away. I stared.

The Repository erupted, crackling, burning, what was left of it. Only the storage place stood untouched.

'You silly buggers!' I yelled at the night sky, at the fires, at the beautiful building smashed to blazes in a few seconds. 'You stupid sods! Couldn't you have. . . ?'

Couldn't they have what? They'd destroyed the syndicate's fakes, by the hundred. All of them, torched to oblivion. The result of all those child-bondeds. They'd created slave-labour factories, gone to absurd lengths to have the fakes accepted in the Repository, then blown them to oblivion? Not to mention hiring a mob of ex-Legionnaires, with the Legion's famed 'battery flash' of six one-twenty mortars. Why?

I'd seen it happen. Start to finish. The enslaved immigrant

children, now the flaming rubble. Only the genuine antiques remained. Their building stood unharmed.

How long I stood there I don't know. It was only the sight of those two security motors crawling back to halt in bafflement at the appalling sight that made me move again. I started down the hillside, blundering so fast I missed my footing and several times went tumbling, but got myself up and ran on. Lost my blanket, of course, but who can trace a blanket?

The metalled road's surface jarred under my heel, practically knocking the teeth from my head. No sign of my red motor. I looked left, right. Which way had I come among the trees? The sky glow behind was brighter now, far more than the floodlight's glim, and orange. No clues. Had I angled right, left? I was sure I'd climbed directly up. At least, I was almost nearly certain I was sure.

Right. Only a guess, but that was the way Marimee's vehicles had come. The speed of the thing had been devastating. Famous Foreign Legion stuff, that, the flying column, the swift four-minute unlimbering, shell the enemy with one-twenties, and off. But mortaring the damned place to smithereens?

Something coming up behind me. I ducked into the trees, up a slope, ran and hid. The motor seemed familiar, if one ever can. I gaped as it came at a fast lick, slithering on the snow at the bend. I almost shouted, but something was closing on it fast. They arrived almost opposite me, the motor hitting a pine tree and sliding sideways, lodging there. In for the night, it seemed to say, after that run. The pursuing motor was a jeep. It stopped by simply sticking to the ground, the way four-wheel-drive militaries do.

A man got out, familiar, walking slow. He came at the saloon car. Its engine was still going, lights on.

And Gobbie looked out. Left-hand drive, of course, so he was my side. Marc walked at him, without speaking. He was armed, a long single-barrelled high-velocity job. I drew breath to bawl out, 'Leave him alone, you bastard.' But shouted nothing.

Gobbie must have known what was coming, because he raised his fist to strike at least one blow before Marc clubbed him. Quite ineffectual, naturally. The Swiss simply swung his stock in through the car window, on Gobbie's temple. It splatted on the side of

Gobbie's head, an abrupt, horrid thick sound that made Gobbie dead that instant. He fell away inside the car.

Marc opened the door, casually shoved Gobbie across with his foot, got in, moved the car a few feet to point downhill, and released the brake. He stepped out, watched the motor trundle down the slope. I thought, almost delirious, Hey, hang on, that's Gobbie. And did nowt. Marc drove his own vehicle in watchful pursuit. I saw his red tail-lights go on. And Gobbie's car slid, even where the road curved, straight into the trees. It crumped, burst into a guttering flame for a minute, then erupted with a whoosh.

Marc's motor drove sedately off, its light fading among the trees. My mind went. He murdered a pathetic old man, my pal. And I did nothing. I was afraid, scared, too terrified even to try to distract the killer. Who had stood a second beside Gobbie's car, pounding my old mate with the stock of his hunting rifle, a murderous washerwoman action.

That meant my motor was concealed upslope, my non-functioning brain went, or they'd have seen it, come hunting me.

In silence I waited, snowed on, quiet, still. The sounds of vehicles died. No lights as yet. Why not? Too far from the fire station? No police stations, this far from anywhere? Watchers don't get medals. They get life. Like all cowards. Like me.

A crunch from below sounded. I swear I felt a waft of heat on my face. Something more had exploded near some bend downhill.

My face was unbelievably cold, partly because it was wet. The snowflakes, I suppose, melting on me. You can't keep them off your eyes. Why not, if you can keep rain away? I found my – Guy's – motor untouched, no footmarks round it. They'd see mine when they came, unless the snow got on with it and obscured everything. Except people who carry out a reconnaissance like Marimee'd done, and who could obliterate a mansion as swiftly as I'd just seen, don't tend to leave loose ends. Marc the henchman hadn't. Police would surely have minions combing the hillside for traces of visitors. Snow may be good at footprints, but it's not so good at tartan blankets hanging from a branch. I didn't go back for it.

No lighter of heart, but with a vestige of something growing in me, I drove away from their direction, so avoiding passing the slope where a motor burned, in great haste.

31

The snow was tumbling like surpliced leaves, white and deadening, when I made the hotel. You couldn't see my window from the road, just a sort of lounge with curtains parted above the main doorway. I drove past slowly to check, then got scared. I didn't want Marimee's men, especially Marc, catching me in Guy's car and putting two and two together. I wanted them to continue acting by instinct, now that they'd, well, done their worst.

Making sure the street was clear, I raced up, slammed the brakes on, screeched to a stop a hundred yards short of the hotel entrance, and emerged from the motor whooping and screeching. I left the engine running, and slipped in silence down the alley a few paces off. Then I ran like a loon, coming up winded and sweating cobs, shaking like an aspen. Not as far away as I'd like, but the best I could manage. In my state I darestn't risk a café just yet, certainly not this close.

The streets were clear of pedestrians, more or less. Traffic had dwindled to almost nothing. I leant against the wall to wheeze some breath back, imagining how the sleepy bad-tempered desk clerk would emerge on hearing the racket, see the motor, and go indoors to complain – or not?

It was a good hour of walking before I returned to the area. I actually took a taxi, flagging one down with a tired boredom and telling him the end of the street, paying him off with much interrogation about what notes were which. We had a good laugh before he drove away. By then, of course, I'd told him my name, tried to translate it for him into German – he did an instant and better job, another laugh. And I'd asked him if he'd any antiques because I was an antique dealer. He entered into the spirit of things, saying no, only his cab. I laughed back, saying I'd been lucky in love tonight, tipped him hellishly, complained about his dry old Zurich snow. We parted blood brothers. He'd remember me if no one else.

Nothing. The street was almost deserted. I stood waiting,

uneasy. A car passed the other end, its wheels mutedly crunching snow. Three inches, maybe more. The place was not white, not like our East Anglian snow. Something made it curiously slatey-grey. Was it the buildings, something in the air? Or did you need a mountain for contrast?

Waiting's no good. I walked slowly down the pavement to the hotel. Door closed against the chill wind. Swirls had left small piles by the steps. Guy's motor car was gone. Either Guy and Veronique had recovered from their oblivion and hurried to Needle Park for a shot of Yuletide bliss. Or something else had happened.

Nobody at the desk. That spoiled things, made my return less noticeable than it ought to be. I dinged the bell.

'Hello!' I called, smiles in my voice thrilling all available listeners. A difficult act, trying to look post-coital after what I'd seen. As difficult, indeed, as trying to pretend that one hasn't made love the night before when coming down to breakfast. Blokes manage it, leaving slight doubt in cruel observers' minds. But women can't. They look loved-in. Or not, as the case may be. Where was I? Pretending. 'Anyone there?'

'Please, Monsieur!' somebody called from upstairs.

'Oh, sorry, sorry!' I stepped across to peer up the stairwell at an annoyed bloke with a moustache and specs. 'My apologies, Monsieur. Shhhh!' Finger to my lips, I turned to see a thin angry desk man.

He remonstrated with me. He complained that this night was more trouble than any in all his experience. I wanted to know what was wrong, but stayed jauntily unsympathetic.

'Any messages for me?' I asked. On being given a surly no, I was astonished and not a little narked. 'But surely, Monsieur Solon my friend left the money that arrived for me? He promised to do so. Could you please check?'

He did. No gelt. I resumed. 'But Miss Veronique, my friend's sister. Surely she left my money? It is very important, for tomorrow I must buy a present for my friend back home . . .'

All in all it was pretty good. His lip curled at the mention of my companions. To my relief he told me they'd returned over an hour ago, leaving their car running outside. Accidents are caused by such irresponsibility. No, they had not deposited their keys. No, no messages. No, no envelope for me. No, he had not seen them. I got my room key.

The stairs creaked, telling the world Lovejoy was in action. For once I was legit. I grumbled loudly, authentically everywhere for when the police would come calling if I'd guessed right. I went into my room. My heart was banging. Have you ever had it thumping so you simply can't understand how other people can avoid being deafened by it? Like that. I was shaking. I looked at myself in the mirror, washed my face, went to the loo, tidied myself up. I was worn out. Had my heart pounded this way, my hands shaken this badly, when Marc the killer had used the butt of his rifle on that snowy road?

Half an hour, I moved. Not like lightning, but trembling. I went out, closing but not locking my door – wasn't I simply visiting my friends in the next room? I knocked. No response. I knocked a second time. Nobody. I knocked loud, louder, loudest.

A bloke spoke to me in German from the end of the corridor. He wore a dressing-gown. Different bloke, no tache, no specs. I was relieved at another witness, explained in poor French I was trying to wake my friends who'd forgotten to leave my money at the desk. I tried the door as I was talking, exclaimed aloud as if pleased, and staggered in a sweat of fear into Guy's room. And gagged. No pretending any more, not for anyone.

They lay on the bed. The light was on. A syringe was in Veronique's arm, dangling, partly filled with blood. Guy lay beside her. The stench was sour, acrid. Vomit soiled the counterpane. Both were partly clothed. Bloodstains on their faces and bare arms, as if they'd pawed each other in some terminal dementia. White, white skin, whiter than the Zurich snow. The pallor seemed an aura. Guy's face was buried in the pillow, a pool of vomit forming an ugly meniscus along one cheek. It was Veronique that got me. She seemed faintly worried, as if trying to be serene but knowing something was going awry. This isn't part of the game, her attitude seemed to be telling me, so what's up, Lovejoy? Can't you explain to these men who've come stealthing into our room and who're giving us a dose we don't actually want this time? Yet there was no expression. There never is, in death. It's a vacancy, a marked absence. It was only me again, supposing.

I have no illusions. In that terrible split second when I was reading expressions into her posture to obfuscate, explain away the ugliness of the two bodies' cesspool state, the scatter of needles, the bloodstained syringes, the marks –

For Christ's sake, I'd forgotten to howl. I'd silently practised one before coming to knock. It didn't matter, because I found myself doing it anyway, creating enough noise to wake the – well, being sick as a dog on the landing, going argh-argh-argh like they do in the pulp comics when fighting. Only I was vomiting on the threadbare carpet, reeling like a drunk, panting and trying to do my howl and failing. Always, always failing. My scene, I sometimes think. What I'd not shown for friends, I showed in grief for enemies. Typical me.

Gasping, sicking, pointing as doors opened and the no-tache man went past me and started hollering. I made my way downstairs, hardly knowing any longer if I was sticking to any plan. Pointing back upstairs, I reeled wherever my feet took me. I managed a brief word as the irritable desk clerk climbed slowly upstairs past me. 'My friends. . . !' I got out. He merely expressed outrage at the mess I'd made, and avoided stepping into anything Zurich might not be proud of.

Swiss trains run on time. I don't mean this as a political jibe. They simply do. Not as many of them as I'd like, and jiggery-pokery at borders, but nothing worth writing home about. Into France, into Paris, me kipping all the way, sleep of the just and innocent I shouldn't wonder. Sleep needs six hours a man, seven a woman, eight a fool. The old saying doesn't say who gets none.

Your feet do the choosing, I often notice. I got into a dozy little doss-house within a mile of that glass pyramid somebody conned Paris into buying. Worryingly, I was low on money. And I needed a motor now that, well, now circumstances had changed. First thing I did was get on the blower to Dicko Chave. God, but heartiness is a killer. I staggered from there like a beaten boxer. What with his indefatigable good cheer, his merriment, his stiff upper lip. I'm sure he'd be great in battle, but just to say hello to him was a burden. He'd bring more money over, he told me. Midday flight.

'Looking forward to meeting her. Lovejoy,' he'd said crisply.

'Her?' I'd bleated, in a panic remembering my super new

mythical partner. He'd already financed her once at my Zurich hotel. 'Ah, well, you see old chap – '

'Toodle-oo, Lovejoy. See you in Gay Paree!'

That's all I needed. He was still blabbing cheer when I rang off, depressed. Things were getting too complicated. I wondered if I could reasonably nick a car, decided against it. There was Lysette, of course. Where? Sheer spite must have taken her off in high dudgeon. Being a bird, she'd naturally blame me so she was, frankly, out. My one chance of help, and I had to chuck her. Typical, but I felt utterly panned out, forswunked. It wasn't my fault things had turned out like this.

They'd repaired the ramraiders' efforts. I was pleased at that. The pretty girl – Claire, was it? – had done her stuff. I hoped I'd given her enough heavy hints to get her antiques out of the way. I stood opposite, watching the dealers in and out. It was along here that the ramraider had hated me and someone else, when he'd peered in and called us bastards. Given such a clue, I should have made myself face facts back then. Someone else, with more sense, had. Nobody's more sentimental towards children than a crook. It's a wonder the ramraider hadn't clubbed me there and then. In fact he would have, but for leaving clues, collecting bloodstains. I'd escaped such a fate, of course; lucky old me. Somebody else hadn't, o.c. Lucky old me.

'Monsieur Lovejoy?'

Somebody touched my arm. I fumbled in my pocket for a coin to give to this importuning beggar. You can't be all worked up about child exploitation while ignoring the plights of others. I thought. Here, hang on. How the hell did this policeman know my name? Him and two police cars – so low on the ground, Paris bobbies' motors are – and what was going on?

'You will accompany . . .' Long pause, then he made it: '. . . us.'

'Thank you,' I said miserably, and got into their motor. Best not to say a single word of a foreign lingo straight away, or you get spoken to at such speed you're lost in a trice. To show grovelling subservience I added, '*Merci, Monsieur*. Ta.'

And got driven away to the police station. I wasn't quite ready, but when is ready for the likes of them?

*

The place wasn't some grand Victorian dump, nor some black glass rectanguloid. It seemed no more than a dullish office that looked like a building-society branch office. I'd never seen people smoking like their jobs depended on fags, but this lot were. All except the lead bloke. He was an oddly motionless bloke with an ornate waistcoat, the sort you saw years ago on telly announcers. The rest of him was very, very serious.

'Lovejoy?' he said. Not to me, to everybody else. The police who'd fetched me promised yes, this man was Lovejoy, and got sent on their way. He had a good smile, events such a drag and couldn't we get on with things, please, but I wasn't taken in. Police only have three sorts of smiles, all phoney. They constitute threat. 'You're Lovejoy,' he told me sadly.

'Lovejoy, Monsieur,' I agreed. '*Merci.*'

'Bring the lady in.' English his language, so no cheating.

And in came the beautiful Claire Fabien. She stood carefully away from me. I smiled my very best, innocence radiating from me. I rose, made to shake hands. She recoiled. I faltered.

'Miss Fabien!' I tried. 'The antique dealer! You remember me? I bought several pieces from you. The Davenport!'

'Yes, Monsieur,' to the cop. Except now I looked at him he began to look less and less like a bobby. 'This is the man.'

'Of course I am *le même homme*, Mademoiselle!' I outdid Dicko in heartiness, beaming like him. 'Are you all right? In trouble?'

Waistcoat had not risen when La Fabien entered. I don't like blokes this motionless. Blokes normally shuffle about, hitch, shift feet. We don't stay frozen to spots, unless we've malice in mind.

'Lovejoy. You warned Miss Fabien against ramraiders.'

'Against who?' I asked, a puzzled innocent.

'You advised Miss Fabien to move her antiques, even into a pantechnicon.' The word came out stilted. 'Why?'

'Ramraiders?' I wrinkled my brow, theatrically. Clear the brow and into, 'You have them in France? Good heavens!'

'Very well.' This man didn't waste time on prattlers or phoney excuses. He let me off his hook too easily. 'To the English, crime is an amusing commodity. To the Germans a philosophical proposition. To the Americans a job.' I didn't know whether I was to laugh or not, so did. 'Monsieur. You ordered a large number of antiques for shipment from many antique dealers. Most spoke of

254

your excellent choice. Payment was in cash, by two assistants. Could you please identify them for us?'

'Guy and Veronique Solon,' I said pleasantly enough and quickly. 'I was hired by them. Met them in a motorway restaurant when hitchhiking through your lovely country.'

'How did that happen?'

'Oh,' I said, smiling apology at Claire Fabien, taking so long, soon clear up this misunderstanding, 'we got talking antiques. Don't exactly recall how. They were international buyers. I stopped off with them at one or two places, window-shopping. They admired what little skill I have. I agreed to do a bit of purchasing on their behalf.'

'Why France, Monsieur?' A pause to avoid smiling. 'I believe like your poet, that it's curiosity, not devotion, makes pilgrims.'

'Eh? You mean me? Just trying to find new sources of supply. I'd run into a shortage of stock. You know how it is.' His shrug made an elbow-room of silence. I said to Claire, 'Did you get ramraided then?'

She glanced at Waistcoat. 'It was very terrible. They drove cars in the shop and stole. They ruined many antiques.'

'Kell do madge,' I tried politely, shaking my head. If she'd windowed the ones I'd ignored, the world had only lost a few poor-quality fakes. I looked at her with interest. 'You claimed on the insurance, Miss Fabien?'

Suddenly a little pinker than before. 'Of course,' she said stiffly. So she was pulling the insurance scam. Had to, of course – or admit that her display was muchly fakes.

Was it that give-away that decided Waistcoat? He rose, thanked me profusely, and shook my hand. Deadest mitt I'd ever touched among the living. I began to wonder if I'd landed in the French equivalent of our Fraud mob. I had the sense not to ask.

'Your intentions, Monsieur?'

'Oh, I was just about to look round the Louvre des Antiquaires, Monsieur. I've heard of the *Marchés aux puces*, and your Village Suisse, where many superb bargains – '

'Please do not believe all you read in the guidebooks, Monsieur. Though I am sure you require no assistance.'

'Thank you for your advice, Monsieur. . . ?' I'd see this sod again, I felt uncomfortably.

'Pascal, Monsieur.' He didn't smile. 'Easy to remember, eh?'

'May I walk you to your emporium, Miss Fabien?' I asked, gallantry itself.

She recoiled, no, no. Well, win some, lose some. And that was how I came to be sitting alone in the cold wind of the little square where me and Lysette and one other had met up and talked over what we were going to do. And where I'd made the decision, shutting out the truth and causing a friend to be . . . well, made unable to continue living.

The coffee didn't seem as good. I realized I'd ordered breakfast, this hour. I had it, then wanted soup and some other grub. The waitress was encouraged, brought a menu. I asked for more. She was pleased, said I could dine inside if I wanted. I realized I was the only one sitting in the square, everybody inside looking out. It must be perishing. A light dusting of snow was on the table. How long had I been there?

'It is too cold out here for your lady,' she said. A bonny lass, wanting humanity's loose ends tidying up.

'No, ta,' I said. 'I like fresh air.' I couldn't take Lysette, not at this stage. Not even if she would give me a lift to the rotating mansion of Marimee's syndicate where the great share-out would occur and I'd have something positive to do.

The waitress relaid the table and went in, disgruntled. She would have to brave the cool gale that fanned this glade with my next course. Cool gale? Some fragment of school poetry? What poet, Monsieur Pascal? She came across the square towards me. Overcoat now, I noticed, and different from a few minutes ago. I was shivering, but managed to stop it as she pulled the chair opposite me and arranged herself as they do.

'You will catch your death of cold, Lovejoy,' she said sternly.

'You'll have had your tea.' The old Scotch joke I told you once: Edinburgh folk say hello like that, too mingy to offer any. Friendly Glaswegians give you tea without asking.

'Wrong city, Lovejoy.'

'Where's the boyo?' I gave her, Welsh accent. 'Sure to be near, eh, alannah?' Irish for darling. Anything to strike back before I got arrested good and proper.

'Stop it, Lovejoy. I won't have this daftness. I want to know

256

what happened. Not', she gave me in her best Clydebank reproof, 'what's in the papers, either.'

'Is it already in?' I was surprised, but then I never read them. Avoiding newspapers ensures a better quality of ignorance.

'What is it, Lovejoy?'

'Shouldn't it be Gerald asking these questions, Lil?' I nearly joked about talking to the organ-grinder, not the monkey. 'No good saying it all twice.'

She almost smiled. 'Cheek! Gerald's taking photographs, doing the recordings as usual. *I'm* the SAPAR field agent, Lovejoy, not him.'

I drew breath at that. 'You?' Cunning, to wear the SAPAR gold pendant as if it was a fond husband's gift, when all the time she was the baddy. 'I've never heard of a bird hunter before. Does that mean that when you and me – ?'

'Lovejoy.' She looked askance. 'This is being recorded.' She meant Gerald was nearby with directional microphones on the go. 'Who is the girl Lysette?'

'Mind your own business, you rotten cow.'

Not a quibble, more of a learner's smile. 'Start from the beginning, please.'

'Sod off.'

'It's either me, Lovejoy, or Didier Pascal's unit. He's closing.' She paused. The waitress was emerging with my grub. 'Me, you might get some reparation. Pascal is already on to it. When he moves, the fur will really fly. And he does read newspapers.'

If I delayed the full explanation, disguised as a show of willingness to co-operate, I might yet give Marimee time to do the necessary damage. He was only the instrument, after all. The syndicate was the real enemy.

'Inside, then,' I said. 'Let's go somewhere warm.'

We passed the waitress. I made profuse apologies. She followed us, hating Lilian all the way back in, knowing this change of plan was all the woman's fault. It quite cheered me up.

32

The pity is you don't get many chances. Things should be different, but never are. Some folk make their mark. Like Jules Tavernier, a French painter of the 1880s. One of his paintings hung in Claire Fabien's shop; with any luck I'd call eventually and buy. He was no great shakes, Tavernier. But he made his mark by simply catching the boat to Hawaii. Unremarkable? Not quite – he did for Hawaii what Gaugin did for another exotic place. Now, he's immortalized, the epic painter of Hawaii's sublime and awe-inspiring terrain. See? One decision, glory for ever. Wish I was like that.

I got the taxi to drop me off at the factory I'd been taken to by Lysette and somebody else, the night I'd been made to realize. Shaking like a leaf yet bold as brass I went down the steps and banged on the door. I hollered, yelled, kept thumping, and finally somebody came. He looked North African, though how would I know?

'I wish to speak with the Commandant,' I told him. My ponderous French seemed acceptable, but in the darkness his cataract gave him a wall-eyed appearance. It put the fear of God in me. '*L'homme*,' I added for good measure.

He tried fobbing me off, shook his head. I thought of trying to bribe him. In despair I said the magic word. '*Je désire parler avec Colonel Marimee.*' His expression cleared, apprehension stalking his mind. He was the bloke who'd whopped the children. I could hear the noise going on, that faint bustle, chants, shouts. '*Il faut*,' I encouraged him, and had a go at telling him I'd been summoned by Marimee himself.

Ten minutes later I was in a long saloon motor between two gross toughs. That is, they looked and smelled like pimps, but were lean as laths, wiry and ready for anything.

'*Mon commandant*,' I said to Marimee, who oddly was doing the driving. 'I wish to warn the Colonel, with respect.'

'Speak.'

'I . . . I hate to say this, *mon commandant*, but today I saw sold, at the Louvre des Antiquaires, a piece of furniture that I deposited in the Repository.'

Silence. I cleared my throat, ready to embellish. His goons compressed me, simply leaning sideways. I said nothing.

'You are certain?'

'*Mon colonel*!' I said it as if proud with obedience, trying to be the good soldier I'd once failed to be.

'From whom?'

'It was loaded on a van, Monsieur. I tried asking, then became worried in case . . . in case . . .' His nod was almost imperceptible. 'I failed to get the vehicle number. I didn't know if I should ask Monsieur Marc or not, but – '

'Marc.' Flat, impersonal. 'He was there?'

'Oui, *mon colonel*. He received money. I was anxious not to be seen, you see. I blame myself, sir. I passed the emporium a little earlier, and thought then that some pieces being loaded up looked familiar. But I made absolutely sure of the last item. Should I have made a drawing of it for the Colonel?'

The motor didn't move. We'd simply driven round the corner and parked. The night streets were deserted.

'You asked for me, not Mademoiselle Delebarre. Or others who hired you.'

'*Oui, mon colonel*. My duty. I was assigned to you, sir. Only', I went on in spite of a distinct lack of encouragement, hammering it home, 'it seems to me that if one item was stolen, then *all* may have been sold the instant they were deposited. I cannot understand how or why this could be. It seemed to me my clear duty to the Colonel – ' I'd looked up some words in a pocket dictionary for the purpose of fawning exactly right.

Compressed to silence by my tough book-ends. We stayed there an age. I tried hard not to sweat, tremble, babble, promise not to reveal a thing if only he'd let me go. I kept persuading myself I was a baffled bystander, trying to earn a bob or two, wanting home. Instead, my mind kept wondering how they'd kill me, what it felt like, if they'd use knives, dear God not *knives* –

'You have done well. You are discharged. Cross the Manche.'

Cross where? What's a Manche? The Channel! He meant clear off! I almost shrieked in a relieved faint, remembered to say yes, *mon colonel* and thank you, *mon colonel*, goodbye and it was an honour to serve under –

My foot hardly touched the floor before the car was off. I tumbled, lay there, letting the blissful sweat come as I stared up at the black sky. I'd done it, done it, done it . . .

Done what?

'If you think I'm flying in that frigging thing, love, you're mistook.'

'Lovejoy.' Lilian had an auntie's exasperation in her voice, though she was no auntie. It's the woman's inflexion, a kind of exasperation when a bloke doesn't obey instantly. It's the *I know what's good for you so swallow when I tell you* cadence of the nurse with the grueful spoonful, the *We're going to Bognor for our holidays* voice. 'You've flown in one before.'

'I'd been shot then.' I stood rooted on the airfield.

'You're not shot now.' She was half laughing, half screaming. 'We've ten minutes. For heaven's sake!'

'Helicopters fall down.' Two ground crew waited.

'It's the safest means of travel, Lovejoy,' Gerald's brogue put in. Why did he always sound doleful?

'You're not going,' I spat, narked. He looked offended.

'It's only an hour, Lovejoy. Lausanne.'

'Might as well be a million miles,' I argued. I'd gone clammy in spite of the wind – *wind*! Taking off in a frigging egg whisk in a frigging *gale*! Was the world mad?

'Less than two hundred and forty miles,' Gerald intoned.

'Shut up, you pillock.'

'Don't talk to Gerald like that, Lovejoy!' from Lilian, real anger this time to show me where I stood. Just because we'd made smiles, she was warning me. 'Didier Pascal's people found Lysette Fotheringay at your hotel. She's already on her way.'

To Lausanne? To where? I didn't say. 'You did ask for her to be found, Lovejoy,' from Gerald, fidgeting. I keep wondering how folk become what they become. Like, I'd have hired the meticulous, accurate, single-minded Gerald Sweet any day as a dedicated antiques-recovery sleuth, Lilian his travelling companion. Instead, it was the other way round. Why? I'd not had the courage to ask them if they'd picked me up by accident. I desperately wanted the answer to be yes, so chickened out.

'She'll be there?'

'Yes. They've already been gone an hour.'

'Driving, I'll bet! Why not with us?' So that Pascal could extract news from her in his black Citroën, that's why. 'I get airsick,' I protested feebly.

'She's gone through a lot for you, Lovejoy,' mourned Gerald.

I gripped his tie. 'Listen, you prat. I'm the one who's gone through a lot. Nobody else. D'you hear?' His bald head glistened. He nodded, puce, his eyes goggling. Even in that position he took orders from Lilian, glancing behind me to see what she gestured.

'Aye, Lovejoy. Sorry, man.'

'Aye, well.' It was a private helicopter. That alone chilled my spine. I mean, air crashes are always chartered, never scheduled flights, ever noticed? Or is it the other way about? 'It isn't Air France, then.'

'Lovejoy.' Lilian, the spoon, the Bognor holiday. The last words of the Old King came to mind: *Bugger Bognor!*

Nobody had asked me about a crashed motor on the mountain road above the Repository. In fact, there had been very little news given out about the whole thing, except *Explosion Partly Demolishes Furniture Storage Facility* sort of thing. Lilian had seemed quite proud of the media's inattention, silly cow. I'd told her my version, some even accurate. I had the feeling she'd believed most. It goes to show how poorly women co-operate.

'It's okay for you,' I groused, stung. 'Why doesn't a helicopter have a giant parachute. . . ?'

We fly south-east, the pilot started to tell us as his blades screwed the heavens and the engines deafened the world out. Gerald of course corrected him, giving points of the compass in millibars, whatever. Lilian held my hand unseen in the back seat, her cheek colour heightened at her dreadful temerity. I didn't squeeze her fingers back, having probably fainted with fright. We landed in a trice.

Lorela Chevalier was smart as ever, really beautiful. She greeted me in the foyer of the theme-park hotel as if we were old friends. I'd made it a condition that everybody else stayed away.

'Welcome,' she said, a beautiful slim volume between two attendants. They weren't the same blokes, but wore unresponsiveness like every armed squaddie. Why do weapons confer laziness on eyes, droops on hands, sloth on shoes? Somebody ought to research that. 'How do I call you?'

'Wotcher, Lorela. Lovejoy.'

Her eyes widened a little, settled into understanding. 'I've heard the name. That explains . . . Won't you come in?'

'No, ta.' Somebody was hang-gliding in the distance beyond the picture windows. You could see a couple of horses trotting, a small whiskey with coloured fringes being driven on a hand rein by a beginner, a liveried groom trotting longside. A lake shone through trees. A moneyed holiday location; this was no Bognor, 'Just show me.'

'Lovejoy,' she said ruminatively, leading the way to a lift. The two vigilantes came too. We descended without a starting judder. 'East Anglia? Poor. Unattached. No premises.' She turned her lovely eyes to add, 'Divvy? Like Leon Cabannes?'

'Like Leon Cabbanes *was*.'

She looked at me still. The lift door opened. A small train thing on a kind of rail set in the floor. She didn't move.

'Yes. Very unfortunate, Lovejoy. The old gentleman was coming on to our staff the same week he passed away.' No wonder Troude and Monique ordered old Leon topped.

The train thing had no driver. I stared at it, queasy. I'd already been brave once today. Twice was snapping your fingers at Fate. 'We get in that? How far is it?'

'It's programmed,' she said smoothly. 'It can't go wrong.'

'Like your hiring schemes?'

She stepped in, arranged herself, nodded to three blokes standing about in gold jackets. I sat beside her warily. We started off, just me and her. Smoothest ride ever, down a cement tunnel. She had no controls.

'Tell me, Lovejoy. Was that dead man anyone to do with you? There was a crashed car down a ravine with a body – '

I clouted her, really belted her, grabbed the handrail in front of me to stop my hands throttling. She sat still. The little train was three coaches long, enough room for two bums a coach, six in all. No goons with us. A few moments, then she found some tools and started blotting her face to the accompaniment of that faint rattle their handbags always make.

262

We glided through two intersections, same speed, slowed, then through a vaulted arch. Steel doors rolled away for us. We alighted in a huge arched place. Hangar? On pallets, furniture in covered and even transparent seals. A fork-lifter whirred across an aisle about eighty yards away. Music played softly, Vivaldi's *Four Seasons*. No external exit that I could see. Colour codes, and a stand plan like you get to explain tourist vantage points, but here to show where antiques dollops were stored.

'No, nothing, Jim,' she assured somebody who'd stepped forward with a grunt to start extermination of the visiting maniac. 'It's fine, really.' She swivelled brightly. 'This way, Lovejoy! We arrange things here simply – '

I held up a finger. It was blooded. 'Shtum, love.' My knuckle was unfortunately bloodstained, her cheekbone bruised to hell, though luckily I'd missed her eye. I walked away among the stored furniture.

It took three-quarters of an hour to check a good enough sample. Her blokes unwrapped the pieces I chose in the coded area. They hated me every second. Without her restraint they'd have marmalized me. Marimee's stuff seemed all there, every single fake. *Fake*, observe.

'The genuines?' I asked finally. Odd that the beautiful fakes didn't make me feel sick any more.

'I'm unsure,' she said, determinedly bright. 'I think they're here somewhere . . .'

'Don't frig me about, love. They're not.'

She nodded slowly, appraising me, lips pursed. 'I knew you were a divvy, Lovejoy, when, ah, when you – '

When I what? Painfully I thought back, an all-time first. The penny eventually dropped. 'When I directed the Jamie Sandy antique with the other genuines?'

'We always place one of our own, to mark a large deposit. Banks do the same, I'm told, using gold-bullion markers. Radio-isotope labelling has become routine, even for political documents. The other group are . . . at another of our storage facilities.'

I stood hunched, hands in pockets. It felt cold down here. No snow, no cold winds, no mountainside, no pines plopping snow-falls in earthbound gulps, nothing to melt on your eyes and set your eyes running.

'Get rid,' I muttered to the floor.

Some deep bickering, then her men drifted. You could feel their anger. I waited until I'd heard doors whirr and thump. I looked at her. Her cheekbone was prominent, blueish. I almost exclaimed aloud, asked who'd done that. Me.

'They'll be at you, love. Unless.'

'Unless?' She was composed, thinking away, lovely eyes on me. She had sense, this one. Ready for an agreement.

'Unless you say nothing at all to the authorities. And you can go on as before.'

'Which is how, Lovejoy?' She smiled because she was making me speak frankly when I didn't want to. Women have a nerve.

'You accept antiques at the Repository, show customers how secure your Swiss fortress is. Then secretly van them elsewhere, simply transfer the antiques to secret locations. Like this, under a holiday theme park. Good cover, disguised vans, the lot. There really *is* no Repository, is there?'

'Promise not to tell, Lovejoy?' Ah, good old question time. 'Ouch!'

Smiling had hurt her face. Served her right.

Pascal was filled with mistrust. I've been mistrusted by super-cynics, and can tell. It says a lot for the Gallic character, I whispered to Lysette. She said to shhh, it was impolite to whisper in company. So why was she whispering?

He wanted to make a speech. I'd already said it wasn't necessary. We were crowded into a caravan trailer. Air conditioning whirred. Too many of us. Pascal had three goons along. There was me, Lysette, the Sweets, and some uniformed bobbies.

'It'll tip them off if you go in force,' I'd said when Pascal wanted to call his regiments out. 'They'll not come. You must wait until they're all inside, then bottle them. See?'

They settled for road blocks. On permanent stand-by, to be put in place when I'd given the signal.

'Lovejoy,' Pascal ordered, umpteenth time. God, but I wished the bloke couldn't speak English. They were all bloody linguists, except me. I mean, some Oxford goon's worked out that there's 403 septillion ways of combining letters in English – yet everybody else knows my language better. How come? I was especially

264

narked that Lysette got on really well with Didier Pascal. What sort of a name was Didier, anyway? Sounded like a rocking horse, the bum. He'd already got Lysette to sit next to him, the eyes of a rapist. 'You will signal only when all – repeat *all* – the syndicate has arrived. You do understand?'

'I've said yes three times. How many more?'

The seven uniformed officers sat stolidly listening, though I think they'd already got organized. One asked, 'Where?'

'I'll show you,' I promised. 'Lend me a motor?'

'No,' Pascal said, exchanging glances with Lilian Sweet. I just caught her minimally shaking her head. 'We go together.'

Which was how I finished up sitting in a twitcher's hide watching the mansion house in the gladey garden below. It wasn't going round this time. Its garden was absolutely still.

Two days later, they came.

33

Living in close proximity with somebody you don't know is painful. I'm not one for chat; neither was Pascal.

The bird-watcher's hide was made of logging. No lights, no door for the opening in the wall, no glass for the long slit window. That was it. I'd got a blanket-thick overcoat, and Lysette gave me gloves. Gloves, the old Elizabethan lovers' gift. Binoculars with dulled lenses, and that really was it.

We had a loo outside in a rectangle of sacking, blowing in the wind. Basically sawdust in a large tin. Grub was already prepared for us, cold. Tea in a vacuum flask for me, coffee for Pascal. We had to make do. No talking was allowed, pleasing me.

The mansion house below seemed reduced, now the real deed had been done elsewhere. The garden I noticed was smaller than the Repository's, but the two prominences topping the hillside to our right were about the correct elevation relative to the building, and were wooded to about the same degree. Nicely chosen. I'd explained to Lilian Sweet and Pascal before I'd got stuck in this hole that the scammers' meeting was to be within the week. It only took me an hour to start wishing I'd kept my mouth shut and simply eeled away.

There from ten o'clock onwards, night. Midnight came and went. Twice I'd whispered had Pascal anything to read, got looked at. Faint starlight was all we had to see by. I tried looking down at the mansion house, the gardens, the little stream, through binoculars, but couldn't see a damned thing. Never could. I always used to pretend anyway, when it mattered.

If we wanted to say anything desperate, we were to write it down on a small notepad, pencil provided. No talking.

Within three hours I was starting to wonder what if they didn't come at all. I'd be found in this log hut in God-forsaken countryside starved to death years later, waiting for the syndicate to come. I imagined the scene, with great bitterness thinking of the grub there'd be, the lovely luscious women delirious with joy, flushed with excitement at the vast fortunes they thought they'd made from the scam, Monique queening it over everybody, having justified her barmy political beliefs.

And let's hear it for Colonel Marimee, ladies and gentlemen! With fanfares and party time and delectable birds so edible you'd almost forget to reach out for the grub and sink your teeth –

'Sssss!'

'Sorry, sorry,' in the lowest whisper. I must have groaned. I'd not had a pasty for as long as I could remember. I was famished as soon as we got inside this place.

They'd be readying for the ultimate celebration down there. Servants, I supposed in my entranced mind, by the score. Maybe Katta, with her luscious delectable mouth surmounting that gross pendulous shape. Lovely. And Almira, with hubby Jervis. And those Madagascar folk, so wealthy with their digits sheathed in gold. And the smoothies, Philippe Troude, Monique Delebarre and all. There'd be frolicking and wassailing in nooks and crannies everywhere, even before the announcement.

That would be the peak. They'd get called in to a separate room, maybe some baronial panelled hall with a log fire. Brandy, being in France, would be served, with canapés or whatever those little noshes were, on silver trays. Then they'd announce the sum they were going to claim from Lloyd's insurance. But only after they'd made the celebratory call to the Repository . . . I smiled, got admonished by a nudge. No chuckling.

The night passed. No cars arrived, except one that seemed to be Monique's. No passengers, no visitors.

Odd to think that Paul Anstruther had been Katta's sex focus (sorry, no pun intended) all these years. How on earth had Cissie put up with her? Except I'd learned that Cissie adored Philippe Troude. I began to think about seeing Katta's huge form writhing on the ecstatic Paul. God, but that would be bliss, some bird so vast you could hardly see over her. Would you want to?

But hadn't her reaction been strange, that night I'd unexpectedly eavesdropped on them? When the car doors slammed, Katta'd been really terrified. She'd leapt off Paul, not pausing to wipe her mouth until she'd been reassured – *by hearing Almira*. Then, and only then, Katta had relaxed, paused to tease Paul by giving him that erotic moue. Question: *Who'd she thought was coming?* Answer: Somebody she was *truly* scared of.

If I had a permanent bird, I'd know the answer straight off. I knew I would. It's as if a woman is your missing half. Happen I should get one, some day. Except it never works. I suppose in a way I'm like Dicko Chave, perennial failure. Except I nearly get enough, and Dicko simply lacks any. And settling down for good is impossible. I mean, what if you draw a Cissie? I knew the answer to that for sure.

Which raised the question why my mind kept coming back to her. Ambition unlimited, ferocity unleashed, anything for wealth, status. She'd married us – there seemed to've been no negotiations, just Cissie's determination – because she aimed to harness my divvying skills and gross a trillion. She said as much. She stormed off because I was uncontrollable, and her scheme didn't work.

My head jerked upright. I was stiff from leaning on the log sill. Mostly blackness out there. I occasionally tried standing up, stretching, swivelling like Olympic atheletes do after gulping their anabolic steroids before track events, but you get fed up with fitness so I sat down again. I sometimes looked at Pascal. He was a good watcher. I'd never met anybody quite like him before. Gallic equivalent of Lilian Sweet? If so, I'd seriously underestimated Lilian's talent.

Once, in early daylight of next morning, I woke to find him passing me photographs. Two children, both girls, one smiling doubtfully in a small garden pool, the other standing on the bank throwing a scoop of water, laughing. What, eight and fourteen? Yours? I asked with a pointing finger. He nodded, smiling, asked did I carry any photos? I shook my head, pretending rue. He shrugged, stood again at the slit window staring through his binoculars. And that was that, entertainment for the day.

We had stewed tea and coffee from our row of thermos flasks. One every five hours, our ration. Cold sandwiches of cardboard material. Sausages, well congealed in thickening grease, sliced ham. Couldn't Paris have raised its frigging culinary game? I wanted to demand, but caught Pascal's shrug and made do, trying to prove that I too could be a stoic.

No snow, but pretty cold weather, especially at night. I guessed Pascal's police'd not set up a rota. Rotas work well when sussing a possible place for a rip, until you actually need to replace the old watchers with fresh invigorated new. Then there's trouble. If it isn't a give-away from banging car doors, it's obvious that something changes in the street's pattern. I wasn't too sure about things in the countryside, even though that's where I live, but I knew the French had gamekeepers too. And those miserable sods can spot reeds misbehaving miles off.

Doing nothing's really weird. How do Trappist monks manage? Though I suppose they're allowed to read. Once, this bird actually hired me to do utter nothing. Honest, true. She was really flash, very chic. Wed, of course, she had a lad at boarding school, husband in mortgages. She truly hired me to just be there. And 'there' was simply nearby wherever she was. She even introduced me to her husband, who okayed the whole thing. For quite three days I thought I was a bodyguard, and went in fear of my life, scared stiff, until it dawned on me that I was mere decoration. I even asked Doc Lancaster if it might be one of those afraid-of-loneliness things. He sent me packing, the swine. Really odd. Can you imagine, a woman just wanting a bloke dancing attendance? They're strange. I overheard her being teased by her posh friends, chinless wonders, about her 'bit of rough', meaning me. I was deeply narked. On the way home we made smiles, me like a gorilla, she thunderstruck that her figment had suddenly become bestially real. I resigned that night. You won't believe this, but she thought a lifelong loveship had been sealed, whereas I'd thought I'd been punishing her. See how women insist on misunderstanding? Like Cissie, like Almira, like Jodie Danglass, like Lysette, like Lilian Sweet. They have the advantage of being underhanded. It's not fair. We've got to be honest and upright. Women can do what they want. It should be the other way round.

'Sssss!'

'Ssss!' I went irritably back. Okay, so I might have muttered aloud. No need to go berserk. Pascal settled. He'd only given me one small set of binoculars, but collared four pairs for himself. He was forever stealthily changing lenses, looking for some bloody attachment or other, getting right on my nerves.

Lately, I'd been trying to get my teeth right. Toothpicks always seem one of civilization's good ideas that never quite comes off, though the Romans used them. It doesn't bother me that Juliet only had (honest) four teeth in her head when, aged fourteen, she romped with Romeo. So I'd acquired toothpicks. For something to do I started digging. The best teeth gadgets are those electric rotary brushes you charge up on the mains, but I always lose the little things that go round and round on the end . . . Pascal nudged me. I mouthed an irritable *I'm awake, I'm awake!* and roused blearily to more misery.

The day seemed to have turned itself inside out far more than twice when finally Pascal tapped my shoulder. Something happening. I hope I hadn't snored. It was early afternoon. I looked out, fumbled for the binoculars. He pointed to my pair hanging round my neck. I peered, focused, got it blurred, tried again.

A big Merc. Whatever colour they paint them, a Merc always looks black. Ever noticed? Grandeur, I suppose. Even Hannover taxis look black, and most aren't. A bonny girl, slender as an arrow, arriving down there with a bloke. Servant out to say hello, show them inside. The motor retired, pomp in every line. I ticked the air to Pascal. He nodded. I'd seen them at that party, or in the hotel meeting at that security room. He nodded okay, keep looking. Irritably I nodded back that I was, for God's sake, don't keep on.

They arrived faster, increasing numbers. I started a pattern of gestures. Thumbs up, yes I recognized the couple from Madagascar, the bloke who looked something artistic, the slightly plump woman with too-young dress sense, her besuited banker husband. The German moneybags who'd asked the wrong question of the Colonel in Zurich. Then Almira, her husband. Philippe Troude with – heart in my mouth – a popsie having difficulties in stilt-like high heels on the drive surface. Definitely not Jodie Danglass, multo definitely. But yes, she'd been at the party.

Then, astonishment showing me how astonishment should be really felt, Sandy, in splendiferous garb, gold cloak, what looked like electric Christmas-tree lights flickering along the rim, ostrich feathers in an absurd halo. He looked ridiculous. Still no Jodie Danglass. But Corse the roller, last seen abusing me and the rest of the known world at Josh Sparrow's barn. I grunted with satisfaction.

Pascal was looking at me oddly. I smiled, indicated that all was going quite well. The numbers began to dwindle. Then ceased.

Nudge. He showed me the time. Two hours, the daylight not yet fading but definitely less encouraging than it was. Motors revved, cars lined up to one side of the mansion house. No marquees today, no tents or awnings, no sherry on the lawns. Some uniformed drivers smoked, one reading a paper. All cars were left-hand drive, Continental design. Pascal stirred, hands asking if that was it.

No, I gestured back. I opened my palms, fingers asplay as if holding a large ball. Many more to come, I indicated, though, waggle waggle, I still wasn't sure of the number.

How many, then? He was becoming edgy, scanning the sky. What for, helicopters? Dusk? Some additional help he'd requested should things start to go wrong and the whole syndicate looked likely to escape? Or something much much worse?

He indicated, drawing an imaginary net tight, that he'd got them in the sack, all the evil swine in one. Why delay? I shook my head. More would come, hold on, wait.

No sign of anything flying overhead. No signals from the trees. Nothing that I could think of or see. Only Pascal, finally watching me more than he watched the mansion house in the clearing below. I smiled a bit at him now and then, showing willing, offered him some of my tea, tried his coffee with a grimace. Not a single smile now, nothing but wary glances. It began to nark me. What the hell could I do, with the daylight now definitely losing interest and the mansion-house lights starting to come on, and me stuck up on a hillside in a plank shed with a cop? For Christ's sake, I thought, narked. You're a frigging copper, not Tracker Joe Wilderness. Get a grip, Pascal.

The motor came at last. Paulie's, the same one I'd driven in to visit hospital that day. No need to be prompted now. I was all attention. Without having even to focus, I saw Paulie halt his motor, leap out and scurry round to the opposite door, open it.

She looked smart, trendy even. And stern. She simply gave no acknowledgement of his politeness, and sternly swept by without a look into the mansion house.

Cissie always did run true to form. Katta heaved her enormously beauteous bulk from the low motor, and walked round the back of the building with one of the chauffeurs who'd been having a smoke leaning on the bonnet of his Bentley. I felt glad Katta'd be out of it, when whatever it was happened.

My finger gave Pascal pause. By now he was hopping from foot to foot, less taciturn than he'd ever been in his entire life, I shouldn't wonder. One more yet to come, I mimed, stabbing the air. Keep looking. Wait, wait. Hold them off, whoever they were.

And even as I recovered my binoculars, his motor arrived. Marc got out of the car, chucked the keys indolently to one of the other drivers, and walked into the building. I'm sure it was him. He carried a large suitcase-size thing, not so large he had to trundle it on wheels. I said nothing, just started a slow counting on my fingers, clearly trying to work out if I'd forgotten anybody. No, that was about it.

Still I waited. Why? Nudge from Pascal. He even scribbled me a line on his barmy notepaper, his pencil shaky, all over the place. I went sssssh very softly, read his scribble, frowned at *Maintenant????*, waved a downward palm slowly, take your time, mate.

I wanted his watch. He had an unbelievable three, honest to God, three, ripped one off savagely, thrust it at me. I stared at the hands, counting, my lips moving to show him I was on the job.

Marc would go into the assembly room. Only the syndicate would be allowed in, nobody else. That was their pattern. I saw the whole glitterati lot – can we take our drinks in? How much will the pay-out be? What claim we shall put in to the insurers? Isn't Colonel Marimee coming, then? Shame! Monique gorgeous, lovely, taking the place of honour on the dais. Would there be a rostrum? Lights?

Marc'd be going in now, smiling, handshakes, proud.

They would be chattering, talking of their expected riches. Claim for tons of priceless furniture in the Repository, share out. What were their expectations, really, when all was said and done? They'd have the perfect money machine, for slavery is eternal, pure, elementary, a model of perfection. Everybody's fatal siren call.

One minute fifteen seconds. Tick tick, silent second hand but shuddering me with its mute force. One eighteen, twenty.

What orders had Colonel Marimee given Marc the killer? To activate some switch on the case in the meeting? Probably. Or would the case be on auto? Or externally controlled perhaps? Had he told Marc it was an aiming beam for his famous flash mortar? Marc would believe he'd have a few minutes to get clear . . .

'Your watch, ta,' I said, returning it.

One minute forty seconds, plenty. 'Go now. No more, I'm sure.'

Pascal flipped a switch on a small box thing strapped to his shoulder and yelled into it, over and over again. It sounded like 'Lay-lay-lay-lay. . . !' He hurtled from the place leaving me alone, looking out at the building through the foliage. A motorcycle engine sawed the air, Pascal running like a rabbit through the trees towards the road.

A *crump* sounded. I felt the earth press up slightly against my soles. No waft of heat on my face this time, no blizzard, no residual crackle audible, no sky glow from a fading blaze, none of that, no snow on my face, no whine of Marc's car.

The drivers were bewildered down there. Two had run towards the mansion, then withdrawn. Maids and waiters emerged, scattering, shrieking, pointing. Katta came, smoothing down her skirt, perhaps from some motor parked behind the house.

A man came staggering round the side of the house, blood on his head, trying to wipe it. The drivers took him, shouting, beckoning. Some went to the edge of the drive, peering at the back of the building's west wing. Two thought, dived into their motors, stood free with car phones in action. A few windows had billowed out, sharding on the lawn. No smoke, no sign of fire, no bright flames. One thing, Marimee did a precision job, every single time.

An explosion, I guessed, in the syndicate's meeting. There'd be grave injuries, I shouldn't wonder, even deaths.

Helicopters headed over the trees, shining headlights. Four. Another, distantly, higher. Searchlights of amazing power. Motors shrieked and wahwahed along roads. Police were everywhere. It was very efficient, motorcycles roaring and those sharp-edged police vehicles short on windows arriving by the column. I thought, why am I so cold inside? Why am I not weeping? For Paulie, Marc, Sandy, all the others so recently living?

For Cissie?

I'd probably got time for a walk. Stretch my legs after all this standing about. So I left, walked down among the trees.

Goodnight, Gobbie.

34

'Lovejoy!' The last person on earth I wanted to see, Dicko Chave. He was impeccably dressed, tweeds to his eyeballs, handmade leather shoes.

My heart sank. 'Dicko! Just in time, mate!'

He stood in the corridor, beaming. 'Had difficulty finding you, old chap. Some young lady guided me. Seems like everybody's talking about you there. Made a killing, what?'

'Er, aye. Look.' I was trying to explain my nakedness, towel wrapped round my middle. I lowered my voice. 'The lady – remember my temporary partner, that I want to introduce you to? She'll arrive in half an hour. I'm trying to get ready. Mind if we meet up in the residents' lounge?'

He almost fell over with enthusiasm. 'Certainly, Lovejoy!' He wrung my hand. 'Never forget this, old sport. You're a brick!'

I went in and shut the door in relief. Katta looked up from the bed. Credit where credit is due, a plump woman is real value. I realized I'd never seen her under the bedclothes. A natural counterpaner.

'Khoo theyet?'

'Eh? Oh, friend.' She flicked the towel from me. She stared. She had a smiley kind of stare, the most erotic I'd ever seen. She reached. She had an erotic kind of reach, the most erotic reach I'd ever felt.

'He naye-iss?'

'Aye. Yes.'

As we started to make smiles, and I groaned in bliss at the ceiling and she grunted with divine relish, a strange possibility came into what was left of my mind. I tried hard to register it for afters, so to speak, but failed.

'Lovejoy, *mon ami*.'

I'd been summoned before Pascal, the day after the deaths. He had two assistants with him. Lilian Sweet had Gerald and an official of some ministry. Two uniformed police worked transcribers. I'd never heard so much racket before, not even in a cop shop.

'*Oui*, Monsieur Pascal?'

'Did you know?'

Ponder for a sec. A minefield of a question. If I said no, he'd say, What didn't you know? And thence et dangereux cetera into some Parisian clink. I could joke: Know? That France intended to demolish the Eiffel Tower in 1909, when it was a mere twenty years old, and build on the site. . . ? but that'd nark him. You counter word tricks with a definition.

'Know? That the explosion was going to happen? No, Monsieur. How could I?'

'Indeed. How could you, Lovejoy?'

More mines. I nodded, grave and sad. 'Even delaying so long, I worried lest I missed a couple. That's why I took your watch, allowed myself only two more minutes. Less, even.'

'Marc was gardener-chauffeur at Mrs Galloway's lodge. The place you stayed as her lover when you first came to France, Lovejoy. Had you met him previously?'

Shrug, my own personal ineptly non-Gallic version. 'Vaguely saw him about the place.' I straightened, honour bound. 'But, I do not make any admission about the relationship between Mrs Galloway and myself. The lady's honour forbids me speak – '

'*Oui, oui*, Lovejoy.' He had a knack of making agreement sound disbelief. 'Your firmness does you credit. About the events surrounding the explosions at the Swiss Repository.'

'I was in Zurich when that happened, I believe. But I had nothing to do with it.'

'You observed no similarities between the mansion house of yesterday and the Repository?'

A shrug to dispel surprise. 'Similarities? I knew neither place. When I was taken to the garden party, for reasons that even now are unclear, I wasn't even sure where it was.'

'Lovejoy. There will be criminal charges brought. Their precise nature is yet to be determined. For this week you will remain in Paris. Thank you.'

And I left. They'd booked me into a small hotel near the Panthéon, which pleased me. I was to report three times daily to the bobbies. Each time, Pascal had to be notified in case he wanted me. I realized with a shock that Lilian and Gerald Sweet had an office, a real genuine office, in Pascal's division. Can you believe it? Their underhandedness took my breath away. What's happened to fair play?'

Katta was waiting outside Pascal's office on a bench, a picture of misery. She brightened when she saw me, leapt up and embraced me, cooing. I realized instantly that here was a woman filled with love's natural warmth. She'd lost Paulie, *requiescat in pace*, her precious plaything, and wanted another. Just to tide her over, I said I was free and did she have time for a chat. I'm always ready to do friends a good turn. Anybody'll tell you.

'Listen, Katta, love.' I stopped us just short of the lounge. 'One thing. I'm really happy.' Nothing settles a man's soul like a woman, but how do you tell her? 'What I mean is, ta.'

'Oh, kyoo, Lovejoy!' She simpered, in her thick mascara, plastered lipstick, hair greenish, cheeks really rouged. You have to hand it to birds. They have real style.

'There's one thing.' I hesitated. How to describe Dicko? The truth, when all else fails. Here goes. 'Katta, love. Dicko is, er, new to women. You understand? He simply doesn't know how to, well *cope* with a genuine female.'

'Chee is. . . ?' Her purpled eyes widened. She actually licked her lips. 'Chee feerjeenal? Layke chyoo?'

Virginal like *me* for God's sake? I swear that sometimes I think she's putting it all on. 'Dunno. He's certainly a beginner. Okay? But he's a friend. So, well, go easy, okay?'

She seized me, grabbed me in an envelope hug and forced her lips on to mine. Her tongue rummaged my uvula. Passing hotel staff made approving murmurs. 'Senk kyoo, Lovejoy! Setch er geeft!'

Dicko was waiting in the lounge, bouquet of carnations at the slope-arms position. He shot upright. The poor chap was desperate, expecting another failure.

'Katta, may I introduce my friend Dicko Chave.' I was on my best behaviour.

'Chow doo yoh doow?' Katta got out, coy and shy.

Dicko shook her hand. 'Flowers for a flower,' he clipped out. The daffodils stood to attention.

'Heavens!' I exclaimed. 'That the time?' I left them beaming at each other. A hit!

Exit Lovejoy. I'd keep his loan, my fee for effecting a lonely-hearts intro. Fair's fair.

The street was abuzz with police. I watched from the corner among a small crowd. The factory was being boarded up. Cloaked folk stood gazing.

'It's no victory,' somebody said close to my elbow.

'I know,' I said.

'It will simply move on, Lovejoy. More legions of slave children, different guises.'

'I know that, too.'

'Mrs Sweet tells me there were five in Great Britain.'

'And the rest.' I always sound bitter, wish I knew why. I do try to sound light-hearted and chirpy. I've never yet seen me smile in a photo. I wonder what it is.

'They are introducing legislation . . .'

'Shut it, love.' When law steps in, truth flies out of the window. I watched as the police loaded up the furniture, much partly completed, some hardly started.

'What will you do, Lovejoy? Now Katta and Mr Chave have got engaged?'

That made me turn and look. She tried to give me a hankie, silly cow. You can always trust a woman to be stupid. 'I've already got one, ta. Engaged?' I thought she meant hired.

'To be married, Lovejoy.' She was near to a smile. 'Katta asked me to give you this.'

Hotel notepaper.

> Dear Lovejoy,
>
> *Timeo Danaos et dona ferentes! My betrothed and I shall expect you at our wedding. Do bring a guest, darling.*
>
> *Love from your new neighbour,*
>
> Katta

What had happened to the accent? That's women for you. Me

277

and Lysette strolled off. No good checking on the police now they'd finally got weaving.

'Mrs Sweet wishes to see you, Lovejoy, tonight. She'll call at your hotel.'

'She does?'

'It will take several sessions, I think, from the way she spoke. She has a massive inventory of antiques she wants you to check, before Miss Chevalier arrives tomorrow.'

'Miss Who?'

'Miss Chevalier. Monsieur Pascal told me there's a way to reduce the criminal charges against you, if you co-operate with the authorities here, Switzerland, Great Britain.'

'Meaning co-operate with Lorela Chevalier?' I'd saved her firm, her reputation, her antiques, her job . . . She'd tried to phone me at the hotel a thousand times. I'd finally left the receiver off the hook while Katta, er, swallowed my pride.

'I think so, Lovejoy. And Mercy Mallock will be with you soon. She faxed the hotel.'

'Mercy?' I brightened. 'What'd she say?'

'Her letter is too long, too personal, and impertinently presumptuous. You must have nothing more to do with her.'

We turned into the street gales, par for Paris. This was starting to look sour. I mean, Katta'd served, as it were, her purpose in detoxifying my soul with her unique brand of adventurous love. But Lilian Sweet was a different proposition. Back in East Anglia I'd not last an hour if word got about that a SAPAR hunter had decided to cottage up with me. And Lilian had proved her determination more than somewhat. I'd not shake her off in a trice.

Lorela Chevalier on the other hand had definite possibilities. Lovely, attractive, feminine as a flower. But with the giant responsibility of her great Repository? And willing to offer heaven-knows-what for me to replace old Leon? To live with the glorious Lorela, in utter affluence, comfort, warmth, wealth, surrounded by the densest collection of perfect antiques the world could assemble? I'd die of ecstasy in a week.

No Paradise for the likes of me.

'Are you going to the hotel, Lovejoy?' I'd stopped at the square where me and Gobbie'd met. And Lysette.

'Well, aye.' I felt uncomfortable. I'd nearly said I'd nowhere else to go.

'Miss Danglass is waiting there, Lovejoy.' Lysette was standing close. The wind whipped our coats about us.

'Jodie Danglass?'

'Yes. She's been waiting a while. She said she has urgent offers from a Big John Sheehan, about some glass replicas he wants you to market for him. He's asking after some Carolean mica playing cards he bought from a young widow. It's rather complex, Lovejoy.' Sherry Bavington, the bitch. She must have come calling, nicked the micas from my ever-open cottage. I'd strangle the thieving cow, after I got a lock for the door.

'Aye, it would be complex all right.' With Big John Sheehan it was never easy, cheap, or straightforward. Sending Jodie to France was his way of saying to the trade that he had nothing to do with the child labour – not that anybody'd ever believe he had. 'She mention which? The Portland Vases?'

Lysette's eyes were pure, that ultra-blue you get in Greek paintings.

'Lovejoy. I don't think you should become involved in something new, not just yet. Not with Monsieur Pascal's team still investigating.' Pause. 'Do you?'

'No,' I tried, cleared my throat. 'No,' I said, firmer.

'Darling, I have an idea.' She smoothed my lapel. I hardly felt her hand. 'Paris can become rather crowded. Would you like to stay somewhere else? Only for a short while, not too long.'

'Stay?'

'Yes. Rest, read, have time to visit interesting museums.' She smiled, quite casual. The wind swooshed her hair across her face. She scraped it aside with a reproving tut. 'Some antique shops aren't quite played out. That sort of thing.'

'What about Pascal and Lilian, the rest?'

'Need we tell them where we are going, darling? I think not.'

'We'd never make it.'

She smiled. 'Oh, yes we would, Lovejoy.'

'You're not an antiques hunter too?' It was a joke, but came out despairing. What had I thought, those epochs ago: that too many people were paid but loving eyes.

'Not yet.' Her reply started out serious, emerged as a joke. I felt her smile.

'Let me think.' I stood there. She slipped her arm into mine, and we sat on the curved bench beneath the tree. 'Hang on,' I said. She'd put her arm round my shoulders, pulled my head gently down on to her shoulder. It was the wrong way round. I'm the masterful all-caring protective provider. She was the weaker vessel. 'If Jodie Danglass is here from home, and Lorela Chevalier is offering . . .'

'Shhh,' she went. Her fingertips pressed my cheek, turning me to her. She touched her mouth on mine, very soft.

Applause sounded. The café windows were crowded, grinning faces and salutations everywhere. She broke away, scarlet.

'Look,' I said. 'How about we try that, then? Might as well, eh?'

Took me less than ten minutes to talk her into it. One thing, I'd not lost the knack of persuasion.